I0617686

The Victor's Heritage

Book Two of The Jonah Trilogy

The Victor's Heritage
Copyright © 2015 by Anthony Caplan
www.anthonycaplanwrites.com

Cover art by Bespoke Book Covers

ISBN: 978-0-9815166-5-3

All rights reserved. No part of this publication may be
reproduced, distributed, or transmitted in any form or by
any means, including photocopying, recording, or other
electronic or mechanical methods, without the prior written
permission of the publisher, except in the case of brief
quotations embodied in critical reviews and certain other
noncommercial uses permitted by copyright law.

Hope Mountain Press
810 Ray Road
Henniker, NH, 03242

And of six hundred thousand people on foot, they two were preserved to bring them in to the heritage, even unto the land that floweth with milk and honey.

Ecclesiasticus

To Ezar, Michael, Eve and Grace

One --The Augment

Corrag smiled at the idea of Gurgie in her bedroom on Durkiev Drive across town and the shock of recognition when she realized her friend had signed off on MandolinMonkey rather than go in for the remnant. So characteristic of a truly dynamic soul, Gurgie would say, to quit nonchalantly on the verge. But for Corrag the reality was less comforting. She had ten minutes before her parents called for dinner. It was a more complex fear coming over her -- of facing Ricky and Alana, the stalwarts of St. Michael's Close, the exclusive, tree-lined enclave of Edmundstown where she had grown and lived her entire sixteen years. Her parents, the Drs. Lyons as they were titled in the annual consensus, had implied that this talk would be "important to her future." Whatever that could mean. Something about the boring infinitude of possibilities always just around the corner. Like signing off on the game rather than face the interior of the obelisk, it was easier for Corrag to be present and accounted for -- ride the tide of her parent's displeasure -- than to make a stand by remaining in her bedroom, the private space she continued to carve out of the increasingly imperiled life she was about to leave behind.

She observed numbly as the icon came up on the nanowall, the family crest with the towering crane and the stylized image of the transgalactic, so twenty-thirties, and wished again she'd had other siblings, that Ricky and Alana had been more compelled by the recommendations of the Commission on Demography and less concerned with their augmented careers. But so be it. There were also advantages to being the basket in which were placed all the eggs of the Lyons family name. If only the crest design were more compelling. She hit the kill button before the music could end. It was the theme of HG Wells's acclaimed classic *The Shape of Things to Come,* which she had performed during her sixth grade drama season in a stellar role as Hillary Perron, the Council leader responsible for the withering away of the former state of California, the sclerotic, corrupt vestiges of what had once been democratic governance. Now it just reminded her of her parent's unfulfilled expectations for her development as a young woman about to assume the mantle of augmentation.

She descended the stairs covered in royal blue carpeting and sat at the dining room table of molybdenum while her father, white beard trimmed neatly and his cardigan in the colors of the University of the Upper West, maroon with cream pockets, beamed at her. Her mother Alana continued to talk in that subtle, alluring monotone with hints of New Albion that had entranced uncounted faculty parties on the shores of Mono Lake.

"And I've always maintained that tennis induces a better oxygen wash of the skin than yoga, Ricky. Well. Here she is. Corrag? Where is your file?" asked Alana.

"Can I get my food before the interrogation?"

"Of course you can. Don't be silly," said her father, trying hard to keep the sound of despair out of his voice.

Alana sighed. Corrag hated hurting their feelings, but there was nothing else to be done. This would have to be endured. Not even Alana was going to come out of this smelling of roses. There was probably a word in another language for the moment when a young woman declared her independence from her family without a pre-approved plan in place. Corrag felt herself destined for a new form of singular existence that depended on taking this risk.

"Have you taken a stab at the essay yet? When is it due?" asked her father, once she had served herself from the tray offered by the housebot of the lasagna and truffles.

"In two days," said Alana. "It's getting late."

"I'm having thoughts about it," said Corrag. "I'm not sure."

"Not sure. Thoughts. That's Corrag for you," said Alana. "What is sure for you? Nothing is ever sure in your world. You are the classic case of choice overload. We never should have let her have a PlayCube of her own."

"Let her speak," said Ricky.

They waited breathlessly, the two anxious parents, while Corrag forked some lasagna and chewed without looking at them.

"Didn't you always tell me to follow my desires, Dad? Well, that's what I'm trying to decipher. I don't really know what my desires are. I don't know what I really want. That's my problem. I want to know. I can't just plunge ahead into fine-tuning until I do. It wouldn't be right for me."

"Right for me." Alana repeated. She dropped her fork. It clattered on her plate. Ricky grabbed his head helplessly with both hands. The bot, sensing some urgency, circled the table speedily. Corrag waved it away with her hand and looked at it with a hard stare that sent it back into the kitchen through the energy panel.

"This uncertainty of yours is in total defiance of your education and privilege," said Alana.

"I know," said Corrag. "But it's what I want. Until we reach augmentation, we can choose what we want, right?"

"Within reason, Corrag. The parents still have the final say," said Alana darkly.

"It's unbelievable, Corrag," said her father. "There are no more exemptions. Look at the Calder boy. He wanted to take a year and read the books in his grandfather's library because he said he 'valued the experience' of holding the words in his head instead of instant upload. He tried to argue in the consensus -- you don't remember, do you? -- that the year of reading was worthwhile. But there were no more exemptions. Do you understand? He was effectively exiled. The only thing left to him was the HumInt Corps. Is that what you want? Hundred mile marches in the swamps where not even the bots can go? Certain premature death? No augmentation means no physical corrections."

"That's not true. There are other things," said Corrag, the color rising in her face.

"Like what?" asked Alana.

"I don't know."

"Uugh," grimaced Alana, her face wrinkling like a

prune despite the botulin implants.

"Look," said Ricky. Corrag could see the glint in his eye that told her he was probably in the Cloud. "It's a common condition of human childhood to seek individuation. We try to condition it away, but the vestiges of the trait are stronger in some and may require remedial conditioning. Or else you can choose the VocAg. There are some interesting possibilities. If you like manual work."

"Okay," said Corrag. She'd heard it all before. The path of the conversation had taken a familiar tack that apparently was not remembered by her father. But Alana would not have it.

"Do you know what that is? It's not exactly gravy, is it? Give them run of the greenhouses. How ... utterly tacky," said Alana.

"So? Somebody has to grow the food. I thought we were all in this together. Hail the Federation. Smile all the while."

"Corrag," said Alana sharply.

"What?"

"I can accept that you need time," said Ricky. "You've always been ... different."

"What are you talking about, Dad? I'm just like you. Have you forgotten? You told me about refusing to play football. How your dad took it hard. How you had to find your own way."

"I know. You're different. Yes, like I was once. That's why I love you. We'll continue to support you in your choices no matter what."

"But she doesn't know what she wants."

"Give her a year. What if we send her to New Albion to stay with Geoff and Joan? She can work with them, I don't know, help with the cows and the vegetable garden and get a real taste of life in the Republic. How does that sound, Corrag? It's a world away from here. You haven't seen your cousins since you were oh, two years old."

"I don't remember."

"I agree," said Alana, with the glint in her eye. "At first I thought it was a bad idea. After all, the Republic's ideas on education and adulthood are very different than ours. I just don't know how it will sit with the Council."

"I'll run it by Mitchell Culpepper. There is the youth emissary program. It's usually staffed by graduates of fine-tuning, but they may make an exception for me."

"And I'll get in touch with Joan. There's the risk of course."

"Of course. But paradoxically there are fewer opportunities for young people in the Repho. The reliance on market forces will always prove inefficient as a mechanism to harness the singularity."

"Do call Mitchell."

"I will dear. Tonight."

Ricky and Alana finished their dinner with occasional glances Corrag's way. The matter was closed as far as they were concerned. Corrag watched her parents, wondering at their ability to turn on a dime conversationally once all the options had been thoroughly considered. For her though, a year abroad loomed mysterious and menacing. She hadn't heard them talk about the New Albion family in a very long time, and why that would be the best option for her was not clear. Corrag had, in the back of her mind, figured they would find a way to get her private tutors to prepare for augmentation with some kind of mental health dispensation. Certainly it would have channeled her into the arts, but that was where she felt at home, without the responsibility for determining the way forward for the entire civilization. Just entertain us. That was the mandate for the ArtSmile corps coming out of the Federation system. Most of their recent mindscapes and challenges were pretty bland. The occasional bootleg memes from Sandelsky, the main branding of the Republic that teenaged hackers sometimes spread around the play spheres, far outstripped Democravian productions in technical flair; and they just seemed deeper, somehow more important.

She advanced around the dark corner. The street was empty except for a parked vintage Bundeswehr quadcopter on the right. She passed it and lifted her head. In her hand she hefted the laser pistol and aimed it at the bonfire about three blocks away. The Mandolin headquarters was a square, black obelisk, modeled on a classic Anish Kapoor sculpture. The fire, smelling of gasoline, raged around its doors, and she had to shoot her way through a crowd of ripper monkeys.

They were easy. They always aimed right for your head and all you had to do was duck several inches and fire back at the same time in their general vicinity. The game makers had been recently faulted at a consensus for setting the adversarial level purposefully down market in order to secure continued funding. For Corrag, the subtext was clear. Life was a popularity contest. No matter how efficiently the council liked to think it was doing its work you couldn't do away with the basic human flaws of wanting, desiring and seeking what was out there. Greater RAM speeds and advanced neural networks had never gotten to grips with the pattern-making propensity of the human brain and the magnetic allure of pleasure which threw up the energy-matter continuum all around. MandolinMonkey did a good job of smoothing the jolts of scenic transition and stimulating the pituitary with each new level attained. Still, she found herself impatiently bypassing the obvious level trap with a joystick function and flying down the hallways unmindful of lesser adventures and parallel opportunities.

Above and behind her sprung two Greckels, stoat-like creatures capable of quick dimensional extensions and sharp tears at limbs and throats. She felt a blatantly obvious turbo lift from their move that gave them away. Of course they were Gurgie and Mathew.

"Come with us," said a high-pitched voice.

She had five seconds. She knew she should check the table for power surges at least, but she felt compelled to follow. If they were leading her astray, so be it. She would find a way to dodge an ill end, as the game makers called it. Her avatar, an Elfin, had the power over water and fire and so was a logical complement to the Greckels' slippery land capabilities. What the game lacked was diversity of power source, the ability to shape shift and entertain various outcomes at the same time. But for now it would do. In the end, win or lose, the only thing that mattered was displaying the innovative spirit that the Founders wanted in the future leader corps. Once you had that figured out, everything else was an easy trick. The person that had helped her to climb the ranks Federation-wide was Ben Calder. Where was he now? Was he still alive? Or had the stint in the HumInt Corps in the Basin wars possibly killed him, as her father had suggested? A stab of fear hit Corrag at the thought of Ben dead.

They were in the obelisk. Corrag wondered how they had gotten in. Down the hall the two Greckels paused and stood on their hind feet at a nanowall display. There in a neon gothic font flashed the message:

Be a Vence with us at the Spring Fest.

She had their songs posted all over the soundscape in school. The Vences had painted their faces in ghoulish camouflage colors and had flouted the ideals of physical perfection and the singularity long enough to gain for themselves a diehard following. Gurgie's parents had been fans and so had Ricky, in his youth. But he hated their music now and cringed whenever Gurgie came over for a visit trailing *Blast Me Down Andromeda* out of her loose earpiece.

"Very smooth, Gurgie," said Corrag, pressing the joystick dialogue button beneath the thumb hold. The Elfin jumped and clapped, signifying acceptance of a strange, land-based phenomenon. Corrag smiled at the clever algorithm that had allowed her avatar to anticipate her feelings. Then the Greckels faded into the ether and she was alone. A blank look on the Elfin's severe, drawn face was intriguing, as if she were pondering the significance of life.

Corrag saved and hit the power off with her index finger, before any other competitors could appear to threaten her, and lay down on her bed. Sometimes the Elfin almost seemed to come alive and read her mind. That was the most frustrating thing, the apparent gap between her capabilities and actual human feelings. There were some who believed that bots had already made the transition, but Corrag was not one of them. For a while she had believed, and her parents and teachers still fostered the foundational concept that humans and bots would soon be equals in thought and feeling. But for Corrag the issue was now moot. In the last year, she would guess, she had come down thoroughly on the side that this equality was neither necessary nor desirable. Not that she dared to voice the opinion. It would place her beyond the sphere of Democravian influence and deem her "inconvenient" for continued leadership training. Because the ideal of the Democravian way, ever since the initial founding of the institutional state in 2022, was to raise a cadre of youth who would merge with the bots in order to undergo the transgalactic mission -- colonize the most desirable Earth-like habitable planets, 23 of them, that had been so far identified as potential targets in the Milky Way. And in the intervening two decades since the first councils and consensus meetings, the notion of youth had of course expanded so that almost all citizens with the appropriate formation could potentially qualify for merger. It was this very accessibility to the highest ideals of the state that gave Democravia its missionary fervor, its self-styled exceptionalism, and made it all the harder for Corrag to accept that she was swimming against the stream. Though she knew, in the darkness, under the sheets, about to fall asleep in the silence of the Edmundstown night that she was not really alone.

Edmundstown Senior School was divided into two floors, the Upper Deck and the Lower Hall. On the Upper Deck, Corrag took most of her classes except gym. Miss Schilling taught the humanities block for advanced seniors. They were touching on the literature of the transgressives, in the context of the decline of the West and the rise of the plural. Miss Schilling was a bright-eyed thirty-year old. Mathew and Gurgie sat in the front row and laughed at her references to James Joyce as "that old man in the trench coat hiding in the sand dunes." Corrag sat in the back row between Julian Alvarenga and Prualyse Kopeckwitz. She wondered what was that funny about Joyce. Was it his notion of the circularity of time, so maligned and disparaged? Miss Schilling, with her bright smile and sharp hairstyle, looked at her as if reading her thoughts.

"And of course you have had the night to reflect on the links to our core curriculum factor nine, and that is what? Corrag?"

"Factor nine?"

It had been flashing on the wall at the beginning of the class along with a soundscape by SwiftBoat.

"Oh yes. The need to transcend individuation and internalize utility," said Corrag.

"And how does our study of Joyce tie in?"

"Well, I don't quite know. I mean, yes, there were a lot of voices, but isn't it admirable for a man to try and capture the essence of his reality like that?"

"But the end result is a cacophony. A cacophony that at best yields a meager portrait of one individual's disillusion and bitterness. Democravian artists have dwarfed the possibilities of the transgressives. To end, Corrag, with Molly Bloom reminiscing on the romantic past, I'm sure you'll agree. Such a shoddy counterfeit of reality. When we compare that to the works of the Ontavians, collaborations that we will look at next week that mix the perspectives of symmetry and harmonics, it will all be clear," said Miss Schilling. Gurgie turned around and gave a hard stare.

"But it's about the common people struggling with the weight of history. Isn't that a part of what Democravia represents?"

"It's not good enough, Corrag. Not good enough. It disparages women."

"But so does *The Great Gatsby*. Look at Daisy. Irresponsible and careless and destructive."

"Yes, but Fitzgerald identified the malaise, the lack of tether in the primitive, unwashed American soul, the need for correction. The inevitability of self-destruction. That is a seminal work. If only Fitzgerald had correctly identified Zelda as a collaborator in his life work. The myth of the heroic male was still too strong. There were too many economic factors at work in its perpetuation. You've seen that in your history block. I want you to reference the SwiftBoat parody of masculine artistry. *Nietzche and Me.* You'll find it in Unit 28, I believe, in the Library archives for this course. In your reflective piece tonight remember to present in a visually appealing manner and to comment on the works of at least three of your fellow students. That's all for this morning, students. Smile all the while."

Julian Alvarenga smiled wanly at her.

"Nice try, Corrag. Going for the gusto, aren't you?"

"What is that, Julian? An obscure reference to 20th century advertising? Let me guess. Cigarettes."

"Close. Try beer."

"Try beer. Funny. Very transgressive of you."

Julian was the first of his siblings to attend the Upper Deck. They were a family of former farm workers, the dark-skinned people of the Valley, mostly displaced, like the majority of work sectors, by the first generation of semi-autonomous bots. He had a permeable quality, as if life was just passing through him that reminded Corrag of a sieve. She looked him in the eye to test her theory. He looked her right back and smiled. This was strange.

"Corrag? Can I see you a minute?"

Miss Schilling lifted her head at her desk. Corrag nudged past Gurgie.

"I'll wait for you," said Gurgie.

"By the O tank."

"Fine."

Miss Schilling looked tired. She patted her hair behind her ear and cocked her head at Corrag, who suddenly felt under siege, as if something had popped inside her skull.

"How is that essay coming?" asked Miss Schilling.

"It's not."

"I didn't think so. I've seen this before, you know. I want to help."

Corrag felt like crying.

"I'm taking a year. My father's going to clear it with Axion."

"Looks like poor Corrag is having a crisis."

"You don't need to rub it in."

"I'm a little bit angry, frankly. I offered to help you months ago." Miss Schilling thrust her hands out on the desk, splayed fingers on the console, which was flashing slogans and cafeteria menus and student visuals.

"But I don't believe in it anymore, Miss Schilling."

"Don't believe in what? What you're going through is perfectly natural. Your feelings of nostalgia and ... and anger are the signs of a higher calling. I so much want to recommend you for higher order augmentation. And it's going to raise questions about the entire program here if you don't complete the application process for Axion Fine-Tuning. You can't do that to us, Corrag."

Miss Schilling was sitting straight up on the chair and suddenly looking at her with that eagle-eyed augmented focus that made Corrag instinctively want to squirm. She looked down and away. Again the easy path beckoned -- to follow along and do what she was told and hope someday it would all be okay. That was the subliminal message, the factor X of the hidden curriculum not just of the Edmundstown Charter School but of the town itself. Perhaps even of Democravia.

"I'll try."

"More than try. Put in the Corrag effort that we all know you're capable of. Top shelf stuff. Give it all you've got. Do it for us, for the Wildcats. For Edmundstown. Make us proud."

"Is that all?"

"Yes, that's all. Share with me, please. And Corrag?"

"Yes?"

"Smile. All the while."

Corrag got out through the faulty energy panel that zapped her back with a slight jolt. The janitor, Mr. Breen, was already coming down the hall on the beat up old Segway, his laser torch repair tool swaying dangerously against his hip. At this time mid-morning the energy grid constantly experienced minor fluctuations as the wind either rose or fell, and the water desalination plants kicked in up and down the Kaiser aquifer, giving the bigger power users in the area headaches such as energy panel misalignments and nanowall absurdities. Mr. Breen smiled at Corrag as he would at a senior with some insider knowledge of these sorts of problems. Gurgie leaned against the wall and Mathew looked up and down the hall nervously at the river of well-dressed and contented Upper Deck students in their paisley and Kubik-patterned neoprenes with the various interchangeable logos of self-satisfied Democravian memes. There were few other teachers in the Upper Deck. Most of the classes, conducted via upload and lecture, needed only administrators to assist with student work in the study hall blocks. Miss Schilling had only a few more semesters of small class teaching before she would move on in the Axion system to upload lectures in a regional class encompassing the Western and Middle Southern districts.

At the O tank, Corrag fastened the mask to her face while holding her standard issue ExePad tablet in the other hand. The O had a sweet aftertaste. They added something to it, some kind of anesthetic. That was the rumor anyways. And on some days there was a caffeinated mix that heightened the fervor of students about to embark on a school-wide mission, one of the collaborative, experiential pieces. The last one, to Haiti, led by Mrs. Wilson, the head of the PTA, had been a disaster. Seven students had caught new forms of the pulmonary virus that had decimated the Caribbean and South America and had needed long stays at the Beth Israel Xen Kai Hospital in Matamoros.

"So, Corrag. Do you have anything to say?" asked Gurgie.

"Yes, I saw your visual. And yes, Of course I'll go with you to the Spring Fest. What did you think?"

"Well, you have been acting very strange lately," said Mathew, eyeballing her with mock augmented focus.

"I've had a lot on my mind. I haven't finished my application essay."

"Why not?" asked Gurgie. "You can't be thinking about transferring to the VocAg?"

"I am."

"Jesus, Corrag. You need to come with us tonight."

"Okay. I said I would. But more importantly, how do we dress? We're a team, right? Forget the Vences. Everybody's going to do that. I have an idea we go as Daisy and Tom and Gatsby. I'll be Gatsby. I have the perfect idea for a pants suit that my mother used to wear. It's in a box in the attic."

"But I thought we had discussed going as Joseph in *The Assistant*," said Gurgie.

"No, I was going to be Tobler the Inventor," said Mathew.

"Oh, that's right," said Gurgie, distracted by the sudden thinning of students as the next class began. They walked together towards the cafe. Corrag wondered at how easily Gurgie gave up on the Vences. The changes they all went through were happening way too fast and Miss Schilling was having way too big an impact on their social lives. Outside, a flock of small birds flew in a cloud by the energy panels, distorting and magnifying so as to seem a shade, like a hand drawing down upon the three of them as they walked along.

"The thing is," said Corrag, thinking aloud. "I like Daisy and Tom and Jay Gatz, whereas I don't like Joseph.

He's too pleasant ... and passive."

"Exactly. Just like Gatsby. Only the mask never slips," said Gurgie.

"Well, I'm not feeling very Chinese. But I am feeling destructive," said Corrag with a cackle, turning and leering at Mathew and Gurgie.

"Okay. Spring Fest is our last fling at childish role-play. So you want to celebrate that bourgeois trope of creative destruction. Be our guest," said Mathew.

"I just want to have fun," said Corrag coldly. "Mathew."

"Oh, God. Fun. Right, I forgot how important that was to you."

Corrag's brows wrinkled. Mathew was upsetting her.

"Doesn't mean we all feel the same way," said Mathew.

"You'll feel just like Miss Schilling wants you to feel, which is to say not feel anything at all. Isn't that the preconditioning? Too numb to think for ourselves so we take on the augmented way and don't have ourselves to answer to any more. How convenient."

Mathew and Gurgie looked at each other, letting their confusion about Corrag's defiance of the Democravian ethic of obedience show in the glance held between them.

"Corrag. Okay. We'll go as Daisy and Tom and you can be Gatsby. But we'll be Daisy and Tom as Walser's Chinese, as the assistants, and Gatsby will be the Inventor. We'll turn the two books around."

"That's the Gurgie I love the best." Corrag threw her

arms around Gurgie and spun in the hall. A teacher, Mr. Aarnits, glared at them through the open doorway of his classroom, and the emosensor directly overhead glowed a warning green.

The crowd outside the Taylor Jabones Civic Center seemed to undulate and throb as the Lyons family portagon pulled up to the curb. Mostly dressed in velvets and vintage chambrays and shades of purple and green, the colors of the Edmundstown Wildcats, purple for the Upper Deck and green for the Lower Hall, the students were an unrecognizable and restless mob in the customary spirit of the Spring Fest. Corrag had mixed feelings about the night. She mainly wanted to dance and forget about the issues confronting her at that moment.

"Good night," she said to nobody in particular as she stepped away from the open door of the van.

"What time do you expect to be picked up," said the driverbot, speaking from a juncture of the neckpiece and the swivel-cam head. It was Alana's voice.

"One thirty, please," said Corrag.

"Not acceptable. Twenty-two thirty at the latest. We will be at the loading station then. Please be there as well. Mind your manners."

Mind your manners. That was just like Alana, to remind her of the proper way to behave at a Spring Fest. As if she had not been a rabble rouser before Corrag had been born, one of the late 2020s leading Unoits who had marched on Federation Councils demanding an end to supression of the Vallegos and increasing availability of subsidized mezzopeptide and other corrections to the unenfranchised dwellers of New Canaan, as Democravia had then called itself. Corrag shuddered at the image in her mind of her mother as a young woman just a little beyond her own age.

As she made her way through the sea of bedecked and masked youth of Edmundstown, Corrag kept looking out for the familiar sight of her two closest friends. She had on a mobster fedora over her mass of long curls and a bone white Venetian bauta mask, tight cut Wall Street pants with black neoprene Night Wolf galoshes. A low cut, long, red vintage Hollywood silk coat and in her hands a digital wand-clock with wings finished off the outfit. Somebody jumped into her path with a black Zorro mask and a Spritz gun.

"Who are you?" asked the masked figure.

"No. Who are you?" asked Corrag.

"Your best friend." There were hoots of laughter as the crowd of booters egged the masked youth on. Corrag pushed by the group, and they sprayed their Spritz guns into the air, letting off the rainbow hues of the plasmic concoction. This caused an outbreak of similar Spritzfire around the pedestrian square in front of the Civic Center. Then the real fireworks began from the roof of the Center, and the crowd went berserk with cheering and shouting. Corrag stopped in her frenetic rush to the entrance steps and watched the waves of exploding color fanning out over her and descending on the crowd from the black night sky. The explosions and the crowd's reactive shouts of glee merged into a dull throbbing at the back of her mind. Corrag had a flash image of the fireworks she'd seen in the desert at her grandfather Al's ranch in Sonora. The old man had never been a hand at the consensus and thus remained outside the Democravian orbit until he died. But at his funeral he had been made an honorary recipient of the Arts Benefit Lifetime Award and his books uploaded into the official curriculum of the Augmentation Board, the 14 members from around the world, mostly Republican Homeland and Democravian, who controlled the IPP keys, the core of the Interneural Web, the old INW along whose frequencies ran the entire collective virtual sphere.

Corrag was about to look at her emosponder when she felt a tap on the shoulder and turned around to see two characters from some macabre production of musical theater complete with wigs and vintage paper Chinese umbrellas.

"Where did you get the umbrellas? I love them."

"You haven't said anything about the matching boots," said Gurgie. She pushed out her foot and Mathew rolled his eyes.

"Lizard skin. There was a Yaqui Indian in the family service who made them for my brother and I," said Mathew. His V mask in the dim light of the fireworks somehow perfectly fit him.

"Oh, you guys are absolutely the best. Shall we go in? These Spritz guns are driving me nuts."

"Let's do it," said Gurgie.

Inside, the event organizers had pumped up the O to maximum levels and the band onstage was putting out a synthesized auralscape that was also simultaneously being relayed along a local intranet. Dancers were plugged into wireless ear clips and gyrating along to the pulsating power chord driven harmonics. Refreshments in the form of fermented Maxergy drinks were being dispensed by generic bots laid on by the Western council, and info-point stands along the perimeter of the hall manned by Democravian council workers were representing the various work sectors, including a recruiting officer of the Democravian Military Defense Wing, a cubicle of mimics and aerobesthetes from the ArtSmile Corps, the VocAg table dispensing samples of hormone replacement snack from local Valley growers and *cooperativa* pickles, and of course the Daughters of Harmonious Memory, a social organization that looked after orphans and whose members' ancestors had fought in the New Canaanite wars, were flashing images of vintage industries such as the Hollywood cinema, the primitive visualscapes that had once so entranced the older set. Gurgie, Mathew and Corrag stepped along, driven by the sweep of the crowd into the middle of the dance floor where the lights from the emosensors were pulsating the fastest. The band began playing *Heaven's Gate*, a classic Spring Fest staple. Dancers jumped together, craning their heads back and pumping both fists in the air to the bass line rocking the hall. They came closer together and then fell back like a human wave, the youth of the Valley celebrating the apogee of the year. The rockers with the Spritz guns, along with the girls, many of them costumed as simple sex workers or in jury-rigged uniforms with the insignia and the classic meme of the HumInt Corps, *Ridet Geritur*, linked arms on the outside of the dancers and began to circle. And then the choreographed symbolic imagery was lost, subsumed as the dancers spilled out beyond the circumference of the steppers.

When the song ended, Corrag looked around, slowly coming to her senses. She unsnapped her ear clip and felt her way towards the outside of the dancing mob with her hand. The next song increased the intensity, and the circle of Lower Hall booters renewed their boundary walk. Corrag waited for the right moment, a lull in the energy pattern, and broke out through the human line. She walked over to the refreshment valve and slipped on an O mask. Her head cleared and she felt for an instant a sense of euphoria, somehow almost organic, as if she were suddenly light years away, on a distant moon of her own, with no impinging concerns about the future and what it held weighing her down. She wished she could hold on to the moment. Even better, she wished she could share it with someone.

All the Zorros and Buzzyears and the Hillaries and Eunique Biebers -- they were all kids she would have known from Lightning Leagues or fencing classes or the myriad theatrical productions she'd been in through the grade and middle schools. Corrag found it fascinating that in this sea of familiar yet bizarre anonymity she was free, free in a way that carried an exotic charge of exhilaration. She had overheard parental stories about the dangers of Spring Fest, about kids not being able to distinguish reality from fantasy and jumping from the upper balconies awash in feelings of euphoria and invincibility. This was their first taste of the Augment, after all, of the freedom that came with giving up their childish identities. But Corrag wondered about herself. Would she be truly able to merge with the path and put the Democravian nation's well being before her own desires? Sometimes she thought she was too enamored of her own thought processes, of the way her mind wanted to dig and scratch its way out of the traps the adult world set. She was a feral creature, a throwback to a more primitive way of life. It didn't seem to be something she'd inherited from Alana and Ricky, the two of them epitomes in her mind of the deep-rooted and loyal communitarian ideals that ran in her family. Where did she get it, this unhappiness, this habit of solitary thought she'd secretly cultivated in the midst of privilege?

A boy in a uniform, tall, with a purposeless gait, approached from out of no particular direction, from the darkness. His mask was the same as Corrag's, just a little older, not as shiny in the pulsating flashes of neon, and he stopped in front of her. Corrag looked carefully, noting the moment of recognition with some distance. Nevertheless, her heart skipped a few beats and her mind raced. She didn't expect this. It wasn't fair of him to just show up. Without turning, Ben Calder addressed her, staring out at the dance floor.

"I thought I might see you, Corrag."

"You don't mind rocking the boat. Did you miss me?"

"I don't know what you mean. I'm not supposed to be here."

"You never called. Why is that? Were you trying to forget? And now you're here because you couldn't? You never even called. I mean you have an emosponder, right? They couldn't have taken that away. Why didn't you ever call? I thought you were dead."

"Sometimes I wanted to be dead. But here I am. And you? I hear you're entering your application for fine-tuning."

"Not yet."

She had a sudden need to see his face.

"Come with me. We'll check out the balconies," she said.

"That's not allowed."

"Just come. We'll figure it out."

"Do you know the way?"

"I'll find it."

Corrag led him past the stands to the far end of the hall. Gurgie and Mathew were dancing and looked over briefly in her direction. She pretended not to notice. She grabbed a Maxergy freshener shot, and Ben followed suit and they walked together out past the dancers and the presenters from the ArtSmile Corps lounging and stretching in a circle by an unused energy panel exit. Corrag waited until the music reached a moment of high intensity and then reached swiftly with her time wand and tripped the converter switch on the box like she'd observed Mr. Breen do. This turned the receptor back to the recently phased out digital signal. The panel bars began to throb in a slow rhythm, in line with the less powerful digital pulse. Then she looked at Ben and nodded, and he slipped through the bars of the panel. She waited a few seconds, held her breath and with a sudden movement jumped between the bars to the other side. She felt the hairs on her head and neck rise with the kinetic energy but not enough to set off any alarms.

The music and hubbub from the center sounded distant. The walls of the hall they were in were dusty. The unpainted cement had splotches of water staining down from the ceiling. Ben was looking into the dim distance in some inert way. Corrag reached up and touched his masked cheek, and he recoiled.

"Can you just take it off?"

"I ... you," Ben spluttered. "You don't have the right, Corrag."

He reached up and pulled off the mask. His face looked old, tired. His eyes were dark, and he looked away when she stared. She tried hard to remember the way he had used to look, the memory she had of him the day he'd explained to her that he could wait with his avatar at a crossroad and that if he concentrated he could sense the virtual enemy before it appeared. He had been so alive, so focused and so quick to see a way. Underneath the mask of this face there was that other face, she was sure.

"Where have you been, Ben?"

"In the south quadrant with the Corps."

"What do you want to do now?"

"Corrag, why do you think you can ask me that?"

"You're Ben. My friend."

"No. I'm Private Calder of the 175th Air Infantry Battalion, Mayagua Sector Six."

"So, that doesn't mean anything to me. You're Ben. Why did you come back?"

"I don't know." He walked away down the hall. Corrag followed. She wanted to touch him, to turn him around. Where was he going? It scared her to see him this way. She didn't want to lose him. He was the last link to her childhood, to the hopes, unformed and unspoken as they had been, of a happiness of her own. At the end of the hall, where it emptied into a larger stairwell, he stopped and craned his head around, looking up into the dark.

"What do you see?"

"Nothing. Come on."

"No, Ben. I mean about us."

"About us?" Ben took his foot off the step and turned towards her. He shifted his weight uneasily and looked into her face intently.

"There is no us. We don't exist."

"What about trusting your instincts, Ben? What about finding the way?" Corrag's voice cracked with emotion. She heard the echo of it down the hall and had the sensation of falling, as if she'd been dropped into a time warp.

"Shut up, Corrag. That's just stupid."

"Stupid? Ben, that's what we lived for. Don't you remember? You taught me everything I knew. You were the best gamer ever before you dropped it. Left it all behind. Said you'd be back and we'd figure it out. I believed you, Ben. We can find a way to be happy. In a new way. Our own way. What about all that? Are you going to say you don't remember? Private Calder or whatever you are?"

Ben turned around and walked back towards her.

"You've never been on patrol in the Nicanor. You've never done three weeks on the hunt. You don't know what it's like to be holding a Nicanor prisoner and looking into eyes that just mirror back the hatred. There is no you or me. Just the next day. And the next camp. And the next. You disappears. Me is just a hole to put food into. The Nicanor kills you."

"Don't go back. Stay with me. We'll find work on the *cooperativa* farm. I'll do the VocAg."

"No, Corrag. Finish your fine-tuning. Be what you need to be."

"And smile all the while?"

"Yes."

"Why, Ben? Why?"

"Because otherwise it hurts too much. We never knew pain, Corrag."

Ben took her hands in his.

"I know it now."

"There is no you. There is no me. Listen to me."

"No. I won't. I listened to you before and you lied." Corrag pulled her hands away. She wanted to run back to the dance floor. Forget she'd ever seen him or ever wished to see him again.

"What's a lie?" asked Ben, his voice small, tinny, just a remnant of the fire and humor that had once filled him.

"What have they done to you Ben? It's like you've been augmented, only worse."

Ben stared at her, unable to say a thing.

"What is it?"

Instead of answering, he turned and ran up the stairs, taking them two or three at a time, his legs churning and arms flailing. He'd disappeared from sight in a matter of seconds, just the sound of the boot strikes on the concrete echoing more and more distantly as he ascended. Corrag followed. She climbed at a slower pace, hands on the cold metal rail, listening for the sound of Ben up ahead. But there was just silence. When she reached the top flight, there was a metal door propped open.

Outside, the cold night air rushed by in a breeze from the north. The San Fermin Mountains ranged in a dark silhouette. Ben was standing on the edge of the roof overlooking the Convention Center plaza. The red lights of Federation weather and surveillance drones filled the night sky. Corrag came up next to him and looked out over the city.

"That's where we grew up, Ben. We existed in it. That was real. You and me, we were real, right?"

"Yes."

"But you think I should fine tune?"

"I do."

"But look out there. We can discover it for ourselves. We can be free."

"There's no such thing. All the desires will be reprogrammed and rebooted to the higher order."

"Well, then. Why try?"

"Because otherwise we die."

"But you're going to die, Ben."

"Not if I kill first. In three months, with confirmed kills in the seven hundred or higher range, I can be a candidate for Officer Training School."

"Is that what you want?"

"What I want. It's what is, Corrag. That's all. There is no other way. Some day we can live in the heavens on the planets of Betelgeuse or Andromeda. Our offspring will rule the galaxies, fill the universe with their thought forms and productions. Don't you want that?"

"That's not alive with me. I want to live here and now. With you. Have children, not offspring. Raise them to run and breathe and drink and dream in the mountains and valleys of Earth. That's why I knew you'd come back. I knew you would, just not tonight. I expected you in the summer. That's why I was holding out on sending off the fine-tuning application. I wanted to be here when you got back."

"There's a break in the fighting now," said Ben distantly. "The Naguani have retreated. It's strange. I expect they're gathering strength for a major counteroffensive. We've tried to burn them out. Dry up the water cycle with localized cloud inhibition and carpet napalm bomb the rivers. But they keep coming. They never stop. No matter how many you kill there's always more of them. Especially at night. They can shape-shift and come at you. The jaguars can get by the lasers. In your sleep. That's the worst sound.

"What is?"

"The guys in their bunks being mauled, Corrag. All the guys in the Corp, we just want to survive long enough to get the kill range target and get out. It's as if the war is bigger than we are."

"What about the girls?"

"Well, it's Democravia, right? The girls in the Corps can work their way up to augmentation with a kill rate, too."

"That's wrong."

"Yes, it is. Kind of."

She couldn't see his face in the dark, but wanted to. At that instant she sensed he needed her. The distance between them was threatening to blow up and obliterate whatever they had left between them, any memory of a friendship, any hope Corrag had for the future. So she took his hand and pulled him away from the edge of the roof.

"Let's go. I know where we can go."

"Where, Corrag?"

"Anywhere, I don't really know where. It doesn't matter where."

They went down and out through the dance hall with their masks on again. Corrag tapped the emosponder on her left wrist and picked up Gurgie's avatar on the display.

"I'm going out."

"Where?"

"Don't know. I'm with Ben."

"Please be careful, Corrag. Think about your steps before you take any. Be sure."

"If I did that I'd never get anywhere, Gurgie. I'll be back soon. Don't worry."

Corrag tapped three times on the emosponder, putting it to sleep. Together, she and Ben walked briskly, wordlessly, until they found a zipbike out on the street about five blocks from the Civic Center. After punching in the emergency code for civilian first responders on the meter, Ben mounted it and motioned for her to jump on the back. Corrag smiled. Now they were getting somewhere.

"How long do we have?"

"Three hours showing."

"That should get us to Ysidro."

"Do you remember how to get there?"

"I think so. Go out north on the old causeway."

Ben twisted the throttle, and the zipbike responded instantly, silently accelerating to eighty miles an hour on the quiet streets. Ben braked on the corners and leaned as if he'd just gotten off the speed circuit training ground. Under the Spring Fest curfew, he didn't have to worry about other traffic, and by keeping his headlights off he avoided alerting any police radars.

Ysidro had been Ricky and Alana's favorite camping ground in her childhood. They'd often pitched a tent in the shadow of the canyon land. She felt herself looking for a way back towards those days, the sense of security, satisfaction and rightness of those summers, drinking in the sun on the slippery stones of the riverbed. In her mind the golden glow of the memory was a currency worth guarding. In those years, the wars of the New Canaanite alliance against the secessionist states had still been fresh in Ricky and Alana's memory, and Ricky had always kept a firearm loaded inside the tent in case of surviving secessionist marauders, but they never saw any. Alana had always played up the possibility in order to keep Corrag close by, warning her to not go too far along the riverbed by herself. But one of them had always been there with their old sheepdog Haj, hovering, as she had built her fantasy castles with river stones worn soft in the wettish mud in early June from the melted snowpack, an afterglow of the past. She imagined that somehow Ben sensed her giving directions by shifting her weight on the back of the zipbike, and they did end up somewhere very close to Ysidro, on an old logging road. Ben pulled up on the shoulder and parked. They got off and removed their helmets. Around the corner of the mountain was just a hint of the dawn to come. In a few hours the alarms would be going off and the search drones would be activated. She couldn't see his face very clearly.

"What are you thinking?" Corrag asked.

"I'm thinking you're brave to be out here with someone you hardly know. What would your father and mother think?"

"They already think I'm a lost cause. It doesn't matter to me. Besides, what do you mean hardly know?"

"Do you think you know me, Corrag?"

"Of course. You haven't changed for me. I know you've been through hell, Ben. Don't get me wrong."

"Then help me out here. Shine your light for me."

Corrag knelt beside him with her open emosponder. Ben used his utility tool to unclip the casing on the zipbike's fuse and carefully pull two hair-thin filaments that powered the geopositioning transponder. Then he turned the bike on again and rolled it over to a stand of aspen and behind some rocks where it couldn't be seen from the road.

They hiked up a trail that paralleled the creek in the canyon below and then crossed an old footbridge. The sign for the trailhead was lying on the ground, rusted and overgrown with weeds. Ben said he knew an old hunting cabin that had been used by his uncles before the war. Somewhat hesitantly at first, Corrag agreed on it as a destination. She really wanted to stay on the bridge and watch the water rushing underneath their feet, the way it sparkled and crystallized into the colors of the rainbow. The sun had come out and warmed up the air. Flies buzzed around the body of a dead bird. They marched ahead, Ben pushing the pace, perhaps concerned about getting far enough up the trail to evade the police.

"Gurgie will tell them I'm with you. Mom and Dad won't mind," she said, thinking out loud.

"Colonel Bohjalian won't be so easy-going. I'm supposed to be back on base as of twenty three hundred."

"What will they do?"

"I'll be assigned to care-taker duty for a month once we deploy back to the Basin."

"Is that the worst they can do?"

"The worst is the CDC labor camp in the Ozarks for deserters. I don't think they'll send me there for going AWOL with my girlfriend."

Corrag liked the sound of being called Ben's girlfriend. She thought of her father's rants against girls who relied on their boyfriends for their own sense of acceptance. He wanted her to be more independent and self-reliant, but it was another area where she differed with his thoughts for her. Corrag liked the idea of being important in a boy's life, of being necessary to someone, and didn't think it made her any less of a human being to enjoy or desire it. Alana didn't like Ben for other reasons. She thought he was too smart to be completely trustworthy. People like Ben, she would say, often needed re-education components before being assigned to an augmentation track. This escapade would be further proof of the rightness of her judgment. But Corrag didn't want them, her parents or the school or the Council, to blame Ben for leading her astray. She wanted to be the author of her own demise, if there was going to be such a thing. Let it be by her own hand at least. But for Ben, let it be a mild reprimand, whatever caretaker duty was. It didn't sound so harsh. She didn't want him suffering on her behalf.

After about a mile, the trail took a turn up a steep, rocky face. There was a cabin at the top of a ridge, sheltered from the prevailing wind by the mountain behind it. The siding was faded, and gaps showed between the boards. Scraps remained of the tarpaper that had once protected the wood from the elements. When they looked back, Corrag and Ben could see the desert, the suburbs of Edmundstown and then the city on the eastern edge and Mono Lake far in the distance -- just a dot of iridescence in the foothills. And far off behind those hills was the ocean.

The momentary sense of peace was broken by the barks of a dog and the sound of a door clapping shut. They turned round. An old man, faded into the dirt, had appeared beside the shack. He neither waved nor moved. Nor did his attitude suggest fear. The dog barked again and the old man leaned down and scratched its ears.

"Hi there," shouted Ben, but the old man made no sign of hearing.

"Let me handle this," said Corrag, putting her hand on Ben's arm. "We don't want to scare him." She was thinking of Ben in his uniform, and there was something frail and covert about the old man's quietness. She walked over, and the dog growled as she approached.

"Nice dog," she said as she got close to the old man.

He looked up and squinted. The dog was a mix, with blue husky eyes -- an old mutt. The old man straightened. The top of his head was at a height with her shoulders, and his hair, greasy and long, hid his face. He wiped his hair away with one hand and looked at her with grey, lidded eyes.

"I've been waiting a long time for you," he finally said.

"Who are you?" she asked with exaggerated wonderment, placating his delusions.

"Abel. Abel Marin. You and your friend are just fine. What are your names again?"

"Corrag and Ben. What's your dog's name?"

"Sandy."

"Perfect. Hi Sandy." She petted the dog and the old man began to cry. She noticed he wiped his tears away and let the hair fall in front of his eyes again. Ben came over.

"Ben, this is Abel and Sandy. Why are you crying, Abel? There's no need for that," said Corrag, horrified that he might think they meant to harm him.

"Crying," said Abel. "Is how a man keeps a heart strong. I've been waiting a long time. I thought the world was done with me. And now you're here at last."

Ben looked at her. She gave him a stern look back and shook her head.

"You've come back at last," continued Abel. "Let me give you something."

"No, you don't have to give us anything," said Corrag.

"Water would be nice," said Ben.

Sandy began to bark as the old man moved back to the shack.

"Come in," he called, holding the door open. The rusty springs squeaked as it shut behind them.

"This used to be my uncles' hunting cabin," announced Ben.

"The old boys knew how to live. They've died out now. Nothing left. We need to mourn for the earth and bring back the old ways again," answered Abel.

It was dark once the door closed. There were no windows. Their eyes adjusted, and Abel motioned for them to sit. He brought them two Mason jars of water he poured from a metal bucket. They sat in the folding chairs by the sink. The cracks in the siding allowed some light inside, enough to see. There was a rough plank workbench against the wall piled high with animal skins and bones and dried plants, with wild flowers and dried leaves in bunches. Corrag drank the water. She wondered who Abel thought they were. He was a crazy old survivor, one of the holdouts from the war of secession that the Council had never bothered to track down because he had never appeared on anybody's lists. The fact that he could still be up here on his own was itself an indictment of their claims of control.

"This water is strange. It has a taste of something weird," said Ben.

"Spring-fed mountain water. I'll show you where I get it," said Abel. "When I first come up here there was no water. I had to find it. I was just a little tyke. But I hardly remember that. Anyway it's not important. You need to know, but not about me. I'm just the messenger. It's the earth that speaks."

Ben looked at her in the semi-darkness. He thought Abel was a crazy old coot. But Corrag wanted to keep listening to him. There was something soothing and calm about the shack and his voice. Sandy poked her hand with his muzzle and she petted him.

"What does it say, Abel?" she asked absentmindedly.

"Hmm? I don't know. Listen, you two is hungry. I forgot I need to feed you. Let me give you some food."

He disappeared into the darkness between the workbench and the far wall. Ben and Corrag looked at each other, shifting the folding chairs around to see each other easier. Ben smiled, as if all of this was part of some plan he had foreseen and devised. Corrag had questions about Abel she needed answered. Wouldn't he have needed inoculations against dengue and the avian virus that had wiped out the population of the mountain states? How had he avoided the orbiting aerial surveillance satellites and their heat sensor cameras that spotted the signals of life processes from space? Why was he allowed to survive here on his own? She wanted to whisper to Ben, but she stilled her curiosity. It was all right to not know all the answers. Clarity was over-rated.

When he returned, he brought with him a bowl with dried roots. He peeled them and then scraped with the knife into a mound of flakes. He produced part of a leg bone of some animal from which he cut sinews of dried meat and placed it all back in the bowl at their feet on the ground. Ben got out of his chair and sat cross-legged on the earth floor tamped almost smooth. Corrag followed suit. The meat was tough and hard to chew, but the vegetable matter had some moisture left in it, which almost gave it a palatable taste. They were both hungrier than they realized after the hike. It was about mid-morning but almost pitch black, except for the light coming through the cracks.

"My Mama and Papa come up here from Sonora with a bunch of folks. They were mostly Yaqui. They were not people who farmed or went looking for that kind of work. They were looking for the mountains because they knew the end was coming and the Spanish missions had told them to be on the lookout for signs of the war. They refused to fight for General Walker when he tried to put down the men who wanted their freedom, so a lot of them were put in jail. And then the rest took off in a big convoy for the north, because that way was cooler weather, and in those days there was tremendous heat. You two probably are too young to remember. For a while we were in Arizona. That's where I learned my English in a little school there that was broken up by secessionists who wanted to kill my mother because she was the leader of the group of women teaching them the ways of the medicinals. You're eating some there; that's *lechuguilla* root, which is good for your heart. The secessionists didn't want us helping others to live free and together in nature. They wanted it all under their control in the name of the markets. You remember that part. The markets were going to be the answer to everything. Just put us all on the shelves of the market, you know. So anyway we came up here I was about five I guess by then and the deer were the first to notice. And this was after the big battles in the Mississippi where they loosed the crazy winds and tornadoes that knocked us back; and that got out of control, and then there was sickness on the land for many years. They said it was bird flu and had us put down all our flocks, but then they said it was a fix that all the corporates had put on to starve us out. The deer helped us survive long enough to get our bearings, and we lived up here pretty much on our own, and once in awhile we went down to the highway and just stayed there watching the traffic, waiting for our cousins on a certain date, the anniversary of the lady of the rosary, which is in October, I believe. I've almost lost track of time. What year are we in? It doesn't matter. Time is ending anyway. The planets will sink back into the fire of the suns, and we'll soon see if there is more than one universe. I believe there is because the deer tend to believe that this is not all there is. That's why they don't mind dying and giving up their hearts for us. That is the sign, you see. That is the final sign of the grandmothers that they talked about and my mama and papa talked about and even you talked about the first time you came up here. Do you remember? You always said you would come back, and now you have."

While he talked Ben and Corrag ate. Soon it felt like they'd always been there and it was the most natural thing in the world to listen to Abel's voice telling his stories that opened up into a world they had never known, despite Abel's assurances to the contrary, implicating them in its meanings, an alternate reality that existed in his mind. His voice was so soft, and he seemed so sure. Maybe it was possible he had known they were coming.

Ben's initial anxiety went away, and Corrag wondered whether there was something in the food that was shifting their sense of time. Later, when the sun had risen halfway up the sky, judging from the light coming in the open door, she followed Sandy outside and saw Abel working in the ditch that ran along the back of the shack, perpendicular to the trail that she could see continuing up to the face of the mountain. She wandered over and saw Abel face down in a hollow, through which she could see just the faintest glint of water running. He was mumbling words in a language she was sure she had never heard. Then a black bird flew overhead. She thought it was a crow, and Sandy barked at it. Abel got to his knees and turned to see her standing behind him.

"Hi there, Corrag. I was just thanking the water for bringing you here. You and Ben. After all these years you've returned. And the water always promised. So I'm giving thanks. You know, you can bring the water wherever you go if you remember how. I'll show you later again. I'll show you and Ben."

"I've never been here before, as far as I know," said Corrag.

"Well, there's stuff you're not aware of. Stuff you don't know because you've buried it. But that's okay. It's all part of the plan," he said cheerily.

"Plan? We don't believe in that," said Corrag. She had an urge to test his assurance. "There's a process of space and time unfolding and we humans need to stay ahead of it. We can do that with our scientists who see and measure and analyze. Before the planet dies. What kind of God lets his planet die?"

"The planet die? The planet's just getting started, Corrag. I'll show you. There's no need to look for others."

"Are you saying the scientists are wrong?"

"Not wrong. Sometimes they're looking at the world through their lenses and what have you and a little ant will come up from behind and bite them on the ass. That's God playing with them because he has a sense of humor. That's all. Not wrong. It's what they do. It's good to use what He gave us, and put it all together. But see what I mean? There's a lot of stuff we know that the scientists haven't figured out. Which is why it's important. You know what I'm saying, Corrag?"

"I never knew my grandparents."

"Listen to the grandparents. And the scientists, Corrag. They're both right."

Abel laughed and jumped up from the ditch so that he appeared beside her. His age was impossible to gauge with his wrinkled brown skin and lidded eyes. Other times he seemed barely in his twenties with his strong, sure movements and rapidly shifting facial expressions. Corrag thought he was like water itself -- radiant, sparkling, and larger than he appeared, as if he contained within himself reserves of strength and wisdom.

They walked with Abel and Sandy up the mountain along a ravine. Ben and Corrag trailed behind, and Ben stopped often to look out over the valley from the ledges. They kept going higher up, scrambling over the boulders, barely keeping Abel and Sandy in their sight up ahead. Corrag was trying to explain how she felt about Abel, as if she had known him for a long time. She had never met anybody so strange, and yet she had also never felt as comfortable with somebody in the first moments after meeting. It was as if he had some knowledge about her that was the missing piece of a puzzle she had been trying to reconstruct without knowing it all her life. The school, her parents, had all contributed valuable pieces, but had also missed out some of them.

Ben thought she should be more wary of her enthusiasm.

"Look, there's no way he could direct the water the way you think, with the powers of his mind," said Ben making exaggerated vibrating gestures with his hands like some old vaudeville wizard from the movies. On him the gesture seemed forced. She couldn't think of an immediate answer. She was hurt that Ben couldn't see what she saw in Abel and would so easily dismiss him as some unimportant aspect of the landscape. Ben was focused on seeking advantage in a way that bothered her. As if the default setting in him was the gamer that was always looking ahead to the next junction, always seeking opportunity to gain strength for the next confrontation with the inevitably lurking enemy. But that wasn't the way the world worked. Everything went and returned and the ego was like a dam that held back the water pumped by the motion of the universe. Eventually the mechanism would fail. It was what Miss Schilling had been aiming at in her halting way to teach them and Ben had yet to see. Perhaps the war with the Naguani would teach him.

The trail was invisible except for a slight wear in the line of scrub. They were coming down the backside into a valley of young pines growing out of scrub grass. Abel detoured around the valley and kept along the ridges, hopping from rock to rock like a mountain goat. It was tough to keep up, and even Ben was getting winded. At the end of the valley it became clear why he had detoured. There was a concrete wall, an old dam from one ridge to the next. Corrag marvelled at the premonition she'd had of it. The valley had once been a lake.

"You know what this was?" asked Ben.

"What?" she asked.

"Lake San Pedro."

"That's why they built the desalination plant before

we were born. I remember my Dad talking about it. He said it gave the Federation more control over the water supply then the old hydro system which was rigged for the big farmers and fat cats," said Corrag.

"Yeah. It's pretty dry now."

Abel waited on a flat rock with Sandy. Corrag and Ben took their time climbing down to him.

"Wanted to show you the old world that's disappearing. You bringing the new way. The water flows strong. That's why you need to listen to your tears. It's the water calling from inside. Don't bottle it. Here look at this," said Abel.

The flat rock was the top of the wall. Abel walked them out along it. They could look over and see to the north through the mountains what had once been the old Inland Empire, the agricultural heartland of the United States until the years of drought and secession put an end to the decrepit model of so-called representative government of the people by the corporate interests.

"This was Lake San Pedro," said Ben.

"That's what your people called it. It never had a name," said Abel.

Out in the middle, they stopped and sat on the edge. Abel handed out some food from a satchel bag over his shoulder. It was a dried, almost unpalatable sort of plant matter. He even gave some to Sandy, who wolfed it down whole.

"I know it's hard. Just eat it. You won't be hungry and it will help you see what is really here." Abel didn't say another word. Hours passed, and the sun went behind the western mountain. Corrag fell asleep. In the dim light of the late afternoon, Ben asked Corrag to come with him. He had climbed down the face of the dam and come back up. She got to her feet and followed. It wasn't hard to get down the wall. There were built in handholds and steps. Then at the bottom she could see what he had seen, the crack and the water flowing through, not a torrent, just a trickle.

"He's right. The water is coming," said Ben.

"Do you think it's safe?"

"The dam? It won't go immediately. But eventually it will crumble."

"What now? What about us?"

"What do you mean?"

"Well, we have a choice. He's given us a clear choice. Follow the dam or the water. Which is it?"

"Corrag, I don't know what it is Abel gave us to eat, but I don't really see we have a choice. We can't stay here. We have to go back up and get home."

"Right now, Ben. What's your choice?"

"You're scaring me, Corrag. Don't talk like that."

She could see he was as frightened and confused as she was when faced with the wall of the world and its seemingly inescapable logic. They sat together and waited for the night. Ben leaned over and put his arm around her and hugged her closer. The dam wall grew dim and the black bird swooped down from it overhead.

"Is that the crow?" asked Corrag.

Ben didn't answer. He was asleep.

Instead of the concrete wall, there was a waterfall,

with an iridescent cascade of water broken in a moonlit glow. Deer stood along the banks of the river and tall pines had grown in the surrounding fields. She heard Abel call for Sandy. She heard her father call her name. Where were they?

"Ben. What time is it?"

Ben woke up and looked at his emosponder.

"Oh, my God. It's late. Let's go, Corrag." He stood and pulled her to her feet. Where were they? Disoriented, she followed his voice as he called from above. Then she could see the wall of the dam as her eyes adjusted to the darkness. Where had the waterfall gone? It had been such a vivid presence. But now she felt a gnawing in her gut and her legs shaking as she climbed. When she reached the top of the wall she collapsed in a heap. Sandy barked and dug at her hair with his paw.

"I'm okay, Sandy. I'm okay."

Abel held her by the chin and dribbled in water to her mouth from an old tin canteen. It tasted sweet. Her eyes, ears, even her sense of taste were playing tricks on her. Then there was a loud noise, and the lights blinded her. Sandy barked and Abel yelled.

"Run, Sandy. Go boy."

The lights were followed by cable dropping out of the hatches of the Federation Home Air UC7 reconnaissance choppers, and rappelling soldiers descended to the ground in quick succession. Corrag screamed.

It took about a minute. Working in silence, they handcuffed and blindfolded the two of them and bundled them towards a chopper whose blades were still whirling.

Corrag cried out Ben's name. He didn't answer.

"Keep quiet," said a soldier with his hand on her shoulder. Dirt and gravel kicked up from the downdraft of the whirling blades. Unseen hands pulled her onboard. Then they picked up and flew off into black space. Corrag cried for what she'd seen and for the childhood sense of possibility she'd left behind in that mountain valley. She let the tears flow as Abel had said. She never had the chance to talk to Ben, and for years wondered if he had seen the same things she had: the waterfall, the deer and the moonlit wonders of a reborn world.

Two -- Metamorphosis

The process turned out to be benign given that her family was already on the Stellar Rankbook for potential colonists. Ben was not so lucky. She was turned over to the Testers who scanned for signs of atrophy in the amygdala and prefrontal lobes and conducted reactive surveys for empathetic alineation. Then in conjunction with the parents a plan of remediation was devised. It consisted initially of sessions with Federation attorneys. Corrag's had a bristling moustache and an aggressive conversational style in which all queries ended up leading to Corrag having to declare her agreement with his propositions, arrived at after much initial small talk, that for example Democravian policies on communal property rights, or the war with Basin tribes for resource conservation, were sound and in the interest, as he said repeatedly, with minor variations, of "human progress." Corrag found herself getting nauseous during these sessions. Then they finally released her from the holding cell in Edmundstown's Federation courthouse and she changed out of the orange jumpsuit into a dress and shoes that Alana had dropped off. The guard, a black woman with a frumpy middle-aged face, told her Ben had been shipped out via Tubid to São Paulo that morning for the front line Federation camp in the Basin with his regiment and that he was on probation after having been judged mentally stable but "in need of rigor," which usually meant a demotion in rank. But given that he was a private already, he would be placed on foot patrol for extra weeks, which in the Basin could be a death sentence.

The guard woman's face displayed no emotion even with Corrag scanning hard for it, for any kind of sympathy. She felt it was a kind of monstrous thing not to have any emotion for Ben in the face of this plight that after all was her fault not his, and she wanted to blame somebody else. The guard woman was a convenient target, but she decided she did not hate her. Instead she hated the Federation with its rules and silly processes. That was a hard call because after all was said and done it was still her country, and her family were part of the tradition of communitarian democracy, which stood for a land of multipurpose and the greater good. But the guard woman wouldn't even look her in the eye, although to be fair she had told more than her duty would require about Ben and his fate. But not to see how it hurt her, not to be there at that moment. That was just Corrag being too soft. That was what Gurgie always accused her of, of lacking the killer instinct you needed in life, even despite all the kumbaya they got in the schools and from their parents. You had to be tough to survive. That was what Gurgie said. As if she was in any way tough. Corrag knew she was lacking in that quality. But she had her wits. She trusted in them with no reservations.

"You got a comb?" asked Corrag in front of the mirror in the bathroom. She was the only girl in there. The other women prisoners, mostly in their twenties and thirties, were in the gym walking around or talking together in small groups on a break.

"Nah. Sorry," said the guard woman. She shifted her weight and tried to find something else to look at. She was bored. Corrag used her fingers to pull her hair into a semblance of order.

"Do I look okay?"

"You isn't going to nobody's party."

"Every day is a party in my world."

The guard woman put her hands behind her back and cuffed her. Corrag did not resist.

"Do you really have to?"

"Of course. You still under custody."

Then they walked down the halls and the panel slid open, and there were Ricky and Alana dressed in their formal suits and the Federation attorney and the judge in his robes seated beside them. The guard marched her up to the assembled group, uncuffed her hands, and smirked at nobody in particular.

"Corrag Lyons you have been deemed fit for release under the proviso of Security Code 308 section B," said the judge in a thin, reedy voice. The anti-aging hormones were not totally blocking the effects of advanced years on his vocal production. "At this point your family and Mr. Shearstein will inform you of the state's need for redress and your program of remediation and re-education."

Ricky and Alana were beside her, hugging and kissing her together.

"Oh, Corrag. We've been sick with worry," said Alana. Corrag felt a flush of relief to be free and so glad to see her parents. The nightmare was almost over. The attorney cleared his throat and interrupted.

"We need to inform you, Corrag, that there will be mandatory meetings every two weeks."

"Where?"

"With me."

"Oh."

Alana was crying. Ricky's face had a mixture of repentance and concern that Corrag associated with his public persona as a college administrator. But she was almost home.

"We need you to sign off on the agreement and the admission of guilt," said Ricky. The attorney held out the reader.

"Can I scan it before I sign?"

"Of course," said Ricky.

Corrag took the reader and quickly read the document. There were bullet points at the end, which detailed her misdemeanors:

☒ *Betraying positions of trust*

☒ *Absconding with communal property*

☒ *Inappropriate contacts*

☒ *Evidence of seditious sympathy with unknown intent*

Corrag looked up. Before she could speak, Ricky jumped in.

"There's nothing in there that could impede advancement to an augmentation track. Isn't that right, Mr. Shearstein."

"That is correct," agreed Mr. Shearstein, clearing his throat at the same time.

"That's a pretty low objective. What if I don't sign?"

"Low objective? Low objective?" Alana repeated in an unbelieving hiss.

"Now is not the time, Ally," said Ricky, heading off a fight between mother and daughter within earshot of the judge and the row of defendants and attorneys in the back of the room waiting for their verdicts to be handed out.

"It's the last two. What exactly are my inappropriate contacts and where is the evidence of my seditious sympathy? That seems pretty vague to me," said Corrag.

"We can discuss these at further length and you can certainly have questions. But if you don't sign, that will force us to proceed to a trial date with the judge, and you won't be going home today unless your parents make bail, which has been set at $200,000," said the attorney.

"What?"

"That's just the way it is."

"That's not fair."

"It is according to the articles of status that govern civil conformity in Democravian court jurisdictions."

Corrag swallowed hard. This was the compromise with principles that meant she had accepted to play by the rules. Alana and Ricky would never forgive her if she chose to favor ethical purity and go to trial. She was angry enough to do it. But the idea of a shower in her own bathroom and a night's sleep in her own bed were impossible to resist. Corrag picked up the stylus hanging from the reader and signed on the line. Mr. Shearstein went for the reader, but Corrag pulled it away from him.

"Who gets this?"

"Give it to me, please," said the judge, stretching

down his shaky hand.

In the portagon nobody spoke until they were out on the mostly empty freeway. A crew of internal migrants worked on filling in the shoulder where the last tremors had crumbled the asphalt. Corrag looked at them with understanding and sympathy. Somebody somewhere must realize that the system was corrupt. It would have to crumble. Change could only come from below. From the dispossessed, the migrants, people like Abel. Ricky spoke up, as if he had read her mind.

"No country is perfect, Corrag. At least we try to get it right here, recognizing the common good as the highest ground of social probity."

"Yeah, Dad. That's right. I have no problems with that."

"Give her the emosponder," said Ricky.

"What? You have my emosponder?"

"Yes, I have it somewhere. Did I put it in my purse?" said Alana.

"I don't know. The admin gave it to you, so you have it."

"It must be in my purse," said Alana.

"Oh my God, You haven't lost it, have you?" said Corrag.

The emosponder had an image from Ben. It was a lowdef selfie. His face, hair buzz-cut and freshly shaved, in the São Paulo Tubid terminal. There was a stand for Caipirinhas Del Noreste and several profiles of catlike, feral faces in the background and his large, beige jaw line and smiling brown eyes and underneath he had written:

Keeping it on the wild side, Benjamin P. Calder.

She was lying in bed with the music on, playing a song list from Oomo reflecting her nostalgic mood. Gurgie and Mathew were both at the summer camp for fine-tuning inductees at the UUW campus. Ricky and Alana had planned for an Alaska cruise, and even this situation would not deter them from it. So she was going to be home for the summer with no friends or family, just the scheduled visits with Attorney Shearstein to keep her busy. And Ben was likely to die on patrol in a doomed war with the Basin tribes. And they were all doomed because there was never going to be an interplanetary expedition and none of them were going to live forever in the orbits of Betelgeuse and Andromeda. Not exactly an inspirational tableau, but it was what it was. She was so full of clichés, another sign she was home in the bosom of Democravia and her family. She had had a taste of freedom with Ben on the San Pedro -- with Abel and Sandy. Just a few hours really in her entire life of mental processes unhindered by the Panglossian half-truths she had been reared on. But what could await her, she wondered. She could never fit into the Democravian life plan with its defining motif of self-sacrifice for the common good now.

A knock on the door sounded and Corrag sat up.

"Yes?" Why weren't they using the nanowall, she wondered. That's what it was there for.

"It's me. Can I come in?"

"Yes," she said with what she thought was an air of tolerance.

Ricky entered with his face set in a stern, parental setting.

"It's time for our walk."

"Does it have to be now?"

"Yes. I have a cocktail date later so it will have to be now."

"I'll be right down."

He closed the door again. Corrag put on her shoes. A walk would do her good, but a serious talk with her father was not something she was ever prepared for, especially not now when she was so unsettled in her thoughts, still processing the experiences of the last few days.

They went out on Durkiev Drive towards Unity, headed for the park. The neighbors were in the yard with their dog, tossing a disc to it. The Rosaleses were waving. The desert grasses in their yard were brown and scraggly, despite some rain in the last month.

"Say hi to the Rosaleses, Corrag." Corrag waved and smiled like she had been doing all her life, an unthinking response. The Rosaleses smiled and waved back.

They walked on. She waited for Ricky to speak, with her head down and occasionally looking up to see where they were. He didn't say anything until they reached the park. Parents milled about, typical pairings of post-racial and post-gender secularists. Their bumbling kids were on the jungle moat.

"Remember when you fell and hurt your knee, Corrag?"

"Yes."

"That seems like yesterday to me."

"It's an elastic thing. Our memories. Some of them are etched pretty strong, Dad."

"Having you in my life is etched very strong, Corrag. To me you were, and are, a pretty special, life affirming event."

Corrag remained silent, penitent. This was not an act, she realized. She genuinely felt sorry for how she had hurt him. She should have been grateful at least for still having these true feelings of filial devotion. Then she wondered how much of his thoughts and words were due to augmented impulses. Was he open at that moment? The feedback algorithm sometimes became overridden in time, and, especially in the earlier implants there was a propensity for the back channels to get stuck in the receptive cycle, which meant their clients became "mimes for the machine," as the syndrome was called in the official literature, or Demodummies.

"Your Mom, Alana and I, Corrag. We've always believed in you. You have potential, a future ahead of you. That's what is so upsetting about some of your recent choices."

"Dad..."

"No, I have nothing against the Calder boy. It's not that. I don't want to go over that ground now. Here's what I want to say to you, Corrag. I pulled out all the stops for you, went to Councilor Culpepper and they've agreed to consider sending you as a youth emissary for a year to the Republic. Alana has talked to her sister Joan and you will stay with them at the farm in New Albion."

"Dad," she repeated. She had wanted to protest, but

now was gutted. She felt robbed.

"I just want to be in charge of my own life. When does that happen?" She almost felt like crying. They were at the edge of the park, looking at a stand of azaleas that was humming with late season pollinators.

"I know. I know," said Ricky. Corrag glanced at him. He had aged in the last few months. There were new wrinkles that hid the scar on his cheek, product of a childhood accident. Maybe he knew he would never see the interstellar. It must be hard for him to have to accept reality, she thought. Or did the augmented access keep him informed of a larger vision? Was it something he was using at the moment?

He shook his head and rubbed his eyes and then stared hard at his daughter.

"Who among us is in charge of their own destiny? We all have to answer to a higher authority, Corrag. You know there is no such thing as individual freedom. That is a red herring used by the Republicans to justify their greed. No such thing in reality. You just have to do the best you can in accord with your role, your status in life. Play your part to the fullest."

"Maybe that's true. But I don't like my part, Dad. I'd like to do some revision."

"Why, Corrag? You've had all the best. Democravia has provided for you. All we ask is you give back."

She had no ready answer. She thought of the bees, the circular rounds they made in search of nectar, their orientation in accordance to the seasons and the position of the planet, the awful grind and constancy of their short life spans and the fact that everything depended on it.

"You'll find that there are no shortcuts to fulfillment. Look to make a difference in the lives of others."

"Maybe I can make a difference, Dad. Maybe I can. A real difference."

"I hope so. I am proud of you. I know there are people who are saying you've fallen off the track, but prove them wrong, Corrag."

The track, the well-worn track was what Corrag didn't want to follow. When would he see that and really trust her to find a better way? Maybe he never would. Corrag was more convinced than ever of the rightness of her wish to be free of the compelled thought control that came with adult responsibilities.

"Corrag, I didn't want to tell you, but I feel I must warn you. That dream has come back. Now, I don't believe it means anything. Individual destiny is an illusion. But this dream. Its constant reoccurrence intrigues me."

Ricky's dream. She tried to remember what it was, something that he and Alana referenced from time to time. It got in the way of his sleep.

"What is the dream again, Dad?"

"Corrag, this is something I don't like talking about. It's painful. I don't know where it comes from. I have this dream that you and I are on the beach and the tide sweeps you away before we get to you. And then when it sweeps you back it's along with this flood of dead fish."

"Well, at least it sweeps me back."

"That's not funny. It always scares me awake."

"Well, you're just scared of losing me, Dad. It's natural."

"Overcoming our mortality is the driving force behind human civilization. I sometimes think you might be the one, Corrag."

"Isn't that what your father said about you, Dad?"

"Yes, but he said, before he died, he told me..."

"What?"

"That it would take three generations to overcome the death wave."

"What death wave, Dad. What is that? Sounds like crazy mumbo jumbo from the old days."

"I don't know what it is exactly, Corrag. But Al, he once said something about how he'd cheated death. I ... I don't remember the story exactly. But ... some kind of story about a Mayan tablet and the drug cartels. I never understood it all. He said he wrote it all down, but I never found the manuscript."

"Well, Dad. Someday we'll get some clarification on the fine print of your Dad's dream and your dream. Luckily I don't have that dream."

"Yeah," Ricky laughed and flashed his lop-sided grin that made him look like a grizzled old desert pirate.

"I'll miss you, Dad."

"I'll miss you, too. And Mom will miss you. I know you two haven't been getting along all that well, but she loves you more than anything, Corrag."

"I know."

"Remember. Service to others is the key to success."

"I'll try, Dad."

At the end of the week Alana and Ricky took off in the portagon for the ferry port of Ventura where they were catching the three week cruise in the hover up the coast to the calving icebergs of the Alaskan North Slope. It was the traditional thing to do for the twentieth wedding anniversary. A cadre of UUW faculty and Edmundstown friends and acquaintances saw them off the night before. Alana had a couple glasses of Chilean wine too many and began telling loud stories and bragging about Corrag's achievements, including the escapade in the mountains with "that HumInt boy" as she called him. How was that something to brag about? Corrag decided she would never understand her mother. She retreated up to her room and played MandolinMonkey for several hours. She had fought her way into the headquarters, the obelisk, and been granted access to the highest level, the accelerator, which held the key of cognizance. There she had skipped out, not wanting to end the game too soon. The key would turn out to be a source code, which would provide a year's worth of free game time and access to the entire Federation approved catalogue of virtualscape productions, she was sure. If dreams were an unreliable reflection of anything real, then the virtual world was even less so. But some days she wasn't so sure. Some days, a game could reveal a flash of insight like turning a corner on your own life. Or something like that. She missed Gurgie and texted her anyways, although she knew that as an inductee Gurgie would have been compelled to give up her through-file at Edmundstown school district and take on a new pass code.

There was a list on the kitchen nanowall of chores that she had to take care of while they were away. Charge the housebot for its monthly energy upfill during the nights and get the top floor nanowall resegmented. A municipal utility crew was supposed to come out Tuesday to do that. And of course see Attorney Shearstein on Tuesday downtown in the government complex. The gardener was coming Friday to trim the hedges and mow the lawn, and Corrag was supposed to pay him, as well as the utility crew, from the bitcoin account. And Corrag had gotten permission to buy some summer clothes for herself from Jaceys with the Jaycey card. She thought a bathing suit like the one she'd seen Carson Macroom wearing in that daytime soap, *The Bully of Jermaine Street*, a recreation of the life of an indeterminate and socially unfit Eastern European woman in London at the beginning of the century, would do, given she could stand to lose some weight.

The days went by in a blur of unfeeling and sensory-deprived existence. The work crew was a motley group of amnesty men who looked unwell. They managed to get the wall done, but their fear of the work boss, a typical Democravian heavy, probably a HumInt vet who had picked up some jungle ways in the Basin, was palpable. The boss had Corrag sign for the bitcoin account.

She had no word from Gurgie or Ben. She watched a lot of telly once the nanowall was resegmented and then on Tuesday dressed in a frilly short tennis skirt and yellow blouse that she had bought with the Jaycee card and had express delivered and prepared to catch the subporter downtown.

The day was clear and dry, like every summer day she had ever known in Edmundstown. It never rained in southern Democravia. Water from the Carlsbad desalination plants provided for most of their needs. The last of the Oglala aquifer was being pumped to give them a few more decades of viable life. There were no settlements east of the desert and very little humans aside from bands of desert nomads. From radio signal drones in outer space Edmundstown appeared as a bastion of light in a sea of darkness.

The people at the subporter stop on Unity and Western Ave were mostly middle-aged administerial types, some of them nervously glancing up from their emosponders. The one thing about the subporter was it gave her an opportunity to look around and study people. Everywhere she saw little signs of individuality that were like the water creeping in under the concrete wall of the San Pedro dam: a brown man in a stiff spandex suit chewing coca leaves and checking his fingernails while he daydreamed and watched the new station roll in; the mother and the child who fled from her grasp and laughed when she cuffed and cursed him in a foreign language that sounded like some kind of gypsy slang; the old man who smiled at her when he caught her watching it all. She got off at the government complex and walked across the street past the Taylor Jabones Convention Center and thought of the Spring Fest crowds she'd last witnessed there on their way to Democravian citizenhood giving it up in one last whoop of juvenile energy release. The people on the street were like bundles of energy driven in an actually beautiful and orderly dance that was everyday life. And Corrag decided that it was good and that someday she would like to be part of the dance of these people who proceeded on their strangely non-random, tracked orbits with calm and courage and faith in the order that had been provided by the Federation and its processes of law and justice and commerce. Why couldn't she fit in?

Attorney Shearstein's office was on the third floor in the Public Prosecutor's wing of the Justice Building, an obscure cement block with equally linear expansions in the Brutalist style of the Aquarian Age in which most of Edmundstown's older public architecture had been designed. The prosecutors ranked an adminobot that signed her in with an iris scan, its neck creaking with a thin hiss; its hydraulic head joint needed replacement. Some of the lawyers were milling around the food cart where it had stopped at the juncture of several hallways. The food cart gave off a pungent odor of cumin, as steam from the coils was being vented.

He was in his office glancing through the oddly grayish and boxlike scanner on his desk. She didn't remember the way the bags under his eyes made him seem older than his years, or the way his receded hair gave his skull a lopsided look, as if he might topple over forward as he stood from his recliner with difficulty and approached her with his hand extended.

"Good morning, Corrag. You had no troubles finding

us."

"No. I just autosearched with the index codes and the address came up."

"Very good. Very resourceful. I've had a glance through your files and there have been no previous brushes."

"No."

"You've had the Testers."

"Yes."

"But that was a purely conscious scan."

"What do you mean?"

"I mean you didn't go under, did you? Have a seat and close the door, Corrag."

Corrag did as he directed and warily sat down in the available recliner facing the desk. It put her at his eye level as he sat and looked at her with his little blue eyes that reminded her of a bird. She couldn't see his fingers as he drummed on his scanner, and she felt suddenly lost. Shearstein was talking.

"The advantages of testing of this sort is it shows deeper motivations and inclinations that can lead an administrative council to make directions and recommendations to the probationary child and its parental units. You are still a child in the eyes of the law. Although by my lights a 16-year-old girl is capable of making her own decisions. Don't you think?"

"Yes, of course." She felt he was leading her into a trap. She didn't trust him at all, she decided.

"Would you be willing to undergo deep testing?"

"When? Right now?"

"Yes. Here. I have the apparatus."

"No."

"Okeydokey. That's fine. I could remand you, you understand. It's within my remit."

"Remand. Remit. I don't understand what you're saying. Could you please speak English?"

"We have some time in which I have been empowered to help the council make a recommendation about your status. There are many paths leading to a good outcome. That's all. Do you understand?"

"I guess so."

"Good. The value of deep testing is it's a shortcut to my understanding of what makes you happy, Corrag."

"I don't want you to know that."

"But I must."

"Why?"

"Because without that deep knowledge we cannot make a decision about your placement."

"But my father..."

"Nothing. Your father and mother's credentials can't help you now, Corrag. You are in the hands of the Justice Department. Later we can work with your parents to get you cleared of any wrongdoing. Have the charges dropped and the arrest annulled. But that assumes your cooperation."

"He told me he talked with the Council at the June meeting and they decided already."

"That's not the protocol."

"Well, that's what he said. If you want to mess up the process, go right ahead, but it seems to me that wouldn't be wise of you."

"The final decision, Corrag, will be made at the next closed session. You can either have deep testing or you can read this document. I have a copy. And answer the questions on the study guide and then we can test orally."

He seemed to be done with her. He was focused on the scanner and had stopped drumming his fingers. She took the ragged old tablet with the gorilla glass of Thomas Picket's foundational tome, *Value and Man -- Citizens of a Post-Sustainability Order* and the iconic image of the blindfolded Justice and her crummy old scales, and the stapled pages of the study guide which he had pushed across the desk. She flicked through the initial screens, it was dry and full of facts and graphs, but preferable to the deep testing, an invasive process which left markers in the tissue of various brain regions. She had heard her teachers debating the worth of this book, which had been a major influence on the Founding Brethren. This was somewhat old school and quease inducing, the old tablet and the stapled pages, but she would manage.

"Okay. I'll read this. I guess that's it then." Corrag stood. "I'll see you in a week."

"No, you have to read it here," said Shearstein, craning his head up slowly at her.

"Why?"

"That's just the rule."

"But I'll read it. Who cares where?"

"Somebody does because that's the rule."

"Bend the rule."

He looked at her steadily. His face never showed any

emotion. It was obviously an advantage to him to be opaque like that. She looked around. He had no pictures, nothing at all on the chrome tinted glass walls, no clues about his family, pastimes, nothing about a life beyond the enclosing, claustrophobic office. Dim shapes of figures could be seen moving beyond the walls, but they were invisible to anyone outside. She noticed he was looking at her legs.

"Bend the rule," he repeated. "You have a nice body, Corrag. You should make any man happy."

"Does that mean I can go?"

"What do I get if I bend the rule? It seems to me that a rule is an inflexible, hard thing. It takes a force to bend it. What are you going to do to help me bend the rule?"

"I've already agreed to read this book and do the study guide."

"What else?"

She shrugged. He gave a little laugh.

"Go," he said and waved her away with the back of his hand, looking down at his scanner again.

During the week the wind from the north brought with it a cold chill that the Edmundstown Channel Five newscaster called the methane vortex. Every time there was a major release of methane from the Arctic seabed it brought with it a cold blast from the sea's bottom that spread out eastward and southward. It was paradoxical because the methane locked them into a continuing heat buildup in the atmosphere and coordinated reductions with their Republican partners to avoid the worst-case scenarios of life-ending negative feedback loop for the planet. But for Corrag it just brought the cold. She wandered around in the garden after the gardener had left with a keffiyeh pulled around her shoulders. It had belonged to Ricky. His time in the U.S. Foreign Service had been spent in various Middle Eastern diplomatic posts before the States broke apart. It gave her a sense of solidity, a family heirloom, but it was no use against the strange combination of dread, horror, revulsion and fascination she felt when she thought about Shearstein. He wanted to know what made her happy. The idea of a total stranger becoming concerned with her innermost thoughts in such a casual, heartless manner just sent her into a corner of despair from which there seemed to be no escape. What did make her happy? It wasn't having to spend time in a moldy old office with no pictures, not even a calendar from the corner bakeshop, with a whack job administerial with creepy eyes. That much she knew. The image of his slim, pale fingers drumming on the desktop was stuck in her mind like a bad feedback loop.

There was no rice to make her favorite dish, a casserole with the farmed tilapia in the freezer in its carbon nanoparticle foil from the Super8, so she ordered an express packet of MidwestOrgano long grain. It cost so much but it was worth it. She read the news on the nanowall, tuned to the PNS, the old Pacifica News Service that had become the Federation's Progressive News Source. The farmers' union was complaining that the Federation's latest published price controls were causing feedstock shortages that were unintended and poorly planned, but the business council had leaked a story that there was dissension among the Councilors about the level of eco-tax that was being levied on humanure and the need to think about an outright subsidy from value added taxes for feedstock producers.

Corrag liked to keep up on the news. That was one thing that made her happy, being able to sound intelligent and figure out what made the world go around. Maybe she ought to be a journalist, she thought. She liked it when she and Ben had serious discussions. She liked a lot of things. She sent the housebot out to pick up the package, and that was odd, because she usually liked to do things herself. But it was cold outside, and the clouds were scudding across the sky so fast it made her anxious. Then she thought of Shearstein and his little cold eyes and the thin grey band of hair at the back of his head like some strange animal while the casserole baked in the oven. What made him happy? Or was he like some bot, happy in his role as a functionary of the Federation and its machinery of administration? She wondered while she took the casserole out and it grew dark. She didn't turn the light on, and that was strange also. Because she didn't like to be alone in the dark house, usually, so she asked the housebot to turn on all the lights. Then she put on a summer music recommended play list on the Oomo, but the sickeningly sweet music did nothing to help.

It was strange that she would think about Shearstein at all, never mind what would make him happy. It didn't seem to be right to her that satisfying the most basic appetites could make men happy. Happiness was not even a thing in the Federation's constitution, unlike the old United States. Virtue and sacrifice, yes, not happiness. Augmentation was supposed to override the instincts, but it apparently didn't. Not in Shearstein's case.

She tried reading the Picket book. Written at the beginning of the secessionist wars, it had inspired the generation known as the Founding Brethren to establish the Democravian state on the lines Picket had set out. Critics had always existed, but for Corrag it wasn't the graphs and statistics she quibbled with. It was the reverence the book was held in by her parents and the teachers at the school, although there was a pushback from the younger faculty members. Picket was still alive and living in Buenos Aires, apparently. She remembered reading it somewhere. What did Picket think of augmentation, she wondered, skipping through the table of contents. There was no mention of it directly, although he did have a late chapter called *The Need to Reform the Collective Appetite -- from Scarcity to Abundance*, which was about the educational system Picket espoused. Apparently, competitive sports were de-emphasized in favor of community service in Picket's idealized world, which the Founding Brethren did their best to recreate. They took it a step further, relying on augmented tuning to bring the best and the brightest of every generation into the uppermost circles of service. The augmented elites enjoyed access to privileges and perks that were unavailable to ordinary worker folk, but in return were meant to live lives of ego-numbing devotion to the greater good. In contrast, the Edmundstown Charter School vocational track students had an *esprit de corps* all their own, based on their independence and freedom from the responsibilities that the augmented track kids labored under, the knowledge that their destinies, although limited, were less circumscribed, that their thoughts and desires, although less exciting, would always be their own. For Corrag, that was something she had increasingly wondered about. Somewhere in her mind was the thought that their colorful speech and dress patterns were evidence of a finer, more exalted existence, not a coarser one. Except now she and Ben had stepped off the track, conspired together with inappropriate contacts and seditious sympathies against the interests of the Federation. She just wasn't sure what she wanted. It would be easy not to think and plunge ahead, but that was not an option for her. What she wanted was to know things. But that left her exposed. Knowledge was not a protection against the evil of falling away from the utilitarian ideal.

So she read through that night until the housebot let out a warning note and then said: "Lights out. PS Alert," outside her door and then stayed there waiting for a response. PS stood for power source, which meant that she was wasting energy.

"Okay," she said. "I'm going to bed. Lights out. You, too."

And they both did as they were told.

The next visit to Shearstein, Corrag told him she had finished the Picket but wanted to put off the study guide. She wasn't sure why, maybe she just wasn't ready to undertake the study guide questions and the oral examination, although she had finished reading the book. But she wanted to know more. Never mind about the book. What she really wanted to know, the key to the whole thing was what made *him* happy? She was hunched down in her seat, wearing jeans and a sweatshirt in Edmundstown maroon and white with her graduation year on the front in a Whirligig Bold Italic. Her eyes studied his intently. He was making an effort to be cheery. That bothered even more. That somehow he would modulate his behavior on her behalf was truly scary, that they could be equals, adversaries in that way, on some field of play that she was determined to figure out for herself as quickly as possible, no matter how seditious that might be.

"I don't know, Corrag. Happiness for me is the small things. Like when the food cart comes around down the hall just when I've finished writing an opinion, as if it had been planned that way. Those sorts of coincidences make me happy. When things work."

A shiver went down her spine. She hadn't heard what he said. Something about a food cart. As banal as that.

He was married. Two little boys. He showed her the pictures in his emosponder. His wife looked nice, like a lady who wandered the aisles trying to decide on the very best bargains at the Super8. Brown hair, straightened. The two boys looked like him, with inexpressive, waiting faces. Waiting for what? Perhaps something about to be handed to them on a platter, she surmised.

"They look like you."

"Yes. They all say that."

"That must make you happy."

"I don't think about it."

"Well, thank you for sharing."

"Yes, I have shared, haven't I? Maybe you and I should spend some time together outside. Maybe go to some places together."

"Where would we go?"

"There are places. Do you like ethnic food? There's a great ethnic food place I know."

"Ethnic food, huh?"

"Yes."

"Well. Okay, Mr. Shearstein."

"You can call me Edward. You can tell me about the Thomas Picket you say you've read."

"I have read it."

She wasn't sure what she had decided. Things happened, and it was not for her to decide to be for or against. This was what her education as a Democravian citizen had taught her. To be acceptant of things and to help. Shearstein wanted to meet at the Bazoom Club. It was a notorious dive, one of the only places in Edmundstown where you could hear live music and eat food with circumscribed feedstocks. He sent her a text that she opened at home in the kitchen after speaking with Ricky and Alana on the nanowall from the bridge of the hover where there was a public teleport. They were too cheap to use their emosponder and pay the roving fees. The icebergs were spectacular but the definition from the public teleport was not the best. But one day, she had agreed at Ricky's prodding during the conversation, she would like to visit. Perhaps after she had graduated from the fine-tuning program at the UUW. She didn't mention the date she was going to have with Shearstein.

Shearstein's text was curt: "We will be at the Bazoom Club at 17:30 and we hope to see you for food and drinks." He didn't use emoticons, but he did use the royal we. These were the wrong kinds of flourishes and stylistic choices, in Corrag's usual aesthetics, but the experiment consisted of delving deeper into the exotic world of Attorney Shearstein.

She wandered around the house trying to avoid the housebot, who seemed to be following her. Finally, in the kitchen, she ordered it to stay away while she made a snack from an old roll of bread and the last bit of cheese she could scrape from the foil.

"You need to supplement the stores."

"What? I told you to stay away. That means go back and stay in the hall, by the door. Your usual spot. Put it on hold."

She put on the jumpsuit she had only worn once, to Gurgie's birthday party at the Shallow Center, and made up her face to look older, with blue eye liner. On the walk to the subporter station, she did her best to look everyone in the eye at least briefly, before walking on the downtown bound platform and settling into her seat on the porter that slid in silently and took off again after a whisper of hissing doors.

The Bazoom Club was on a block of warehouse type buildings used to store machinery and equipment. The door had a vintage sign painted in the brick above it, a barely visible silhouette of a woman dressed in high heels kneeling on one knee. Inside at the bar, several men and women in worker suits had O masks on, and at the back, behind the door, was a table with three Japanese tourists, all male, with silk suits and fedoras and another table with Shearstein still in his blue coat and pants from the office, sipping a Maxergy cocktail. The head waitress, an older Latino woman in a black skirt and blouse, studied Corrag intently.

"You how old?"

"Eighteen. I'm meeting my uncle."

"Oh, he's your uncle?"

"Yes, at that table."

"Oh."

As Corrag walked across the floor to get to the table, Shearstein looked past her to the stage where a band was taking its place: three men on electrified clavichords hung about their necks and the singer, a woman about thirty, with thin arms in a sleeveless, cotton Gotzeitgeist dress. Corrag slid in to the restored pleather bench beside Shearstein, and he finally wrinkled his eyebrows awkwardly at her.

"You came."

"Of course. Didn't you think I would?"

"I had my doubts."

"You're not concerned?"

"About what?" asked Shearstein, stifling a yawn.

"Me being here and you being here."

"You and I are free Democravians. I am fulfilling my duties as a state attorney to ensure you're back on track."

"Yes, but the Bazoom Club? And couldn't this be seen as undue influence on your part?"

"No, not at all. You must understand the algorithms are constantly modulating in favor of greater human intercourse as one reaches the status of augmentation. You should be flattered, not be attacking me."

Corrag nodded. She thought she should appreciate his candor. The woman began her song after a brief confessionary introduction, with coy gestures using her arms and hands turned palms upward. It was a bluesy number about living on skid row in the nineteen thirties, with mentions of Prohibition and Al Capone in a gun battle with the feds. Prohibition and Al Capone were signs of the decadence of the old institutions, of the inhumanity of the old United States, according to Miss Schilling.

"What kind of place is this? How does it get away with this kind of entertainment?" asked Corrag.

"The Cloud Councilors are tolerant. They have to be. They are slowly proceeding with loosening some social restrictions. It's progress."

"Who are the Cloud Councilors?"

"Nobody is certain. I, of course don't know."

"Aren't you an attorney?"

"Yes, but my level of augmentation is only Code Blue."

"Why?"

"I like my privacy."

"So the higher your level of augmentation..."

"Yes, the more open your mental process."

"Until..."

"At the highest levels you are basically one mind with the Cloud Councilors."

"No-one ever taught me that."

"No. It's not widely understood. There are some things that the people don't need to know."

The woman finished her song. The Japanese tourists stood and clapped effusively. They were heavy-duty fans of the band. The head waitress came by and asked if they wanted to order. She gave Shearstein two old-time plastic menus. He gave one to Corrag and asked the waitress to come back later.

The entrees included poached salmon and beef sirloin in a wine marinade. That was unusual, particularly wild salmon. How did they get their hands on prohibited feedstocks? Corrag decided to order the salmon with asparagus and a kumara and risotto soufflé. Shearstein wanted glazed roast jabali and rainforest snails in a duck sauce with a parsnip salad. He returned the menus to the waitress.

The waitress arrived with their orders and served them silently while they listened to the singer continue with her set of songs about life on the periphery of the social world. The food came almost instantly, although it was supposed to celebrate old-fashioned cookery, according to the blurb on the menu. They ate together without talking. Corrag had never tasted such delicious food, the meats and rich sauces and fresh vegetables. It was a bounty that the Democravian elders had decided could only be available on a limited basis, not trusting that the old greed would not reassert itself in the absence of limits. The music too, was a throwback to older pleasures and thus a subversion of the Federation's puritanical aversion to frivolous, corrupting entertainment.

"This is good," said Corrag, at last, suppressing a burp.

Shearstein smiled enigmatically.

"Tell me about the Picket book."

"It's good. I like it. I like his style. What he has to say."

"Do you appreciate the basic assumptions about the rise of Democravian order."

"I do understand. Of course. I just am not ready to sacrifice myself to it."

"What do you mean? Sacrifice seems like a curious word."

"But what about happiness? That's curious to me because it doesn't get represented at all in the graphs or the numbers. There's so much I want to see and hear and taste. Don't you have doubts?"

"Of course I have doubts. Everyone has doubts. But look at me. I'm happy. There's much I am still learning. You never stop learning."

"Yes, but how free are you? Okay you're Code Blue. That still supposes some level of directed thought."

"Not much really. Basic alignment with the Federation goals. That's all."

"I'm just not sure. How free are you? Really," insisted Corrag.

"I'm proving it to you right now. What do you think this is about?"

"I'd like to see you show some emotion, Edward."

"You are a piece of work. Do you know what I mean by that?"

"Sounds like something Alana would say. My mother. She says I've inherited a propensity for drama."

"Well, Corrag. A sense of drama can be a good thing. The Federation needs the passion and energy of young people such as you. But freedom, is that what you're talking about? Freedom is nothing. You hold on to nothing in order to be truly free. *The ideals of an advanced society can be measured in direct correlation to the absence of desires.*"

"I know. That's what Picket says. The negative wellness correlation. What someone once called the zombie society. 'Cause it's dead and doesn't know it."

Shearstein looked at her intently, and Corrag felt that she could intimate what he was thinking. He was determined to get to her, to make an impact, make himself felt as a man. This was beyond his normal duties. It was something he was taking on as a goal for himself, and she was flattered, although scared also. It verged on anger, what he was thinking. She was like some project or something for him, and if it failed, if it blew up in his face, if she rebuffed him, what then? He had insisted that there was nothing untoward, that he was interested solely in her education, but should she trust him? Would he recommend her for the VocAg track instead? Would she not be allowed to travel East? Maybe she'd be compelled to take up a place in the HumInt Corps and fight in the Basin against the tribes. She remembered what Ben had said about the shape shifting capabilities of their enemies, how it had seemed he and his companions were hallucinating when under attack. That's what she felt now looking at Shearstein look at her. She was under attack and he could shift at any moment and take on another, more monstrous appearance. But then that thought went away and another took its place. He was a door, a portal to the kind of knowledge she had never learned in school. She wanted to keep that door swinging open.

They stayed for the singer's final set. The songs took on another feel, just as nostalgic, but more ballad-like, more personal. There was a song Corrag really liked about a mother mourning the loss of a son who had gone away to war, and it seemed like a pro-tribes song. More people showed up in the club by the end of the set, a motley crew of men and women with aged faces and lumpy bodies, obviously not being cared for by the Health Administration. Shearstein made several drumming motions with his fingers when they all came in. Then he motioned for the waitress and paid the bill with a swipe of a personal account bitcoin card, not the Justice Department employee ID.

"Let's go," he said, and he waited for her to stand before leading the way outside.

He stopped and turned on the sidewalk, waiting for her. The air was cool, and there was a rising full moon behind him coming over the tops of the warehouses.

"Let's keep walking," said Corrag.

"No," said Shearstein. "Aimless wandering. That will alert the algorithms. We want to go someplace specific. The Hotel Junipero. They make an excellent coffee gelato."

"Well, sure," said Corrag, sounding to her own ears false, overeager and childlike.

"It's just a few blocks," said Shearstein.

They walked side by side on the mostly empty sidewalks without touching.

"Did you see the people who came in?" asked Shearstein.

"Yes."

"Anti-war disaligners. Want to take us back to the days of the old United States when such protests were allowed. You know what dissension did for us then. Anybody learns about that in school."

"Why are they allowed to?"

"To what? Associate?"

"Yeah."

"A few protest songs and they can be mollified. Believe me, Corrag. The Federation knows what it's doing."

The Hotel Junipero was a block from the Taylor Jabones Convention Center and was the oldest structure in the city, built in the 2020s by a billionaire tech tycoon as a museum cum residence. It boasted unique Botero sculptures in the atrium and huge, ornate glass chandeliers throughout the first floor. The bar was full of people in suits and fancy jewelry, milling around in a muted, sophisticated buzz. They seemed to be travelers, coming and going to and from exotic locales. Shearstein greeted men and women on their way to the bar and stopped for several seconds of an exchange with a man whom he said was also an attorney. The other man's attitude was breezy and cocksure, and it seemed artificially merry inside the place. Corrag decided that they must have had the O levels turned up. They both had gelatos. They didn't talk much. Corrag felt that Shearstein was nervous.

"The usual quid pro quos don't apply any more, Corrag."

"What does that mean?"

"Do you have any questions for me?"

"I have lots of questions. Why are you taking all this trouble at my expense?"

"Because I care about you? Why wouldn't I?"

"Is that all?"

"Yes."

That wasn't enough for her, but she followed him out again to the lobby. He seemed almost handsome in this place, surrounded by the ornate decor and serious people, testimonies to a former era's extravagance. Someday again there would be opulence, was the promise of the Hotel Junipero, amidst the Federation's egalitarian ethic of utility above all. But Corrag, although interested in this forbidden world, was intent on a different wisdom.

Out on the street he kissed her. He tasted metallic, slightly bitter, as if it was his very essence she could taste. And he didn't know how to kiss, just pressing himself against her mouth and sticking his tongue bravely forward in an expeditionary, ambitious way.

"Okay. Now what?" she said, balancing on one leg.

"Don't be so quick, Corrag. You're too linear. Obviously you need fine tuning."

Corrag felt her face flush, even in the dark.

"What does that have to do with anything?"

"The Federation augment provides superior insights into human behavior, believe me," said Shearstein. "You can't know because you have no access. But someday…"

"Well, I guess that's one upload I'm lacking." Corrag's sarcastic tone was meant as a subtle chide, a moment of intimacy, but Shearstein did not take it that way. He seemed offended, suddenly agitated. He hailed a taxi with an abrupt wave of an emosponder.

They rode in silence back to St. Michael's Close and Durkiev Drive. He seemed to be punishing her with his lack of words, but Corrag was confused. She couldn't think of what to say to break the spell of gloom that had come over Shearstein.

The cab stopped in front of her driveway.

"Wait here," said Shearstein to the driver, a bot. They both got out of the cab and walked up the drive to her door.

"Well, I guess this is it," said Corrag, stopping.

"Corrag, don't you realize what is going on?"

"I do. You're angry. I'm sorry."

"I'm risking everything for you -- my reputation, my family. This is crazy. For what? For who? You're just a girl. A silly, spoiled girl." His words came out with a hiss, and the anger had transformed his face, twisting it in the dim light of stars and streetlamps.

Corrag felt herself get hot with anger. But instead of fighting back, she thought suddenly of Abel.

"You risked it all for me because there are some things that you can't control. You should be grateful instead of angry. I wish there was a way I could make it better for you."

She looked down. He stepped aside. When she looked up at him again, he was staring at the night beyond the roof of the house. It seemed like he was in pain. Clearing his throat, he finally spoke.

"Yes, you're right. I should be grateful to you. Good night."

Then he turned and walked down the driveway.

She heard the smooth hiss of the metallic tires on the magnetized carbon fiber road surface as the cab with Shearstein drove away down Durkiev Drive, and perhaps with it all her chances for advancement.

What was he really thinking? Had he been augmenting when he finally spoke? These questions were a torment to her, made worse when she finally got up to her room and switched on the nanowall to have Ben's low def selfie on the home page there with her. His mischievous smile seemed a beacon of goodness in the dark. She sat in bed wondering and confused. The muddle she was in could not be any worse. If only she and Ben could have made their way to the hinterlands together. Life as outcasts was preferable to the torment she felt, the torture of having her fate hang in the balance, decided by the whimsical moods of the Democravian

Cloud Council. Even if Shearstein cleared her for travel as a youth emissary, would their illicit association sully his recommendation? She felt incredibly vulnerable, with nowhere to turn for help. There were too many questions to contemplate and she couldn't bring it up with anybody at the moment. She texted Ben.

"Wish you were here," she typed, adding the emoticon for fear, a dragon's wing. She sat in bed watching reruns of old reality series. There was no answer back. She turned off the nanoscreen and curled up in the dark. Someday she would not be scared, but that night fear ruled her, running up her back like cat's claws and shortening her breath as if the air itself had curdled.

Three -- New Albion

They were running late, as usual. Alana yelled at the housebot because Corrag's plaid skirt wasn't ironed to her satisfaction.

"It's okay, Mom. It'll be fine," said Corrag, trying to keep her emotions under control. It felt so strange to be leaving home, like jumping off a moving portagon. It had all happened so fast, she hadn't had time to process. A few days after Ricky and Alana had returned from their Alaskan cruise, the council met to handle a complaint about export quotas by the fruit and tree nut growers association. Ricky, as a tenured professional and a close friend of Councilor Culpepper, the former president of the UUW, had managed to jump the list and bring up his daughter's petition for travel to the Republican Homeland as a youth emissary in the public session. The petition had been granted unanimously without preconditions, based on the recommendation they had received from Attorney Shearstein. For Corrag, it was a triumph, and for Ricky and Alana, a huge relief to have Corrag once again back on track. Ties with the Republic were always fraught with complications. By not setting preconditions, Alana fretted that perhaps they had not valued Corrag's potential contributions as an augmented adult, but Ricky was certain that it showed they had absolute confidence that she would return a committed Democravian after her sojourn in the land of the unreconstructed free market jungle, as Ricky termed it.

For Alana it was a chance to prove to her family once

and for all that the superior way of life was to be found in the enlightened haven that was the Democravian Federation. Corrag would shine the reflected light of her mother's rebellion against the staid and unreconstructed generations of settlers that had come before her. She reminded Corrag at breakfast for it seemed the thousandth time that as a youth emissary she was counted on to hold to a higher standard of behavior than the cousins she would soon be meeting. They sounded like a bunch of ignorant hicks to Corrag, but she knew that Alana tended to exaggerate.

The housebot ironed the skirt one more time and brought it up to her room. As she put it on, she felt a twinge of regret, thinking the old housebot would probably be traded in by the time she got back for a newer model, one of the perks of their family status on the Rankbook. Her bag was packed with clothes and toiletries. She had stuffed in some of the little childhood mementos from the top drawer of her desk. But her emosponder had thousands of photos of the house, the garden, Durkiev Drive, the Rosaleses, Ricky and Alana and of course the Rosaria beach, everything she needed to keep her strong. The trip back East was still like going into enemy territory, despite the decade or so of peace between the continental rivals, and she wanted to fortify herself against the temptations she was sure to find. Although the council had affirmed, and her parents strongly still believed that Corrag was a loyal and heartfelt Democravian, the truth was she wasn't sure who or what she was, and this wavering sense of belonging, she thought, could possibly be her downfall.

Ricky insisted on driving to the Lax tubid port. It would have been easier to take the subporter, but he wanted to drive. The tubid port was up the coast, halfway between Edmundstown and the Bay. It was packed with vacation goers headed to the Federation Cup in São Paulo and soldiers headed home or back to base. Corrag scanned their faces, seeing in them some of the changes that she had seen in Ben, and thinking also that he might be dead at that very moment. She had not heard from him since the text she had sent after that outing to the Bazoom Club with Shearstein. She had still not talked to anybody about that night, the loneliest of her life.

She looked at Alana across the table at the deli. The lines of mother worry softened for a moment. Corrag felt like she would cry. There was so much she held back from Alana, but she would miss her. Soon enough she'd be home, and perhaps then Alana would accept her as a person in her own right, not some projection of her own desires.

"Wipe the jelly from the corner of your mouth, Corrag," said Alana.

Ricky smiled.

"Look at you about to make your first trip on a tubid. Our little Corrag."

"Okay, Dad. That's enough."

Corrag dabbed at her mouth with the napkin. This was the right time to go. All three stood.

"I'll miss you," she said, stifling a sob.

"Aw, baby," said Alana. "You'll be home for

Edmundsday."

"What about Thanksgiving?"

"If you want. Although the Hunnewell Thanksgiving is huge. Not to be missed."

"They celebrate Thanksgiving?"

"Yes, of course. Thanksgiving. Christmas, Hannukah. But we have Edmundsday in February. And Spring Fest."

"You are going to have a great time. Learn as much as you can. And remember, there's good and bad in all groups of people. That goes for families and nations," said Ricky.

Going through the security check, the clearance guard eyed her documents and checked her eyes with the mobile scanner. Her encephalograms and iris prints and other biometrics and psych testing since childhood were property of the Federation, and as she was waved through she truly felt that she was going forth on a special mission to the country that had turned its back on the ideals of liberty for all. Even though the Statue still carried the torch in the New York harbor, it was a dead icon in that water. Her light had been passed to the other side of the continent.

The steward showed her to her seat. She put it in the upright position and strapped herself in. The display overhead listed some of the entertainment options. She might be interested in some of the Oomo channels later on which looked like they might include some of the Indie music scene coming out of the Repho. Federation entertainment boards heavily censored this music. But some of it was being allowed on the tubid. Then a young man in spandex took the seat next to her. He peeled off his overcoat and rolled it to put away in the overhead compartment. He was in his late twenties perhaps, with the Mohawk buzzcut that told her he was not a Federation citizen.

He sat down and looked over at her before closing his eyes for a nap. Then he fidgeted awkwardly in his seat and his eyes opened.

"Oh, Jesus," he said. "I forgot my Dopatin pills."

"What are they?"

"Oh, you people and your quaint mental waves. What is it they put in the water in the Fed? Haven't you heard of Dopatin?"

"No," said Corrag, defensively.

"It's a sedative. Releases dopamine. Like eating a wad of cheese. Helps me sleep."

"Okay. Sorry for asking."

He stood and pulled out his coat from the overhead and took out a sleek black headband from the coat pocket. Once the coat was back overhead and he was seated, he put the headband on and finally relaxed. He closed his eyes and seemed to be asleep. When the steward came by to make sure they were strapped in, he made no motion of recognition. The steward smiled. "Got his head on," he said knowingly.

Corrag looked around at the other passengers, a mix of foreigners and natives with a commonality of dress and sophistication that left her feeling underprepared. She remembered a slot on the nanowall's evening news about the headbands that were popular in the Republic for stimulating the pleasure centers of the brain. They were out of the reach financially for most people and were the desired objects of thieves who would sometimes kill to get their hands on them. Their overuse often led to addictive behavior, apathy and mental unfitness.

The pilot's voice came on describing the itinerary of their trip. They were due into Ryan Port on the Great Lakes in about an hour. There had been reports of sabotage activities against the tubid infrastructure in the hinterlands, but the pilot reassured the passengers that security clearances had been guaranteed by both Repho and Federation switches on the Transport Board in that morning's report. Then he asked them all to relax and enjoy the journey. The steward came by with Maxergy snacks and carafes of vintage wines for topflite sections, and then the lights went out for the fifteen-minute power up. They heard the pilot's communicator crackling for clearance. Then there was a pull as they catapulted into the vacuum through the transport tube. The lights came back on after about five minutes of hyper-speed travel during which the hum of air compressors located in the nose of the car were the only audible sound. Corrag could hear the buzz of conversations slowly grow as they glided along at a comfortable velocity. The passengers in the middle row next to her were speaking French. France and Germany were the two leading Euro CRA nations that had briefly sided with the Federation during the early years of the war, but they were now firm allies of the Republic in their common fight against the Jihad tribalists of the Middle East. Her neighbor, the young man in the seat next to her, rolled his head and opened his eyes. She pretended not to notice. They were slowing down for the long glide into RyanPort.

"First time East?"

"Yeah."

"I could tell. You look like a newbie. You'll do, though, once you get the hang of things."

"What do you do?"

"I'm in trade. Fruit and nuts. The Russians are going crazy for almond, and their suppliers in Turkey have trouble meeting demand. So I get to negotiate with the Federation trade people. If you can call them trade people. All that retro augmentation. So slow. You people have to do something about your storage."

"Federation rule is imperfect, but it leads to the best outcome for the most people," said Corrag.

"Don't get defensive with me, sister. Just saying."

Ryan Port saw an influx of new passengers get on. Half of them dressed in exotic foreign garb, the men's heads swaddled in turbans and the women in floral print saris, and the other half, college age, dressed in indigo spandex and rainbow Gotzeitgeist gear, laughing and falling against each other and tumbling heedlessly into their seats. Now the tubid was full. There was a short power up and they were off again into the blackness. After a silent jaunt at top speed in the vacuum of the tube, they began to glide and quickly slow for Grand Central Station.

This was the legendary port that had been reconstructed from scratch after a crude waste bomb set off by animal rights terrorists had sparked the first co-evolutionary troubles. It was only after their capture and imprisonment in the maximum-security compound in Washington State that the secession movement leaders, Joanne Kissim, Wally Delamare and Tracy Durkiev had managed to gain traction. Enough to organize and begin the rollout of their last stand for planetary sanity during the years of the second Ryan administration.

The customs line was short. Most passengers went through the passport check for Republican citizens. The French family was ahead of her on the line for Visitors and Transeints. That was how it was spelled in the Republic. Transeints. That reminded her of one of Ricky's rants about the Repho's academic journalism. She suddenly felt a sense of kinship with her father, and wished he were there with her.

The man in the booth gave her a long glare, looking up from the document. Then he ordered her to look into the scanner for another encepho. Corrag took a deep breath and did as she was told. Curiously, the home page on the encephalogrammer showed a grainy segment of historical document footage -- immigrants in Ellis Island, lousy bands of huddled masses. But Corrag came up clean of scannable defects.

"Baggage check on level three for you," said the man, smiling curtly to show his platinum inserts for front teeth. He was long past a decent retirement year. There were no labor unions in the Republic, so Corrag did not understand why a bot did not take the job. There was so much she did not know.

"Final destination?"

"New Albion."

"Nice up there. Family visit?"

"Youth emissary."

The man nodded.

After picking up her travel bag from the distribution rack on level three, Corrag began to look around. There was a balcony overlooking the main floor and street level entrance, and she slowly made her way over to the marble rail and looked out over the space. The transit of people across the station made an undecipherable pattern, not unlike the movement of people across Edmundstown's public spaces. On the ceiling, a large nanowall showed a political advertisement for Mayor Twombly Gheko, who was running for reelection for a record fifth term. She checked her emosponder. There was Alana, online at the time.

"Any luck?"

"No. Who do I look for?"

"They're sending Beithune. Just stay where you are and put a reader on."

"Okay."

"I love you."

"Love you too, Mom."

She set the emosponder back in her bag's outer pocket. Standing against the balcony, Corrag watched the people and practiced keeping her thoughts still and private. She thought of the advanced language students who learned through augmentation to read facial cues and didn't even need to see a brain map to know what you were thinking. Corrag liked to think at least some of her thoughts were inviolable.

Beithune was the boy, a year and a half older than her. She tried to keep her thoughts simple and quiet so as not to be surprised when he appeared. That was what she was supposed to represent as a Democravian, that willingness to sacrifice individual needs. She wasn't sure she believed in it any more, but the practice of it for so many years was like a track laid down in her mind from which it was hard to break clear.

"Hello, there."

She turned to see who had addressed her. It was a boy, almost a man, with a beret on, and straw yellow hair sticking out from under it in ragged bunches. He came up and stopped and cocked his head. He was short, a little over one and a half meters tall, thin, with sparkling blue eyes and a brilliant Hunnewell smile with a hint of malevolence around the lips -- an ancient, twisted bit of hunger that had eventually been tamed.

"You Corrag?"

"Yes. Hi, Beithune. I was expecting you."

"Hi."

"Nice to meet you."

"A pleasure, cuz."

"You look like you did in the photos Alana used to show me."

"You look kind of what I expected a Federation chick to look like."

"How is that?"

"Well, natural like. And strong arms. Surfers." He

smiled.

"Oh."

"Come on. Before we go back there's something I have to do."

Corrag slung the bag strap over her shoulder and followed Beithune to the escalator ramp down to the entrance of the station. They made an odd pair, the short, cocky boy with a swagger and the tall girl stooping forward with the weight of her bag in an oddly confident way. But an observer would have noticed a family resemblance, something similar in the way they walked, an alignment in their thought patterns that immediately caused them to mesh their gaits. Beithune slipped through the crowds milling on the docks outside with a practiced familiarity, as the water ferries and luxury craft plied the canals and sped along on the open water of the harbor. Corrag had never seen nor heard such a loud spilling over of human wants and needs as she observed leaving Grand Central Station. She was seeing for the first time the busy waterways of the Big Apple and the once majestic, now disheveled skyline of skyscrapers piled far in all directions. A rainbow-hued horde of youth was running the show on the dock. They hustled water taxis, gathered and pointed and scattered at the approach of the police on armored harbormasters -- self-propelled and lightning quick electric jet skis. They whispered sales pitches for home-brewed crystal speed and liquid oomo, as Beithune smiled and shook his head. He and Corrag jumped on a ferryboat and held on to the piping overhead as crowds piled in and out. After they had gone several miles north along the main Broadway Canal, Beithune jumped off and waited for Corrag to catch up. They were on the edge of a plaza. A large sandstone building stretched for several blocks, with sharp edges and glass in the upper towers that reflected the fading sun.

"This is Sandelsky."

"Wow, I'd never believe it."

Sandelsky, the premium Repho game designer, was famed around the world for its innovation in artificial intelligence products and training aids. MandolinMonkey, for instance, the favored game for Federation youth circuits, still owed its patent to Sandelsky, although Federation testers had long ago bought out its functionality. She had always imagined a sleek, squat look for the main office when she thought of the Sandelsky brand, something like the MandolinMonkey obelisk. Although old, this building was part of a complex that took up at least an entire city block and included a bay on the canal for boats. Bored Repho military police mixed with pedestrians at the bridge going over to the plaza.

She and Beithune climbed the steps to the revolving glass of the entrance. She squeezed through with her bag and almost spun out on to the floor on the other side. Beithune had moved rapidly ahead without her. A group of longhaired twenty somethings that looked like they smoked khat and slept in portagons sat at a greasy old circular desk. They laughed out loud at her stumbling entrance. The room was large. It had been once an old garage belonging to the Metropolitan Transit Authority.

The walls had never been redone, still covered with graffiti and relics of the days of oil before the collapse of the permafrost and the floods of the late 2020s.

Beithune took something out of his pocket and threw it onto the circular table in the midst of what Corrag guessed was a Sandelsky design team. Several of them pushed back in their seats and swiveled to see who it was that had challenged with this gesture.

"It's rigged. I know how you do it. Do you want to see?" asked Beithune.

"Woah, there. What is this you've chucked here?" asked a bearded, burly blond giant, slapping his hands on his knees.

"That is the vertglove you sent me for *Fire*. I know how you do it. There's a built in lag, just microseconds, which is enough time for the high frequency transmitters to work around any move I make."

"Ah, so you're saying the game can read your thoughts before you do," said another man, with wide Mongol eyes and tattooed, sinuous arms crossed on his chest.

"Yes, but I know how it's done and I can show you."

"Can you beat the *Fire*?"

"Not yet."

"Let us know when you've beat the *Fire*."

A young woman with green hair snickered. Several people at the table restarted conversations among themselves.

"Hold on," said the blond giant, holding up Beithune's leather vertglove. "Here. Show me what you mean."

Beithune took the vertglove and laid it on the table. With a tool he removed from his pocket he undid the lacing and revealed the inner circuitry. Corrag moved closer, shifting her bag to the ground as she looked over his shoulder. She couldn't hear exactly what he was saying, but he pointed out something on the circuits laid down on the inside of the glove.

"Hmm," said the giant. "Do you think the transponder is cuing from the electrical impulses on your skin?"

"Yes, and the conversion is happening at about a four microseconds gap. See? Here are the two branches coming together. That gives you guys an unfair advantage. But I'll beat it anyway. Just give me some time."

"That's actually a pretty impressive piece of sleuthing, kid. If you're right, you deserve a new vertglove."

"Thanks. And there's another thing." The table went silent again. Beithune stuck his hand in his pocket and pulled out an emosponder stuck together with metalized synthoduct tape. He looked at something and pulled his head up.

"*Absolution.* I'd really appreciate some in tabs."

"That's strictly still in the works," said the giant.

"Some players are already going in."

"Do you know that for a fact?"

"Yes."

"This certainty is impressive in a youngster, if a little presumptuous," said the giant.

Another chair pushed back and a boy stood. Older than Beithune, but not long past twenty, he had a typical sort of face and build but with something slightly dark about him, some mysterious heritage.

"Barrier challenge," he said in a gruff voice, the kind of voice that didn't play much with words. Corrag had heard of barrier challenges. They were illegal in the Federation. She couldn't believe what she was hearing. Occasionally Republican gamers sought to recreate aspects of their favorite virtual settings in the outer world in order to continually blur the distinctions between the two. For the Federation, they were simply much too dangerous, with casualty rates that were not worth the extracurricular experience points.

Beithune smiled, showing a mouth full of crooked teeth. It seemed oral perfection was not an imperative in the Republican health care system. Another difference. In the Federation, gleaming, perfectly straight white teeth were an expectation for Axion streamed children. The sight of Beithune's smile was an unsettling shock to Corrag. But she cheered for him in her heart and tensed her body, as her cousin stepped up to the other man.

"What'll it be?" said Beithune.

"Board, wall or ball? Your choice, kid."

"Ball," said Beithune.

Several people at the table cheered, including the woman with green hair. Beithune looked at Corrag and tossed her his emosponder.

"In case," he said. "Check the finder history and it'll get you to our zipcar and home."

Corrag nodded with the full weight of the realization that Beithune was facing real and imminent danger, including possible death. She looked around for some responsible adult with a frowning countenance to step in and put a stop to the scene, and she listened for an emosensor alarm at the very least. But there was neither.

"Give him an asskicking, Shulder," said the giant calmly.

Shulder led Beithune out towards the middle of the floor. There was a blue ball on the ground, old and dusty. He poked it with his foot into the air back to Beithune, who caught it on his chest with a quick jump. He let it roll onto his shoulder, popped it up behind him with his head and flicked it with a back heel over his shoulder. He caught it with his left instep, balancing the ball on his outstretched foot for several seconds before flicking it back towards Shulder, who caught the ball in the air with two feet, landed with it still pinned between his ankles, and flipped forward in a handspring, flinging the ball towards the wall by releasing it from his feet at the top of the arc. Beithune followed the flight of the ball and gave a slight stagger forward as it thudded with full force. It hit very close to a target painted there in red. The cheers from the group at the table grew louder.

A metallic pincer jaw dropped from the ceiling on an extendable lattice and gripped the ball. The pincer pulled the ball out to the middle of the floor again and both Shulder and Beithune walked over to the pincer over their heads, its spotlight falling in a radius of about twenty feet. The rest of the space went dark.

"Come on, Beithune!" shouted Corrag. She dropped her bag and rushed with the others to the edge of light.

The ball dropped. Beithune gained first possession, spinning with it on his left foot in a tight radius. His hat fell off and his long hair flowed behind. Shulder was on his back, no delay in his reactions. His face registered a focus that seemed demonic, superhuman. His shoulder went down and with a grunt he forced Beithune aside, leaving the blue ball exposed and rolling. Sliding, both of them went after it, but Beithune, lightning in his reflexes, was up quicker. Corrag's heart was in her throat as Beithune leapt after it and cocked his left leg for a try at the target lit up in a bright spot on the wall beyond. Shulder let out a desperate war cry and spun, his foot aimed at Beithune's head in a swirling sidekick. Beithune ducked and stopped, foot on the ball, and reversed himself, spinning against the direction of Shulder's kick. In three quick leaps he was at the wall, but instead of flicking at the target, he reached for the tool in the pocket of his homespun pants, reached down and stabbed the ball, popping it, then pinned the flattened skin against the wall in an impressive arm strike. This was a sign of relent, and despite the defeat, Shulder's life was automatically spared. The lights came on. Shulder stayed down on the floor, his face, contorted in rage, hidden by his two hands.

The giant came up to Beithune and Corrag next to him.

"I must say I speak for all here. That was a hell of a good barrier challenge. As a prize, here's a new vertglove." The giant held out in his hand the vertglove dyed in rainbow colors.

"Oh, and something else with that."

Beithune reached out his hand again and took the vial the giant was handing him.

"Be easy on these. Like I said, this is still in the rollout phase. Someone with your capabilities should be okay, but never overconfident. Got it?"

"Yes, I do," said Beithune, smiling.

They were walking across the bridge to the western wastelands, Beithune and Corrag, in the late afternoon. Behind them were the blocks and blocks of burned out tenements and refugee camps smoldering with scrapwood cooking fires. Corrag stopped and scanned the horizon behind them. Such a landscape of human suffering hadn't even existed in her imagination before. The subporter had taken them through the tunnels and spit them out at the foot of the bridge, but even there, in the bowels of the city's infrastructure, in the higher elevations that had been spared the destruction of the Great Flood, she could still smell the rot, the waste of life on the streets that permeated the old concrete and sank into the ground. Ahead were the parking lots for commuters. They'd been quiet since leaving Sandelsky, but Corrag wanted to talk now.

"Why does the Republic allow all this?"

"You mean all the poor?"

"Yeah. It wouldn't take that much to build it better, at least. Put nanofiber road surfaces down. Plant some bamboo as a carbon soak."

"It's called co-dependence. You don't want people to

rely on caregivers. Then they can't fend for themselves. We want a land of the free."

The zipcar was in lot 49. Beithune stashed her bag in the trunk. He helped Corrag adjust the reclining seat. She felt suddenly like she could sleep, but wanted to stay awake to watch the new landscape. Beithune fitted his emosponder to the rearview mirror and placed his beret and the new vertglove in the glove compartment. Then he spoke into the emosponder.

"Home."

The zipcar started rolling, and within minutes they were out of the parking lot and cruising at a comfortable, constant speed up the northern highway. The houses were metal prefabs, with occasional wooden survivors of the megastorms that habitually whipped up out of the islands. There was constant road advertising, selling everything from nano-milk to Kleenex. Apparently Kleenex was a panacea for fitfulness and instability, to be used to wipe away imperfection and liquid mess, especially for older people. Corrag had never seen age as a demographic component, but that was because in the Fed it was supposed to not exist anymore. But here in the Republic, home truths were not kept secret. They were an opportunity for merchandising. And older, poorer Republicans were the main targets of commercial remediation.

They stopped at a roadside refreshment kiosk and recharger. Beithune plugged the zipper in, while Corrag used the vacuum toilet and then wandered around the kiosk. There were videos on the nanowall screens here for popular items such as the Klondike Tours voyages to Kazakhstan with celebrity guides like Eunique Bieber. Beithune appeared at her side silent as a ghost while she listened to Eunique Bieber plug the service.

"Some of this stuff is pretty cheesy," he said.

"Why is that?"

"Mostly geared to old timers with the mullah to buy such garbage."

"Young people don't?"

"No. There's high unemployment for our generation. We have to fight hard to get jobs and move away from home. Save money for a house. Pay off the college debt. Buy a solar charger and the portagon. Getta hold of the dream, don't you know? That's the Republican deal."

"Yeah, we have it pretty easy in the Fed. No advetising, and no false hopes."

"I'll say. But then you don't have as many options. Freedom of choice is the rock solid foundation of the Repho. Limited choices means no freedom."

"Maybe. What are your choices?"

"Finish college and find a job. Just finished my freshman year. I'm on a co-op semester. Supposed to be doing an internship."

"With who?"

"The family business. I'm a design consultant."

"The family business?"

"You'll see. My mother runs it. So it can change pretty quickly from one week to the next. My consultancy work consists pretty much of staying one step ahead of her whims."

"Okay."

"Yeah."

They got back in the zipcar for the last couple hundred miles of the journey through the woodlands of the great North. The trees were genetically modified pine and hardwood, grown to immense heights under the carbon-charged atmosphere. The forest was meant as a reservoir for carbon uptake, but the giant trees often toppled due to the pulpy fiber of quick growth. Several times they slowed for roadside crews working on sawing up the thick trunks that had blocked traffic. The crews were young men and women, laughing, with bronzed faces, and their zipbikes and zipcars were parked haphazardly nearby in a clearing, as if they'd been summoned in a hurry to take charge of the problem.

Beithune slowed and exited the highway at St. Albans. Then a series of back roads ensued, until they descended a steep hill towards a river valley, crossed an oxbow of the broad, black river eastward on an old covered bridge reinforced with titanium inserts in the beams, and ascended the switchback on the other side into a hill country covered in windmills on the ridges.

The Hunnewells lived on the farm that had been in the family for five generations, starting with the original internal migrant in the mid-1960s who had moved up from the cities, bought the failing dairy farm, and taught music in the local school while reworking the land into an alpaca and wild boar reservation. Since then, the farm had raised Highland cattle and tilapia, white fish, prawns, and mealworms -- all sources of protein and high energy value as food stocks for the food and entertainment industry. With the growth of synthetic printing, they had been forced to adapt once again and now were experimenting with varietals of maple syrup for the export market.

The family house was a large, turret style Fortress with glass walls on the south exposure leading out to a lawn studded with artificial ponds and artifacts from local studios. The zipcar parked itself on the gravel drive, and Corrag got out and stretched her legs. The housebot was stepping down the tiled path from the house, but Beithune stopped it gently with a simple hand movement and a few words and directed it back the way it had come. On the trail of the housebot came a barking yellow dog. It jumped at Beithune, who ordered it down and laughed at its antics. Then the dog ran ahead, and Corrag and Beithune followed to the back entrance through the garage filled with a variety of modified farm implements and up the steps to the door, where the large silhouette of Joan Hunnewell stood outlined in the frame. She wiped her hands and held them both out.

"Corrag Lyons. Welcome to our home," she said, her voice cracking with genuine emotion. Corrag pressed up into the door and dropped her bag. Joan hugged her in her meaty arms, damp from recent exertion.

"So good to see you."

"Yes, and here. My mother sent this," said Corrag dropping to her knee and unzipping the bag to find the ball of California crystal prized by collectors.

"Oh, my. This is wonderful. And you are a great

beauty just like your mother."

After more pleasantries, Joan introduced her to Wennill, Beithune's sister, a shy fourteen year old with weak eyes who looked up from her screen on the couch in the living area and attempted a smile. Jeoff Hunnewell, Alana's brother, was away on a business trip and due back later that evening.

"We'll eat now since you must be hungry. Wennill, off the couch and help set the table."

"I'm not hungry."

"Doesn't matter. You'll eat with us. We don't usually. But today we have a special guest."

"How long is she going to be here?"

"I don't know. Doesn't matter. Get off your butt."

Wennill and the housebot set a table in the dining room. The original beams from the first house on the site had been used in the ceiling. One wall was lined with shelves that held some of the farm's mementos: prizes for 4H club livestock from the last century, a taster's gold medal from the Vereniging van Cider in 2038, and the original Homeland Export License of 2032, were among some of the items Corrag noted. There was no nanowall. She wondered if they couldn't afford one or maybe it was a matter of choice.

"How was the tubid?"

"It was fine. No major delays," said Corrag.

"Your first time?"

"Yes."

"So amazing, isn't it? All the advances we've made and the two families never visit. After all these years. But things are looking up now with you, a youth emissary. That is quite an honor for a Federation girl."

"Well, it was more a matter of expediency, to be honest. I was in a bit of trouble with the law."

"Oh, the law is an ass. You have all my sympathies, girl. It's in the Hunnewell genes."

"Well, we believe that genes need the right conditions to express themselves."

"Right conditions are bound to come along," said Joan, cryptically.

"What's your boyfriend's name?" asked Wennill

"Boyfriend?"

"The one you got in trouble for. I assume that's what you're on about."

"Oh, Ben. He's in the Army."

"Do you hear from him much?" asked Joan.

"No. Not much."

"Par for the course."

"He's probably a little busy, Mom."

"Well, that's true. It's the same with our boys and girls fighting those Jihad natives over there so they don't get ideas about attacking the Homeland. We should really join together again. We were much stronger before the secession.'"

"I wonder if that would ever happen," said Corrag.

"Fat chance," said Wennill. "Not while President McKinsky's in office. His cronies have too much invested in keeping us apart. Imagine if we got all the deals you get over there as part of our package."

"There's something to be said for working for your

benefits," said Joan.

Ben smiled during the entire exchange.

Dinner was macaroni and cheese that Joan served in a hand turned, curly maple bowl. They sat at the island in the kitchen that still had the old granite countertop that Jeoff's great-great-grandfather Dwayne had installed in the original farmhouse. Jeoff showed up halfway through the meal with a carton of ice cream he had bought on his way home from the tubid port of Norm Laveque, named after a hockey star and Quebec academic that had led negotiations formalizing the independence of Canada from Repho in 2042. The ice cream was a maple flavored variety that had been made with their carob maple syrup, a flavor patented and sold to the company in Toronto that manufactured the ice cream and sold it around the world. Repho exporters had perfected printing techniques that enabled duplication down to the photon level of feedstocks, something the Federation was only now beginning to emulate. Jeoff had flown in from Brussels where he had been consulting on agricultural patents with a Belgian company that built dairy farms, mainly in China, and used recycled methane to power worm composting facilities. The worms and the byproduct were used to provide feedstock for South Asian markets. Jeoff was a graduate of Dartmouth with a PhD in Finance and Ethical Markets. He mentioned all of this between spoonfuls of the ice cream and questions about Corrag and her mother and father. He reminded them all that his sister Alana had also been a brilliant scholar, with an advanced degree in Game Theory. She had met Ricky at an intercontinental conference in New Orleans in 2029, the year before the hurricane that had finally destroyed that Southern city, last of the Repho gulf hubs to hold on to a population base. Jeoff tended to dominate the conversation, and Corrag discovered later that was the reason they rarely ate together, even when they were all home.

There was silence when they were done. Jeoff went over to a cabinet and brought out a bottle of a maple syrup liqueur that had the family name, Hunnewell Northern Lights Saffron SugarShack. Beithune and Wennill brought over the glasses and Jeoff poured out the concoction with the long-winded title in five crystal goblets. Corrag politely exclaimed at the amber color and held up her glass, savoring the moment.

"To Corrag, may her stay with us become a long-lasting foundation for peace," said Jeoff.

"Amen," said Joan, downing the glass in a quick shot.

Corrag's room was on the top floor, a loft above the media space with shelves of old books collected over the generations. The books reflected ancient family interests. There was a thin, well-thumbed volume of poems about trout fishing in America and another paperback about a cowgirl with big thumbs and then there were old movies catalogued by year on a rustic wall chart. The housebot that showed her upstairs had several recommendations for her.

"How do you know what I'd like?" Corrag asked the bot.

"I infer tastes. That's one of the things I can do.

Federation bots are not as advanced. You have an interest in family and societal critiques with a thrilling and harmonious musical track."

"I see."

Everything seemed to be better in the Repho household of her cousins, even the bots. They undoubtedly cost a fortune and were therefore only used in the homes of the wealthy, or as in the case of the Hunnewells, the aspiring, as opposed to the widespread dispersal one could find across the Democravian demographic. But the underlying truth was that there was an air of something not quite right, of people tumbling over themselves to avoid the glaring, obvious unhappiness that she could already sense.

Corrag was left alone in the bedroom after the housebot was called back down by Joan to help with cleaning the kitchen. She lay in bed and looked at the texts on her emosponder. Finally Gurgie had gotten back to her with her new Cloud ID. She sent a quick text back to the new address:

-- Hi G. Let's see each other on MM. I can get on if you want.

A few minutes later there was a ding of an answer.

-- I can't. We've been cut off from all the old games. Part of the induct. Higher learning means remapping old pleasure centers, C. Someday for you too, I hope. Do you hope also, C?

Instead of answering, Corrag thought. What was it she hoped for? Something unnamable, a place she imagined. Its existence would allow her to feel comfortable with herself. And friends and loved ones, a family around, encircling her. Corrag slept soundly. She was awakened the next morning by the dog, Teddy, poking her foot with his nose. The sun was streaming in the window above the bed, and the morning light glinted on the wooden floor with the promise of new discoveries. Corrag wandered downstairs and served herself some breakfast, a bowl of quinoa and blueberries and a black coffee from the Ethiopian highlands. The house was quiet. Then Beithune appeared in a doorway and called her over. The door led to a wing of the house, a hall and several rooms off of it. In the first door, Jeoff sat in his office with a bud in his ear conversing to a group of people displayed in holographic three dimensions before him at his desk. The three were Africans dressed in desert garb. They were exporters of Guaniba, a bean from the Mandarke tree that was used in the production of everything from emoenhancers to biological weaponry, explained Beithune. They were speaking to Jeoff from the conference room of the tribe's headquarters in Ngauoundal. Down the hall, Beithune had a sterilized lab.

"This is where we develop taste modules for our products. It's pretty cool," he said.

"Can I help?"

"Yeah. I can train you in the techniques we'll use. You'll work with me here if you want. Then when I go back to school you can take over some of the projects. Which will free Jeoff up to do some more consulting work."

"Sounds good."

Corrag trained with Beithune in the production of taste modules. In a month they produced several new varietals of maple products for the luxury market, salad dressings, deserts, a barbecue sauce and Corrag's favorite, a chewing gum. They worked hard with only a half hour break for lunch on most days. Orders flowed in from major restaurants and gastronomic clubs across the Repho sphere. Beithune believed the Federation would eventually have to begin allowing imports of molecular modules, which were still a forbidden food in her country.

"It only stands to reason. How could you keep this out?" asked Beithune rhetorically, his hands busy with a boiling vat of calcium carbonate solution.

"It doesn't come from the ground. Federation feedstocks must be organic. Look at all this stuff we use. Alginates. Nitrous oxide. Monosodium. Methane hydrates. It can't be good," said Corrag, allowing her thoughts free rein, despite their critical tone.

"Yes, but it's delicious. That's what people want. Choices, Corrag. Have to give the people choices."

"How can that be, Beithune? *'A plethora of choices has ruined the contentment of the American people.'*"

"Who said that?"

"Wally Delamare."

"The man who dared to torch the halls of the Senate? We made the wrong choice when we spared his life."

"We call him a prophet of the new world order. One of the Founding Brethren."

"Corrag, I hate to tell you, you've been brought up in

a backwater. The world is definitely not going the Federation's way."

Corrag held her tongue. Beithune, like her, only half-believed everything he said in defense of his country. In his spare time he was cultivating a freer, more iconoclastic world view that was setting him up for an inevitable confrontation between what he truly believed and what he was expected to espouse. It happened sooner than anyone could have predicted.

Beithune came to her one night and said he needed to talk to her about his gaming. Having been with him at the Sandelsky office and the successful barrier challenge with Shulder, she was privy to an aspect of Beithune he kept hidden from the world of the Hunnewell farm and its subsidiary businesses. He had the latest headset, a Weimar 2.8 and a spare, an old Oculus that he synced to the gaming cube he had hung on the back door of his clothes closet. He invited her in and they sat together on his bed late at night while the rest of the house slept.

The two of them scrambled over the wreckage of an air strike looking for survivors among the Supermen. Corrag quickly became adept at listening for the sounds of groaning and reaching for limbs. But the stench of rotting flesh was a shock to her, and she could barely keep herself from doubling over and retching.

She found the heat imager before Beithune. He came back to her and they both ran up a side street with a little boy in front of them leading the way. She could sense that the point of the game would have nothing to do with the ideology of the Supermen or the Law but simply survival and being on the right side when the final strike came down. Beithune had her along as an ally and to see how she handled herself. So she stuck by him.

An outside observer would have seen the two of them sitting upright against the headboard side by side without touching, watching the space ahead.

On Sundays the Hunnewells went to the church in Hanover, the Unitarian Church of Her Lordship. This was a novel experience for Corrag, who had been brought up in the strict, secular world of a leading family of the Federation, where mention of religion was inevitably followed by talk of jail time. But here in New Albion there was a wide assortment of religious choices, from militant atheists to a temple of the New Israelites.

The Unitarian Church of Her Lordship's pastor was a young man, the Reverend Shellay Hustice, and a Sunday late in the summer he spoke of Her Lordship's exhortation to seek out the truth for themselves.

"'Can the blind lead the blind?' asked Our Lady. And of course the answer is not. You need training to be a leader, and where do you get the training? Through the right connections. Which is why we work so hard to afford the very best augmentation we can get for ourselves and our loved ones! We trust She is showing us the way hard work and the grace of the right connections can pave the way to eternal satisfaction. And so we end our ceremony, brothers and sisters, with the following hope. May your week be filled with productivity and may you bear the good fruit of the righteous in the unified way of our Republican heritage. Amen."

"Amen," responded the congregants.

After a final hymn and the exit of Reverend Hustice, the Hunnewells shuffled out the church door into the bright sunshine of a cloudless August day. Wennill smiled at some friends and Beithune held his breath until they could get to the corner where Jeoff had parked the family portagon. In the car, Jeoff praised the sermon. He had found it very moving. Nobody else said a word, not even Joan. Finally, Jeoff asked Corrag what she thought, hoping to get some support from a neutral party.

"It was okay. I don't really understand the point, though. We're supposed to praise an individual's effort, but if we're all individuals, why do we have to get together once a week rain or shine to remind ourselves of the importance of maintaining our individuality?"

"It's because, like Her Lordship says, we need the right connections to be fruitful, but we still need to be strong and respect an individual's rights," said Jeoff.

"That's ridiculous," said Beithune quickly. "It's because we like to belong to something that reflects well on us. But that Reverend Hustice is so lame, Dad."

"He really is. Why can't we try the Baptist church like you promised? The entire crew team goes there. At least they have good clubs," whined Wennill.

"Maybe. Maybe we will," said Joan, trying to still the turbulent water that Corrag's response had seemed to set in motion. Jeoff exasperatedly overrode the driving function from the portagon, screeching the wheels too fast on the winding road back from the town.

Once in the house, the Hunnewells retreated to their respective rooms. Corrag went outside and played with Teddy, tossing him a beat up, old racquetball she found with her foot under a pile of molecular compost in the rose bushes. At least the dog seemed clear in his affections and motivations. She couldn't say the same about the Hunnewells that owned him. Jeoff came outside, still in his Sunday clothes, a lightweight PET outfit that did little to hide his gut. She wondered why he didn't have remedial surgery. In the Federation it would have been mandated for someone in his position, and his diet and exercise regimes would be supervised until he could bring his weight under control.

"How are you?" asked Jeoff.

"Fine, I guess."

Jeoff nodded. "Feel like a walk?" he asked.

"Sure," said Corrag. He seemed lonely, isolated in the family, and she felt suddenly sorry for him. She could see in her uncle some of the traits she found so exasperating about Alana -- the stubbornness, the yearning for some completeness that was never quite there, the lashing out in quick anger that only fed unhappiness.

They walked down the hill towards the conservation land that was administered by the New Albion Land Trust. The leaves in the beeches, maples and oaks were beginning to turn, and some of the bottomland trees in the beaver swamp were already flush with vivid shades of oranges and reds that Corrag loved with a strength of feeling that was mysterious to her.

"Nice here, isn't it?" said Jeoff. He seemed calmer. The walking did him good. He was a man of action, when all was said and done. Limbs moving meant the world was under control.

"It really is."

"The seasons are a constant. For about ten years we saw some dieback in the forest, especially the birches. Don't see as much damage the last few or so. They seem to be adjusting. Even moose numbers are coming back thanks to the rebound in the wolf population. That's somehow counterintuitive, but you know about the way the ecosystem operates."

"Yes, the Gaian paradigm is something we learn in grade school."

"You tend to stress the role of human stewardship while we understand the deeper symbiosis, but never mind. It's splitting hairs, isn't it, Corrag?"

"Well, those things are important."

"You're like your mother. She was a true believer. We're more pragmatic in the Republic. Getter done and all that. And at the same time we trust our ancestral intuitions about the deeper meaning of it all."

"Yeah. I can see that. There's something to be said. And yet, it does allow for more misery. We don't tolerate misery well. It's smile all the while in Democravia, Uncle. That might seem trite. It used to be for me, but now ... I don't know. I'm not so sure of my former certainty."

"You miss home, don't you?"

"A little."

"Well, I think you've been a great emissary. If that

helps."

"I suppose. This will get me on the track again for Augmentation."

"That's important. If it's what you want. Do it for the right reasons. Plenty of people get augmented but the underlying reference points are all wrong, and it gets them nowhere. Your thought determines your actions, Corrag. If what's in your mind sets the course for you, it's most important to put the right thoughts in your mind. Don't let anyone else put them there for you until you know what's there first."

"But how do you know?"

"Know what?"

"What to put in your mind?"

"By contact with stimulus that brings about awareness. Life experience and struggle with adversity. That's why, in my opinion, Corrag, the Republic will reach star exploration first. Our way is clearer. Buy the augmentation when you're ready for it yourself, not when some council determines you are fit for it because you suit their purposes."

"I like that, but I just see the unhappiness that results from the adversarial system, the lack of planning, and I'm ... well it makes me sick sometimes. Honestly."

"Unhappiness is just a cloud, Corrag, a passing cloud. Don't think that the clouds block the sun. They pass."

"Well, that's easy for you to say."

"How is that, Corrag?"

"You have it all. You're one of the lucky ones."

"Lucky. That's not the word that I would use. We

worked hard for everything. The grace of Our Lady comes to those that contend, Corrag."

"Everyone does in their own way. It is a common struggle. *'The cause of humanity lifts all boats.'*"

"You like a good quote, don't you? *'The stars are for the victors.'* That was also Tracy Durkiev, right? We only have so much time. Use it wisely."

They walked on down the hill, winding until Corrag had the sense they were facing back into the hill, as if corkscrewing into themselves. There was a cascade of water coming off some rocks and ferns and brambles lining the road under the shadow of the giant trees. Corrag had the sense that she was a part of everything that she had ever seen, as if the true augmentation was just being alive. As if everything that had evolved had been designed with her in mind for that very moment. She recognized this as the illusion of singularity, an example of a fault in the hard wiring of the human brain that could be overcome with augmented life-long education, but still the pleasant sensation lulled her as she listened to Jeoff and walked along in the strobing shadow and light of the dappled forest.

"... And then when you get married and start a family it's all about the children and there's no more time for yourself. That's the time in my opinion to get augmented. That's when you need it."

"For yourself?"

"Of course."

"But augmentation means you lose individuation. That's what I learned from Shearstein in the remediation process. The higher you go, the more you turn over to the Cloud. Isn't that true here also?"

"Who told you that?"

"My attorney."

"That's a strange thought. Of course here in Repho we believe the individual should always maintain control. The privacy safeguards to any augment are ironclad. No matter what company you opt for. That's one of the control mechanisms we still hand off to third party non-profits."

"What are they?"

"Third party non-profits are appointed by the executive by two thirds majority," droned Jeoff. "They are made up of retired executives who volunteer. It's considered an honor. My father-in-law, Joan's dad, Peter Stirling was on the Milk Board, that's a third party non-profit that drew up the list of rules for feedstock certification back in the 2020s."

"So there's still oversight."

"Of course. And there still are criminal abuses of the system. Some things are never going to change. My best advice to you is to be conservative. Don't go for the flashiest augment outfit. Some of these kids trying to prove themselves end up slaving away for the outfits they buy into. The back doors can be impossible to see. Make sure they're as transparent as possible."

"In the Federation there is only one augment. That's the Democravian Mind Ministry, the DMM."

"Yes. You know what you're getting with the DMM."

"Top quality access to scientific culture."

"Pretty bland stuff if you ask me. There's no art, no crossover, nothing dangerous or unconventional. Believe me there's a lot of the Federation elite that swing on the Repho augment when they get a chance."

"How?"

"Brazil and Alaska. The cartels that cater to vacationers, hook them for a fee and a three-day sample. They've perfected the cookie wipes using nanobots in the bloodstream. You get an IV transfusion on the last day and away you go back to San Jose and no-ones the wiser."

They walked back to the house. Corrag forced herself to put the conversation with Jeoff out of her mind, stored away for another, more reflective moment, purposely focusing on the details in front of her -- Teddy's dash across the grass, the housebot's confusion, Wennill's cry of exasperation. She had a sudden sinking sadness in her gut. The day had wound away again and she was no better off, no closer to clarity. She excused herself from Wennill and Jeoff. They were looking at the summer science camp art project Wennill had assembled on the picnic bench, a polymer foam model of the tides. The housebot had retrieved the wrong kind of glue from the laboratory, apparently, and Wennill was dramatically inconsolable about the impossibility of ever getting it right in her life. Corrag couldn't help thinking she was overly dramatic.

She had the sense of having outgrown some of the melancholy of her own adolescence. She looked out the gable window of the guest bedroom at Jeoff and Joan in the yard with the housebot circled around Wennill as she finally pumped the right kind of glue from the glue gun.

They tried so hard to please her. Corrag was reminded of her own parents and the ways she had disappointed them. Maybe Joan was right, maybe the Hunnewell genes were stronger than any child-rearing techniques or beliefs. The best outcome from her travels might be to instill a sense of duty, thought Corrag.

She was reading a book from the library called *Conrad,* a historical romance of the Scottish Highlands. In it, the warrior clans united behind Conrad, a time traveler from the future, as they battled the English troops under General Cromwell. Cromwell was depicted as suffering from severe self-doubts and an inferiority complex that led him to torture his enemies as a way of self-soothing, a sort of monstrous addict. Corrag lost herself in the words of the story as the daylight faded and the lights of the bedroom automatically increased their diffusion. Was she like Conrad, she wondered, forever wandering, unable to find pleasure in the small moments of life? In the end, Conrad came back to himself in his former life and was reawakened to the possibilities and mysteries of the ordinary world.

She lay her head back on the pillow and put the book aside. The days were getting noticeably shorter and there was a chill in the air, more like a bite really, once the sun went down. Corrag got up and went over to the closet and wrapped the wool shawl Joan had placed there around her shoulders. A knock sounded on the door. Such an old-fashioned sound. Corrag still marveled at it, the knuckles against wood that conveyed so much more information then the nanowall at home in Edmundstown.

By this particular rap she knew it was Beithune, and by it's exaggerated, leisurely one-two she also knew it was important.

"What are you doing?" he asked after she opened the door. He was disheveled, as if he'd been sleeping all day.

"Just reading. What about you."

"Can I come in?"

"Sure."

Beithune stepped inside the room and looked around, scratching his head. He seemed uneasy, but he looked at her with a determined glint in his eye.

"Tonight it's on. Are you up for it?"

"Do you think we're ready?"

"I think so. It's a big step. This new game is supposed to involve a new kind of biological augment. I've held off, but I want to try it. It's a challenge, a real challenge."

"Do you know the setting?"

"No."

Corrag paused, thinking. A biological as opposed to chemical augment sounded scary but she was definitely interested in trying the new game. The top of the line Repho gamers were hired for the Sandelsky design teams, and gaining access to their thought system had to be an asset.

"What's the downside, Beithune?"

"Losing. That's always the downside. Once out of the ranks, you will never be invited to another opening. The discussion boards will be closed to you forever."

"However, the augment goes away if you lose, right?"

"I think so. The truth is nobody knows if there is even

such a thing as a biological augment. I did an analysis of the in pills."

"And?"

"There are polymeric nanocarriers that may be able to overcome the subcellular bottlenecks. CMD comes to mind, but so far none have yielded gene expresion in any reported findings. But there's always a chance that Sandelsky may have hit on something and are taking it to the field."

"So you think it might work."

"There is a carboxymethylated dextrans in there."

"It couldn't be that big, then."

"Yes, it could. There are Japanese nano designs that unfold once they get released into a solvent with the reticulocytes of normal red blood cells."

Corrag paused to think hard. Doing the right thing was important to her future. On the other hand, taking chances was the hallmark of winning any game. The question of a contraband augment, in the Federation's eyes, hardly bothered her. The Council would certainly be disapproving, but that was the point of having envoys, to bring back and incorporate difference. The core of consciousness was an acknowledged mystery still. She felt confident in its ultimate safeguard capabilities.

"Okay," she said at last.

"I need you with me as a tether just in case. Are you sure?"

"Yes. Let's do it."

"You could just belay me without the in pill."

"No, I want to go in."

"Then here."

Beithune pulled the vial he'd received from the Sandelsky giant from his pocket and shook out two pills into the palm of his right hand. He held it out. Corrag took a pill. Beithune took the other and put the vial back in his pocket.

"We'll take it now, and after dinner I'll meet you."

They looked hard at each other and both swallowed their pills together. There was a slight bitterness that lingered in her throat. She felt immediately queasy and sat down on her bed. Beithune walked out and closed the door behind him. The dizziness ebbed, as did the ringing in her ears. Eventually she stood up from the bed. The solar-electric stored heat had come on, and the wood floor was warm under her bare feet. She wrapped herself in the shawl again and looked at herself in the mirror. She could hear Wennill's voice and the housebot as they descended the stairs together. It was time for dinner. She had a strange fear of taking a step outside the room, and her depth perception was slightly skewed. She held the old book she had been reading in front of her face and attempted to read from the page. The words registered but then somehow vanished from her mind instantly. Then she put some music on her emosponder, picking a song she knew always got her into a dancing mood, *Carnivaleo* by Tizziano Pellegrino, to check her emotional responses. The song came on and she felt a strange nostalgia for the past and a desire to be in the dark. It was very strange.

Corrag skipped dinner. She wasn't hungry. The

housebot knocked on the door and then went away. It was late when Beithune knocked. Corrag let him in. He had the two headsets and the cube. They set up the cube on the end of the bed and sat together against the wall, adjusting the pillows.

"Are you ready?" asked Beithune.

"Yeah," said Corrag. But the truth was she wasn't sure. She feared it would turn out badly, that Beithune and she would be lost in the virtual space and there would be no getting back. It was a strange, primitive fear that she quelled, like a fear of spiders. She had learned with Ben that fear itself was the biggest threat.

Beithune turned on the cube. They put on the masks. There was no intro, just blackness. Then they were plunged into it and falling through bubbles and cold.

Sea was all around them. When she tried to breathe she got a lungful of water and choked. They had on some kind of weights strapped around their waists and were sinking rapidly into greater blackness. Corrag counted four other bodies in the swirling water with her. Beds of kelp shadowed above and swayed all around. Corrag felt the full throttle of panic. There was no way to breathe. This was a sudden death before the game even got started. In the murky depths of the ocean, Beithune turned and looked at her, squinting. She felt lost, totally disoriented, and stricken with a paralyzing, overwhelming hysteria.

There in the distance was a glint of color, a golden eel swaying by a rock, the entrance to its cave. Corrag kicked and was suddenly made weightless. Her effortless movement gave her hope. Menacing, the eel opened its wide, evil mouth, showing its rows of teeth, and thrust itself at her in a wriggling lunge. Corrag arched her back, feinting, and kicked hard, swooping to grab a blue stone on the floor of the cave behind the eel. She turned and there was Beithune behind her. She grabbed Beithune around his neck with her free left hand. They both could breathe; the blue stone was a kind of exterior gill. The eel made one last lunge at them from the corner of her eye, but they swam away unscathed, Corrag holding onto Beithune, sharing the stone's life-giving oxygenation.

It was cold, and the murky water made picking a direction difficult. Now they were alone, sinking deeper into the cold. The others had drowned, their useless avatar bodies hitting and bouncing on the bottom sand. Holding hands in order to share the stone, Corrag and Beithune swam carelessly, letting the current carry them over a ledge. In the distance was a hammerhead shark. It lunged, circling back once it sensed them. There seemed to be a shipwreck below the ledge, the remains of its cargo strewn over the seabed. There were trunks and books, pages waving, the words on them printed in some strange forgotten language, candelabra and shoes encrusted with barnacles and sea life.

They drifted over the wreck. Beithune tugged at her. It seemed he wanted to explore. Corrag resisted, but then relented, not knowing exactly what he saw down there.

The boat's name was Aschelon -- *written on the stern and the steam stacks, and its home port was Le Havre. Time was no longer relative for those onboard. Skeletal victims were scattered randomly, tatters of clothes still hanging on most of them. Whatever accident had befallen the ship, it must have occurred instantly, trapping the passengers forever in the poses of ordinary shipboard life: eating meals, lying in bed or playing cards around small tables in the berths, stuck in the passages where the water had risen instantly around them. Beithune picked a door and pushed against it, then kicked it open. He motioned for Corrag to follow and she did, grabbing him by the hand so he could breathe again.*

They drifted through the ship's labyrinth of halls and decks, eventually finding themselves in the captain's quarters. Beithune gathered up a knife and an astrolabe from the floor. An open closet door revealed a book with Hebrew letters on its faded cloth covers, swaying languidly in the invisible currents. Corrag examined it and heard a voice. It was Beithune.

"What is it?"

"I don't know."

"Keep it."

Corrag stashed the book in a pocket of her vest. Then they slipped out the door and drifted, welling over the deck of the ship. Appearing out of the murkiness, the shark dove at them. Corrag tilted her head, sensing its approach, its cold eyes. They were prey now. It shot forward, no longer circling, with hunger-sharpened senses. Beithune kicked and struck at it with the captain's knife, tearing its throat. The shark made a serpentine struggle in retreat, swimming away, trailing a silty ribbon of blood. Beithune tugged at her, and they followed the shark's trail of blood into the blackness of the deep.

They kicked against the upwelling of the water, attempting to swim deeper. The blackness was broken in the distance by a faint luminescence. The lights were coming from a stone structure, turrets and a tower in the center -- some sort of castle. Beithune and Corrag descended and slowly drifted around the castle wall until they came to a set of ruined stone stairs at the top of which was a set of ominous doors. In front of the stone stairs loomed a sword, its blade encased in flames. Corrag dropped the blue stone in the pocket of her vest and held the book instead. She approached the sword and with her free left hand reached for the flaming blade. She gripped the blade and pulled. The doors opened. She dropped the sword and swam for the inside, holding her breath. Beithune followed, barely squeezing through before the doors swung shut again silently. The two of them stood in the courtyard of the ancient castle, surrounded by warriors in armor slumped against wooden tables and flat out on the floor, seemingly either dead or asleep. The warriors began to rustle, awakening. The two of them could breathe unaided again as if on land, but Corrag's breath came raspily, as if she had a cold.

"Where are we?" asked Corrag.

"The King of the Underworld. All the dead heroes are coming back to life because we found them. It's been thousands of years for them asleep. They will probably try to kill us. Look in the mirror," said Beithune.

He dragged Corrag over to a mirror on the wall besides one of the banquet tables. They both were dragons, reflecting scaly green skin and claws.

"What do we do? We'll never be able to fight them all. It's not like we literally can breathe fire."

"Let them kill us. And whatever you do, don't think of yourself as Corrag or think of family or home. You'll never get back," said Beithune. He took her hand to reassure her.

"I'm scared now. This is exactly what I feared," said Corrag.

"Don't be scared," warned Beithune, his voice rising.

The first of the warriors rose silently now and rushed around the hall, spreading the alarm. The dead men all grouped as one and surrounded Beithune and Corrag. One old man with a javelin approached tentatively, and Beithune jumped at him with a swirling kick as the old man lunged with the spear. The warriors rushed in with swords drawn, hacking at the two of them. Corrag was surrounded. She curled into a fetal ball, holding her breath, as she felt the swords in turn falling on her, cleaving her legs and shattering her ribs. She could hear the thudding of metal against flesh, the spurting of her blood and the gore of her dragon body spattering against the walls and the armor clad bodies of the furious warriors. She listened for Beithune's voice to tell her it was all right, but she didn't hear him. She fought against the desire to hold thoughts of her parents, Ben, the Hunnewells of New Albion. Instead she concentrated on feeling the book she held in one hand and the blue stone in the other, and blocking out the furious blood lust of the undersea castle's ancient heroes.

Awakening as if from a dream, Corrag opened her eyes and looked around. There was Beithune lying next to her, *and now the sun was out. It was midday and hot and the ground was dusty, and the noises and smells of people and animals, sheep, goats and donkeys, pigeons in boxes, erupted into her consciousness. They were both covered in scratches as if they had crawled through thorn bushes, and their clothes were torn and in ribbons, hanging on them like old skins off two snakes. Standing, they both did their best to cover themselves. They were beside a stall selling fabrics in a busy market on the outskirts of a great city in the desert. The sun was huge and broiling. They looked for shelter under the shade of a tent, flapping white cloths held down with stakes in the sand. The wind kicked up, and clouds suddenly swept over the surface of the sun, blackening the day.*

Inside the tent, a crowd of people surrounded two men, one standing and the other on a pallet raised above the ground. The lying man had his eyes closed, and the standing man spoke in soft words, addressing himself to the crowd of onlookers. Corrag could not hear the words he was speaking, but was curious. Who was he? She felt she needed to hear. She thrust forward through the crowd. The standing man turned and addressed himself to a redheaded woman who knelt by the pallet. Corrag couldn't hear what he was saying. He seemed to want to console the woman. Then he turned his attention to the man lying there before him lifelessly. He held his arms over the man and turned his palms upward, in a begging pose. The crowd continued to buzz expectantly, as if this was all a show.

The dead man sat upright, and an audible gasp rose

through the air. Corrag turned to Beithune who had reached her side. They exchanged a knowing glance.

"Now what?" thought Corrag.

"I don't know. Let's wait and see," was Beithune's corresponding response.

Down from the tent's roof beams came a rope, and a young boy swung into the room from his lookout post on the roof. He shouted a warning, and the crowd slowly began to disperse, leaving the sick man, the healer and several dozen disciples to face the coming danger. A group of soldiers burst in through the side entrance as the last of the crowd disappeared back into the streets of the town. The soldiers carried drawn swords and advanced in an orderly, aggressive phalanx to surround the bearded prophet and his party, Corrag and Beithune among them, blending in easily by their wounds and ragged appearance. The sick man rose from the pallet and with the aid of crutches calmly approached his healer and kissed him on the cheek. Afterwards, he made his way quickly through the crowd of disciples. They stepped apart for him. At the tent's exit, a soldier dropped a handful of coins into his palm. That was the signal for the regiment to round up the remaining people and force march them through the streets of the town to a hill on the outskirts.

The prophet seemed to accept his fate, carrying the nailed wooden beams on his shoulders slowly, but without stumbling. In the distance, they could see a body of shimmering water, silver in the late afternoon. The boy who had warned of the soldiers tried to help him, but a soldier knocked him in the back of the legs with the swing of a poleax, and then stomped his back where he rolled on the ground. The crowd marched solemnly on.

Corrag stopped at the boy's side. She could hear his sobbing as she leaned down and put her face next to his. She touched the warm blood on his cheek where he'd been kicked, and put the cool blue undersea stone on his face, rubbing the bloody wound with it.

"That's good," Beithune's thought registered.

Corrag slowly stood along with the boy. The three of them made their way up the rocky trail to catch up with the crowd. At the summit, she could hear the groans as the prophet's body was nailed to the wooden cross and hoisted in the air. The dazzling light of the harsh sun made her blink and doubt what she was seeing, but the faces of the onlookers, their distress and suffering, convinced her that this was the crucifix of the Lord Jesus she had heard vague mentions of all her life. She and Beithune sat a distance away and watched silently, until they took his body down. The rumble of thunder indicated a coming desert storm. Corrag smelled wild flowers as the rain began.

They followed to the tomb where they laid His body, and then the crowd dispersed with the rain and rising water in the ditches of the road.

In the night they found themselves back out on the same road trying to find the tomb. The storm had passed, and they could hear the gurgle of water in the ditch. Stars and a crescent moon provided just enough illumination to find the road underfoot.

"I don't know if we'll find it out here," said Corrag. She was cold.

Beithune smiled. He held out his astrolabe.

"This will help," he said.

"Are you sure this is the right move?"

"Aren't you?" countered Beithune. They were out on the rocky edge of the mountain. The smell of smoke wafted up on a draft of warmer air from the valley. Down below were the fires of shepherds, and across on a nearby summit were the outskirts of a walled city. They could see a man approaching over the rocky terrain. When he reached them he stopped.

"Are you travelers from the islands?" he asked. They couldn't see his face.

"Yes," said Beithune hurriedly.

"And what is it you seek?"

"The tomb where they've buried the prophet," said Corrag.

"Treasure seekers, then," said the man.

"Yes, absolutely," said Corrag.

"Follow me," said the man.

He led them across the mountains. They walked for hours until the dawn came. His pace never wavered during the trek. Corrag felt an immense weariness overtake her and waves of nausea and dizziness as they reached the rock in front of the cave where the body had been laid. The man turned and smiled.

"We're here," he said. Beithune and Corrag slumped to the ground, exhausted.

"We need to move the stone away," said Beithune, finally looking up.

"Ah," said the man. He looked at Corrag. "Do you

agree?"

"*Of course," said Corrag.*

"*Go ahead, then," said the man. He sat down cross-legged on the ground and waited. Beithune and Corrag looked at each other. Corrag walked around the stone, examining it and testing it, pushing. It was massive. Beithune and she strained with all their might against the rock but did not budge it. They stepped away, defeated.*

"*Try one on one side, one on the other," said the man.*

They got on opposite sides of the stone and alternated pushes, but that didn't work either. Corrag stepped away, and Beithune wiped the sweat off his face.

"*Here," said Corrag. She handed Beithune the blue stone and he wiped it on his forehead as she had done. It calmed them down.*

"*You need to help us," said Corrag, turning to the seated man, who was looking past them into the distance.*

"*You had to do it yourselves," he said.*

"*Well, we can't. We need help," said Corrag.*

"*Well," said the man, standing slowly and stretching his arms behind his back.*

He got on one side of the stone and pushed. He was much stronger than the two of them. Single-handedly he rolled the stone a complete circuit and stepped out of the way, revealing the entrance to the tomb. Corrag rushed inside, followed by her cousin.

When their eyes adjusted to the dark, they could see the Teacher seated on a rock ledge inside the tomb, holding his head in his hands. The wrapping on his body had fallen away from his face and upper body, but his hips and legs were still swaddled in cloths. He held his hands, wounded and bruised. He looked at the two of them. His eyes were filled with an eerie green light as he smiled. Darkness overcame his features.

"Flee chilren. The devils are coming," he said.

"What about you? Will they come for you?" asked Corrag.

"About me only the Father knows. He lacks a sense of urgency sometimes."

"You need help," said Corrag.

"Child, I will have help. You have played your small part. Now flee before it is too late."

"Here," said Corrag. She handed him her prize, the blue stone. The teacher took it and held it in gratitude. Then the first reports of the mob approaching reached their ears, high pitched lurid wails, like a pack of wolves with a scent of blood bringing them on. In a second the first pair of eyes stared into the cave entrance.

"You're late," said the Teacher, standing.

Corrag and Beithune ran from the entrance towards the back of the tomb. Corrag searched with her hands for a place to hide. The noise of metal on metal and groans of pain signified the battle had ensued. When she looked back she could see the flashes of light glancing off the shields of angelic warriors.

"Here, Corrag." Beithune reached out for her. She grabbed his hand, and he pulled her up through a chamber, a hole in the rock. They were rising in a well of water, breathless, toward the surface light, the two of them holding hands and then separate but somehow linked in

their thoughts. She could hear Beithune laughing.

She removed the headset. It was morning. The game was over, leaving her the vivid memories, stronger even than real life. And there was the lettering tattooed on the palm of her left hand: מנא, מנא, תקל, ופ רסין.

Beithune slept on the floor at the foot of the bed. The clear, cold light told her it was just beyond dawn, and there would be nobody awake yet at that hour. She got out of bed and crept across the room, put on some clothes and walked carefully down the hall and downstairs. She walked down the hill, through the woods and back up the next rise to where the road crossed a small creek.

Thoughts of Edmundstown filled her head: Ricky and Alana, the high school, her friends Gurgie and Mathew, and of course Ben Calder. She missed her old room and the comforts of her old routines. Now in this new world there was nothing that was easy. She liked learning new things and new ways, but a sudden dread had seized her with the thought that she might never see old friends, never find her way back to the security of a Federation childhood. She sat on a rock and looked at the photos in her emosponder, especially the one of Ben in the selfie he'd last sent her. She hadn't heard from him in months. She searched for news accounts of the Basin fighting. There were detailed articles about several recent skirmishes and the new strategies Federation military spokesmen publicly acknowledged were needed to gain an advantage over the indigenous fighters and their low-tech, shamanist, insurgent tactics. She did a search for

Ben Calder on the lists of dead or wounded from publicly available HumInt Corps press releases. There was nothing. Then she typed in a quick text to his profile: "*Now I'm in a world apart. Except my heart.*" This was from the Vences' song *A World Apart* from their album *Green Gas Works.* She knew he had the song on his playlist, and so her text would be highlighted on his Oomo. She sent it and then sat on the bridge as the water ran. Her pain and loneliness were probably a necessary corollary to growing up, but she wanted some small amount of feeling pampered and cared for. If only Ben would send her something, anything. An acknowledgement of her existence would have been enough. But nothing came back from him.

When she got back to the house it was almost noon. Joan was watching her from the kitchen window. She came out on the back porch as Corrag walked across the freshly cut grass with Teddy jumping at her.

"Where were you?" she asked.

"Just out for a walk."

"We were starting to wonder. Are you okay?"

"I'm fine."

"You missed Jeoff. He's off to Athens this week. Back on Friday. He took the portagon to Norm Laveque. So you and Beithune will have to take the zipcar into Hanover for that lecture you want to attend tonight."

"That's right. I'd forgotten about that."

Beithune had mentioned the lecture on the ethics of food manipulation by a visiting scholar and former Republican general, Stonewall Sikorsky, who had run for

Repho President unsuccessfully on the populist Blue Planet platform in the last election three years ago. But his running mate Eddie Slawdog Wilson had been caught cheating on his wife with a semi-pro basketball cheerleader in the final weeks leading up to the vote. Sikorsky still had lots of fans in New Albion for his stance on food export manipulation, and Beithune had said they would run into some of his old high school friends at the lecture.

"Why don't you have some breakfast before you get started on the lab prep?"

"I think I will."

Joan poured out a bowl of cereal and some raw milk over it and served her at the granite countertop. Wennill was just finishing up her breakfast, with her face buried in her emosponder.

"What are you looking at?" asked Corrag.

Wennill looked up and frowned. "It's just a video from my school about the first days."

"Let's see."

Corrag scooted her stool over and Wennill ran the video for her. The school principal, a portly woman in a standard spandex suit with a permanent open-eyed grin spoke about some of the joys of learning and the pleasures of engagement.

"And remember to have fun with your class selections," she said in closing. Wennill took the emosponder back as Corrag looked up at her with a questioning expression.

"I hate it when they tell you to have fun with your

class selections," said Wennill.

"You're so lucky, though," said Corrag.

"Why? I don't see you signing up for it."

"You get to be with your friends."

"Yeah, and we can wander around all day together."

"They need to turn up the O levels in your school."

"That's not the way we do things in the Repho," said Wennill mockingly. Joan scowled.

"That's enough, Wennill," she said. Wennill made another face and took her bowl to the sink.

Wennill's opening days video served only to make Corrag more aware of the passage of time and the conflicts inside her impeding emotional progress. She was almost ready to ask Joan about possible medical treatment. But she stopped short when she considered that health care for the Hunnewells was an expensive proposition, and also that in the Repho emo manipulations were considered a responsibility and prerogative for family units, not a medical necessity. At home, Alana's medicine cabinet was stocked with subsidized boosters and dampeners. Federation government policy mandated medicated manipulations for elite adults and preschool children in order to maximize augmented connections. Corrag had grown up with Prednizac and Duloxetine supplements in their familiar butterfly shapes with every breakfast, until a sixth grade counselor, Ms. Swedlock, had suggested the value of medicine free middle school years for optimizing prefrontal lobe development. Those had been some especially moody years. Now Corrag would have loved just the slightest hint of the freedom from mental turbulence that Federation medications provided. For her it was simple -- if you had a cut on your finger you put a bandage on it. If you felt suddenly fearful of the dark you took a little blue Alprazol that fizzed in the water with that comforting green sheen.

The lab prep consisted of cleaning out borosilicate dishes of yeast samples, setting out the ceramic containers of powders and syrups and setting up the laser spectograph that Beithune would use to measure proportions. After doing all that, checking in with Alana and Ricky seemed like the thing to do for her. On the emosponder she punched in the call code for intracontinental and the number for the house on Durkiev Drive and got the icon for the Lyons intergalactic in the upper right hand corner that meant they were in and that soon her image would be showing up on the downstairs nanowalls. She could imagine them in the kitchen in the hour before Ricky set off for work, freshly manicured and shaved in his maroon and cream coat, Alana in her silk bathrobe and the housebot scurrying around to get the buckwheat baguettes on the table. Then her parents appeared together in front of the molybdenum table onscreen. The image was a far cry from what she had imagined. Alana was red-eyed and frazzle haired and Ricky was unshaven, wrinkles on his forehead and in a baggy guayabera that made him look like a Republican bot salesman.

"Corrag. You've been a good girl, I hope," said Alana.

"Yes, mother. What happened?"

"It's been very tough on us. Your father has been dissed for recontracting."

"What? How can that be? He has long tenure with UUW and the Council."

"I made a hasty decision to publish, Corrag. The Augment led me to believe I was within the bounds. I think I was hacked," Ricky said, cracking his knuckles in a nervous gesture. Corrag had only ever seen him do that once, when the housebot broke down and started a fire in the kitchen. She must have been in second grade. The firemen had come and it had been all right, but for a few weeks they had been without a bot, and Alana had almost overdosed on Duloxetine.

"What was it?"

"A reform piece, clearly an activist element of my research and within the bounds of a professor's responsibilities, calling for diversification of the educational tracks and subsidized extracurricular options on the Augment open to all students through the first two years of college."

"That would include fine tuning?"

"Yes."

"Awesome."

"Not so awesome, honey. We're going to lose the house," said Alana.

"How do you know?"

"Unpatriotic writings. His name in the Council minutes for the August closed session for delisting."

"How can they do that? That's terrible."

"I know. There's nothing we can do. What the

Federation gives, the Federation takes."

There was a long silence. Corrag thought she would have to come home. There didn't seem to be any other options.

"I guess I'll come home," she said.

"No," said both Ricky and Alana. "No, no," continued Alana. "You're better off there, honey. Stick to your plan. We'll be fine. By the spring we'll be up on our feet again."

"What are you going to do?"

Alana started to cry. Ricky put his arm around her shoulder and pulled her closer.

"Your mother will find work in the greenhouses. She has already put her name down for shifts. We won't be total wards of the state."

"What about you, Dad?"

"I don't know yet. I don't know what I'll do. My augment has been curtailed; it's in holding status, giving me some static. It's going to take me some time to get my bearings. I won't say anything else. We are probably being monitored."

"Probably?" Corrag could not keep the angry tone out of her voice. "Everyone knows there are no privacy controls on Federation networks."

"I guess we just never thought about it that way," said Ricky.

"Be strong, Corrag. And pray," said Alana.

"Pray for what?" asked Corrag.

"That we'll see you again soon," said Alana.

The screen went black as Ricky stepped forward and

put his hand up as if to touch her. Corrag sat back at the desk dumbfounded. What did Alana mean, asking her to pray? They had never even discussed prayer before. She was reverting to her Hunnewell roots in times of stress.

Corrag's childhood home, the symbol of her link to the Democravian promise of a purposeful adult contentment, would be taken from her. It was a catastrophe. She felt oddly calm, not numb, but resolute, thinking of the clarity that the news of her father's ouster from his position gave her. It was as if the veneer of stability and timelessness had been ripped from the picture of her family's life together, and the reality of their tenuous journey through life had been revealed.

Beithune appeared. He was late. Despite looking like a tsunami survivor with his uncombed hair and deep-set eyes, his expression somehow still retained something childlike. He got to work wordlessly. Corrag looked up from her seat at the main desk. She had been going through files on the desktop for Hunnewell Northern Lights accounts going back as far as 2014. The farm had prospered during the secession years, providing food and dried raw milk powder to US military contractor Bechtel. There had been a definite slump in the 2030s, after the farm's raw milk sales had plummeted. That must have been when they sold off the cows, she thought. She had always heard Alana's stories about growing up with the cowherd, but they were no longer a part of the farm's operations. Beithune had on his lab coat now and didn't seem to want to talk. Hours went by in the lab and Corrag felt like a bot, concentrating on following the instructions

Beithune passed to her without comment. At some point she couldn't contain herself.

"What's wrong with you?" she blurted out, passing him a syringe loaded with glutamate.

"What do you mean?"

"You haven't talked to me all day. Why are you ignoring me?"

"I'm sorry."

Beithune put the syringe down and turned to her.

"I have to tell you, Corrag. I'm leaving. I didn't want to tell you. But I can't keep it a secret from you."

"But you can't do that. It's not time for you to go."

"I'm not talking about school. I'm talking about the city. I'm going for the inside."

Corrag looked at him closely.

"Do you have plans, connections, any ideas? You don't just walk inside, you know."

"Nothing like that. It's just right. After last night I can feel it. I think I can take it on. Climb to the top. That was the most vivid virtualscape ever, Corrag. I touched a chord of destiny that shifted the game forever. I mean we did it together, of course. But it convinced me that now's the time to scale the inside barrier. When the game merges with the deepest levels of your unconscious, you're ready to shape your destiny."

"Those are just stories, Beithune. Nobody does that in real life."

"Last night was strong enough to do it. Didn't you feel it?"

"More than felt it."

She turned her hand to show him her palm tattoo, fading but still legible.

"Wow," said Beithune. "I'd ask you to come with me, but I know you have to stay here and finish out the emissary year gig."

"No, I don't."

Beithune studied her face.

"Then come. We'll take it on together. A shot at fame and glory. How about it, cuz?"

Corrag considered for a brief second. A flood of emotions overtook her, but the strongest was a desire for freedom. She wanted to make a run with Beithune. It was crazy, but the sheer improbability of his ambition, to ascend to the top of the Sandelsky gaming world with its Byzantine connections to the Repho power structure, was dizzying in its allure.

"I'm in."

She couldn't believe the words she had just uttered. They finished up the job and cleaned up the work site together. Wennill opened the door and asked if they were hungry. There were sandwiches on the island. They ate, seated on the stools still in lab coats while Joan and Wennill hovered nearby. Wennill was brushing Teddy, and the bot was loading the dishwasher behind her. Joan made coffee. Beithune and Corrag smiled together at her conversation with an air of complicit conspirators. Later in the afternoon they packed bags and took them out to the zipcar separately through the garden and around the side of the house. The bot followed Corrag, but she turned to order it back to the house.

"I know what you are doing," said the bot. "You are running away. Beithune and you."

"No we're not. We're just going on a camping trip."

"You can't fool me. My parallel processor tells me you are running away."

"Listen to me. You can't possibly know because we don't even know what we're going to do. You have to stay silent. Otherwise you will be spreading panic. You don't want to do that, do you?"

"I will miss you."

Corrag looked at the bot closely. Her angled cube of a head gave her an air of humility and sadness. Was it possible for a bot to really feel human love? She laid her hand on the bot's grasping appendage.

"I'll miss you, too."

Later in the early evening, as the last of the leaves were falling off the trees in a strong wind, she and Beithune got in the zipcar's back seat, their bags in the front pushed down so that no-one could see them. As they pulled out the drive, Wennill and Teddy moved out of the way. Wennill stopped and waved and Corrag waved back. Beithune kept his eyes on his emosponder. He was still just a child, Corrag thought again. A pang of remorse hit her for not having said goodbye to the Hunnewells. She vowed to herself someday to return. She looked out the back window. Wennill was walking back to the house, and Teddy was running along the ditch chasing a squirrel. In the distance, in a window, she imagined she could see the bot staring after them, but that was probably an illusion caused by an overactive imagination.

The Green River bus station was an architectural and cultural relic of the pre-secessionist era. The riders waiting in the plastic seats of the terminal seemed timeless in their decrepitude, as if they hadn't moved since the waves of cheap heroin addictions had swept the old New England at the beginning of the millennium. These waiting passengers hobbled by old age and failing health were the children of the great old liberal vision that had failed to hold the United States together, victims of poor choices made by and for them, with lives and bodies that had been scarred by hardships. A middle-aged woman in a print cotton tee shirt with the name of some ancient rock group and faded pajama jeans on her balloon-like legs climbed the steps of the bus, taking them one at a time. Beithune and Corrag made their way all the way to the back. The lights went off. Outside it was also getting dark. Corrag felt a curious sense of relief, as if riding along in this faceless herd of humanity on the dark bus was a protection against fears both real and imagined.

Four -- A New Reality

The winter in the Williamsburg walkup was an endless wash of water and roar. The ceiling leaked, and the drip of water was only ever silen~~...~~ ~, the nightly fights in the apartments above and around them in the former tenement housing. Outside there was little respite from lapping seawater on the sidewalks and the constant barrage of acidic, gritty precipitation. The sooty skies tinged Corrag's days, and her nights were filled with the smells of sewage and rotting meat and the gnawing pain of hunger in her belly.

Beithune had been rejected for three job openings. The last had been with Sandelsky as a design intern. The personnel director had communicated with him at the end of the last round in a curt post interview session on his emosponder and told him he wasn't sufficiently prepared in the coding standards of Motran 397, the language of choice for Sandelsky designers, but Beithune had laughed ruefully in her face and terminated the connection. When telling Corrag the story later that night, he showed her some of the quantum applications using Motran he'd rigged up with his gaming cube, but she already knew what he was going to say. Their ability to communicate without using words had continued to expand in the days and weeks following their *Absolution* win. It didn't happen in any predictable or orderly fashion, but sometimes she just knew what he was going to say and would let the silence lie between them. Corrag felt his despondency weighing on both of them, but the city was an unfolding panoply of sensory experiences sharpened by the razor thin margin of survival they were skating on.

Corrag's job as a welcomer at The Meadowbrook Spa and Gun Club paid the rent with a little left over for food. Despite their shortage of bitcoin, they were heading out for a night on the town, to a party with some people Beithune had met at the Butterfly, a houseboat tied up to the Unisphere at the Flushing Meadows piers. The canal porter was filled with nightlifers looking for action, headed for the casinos and the smokehouses of midtown. Corrag and Beithune got off at Corona and walked out along the rickety old jetty. Beithune's big leather boots made a clopping noise in the puddles, while Corrag slumped along behind him wrapped in her keffiyeh. There were hollers, as a boat of pleasure seekers steamed slowly out towards the harbor lights. At the ramp up to the houseboat, two young men in long hair and bellbottoms with chains hanging off their waists slouched against the hull. The cabin rocked gently, and the swaying lights cast the long shadows of partygoers out on the dark, rippled water. A bearded man held court on the deck, proclaiming loudly to anyone who would listen with the news of his own importance. Three young men in variations of flannel shirts smoked from a bowl of khat and snickered, spitting out over the gunwales. One of them, tall, thin-lipped, fox-eyed, with curly hair spilling out from under his cap, separated himself from the group and approached Corrag. Beithune was right behind her, and Corrag could hear him whispering a warning in her ear.

"A nobody. Don't pay him any attention."

"What do you call when the whale jumps the chump and you're in the way of the paywall?" he asked.

"What?" said Corrag. She had no idea what he'd just asked her. The whale was slang for the Repho and its increasingly autocratic policing, she figured. But all the other references were beyond her understanding. His breath stunk of the sweet smoke, and she wanted to get away, but he was blocking her access to the rope ladder leading to the wheelhouse, where a group of people were hanging out, men and women drinking from long-stemmed glasses, surrounding the man with a beard whose laughter rang out in the night with a large-bellied self-assurance.

She turned around. Beithune was nowhere to be seen. She wondered if she'd imagined his voice whispering to her.

"Not cool," said the young man, barely more than a boy, in the flannel shirt, as he moved away to the bellowing snickers of his companions.

Corrag climbed the rope ladder to the wheelhouse and walked out to the edge of the deck, skirting the crowd. The lights of the city glowed out beyond the harbor. It was a pulsating organism with a life of its own. If only it wasn't so hard to find out the secret of its vitality, she thought. She and Beithune had imagined they could tap into its core, but there was something resistant and slippery about it, an oiliness that prevented headlong inquiry. A woman with black hair pulled back in a bun on the side of her head asked her something.

"I don't know," she heard herself answering, as if from a distance.

The woman's mouth moved, but no sound seemed to be coming out. Instead she heard a tinkling sound like glass breaking. Corrag shook her head and moved away, but the woman followed a few steps behind. She held out her glass.

"Here. Have a sip. You look like you're going to faint."

"I'm sorry."

"No, don't be sorry. Go ahead."

The babble of voices onboard came and went, like waves breaking inside her mind. The drink the woman gave her was good.

"What is it?"

"Just sarsaparilla and moonshine. Home brew. It'll clear your head, though. My name is Monica."

"Corrag."

"Corrag. Who'd you come with?"

"Beithune. My cousin."

"I haven't met him."

Monica's hand shook a little when she took back the empty glass. Corrag estimated she was about thirty, with a thin, nervous face lined from mental effort. Corrag was grateful for her kindness.

"I don't know what happened. My hearing is doing strange things. I think I need an intervention."

"You need some rest and some food, child. What have you eaten today?"

"Not much. Some dried apple."

"Where are you from?"

"Democravia."

"I thought so. We don't talk about interventions. Unless you're a one percenter."

Monica's voice was soft with sadness to it and a mountain lilt that gave her an air of old wisdom.

"What do people do? The ones who aren't top percenters."

"Survive. In my family there were ten of us. Only three alive today. Of course two of my brothers were drafted for the Repho overseas and died."

"Democravia takes care of her children. And our forces are largely volunteer."

"Yes. You're lucky."

Corrag wondered if she was lucky. Did she owe Democravia or was she free? The answer was as unclear as the water of the harbor. There was pride still in her heart for the land of her childhood, but her anger at its recent treatment of her parents was weighing heavily in the balance. Also, she felt herself picking up a new sort of distrust of authority from the air of New York, whose residents imbibed a piratical code of self-preservation that owed no allegiance to any order higher than the rule of appetite.

Monica was telling her more about her life. Her husband was the bearded man in the center of the crowd of people at the wheelhouse. Mike Shannon was a Nenkaja survivor, a former prisoner, and now, in the last few years, a community organizer. Monica saw herself as operating behind the scenes to complement her husband's work.

"Women can do things men can't. We can work in our own way to make a stand in this system. Yes, we are second-class citizens in many ways. But that can work in our favor. We're not tracked as heavily." Corrag was silent, absorbing her words. The fact that women did not enjoy equal rights in the Repho, given the influence of fundamentalists, was not news, but it still upset her.

"Mike has many enemies, and the Gheko administration would love to see him locked up again," Monica said.

"'So you and Mike are activists? Disaligners?" asked Corrag.

"We're working for deep changes. What do you and Beithune see as your ambition?"

"Ambition?"

"Yes, everyone has an ambition. Are you earning for an augment?

"No. I don't want one."

"Good for you. Hold out as long as you can. There are few free men and women in the Repho. But some kids like you, fighting for a way to get free of the whale."

"What's the whale?"

"The whale is the system of things. Many people in the belly of the whale are dreaming, sucked up by their augments. The free men and women are awake. You need to stay awake."

"Maybe that's my ambition."

"That's great. Will you promise to stay in touch with

me?"

"Of course."

Monica brought her a glass. Corrag enjoyed holding the long stem with different combinations of fingers, switching from hand to hand sophisticatedly. The act of drinking and keeping her eyes fixed on some spot in the room where the action was afoot was also a new sort of excitement. She wandered through the party boat. Some people shot her looks that told her it was okay to be alone without being lonely. These were the people who had abandoned the collective dream of the Republic.

She found Beithune at last in the hold in some sort of conspiratorial grouping. The boys in the flannel shirts were there, but they seemed engaged in an exchange of important information and otherwise harmless.

Beithune saw her. She was staggering, a little bit drunk from the moonshine.

"We can go now," said Beithune. But had he really said it or had she just heard him think it? Maybe it was a trick he was pulling on her, some sort of ventriloquist's practical joke. She sometimes thought he would be better off finishing up at college and staying with the family business. She thought she should tell him, but in a while, not right away. She really loved Beithune. He was the brother she'd never had. Beithune grabbed her by the shoulder.

"Why are you crying?" he asked.

"I didn't know I was," said Corrag.

"Hold it, bro." It was the curly haired boy speaking, the one with the foxy eyes.

"You didn't answer my question," he said.

"What was it again? Oh, yes, the whale. What would I do with the whale? I think I would cut it up into little pieces and melt the blubber down to make oil."

"Not a bad suggestion. Here's my follow-up question."

"I don't do follow-ups with people I don't know," said Corrag.

"Well, that's a shame."

Beithune got them out of the hold somehow. He really was good. She didn't recall later how they'd climbed the ladder to get away from the flannel shirts. To save coin they walked instead of catching a water taxi. The canals were splashing over the sidewalks at high tide, smelling of dead Repho children and their spoiled dreams. The streetlights were still on; they never went off, powered by the smoldering Long Island nuclear turbines. The bridges groaned under the weight of the infinite tide of oceans and peoples. Black men with scarred faces and eyes that wouldn't look and Chinese bands of thieves sold khat and oomo and got away from the police in little boats under the bridges with outboard, old school motors that revved away in the darkness. Lovers stole last kisses from each other at the corners outside the chrome-barred storefronts with the nanowalls still blaring yesterday's headlines.

Later in the apartment with the light fixture lodged in the crack of the wall, giving the kitchen the air of a medieval cloister, Beithune made tea while Corrag slumped in the scuffed recliner beside the door. They could hear sirens and explosions of gunfights on the Atlantic Avenue canal. There were turf wars going on in the city between criminal gangs vying for territory. The police occasionally chose sides, but usually maintained a neutral stance, partly because they were outgunned and outclassed, but also because the city's rulers benefitted from much of the criminal activity. Beithune handed Corrag a mug of steaming tea.

"Here you go," he mumbled.

"Thanks."

"That Lars. He's a dubious character. Sorry you had to deal with him."

"Not a problem. Just a typical scene. Not as cool as he would like to think."

"He's had seven barrier challenges."

"I don't care, Beithune."

"I know, but he's good. He's going to get us in."

"Us? In? What are you talking about?"

"It's a Corona Heights posse. He wants me. And you."

"And me. Right."

"I'm serious. He specifically invited you. You need to be a part of this."

"Why?"

"Why? You need to ask why? This is the opportunity we've both been waiting for, Corrrag. And you especially should be flattered. Not many Repho girls get invited to join a posse."

"He's a creep. He makes me sick."

"Oh, get over it. He's plugged into things."

"And that's a good thing?"

"Yeah. Most definitely is. How can you get anywhere if you're not plugged in."

"He doesn't seem very awake to me, Beithune."

"He's awake. Don't worry about that. Did I mention seven barrier challenges?"

"You did."

Corrag woke late. The alarm on her emosponder had been buzzing for several minutes. She worked the early morning cleaning duty and needed to be up by 5:30 in the morning to get to work on time. The apartment was dark and the canal outside was just beginning to come alive with the sound of the garbage barges making their way slowly along, picking up the stinking refuse of the night's excesses. She dressed in a denim skirt and a charcoal black pea coat and half stumbled outside with her satchel hung on her back. She looked like a young woman entrenched in the business of earning her way in the world, but she felt evanescent, weightless and lonely, avoiding eye contact with everyone on the canal porter for the three eastbound stops. The sky was grey, and seagulls scudded across it looking for leftovers on the sidewalks and on rooftops. They were survivors like her. The affinity did not make her feel better about herself, but she did look kindly on the seagulls. They had no choice but to live off what they could find. Corrag had once had options, but for the first time felt the limits of her immediate future startling in their granularity. Still, it was just a matter of adjusting her sights, she thought. To focus on the future was an act of faith, and faith was a good thing, perhaps the only thing that was necessary to live.

At The Meadowbrook, after she was done with the locker rooms and had set the bots up on some mopping on the second and third floors, she took a break in the employee coffee room. She enjoyed mastering the mindless routine of the cleaning, and then the rest of the day was about staying on her feet and responding to the needs of the two women who really ran the place, Lana and Greta. Chuckie the owner usually came in two or three times a week maximum just to make sure things were ticking over satisfactorily and swim a few laps in the pool. He was an interesting man who'd grown up in Democravia like her and gotten east through sports. After a collegiate football exchange one fall he'd missed the tubid back with his University of Phoenix teammates and worked his way up through the health club circuits with his good looks and sun-baked manners.

Lana caught her eye and called her over to the entrance where a table was piled high with boxed food and sweaters left behind and never claimed. The boxed food was the legacy of a charity drive begun at Christmas. Chuckie had told the front desk girls to go ahead and take the food home, but nobody had dared. The Meadowbrook clientele was composed predominantly of rich matrons, the daughters of tech barons that had settled in the enclave and never left home, stranded in their natural upward mobility as colleges across the United States, unable to prevent attacks against students and research facilities by the ecowarriors of the secession movement, closed their doors after the first few campus nuclear waste fire bombings. It was only recently, in the last decade, that Repho educational establishments had reopened for business under scaled back conditions.

"Take some, Corrag. Look at these peaches. Delicious," said Lana, holding up a container to the gamma ray scanner on the front desk to check for nuclear materials. Even years later, businesses in the Repho scanned clients and their possessions for contamination.

Corrag thought about it. She didn't like being labeled as someone in need of charity, but then again it had been a long time since she and Beithune had enjoyed anything as nice as a treat of canned peaches. She tucked the container into her bag and smiled at Lana. There were very few clients in that day. A couple of women, local teachers, were lined up outside the office of Greta, the Swedish masseuse, holding their discount cards from their health exchanges in their hands and engaged in a breezy conversation about nothing much. Corrag listened as she wiped the glass of the front doors with anti bacterial swabs.

"Did you say Jamie's transfer was postponed?" said one woman

"It was. Her husband, you know Bob? His augment was delayed. Heavy drinking involved."

"I didn't think that mattered anymore with Gheko."

"Well, she says there's politics when it comes to the Androids. Sandelsky not so much. But Bob? He wasn't on the swim team and ever since then, well, it's been frankly like shit for him. Jamie's thinking of jumping ship."

"It doesn't pay to jump ship. I always told her that.

Stick to Apple Nuova. It's an Android But they're in the whale."

"Yes, but who knew Bob was a heavy drinker."

"Well he likes an occasional Poo Poo at the Jin Jin."

"Well. Who doesn't?"

"Yes. My sentiments exactly."

"Did you hear? They say Gheko has chosen an ally. Speaking of ships."

"He has? What's he intend to do next? Annex Democravia?"

"That's no joke. It's Chagnon."

The insider talk about Repho politics gave Corrag a jolt. The Repho augment was held out as a hope against death itself, with recent official pronouncements about cryonic upgrades available to the most select customers. These would allow upload into top line bots built for achieving some kind of unspecified state akin to immortality. The lure of that most exclusive of neighborhoods was a boon to the companies at the forefront of the technology, Sandelsky among them. There had been rumors in several of the more lurid social media outlets that Samael Chagnon himself had already had himself done and that his doppelganger was among them, walking the streets and riding the canal porters unannounced.

The panel slid open silently to Greta's office, lined with foam pads. One could hear Tibetan monks chanting over the plaintive sounds of the Northern right whale on its annual migration through the Gulf of Maine.

"I'll see you later, honey. Make an appointment with

the desk."

Greta's voice was languid and neutral as she let her customer out into the foyer. The woman's face was puffy as if she'd been crying. Her hair was hidden under a scarf, an old Gotzeitgeist paisley print scarf that Corrag recognized. Alana had once worn a similar one. The crying woman's face and the memory of her mother startled Corrag into a moment of motionless reverie, and as the woman slipped out into the rush of midday city traffic, she could hear Greta calling her in less than mellifluous tones.

"What is the time that you can waste like this in such deep pensive thoughts?"

"I'm sorry," Corrag apologized. "It's just, I was thinking of somebody."

"We all have these memories. What is that now? Memories are like flowers. They are worthless and stink after you've had them. So stop thinking so much."

"How can I stop thinking?"

Greta looked at her with a hard, hostile stare. Corrag wondered how she could be any success as a healer. She was a woman who had seen the worst of the European fighting with the United People's Army of National Sovereignty, UPANS, which eventually morphed into the Carlist Reserve Administration, CRA, against the Eurasian monolith that was the Sino-Rus Alliance. The CRA still governed most of Northern Europe including the Iberian Peninsula and parts of the former Yugoslavia and all the way east to Moldova.

But now she, Greta, had lost most of her former

idealism. She had undergone augmentation the previous summer, according to Lana. And the initial flush of health had given way to a wary and edgy sentimentality, like a plant that fleshed out its fruit in a rush of summer growth. Greta smoked and drank in secret and sometimes on the job. Lana had suggested that Chuckie knew about her obviously dubious lifestyle, but looked the other way in exchange for sexual favors.

"Find yourself a man. He'll take care of that problem."

"I have no idea what problem you're referring to," said Corrag. Greta gave another hard look and closed the door back on the rest of the world.

Corrag's days usually went by in a rush. After cleaning the pool and distributing the clean towels to their places of disbursement outside the stations, she busied herself swabbing surfaces with antibacterials and then took a shift at the desk as the after school mothers came by for the exercise club. They danced an aerobic routine in the second floor gym under the tutelage of two Brazilian capoeira artists, a transgendered couple who were indistinguishable from each other. Corrag wanted to catch them before they left. She wanted to ask them about the fighting in the Basin against the tribes. She wanted to know how the locals perceived it, not how it was presented to the people of Democravia. In the Repho, nobody even knew there was a war between the Democravian Federation and its southern allies against the rainforest tribes. There was such ignorance of their fellow North Americans' external affairs. On the other hand, Corrag admitted to herself that she had had no idea until recently of the Repho's continued involvement in unsavory Middle Eastern adventures and lingering European covert operations, such as the coup against the democratically elected government of Scotland, or the decade long war with the Sino-Rus Alliance that was just now ending. She learned the hidden history of the Repho through Beithune and his friends from the Butterfly Club.

On this day there was a slushy rain falling from the sky. Many of the mothers tracked mud across the floor. Corrag thought it would give her a chance to do something slightly more active, to get the bot over there and use the disinfectant on the tiles. The mothers and several curly headed little children trooped through the turnstiles and signed off with eye scans administered by the headset. The joke was it was not functioning and Chuckie had insisted that they keep up appearances by jacking off the cover and replacing the infrared bulb with an LED. The LED's hazy vibration was enough to set anyone's teeth on edge, but most of the mothers, the second generation of Meadowbrookian refugees from the Repho's oligarchical circus, hardly passed it a glance.

Corrag shared front desk duties for the remaining hours of her workday with Lana, a three-year veteran of the health club. Lana chatted with clients passing through the turnstile, especially with the men who came to practice in the challenge room. Many of them worked, or aspired to work in the futures sector, buying and selling shares, the heart of the Repho's service economy. Lana called them come-uppers. They usually started appearing soon before it was time for Corrag to take off for home. She didn't mind missing out on these interactions, which meant a great deal to Lana, the chance to pass a few words and get noticed by some of the futures boys. Corrag thought many of them were attractive physically, with sculpted bodies formed by nutritional supplements and plenty of time in the challenge room, but found their egos a serious turn-off. She enjoyed her work, but was always happy at 3:30 when it was time to leave. She was glad to get away from The Meadowbrook and its overwhelming air of dissatisfaction.

The sidewalk was full of real people of all ages and stripes on their way home, arms full of shopping bags. Little children ran along behind a bot leading them to the canal porter stop. The sky was grey and the water of the canal reflected back a dull sheen of contaminants and antibacterials run amok. The smell of the canals still struck hard. It was only in the heart of the winter months that the water ceased to give off a deathly sulphurous odor, as the biological reagents sunk into the harbor sediments. Soon the cold would clear the air. It was late November and the chill made Corrag rub her arms under the black pea coat.

She walked around the block to the bitcoin booth and replenished her card. Next door to the booth was a small Spanish grocery store that carried bread and cheese and coffee. Corrag also splurged on a whole chicken and some Italian coriander sauce and a bottle of maple wine for Beithune. He needed a lift of the spirits. It wasn't great, but it would have to do. She hoped he'd find some position soon, although his dream about a place inside Sandelsky was rapidly fading. As she stood at the checkout waiting for the bot to scan her purchases, she saw the two Brazilians from The Meadowbrook push through the glass door. Corrag smiled at the woman as they walked by her in the checkout and up the drinks aisle. She paid for her purchases with the card and walked out. Someday she would introduce herself to them, she thought. It would be fun to take classes. She had always loved the music and had several classic Brazilian pieces on her emosponder. Outside it had gotten colder. With all her educational possibilities and here she was scurrying along the sidewalk to catch the canal porter in the midst of the subsistence crowds, not the kind of people Alana would approve of. Ricky was more understanding of her dreams, her desires to experience the fullest kind of life. But Alana dreaded a fall from the comforts of the Axion class. Ironically, now she was working in the Rosaria greenhouses while Ricky reconfigured for a new career. She would see her parents soon enough. A couple of months more and then Beithune would come to his senses and head home and she would catch the tubid back to Democravia.

She felt dizzy. These spells that came over her were caused by lack of sleep, she was sure. She just had to sit. There was a step outside the door to a townhouse. The Jackson Heights Canal porter stop was straight ahead. A crowd was forming at the gates as the porter pulled into the jetty. She sat on the step and placed the bag of food next to her. She would catch the next boat. It wasn't a big deal. As she was sitting there a couple approached, walking up from the crowds along the jetty. The man jangled his apartment keys while the woman chatted and then went silent when she realized Corrag was not getting up to get out of their way.

"Excuse me," said the woman.

"I'm sorry," said Corrag, trying to stand. She went for the grocery bag and slipped, falling and spilling the bag's contents over the sidewalk. The frozen chicken in the nanofoil bounced and rolled into the path of a bot pulling a cart full of water bottles.

"Oh, my God," said the woman.

The man leaned down and stared into Corrag's face.

"Are you all right?"

Corrag did not answer. In her mind she was searching for the right words. The words that could explain her predicament, explain why Ben was fighting with HumInt in the Basin and why she was unable to accept fine tuning like the other children, why her father was no longer the man she remembered and why Beithune's dreams were destined to end up failing, and mostly why she did not feel like herself, as if Corrag were a stranger, an imposter, somebody else's sham version of the girl she could never be. And who was that girl? Corrag suddenly remembered. The real thing, the Democravian ideal, her teacher's idealized version of sacrificial and charismatic female leadership, her parents' vision of an accomplished, mature, responsible and serviceable womanhood. But the words did not come. There was a gap between the images in her mind and their utterance in a language anyone could ever understand. And now there was not even dinner, as the frozen chicken in the nanofoil disappeared under the wheels of the water cart.

"She's not okay," said the man.

"Call the cops," said the woman.

"Really? You think the cops?"

"Of course. Why take the chance? She could be a disruptive."

"Oh, come on. Look at her. She's not a disruptive."

Disruptives were the sort of people that would break into your house and steal the last few cans of food off your shelves to sell for a quick brain fix. Corrag was offended to be associated with that class of people. She stood awkwardly. The man put his hand on her elbow, and she shook it away.

"Look. Let's bring her inside. Who knows? She probably has people looking for her. She's a runaway, Yula."

"Jesus. You and your intuitions for the blessed motley."

"Oh come on. Please come in. We'll get you something to take the place of this, this ... We have vindaloo. Yes, and some pastries. Isn't that correct, Yula?"

"Technically, it is." The woman made a gesture with her hand, pointing vaguely to the scattered groceries. Corrag tried to pick up the bag, but the maplewine bottle had broken and she cut herself on the shard sticking out of the side.

"Crap," said the man. "Look at this, Yula. Look at this."

Corrag thought he might cry. She sucked at the hand to get the bleeding to stop.

"I'm okay," she said, coming to her senses with the sight and taste of her own blood.

"No, no. Please." Yula had the door open and was waving her inside with her fan-like, hypnotic, well-manicured fingers. Beithune would never get the maplewine. It was the thought of this, the failed gesture of charity, that drove her inside, not the opportunity afforded by the open door or the couple who lived beyond it.

The apartment was cluttered with furnishings. Esoteric sculptures of mythological Hindu gods and elephants abounded on dark wooden, well-oiled side tables, and there was a bar with vintage Cleo glasses. Dark green curtains were drawn shut. When her eyes adjusted to the dim track lights, Corrag could see a grey cat reclined along the edge of a leather sofa with a painting of a nude woman on the wall above it. Yula drew her to the kitchen with a hand on her waist and ran the water from the sink over her cut hand. The water was tepid, and there was a faint, sickly smell of vinegar coming from the sink that for Corrag was the smell of New York. They all had it in their hair and on their clothes. Even the smell of the canal water could not overpower it -- the collective sickly sweet smell of the New York kitchen sink.

"The key is to keep it elevated. The power of the healing body will take over immediately."

Yula was talking to her, she realized. She had a freckled face and green eyes under a black bang that swept down on one side of her face. She looked away as Corrag took her hand out of the water and wiped it on the back of a towel draped on a chair. The man came into the kitchen.

"And how are you now? Feeling better?"

"I'm fine."

"We have not met yet. Allow me the introductions. My name is Antonio. And this is Yula."

"Corrag."

"Corrag. Will you eat with us?"

"Yes. That would be fine."

"Splendid."

Antonio spread a tablecloth out on the table that came down out of the wall in the living room. There were extra folding chairs in a closet. The silverware came out of the bottom drawer under the sink. Corrag sat down on a chair and held her hand tight to stop the bleeding.

"We don't have a bot. It's so liberating. Don't have to worry about hurting their feelings, including them in any plans we make for the weekends. It's frankly great," said Antonio.

"My parents keep sending their bot for resegmenting. I tell them just to upgrade. It' s difficult. They get attached, the poor things. Soon they'll pass us in capabilities, but they'll keep on out of sentimental reasons. Don't you agree?" asked Yula.

"Yeah. We have a bot at home."

"And that is where?"

"Edmundstown."

"Democravia. Of course, I should have guessed. And

you're making your way in the big city. Did you run away? Kidnapped by the Ozark mountain gang?"

"No, nothing like that. I am an emissary. My cousin and I came down from New Albion. He wants to crack the Sandelsky. Get inside. It's his dream."

"Is he augmented?" asked Antonio, pausing from his chores, which kept him going back and forth from the kitchen to the dining room.

"No. And neither am I."

"Well, it's the only way inside, but it's not worth it. Much better off cracking a niche for yourself. Look at Yula and I, together for fifteen years now. It's not a bad life. Most people are crazy for the Augment. They've been duped," said Antonio.

"Immortality, the false lure of forever. Better than sex." Yula interrupted them. She was carrying a steaming pot of curried stew. "Although the alternative, confronting the universe on one's own terms is sometimes too daunting for words. I wake up some mornings and I just want to say no. I'm not ready. Who is? If you ever feel like you're ready for this life, Corrag, watch out. It truly means you're ready to take off for the next installment. Here it is. The matrix of mother love. This is what you really need. Hope you like it, Corrag. Charming conversationally after all, isn't she, Antonio?"

"Yes and a real striving kind of story. You should hear her tell it."

"Is that right?"

Yula settled herself in at the head of the table and served them the curry. There was also a kind of soy and miso extract as a beverage. Yula worked for a publisher of digital texts, fiction and esoteric works of metaphysical content. She worked on the marketing side, making presentations to reading clubs in retirement communities and in the few libraries that were still funded in some of the wealthier suburban aggregations such as the Charlotesville/Roanoke and Tampa/St. Pete areas. But she was interested, she said, in stories that could help the power of words make a comeback against the deadening bureaucratic spirit of the age. She had a few of her own, collected in a thumb drive. She wanted to show Corrag later, bring them up on the small nanowall that came with the apartment. Antonio was working on an expansion rig. Antonio and Yula were also committed to living augment free, or at least as free as possible, given the fact that the Repho was increasingly becoming a police state and infringing more and more on civil liberties. Which is why they only drank bottled water straight down from springs in the Adirondacks.

The talk of water reminded Corrag of Abel Marin and the water of the Ysidro canyons he'd given her and Ben to drink. That water had been clarifying of so many things.

"I knew someone once who only drank spring water. You would have liked him."

"Really? Who was he?"

"He was from Sonora. A Yaqui Indian named Abel."

"So many stories, Corrag. We must introduce her around at the next party," said Yula.

"Oh, gosh. Yula and her parties. I'm so lucky I get

invited."

"Having no social skills doesn't seem to hinder you."

"Only because I'm with you, usually, Yula dearest."

"Antonio exaggerates. It's why I've never encouraged his literary ambitions."

"Oh, please. One person in the house with that sort of deficit is enough."

Corrag liked the two of them. She found herself telling them about Alana and Ricky and her fears of having lost her childhood home. They were compassionate but not moved to a frenzy of concern, having seen and heard much worse. They warned her that life in the Repho was not a haven for seekers and non-conformists. It was easier than Democravia to live according to your own lights, but also easier to fall victim to the depredations of various types of connivers.

"It's getting late," said Corrag, looking at her emosponder. There was a message from Beithune marked with an urgent emoticon. She would listen later, once she got out of the apartment.

"I'll walk you to the canal stop," said Antonio, looking at Yula.

"You don't have to."

"Of course, Corrag," said Yula. "But first give me your contact. I want you to come with us to meet the writers."

"I'd love that," said Corrag.

Antonio zipped his spandex coat up to the chin line. The night was frosty cold. Celebratory shouts and the pounding rhythms of jihad rap came from passing boats on the canal. Overhead a drone silently fed the police with live feed, giving away its position by the blinking of the red lights on the rotor shaft.

"It's cold out," said Antonio.

"Yes, it is. It feels like the season has changed."

"Yes, every season is a new reality, Corrag," said Antonio.

They walked quickly ahead, ignoring the jostling crowds along the slippery walkway. Corrag was still amazed at the ability of native New Yorkers' to converse and manage the sidewalks at the same time. She was able to stay abreast of Antonio, though. He seemed to want to speak his mind. Steps away from the canal porter turnstile, he stopped and faced her. His eyes shone, even in the dark of the night under the dim streetlamps.

"Well, here we are."

"Yes."

"A pleasure to meet you, Corrag. I hope you weren't offended by us and our silly talk."

"Oh, not at all."

'New York is a funny place. You have to look out for your own interests. Be selfish, Corrag. It's the key to your survival. Augment or not."

"But you and Yula take care of each other."

"We've reached a temporary understanding of mutual interest. Everything changes, though."

Antonio's eyes were piercing and bright. He seemed to devour her body with his eyes.

"Well, I've got to catch the boat now."

"I'll see you again soon."

"Yes, of course," said Corrag.

On the boat there were two groups, partiers from the outer precincts riding the canals with their emosponders blasting music and commuters coming quietly home from Manhattan jobs and perhaps a bit of social time in the bars and smokehouses. The porter tenders did their best to keep the two groups in line, but occasionally tensions flared. Corrag hoped this would not be one of those times. She wanted to be with her thoughts about the party on the Butterfly and meeting Monica, her illuminating dinner with Yula and Antonio, especially the impression left on her by Antonio, and then Beithune and his dreams. But how to hold it in her mind? She could understand why people would prefer the Augment with its clean lines and easy access to a tried and true knowledge base. But still, she would insist on constructing her meaning from a life that was her own, no matter how scattered it could seem, how empty of a thread through it all.

The music from the emosponders was loud, vaguely threatening. She could also hear Beithune, calling from a distance, almost unrecognizable. She listened closely because she wanted to believe that the two of them were communicating. He seemed to be complaining about a pain in his shoulder. She would ask him about that when she got home. She listened to his message on the emosponder.

"Corrag, where are you?"

That was it, just a question. She would answer soon enough in person.

In the apartment, Beithune was fiddling with the

wires on his vertglove, sitting in his coat and ragged jeans at the kitchen table. The apartment was in shambles, their clothes strewn over the floor and on the bed, boxes of rotting food lying out on the floor. The dim tracking fixture in the kitchen was the only light on in the dingy apartment. Beithune was shivering, his face pale and drawn.

"Why don't you turn the heat on?" asked Corrag. "Is your shoulder all right?"

"I don't need it, Corrag, My shoulder's fine. We're already two months behind on the bill. I need your help, though."

"With what?" asked Corrag, hanging her coat up in the closet, dreading the thought of cleaning up before getting into bed. She just wanted to sleep.

"There's a new trial from Sandelsky. They've turned ugly. Lars has got his hands on some bootleg in pills. Corrag, I don't think ... I'm ... I'm not good enough on my own. I want to go back in with you."

"Why, Beithune? I mean there's so much that we need to do in the real world."

"Like what?"

"Like a job, like meeting new people," said Corrag, no longer able to hold herself back. She hoped Beithune would not crack.

"There's no hope if you don't see how important this is."

"How is it more important than taking care of ourselves? This city will eat us up, cousin. Look at you. You need to eat. You can't go on dreaming about conquering the inside."

"No. It's not just about inside anymore, Corrag. The alliance we all feared is taking over the city. Monica and Mike are in jail. Haven't you heard? There's a crackdown."

"Well, what's behind it?"

"Chagnon. He has a background in neural architecture from his days at Carnegie Mellon. It makes perfect sense and fits his sweeping ambitions. I need to go back in and see it. I think I can crack this new challenge before it's street-proofed. There will be flaws that will tell me what their aims are."

"Who?"

"Chagnon. Gheko too."

"That's crazy."

"Do you see now? This is important. We can stop them or at least learn about their aims and methods. We can clean up and make some dinner later. Come in with me now."

"Monica and Mike are in jail?"

"Or dead. Nobody knows and there's no way to get any information out of the administratives or the police. Not even the human rights desk of the Consumer Protection Board. Lars and the boys have gone underground. It's very bad out there tonight."

"Let's lay low. Just for tonight, Beithune. I'll make dinner."

"No. If you're not coming in, then I'm going out. I can't stand it here."

All the sounds in the street seemed to be emanating

from the soul of the planet, older than water, creaks of the forces that were fighting to control the spin. Why did they have to be in that spin? Corrag felt herself falling. She sat down on the bed and cleared a space for herself. If only she could just curl up for a few hours. The world would go on without her, without Beithune. It had nothing to do with them. Their reality could be cleaner, independent of the influences shaking out in the back rooms, in the roots of money and power. Beithune peed in the bathroom and flushed the toilet. Going on a challenge of this kind would inevitably drain her beyond the capacity of a night's sleep to remedy. She had to work, and besides, there was the danger of coming across an unexpected dimension in this kind of unproven challenge, of not being able to ever recover, of losing your mind.

Monica would know what to do. The memory of her voice, its sure tones, came to Corrag's mind. She wondered if Beithune was right. She was in jail, he'd said. On what charges? Wasn't Mike supposed to be in the mayor's task force on community organizing? Certainly, there would have to be protests to secure their release from whatever trumped up proofs were being used against them. She stood up to get her emosponder and began to look up her contacts. She did have a number for Monica.

"No. Don't do that!" Beithune sprang across the darkened room, from his side of the bed to the dresser where Corrag was standing. He tried to wrestle the emosponder from her, but she held onto it and managed to twist away. His feverish look galvanized her resistance. She thought he might possibly already be in the throes of some hunger-induced psychotic break.

"Beithune, calm down! Our contact list is already compromised," said Corrag.

"Yes, but there is a Code Green out for anybody on Monica and Mike's communication folders. They will come down tonight, Corrag. There's a chance they are already on their way. If you hear a knock on the door, our best bet is to throw the emosponders down the toilet As a matter of fact, I'm ditching mine now. You can come with me if you want."

"Where are you going?"

"Water side."

"I knew that."

"You too?"

"Yes."

"See? They've already hacked their way into our heads."

"What can we do?"

"I don't know. Don't think too much about it."

She and Beithune walked silently along the Atlantic Avenue canal for uncounted porter stops. It was good to breathe the sea-laden air and hear the sirens and zipping motors of the watercraft. It didn't seem like there was any way to stop the wild flow of city life, but that was precisely what the alliance between the Gheko administration and the Sandelsky gaming empire was all about, according to Beithune.

"There is a war here. Just like the one in

Democravia," he explained, exasperated. They had stopped at the foot of the Brooklyn Bridge. He took out his emosponder and threw it far into the river. Corrag kept hers.

There was the thin line, the division between the skyline of the city and the dark night behind it. For Corrag, this distinction marked her ability to see things the way they really were and the impossibility of ever being sure of what was there. She wanted to believe in herself, the Democravian girl who stood for doing things the right way, for the good of the greatest number. She put off her own pleasure for the sake of others, and now the others were proving her wrong. This fighting, the mysterious power struggle that was the black behind the night, the ground of all history, was confounding her desire for a proving ground. The Repho was going to be the place she and Beithune made a mark. Now the struggle was to find a way forward. They were lost.

They walked out on the bridge with the other pedestrians, the flow of seekers all wondering where the action was, when it was in the black of the night sky just beyond the light of the known. They all seemed propelled by a common cause, runing blindly towards a shared fate. Someone somewhere surely pulled the strings that made the city jump. She looked at faces, trying to gauge the modality of thought in each look of recognition, each spark of acknowledgement spreading equal doses of fear and excitement. On the other side was Manhattan, the reservoir of the rich and playground of the elites.

They reached Ayn Rand Center Park. The city police

had set up an instant wall of corrugated lithium boards and were beginning to pull people aside and into the police transports that zipped away to the mother boat out in the harbor. Smaller police boats swarmed in the canals, waiting to pull alongside the pilings and take on prisoners.

There were shouts, explosions, a break in the orderly process, and the crowd surged ahead as Corrag and Beithune made for the lithium barrier and the bright lights of the Ayn Rand Center behind it. They had a common thought -- to follow the crowd and reach the city. The police were standing in the way of the mob's will to enjoy the night that belonged to them. But Corrag thought there was something else, something wrong. The police were unusually focused and were not just herding them for the simple purposes that the herd could understand. She sprinted behind Beithune. He had seen a way, and he dodged with the quickness of thought that was his trademark. She had to trust him. She could not see the openings as well as he could. Her heart pounded and her legs pumped. Then it was over as quickly as thought itself.

The cracking sound in the air knocked her to the ground. The smell of burning flesh filled the park. The blue light of ion fields crackled in the sky above her. Corrag gritted her teeth in pain but was unable to move her limbs. Everywhere that she managed to see there were bodies pulled down by the jolt of the lithium panels. Police units in full-body insulated suits were walking among them, pulling people aside and dragging them into the boats. Corrag felt someone lift her by the arms and drag her away. She looked for Beithune and thought she saw him lying on the ground.

"Beithune, where are you?" she screamed in her mind as she was dropped into the boat.

"Sandelsky," she heard from inside her head.

The police transport moved slowly in the bay, silently chopping through the water. Police officers moved down the rows of prisoners sitting on the grooved deck, asking questions and examining emosponder documentation. As the effects of the lithium blast wore away, two sub Saharans and an Inuit looking woman, illegal refugees, went for the water. The floodlights turned on the river and machine guns strafed the area.

"Emosponder?" asked a policewoman in blackface and camo.

"Not on me," said Corrag.

"What's your name?"

"Corrag Lyons."

"Spell the last name?"

Corrag complied.

"National identification number?"

"Democravian Federation. I'm a youth emissary. My father is a council member in Edmundstown."

The policewoman looked at her. She punched something into her tablet and walked away. A few minutes later she came back with a man in a blue captain's uniform and a HINTEL Homeland Intelligence baseball cap.

"Hi, Corrag."

"Hi."

"We have a problem. You know that."

"Why? What's the problem?"

"You're not supposed to be here. You've violated the terms of your entry. What have you been doing?"

"Working at The Meadowbrook Health Club. On Atlantic Avenue."

"Follow me."

Corrag stood and made her way behind the officer on the slowly pitching deck, stepping between the bodies of the fellow passengers. She felt in her pocket for her emosponder. It was lost. Her heart sank. She thought of jumping in the water, but she held back. The black waves promised a quick death by either poisoning or drowning in the toxins.

Inside the cabin house, the Homeland Intelligence officer sat her on a bench and ordered her to wait. He went away after promising to return. Other police came and went, and the boat seemed to circle in the water. Drones and choppers flying overhead filled the sky with blinking lights. Corrag watched out the open door of the cabin house. Despite her fear, she was hoping her special status would prevent her from falling into a worse situation. She didn't know what that situation would be. The police had not arrested her, but being on the boat entailed a loss of human standing. The prisoners were being kept down, physically restrained in a way that was unimaginable. One man tried to stand but was tazed by an officer.

"Get down! And stay down!"

A woman sat up and screamed something unintelligible. Her meaningless wail seemed to sum up the absurdity and the terror of their indeterminate status.

The lights of another, smaller boat coming alongside played across the deck, and the wake from this boat made Corrag grab for a hold. Two female officers, possibly transgendered, came into the wheelhouse and took Corrag, one at each arm.

"Come on," said one.

"Where?" asked Corrag. They seemed rough and uncaring, and she demanded a better approach. They were not providing her with what she needed.

"Out of here. Don't ask questions. Just relax. Don't make it harder on yourself. You'll be fine," said the other.

They pulled her along. She stumbled and excused herself. The other boat was tied off, and they dropped Corrag down with a rope ladder on a cable. The two officers stepped back and one gave a thumbs up as she ducked away. Corrag felt herself falling towards the new boat and arms catching her. The new boat pitched and rolled beneath her.

Nobody said anything to her. She seemed to be the only civilian on board. The soldiers were busy getting commands through their helmets. Once they sat her down in the stern on a berth they left her on her own. She could hear the crackle of the radio communications with the pilot and she could smell the slightly acidic smell of the munitions, lightweight automatic rifles that were carried onboard. A few minutes later they were coming alongside a jetty somewhere uptown. A group of men and women in lab coats had assembled on the dock and surrounded Corrag as the soldiers lifted her out. The boat started up its engine again and moved away, enveloped in darkness, into the current of the river.

"Where am I?" asked Corrag.

"Ward's Island Rehab," said one of the doctors, a young man with a worried face who pushed the glasses up on his nose.

Corrag was speechless. All she could do was look at the doctors and hope they could understand her feelings of despair.

"You'll be assessed for placement. Don't worry. This is a good place," said the young doctor with glasses. The other doctors consulted with their emosponders. One woman smoked a cigarette.

"There's nothing wrong with me," said Corrag at last, as they began to walk across the yard from the dock towards the complex of pale buildings silouhetted against the sky and the flash of explosions downtown.

"No, of course not, dear," said the woman, snubbing out her cigarette on the dock with the toe of her shoe.

Corrag was placed on the sixth floor in what had once been the youth wing in the heyday of the hospital's medical glory. Most of the people there were non-violent. In the subsequent days she would learn their names. A team of doctors came around in the mornings and administered medications and took measurements with the spectrometer and abdominal scan.

Mendez, a thin man with curly hair, shared cigarettes with everybody. He whispered to Corrag.

"You smoke?"

"No."

"That's okay. Listen, you new here, right? You going to need some information that the doctors and folks won't be giving to you."

"Like what?"

"Like how to stay alive in this joint."

"Okay. I'm listening."

Mendez advised Corrag that first morning to lay as low as possible when the doctors came by. Every week they chose one of the patients on the basis of indecipherable criteria, and this person was never seen again. Mendez said they underwent a forced augmentation that rendered them essentially into human bots and were then programmed to re-enter the stream of life in the city to act as informants and mood swingers. There was a lot that he told her. It was hard for her to retain it all.

Every night the people on the ward who were still left came out and played ping-pong under the thin LEDS that were left on twenty-four seven. The ward guards, men who spoke with no decipherable accents, they might have been bots even, Corrag wasn't sure and neither was anyone else she asked, usually turned a blind eye as they dared to make conversation between games. Most of them had been picked off the street in the last few weeks, but there were two patients who had been on the ward full time for at least ten years. City administrators had placed them there for behavior deemed categorically sub-competent. One was a girl with red, frizzy hair who cut herself when nobody was looking and the other was a Puerto Rican boy who had shot his brother in the chest while riding his zipbike. Both of them had been experimented with until their brains were Swiss cheese. Neither said much.

After the first day, Corrag stopped going up to the doctors to ask for information and advocate on behalf of herself. Mendez, who believed that this was the type of behavior that marked people for the covert augment program, discouraged her. The less vital signs the better, he said. Mendez had been through the wringer. When Corrag learned his story she was even more terrified than before. He had started out as a teacher in the South Bronx, but he'd run afoul of the system administrators. A lot of his students had needed special services for dioxin poisoning. A substation of electrical transformers was under their building, and the tainted water had bubbled up into the taps in the apartments for years. He described the students. These students, said Mendez, their hands were useless and their eyes were smoking holes of nothingness. But instead of giving up on them, Mendez had wanted to save them from the vocational school, run by a company with ties to the Gheko administration, where they were worked to death manufacturing nanotube chains, which required them to push buttons on the consoles with their foreheads when they heard the piped sound of music that marked the beginning and end of the printer's run.

"This is the true ideology of these people. Money," said Mendez. "We the people is out the window."

"Why are we here?" asked Corrag.

"Because," said Mendez impatiently, as if she were a three year old. "It's a crackdown, Corrag. Whenever things get out of hand on the street, they come down hard on what they perceive as threats. They'll use all sorts of excuses, enviro threats, what have you, but basically they don't want any opposition that stands in the way of the augmented class. Absolute control is what they want and there's lots of stuff that don't wash in their world like independent-minded people like you and me. We are unfit and sub-competent. That's what it is. Unfit and sub-competent. That means people who is just garbage to them. This is where they put the trash, Corrag."

"What can we do?"

"Follow my advice. Get out of here if you can. Don't let the doctors get a holt of you. Play dumb."

"Why are you still here?"

"A -- it's hard out on the street. I get three square a day here. And B -- I'm researching the situation. I'm writing a book."

Corrag took his advice. The testing for several days consisted of standard intelligence measures she was familiar with from schooling in the Democravian system. She was careful to be wrong on at least a quarter of the multiple choice questions, and on the open ended drawings she limited herself to simple stick figure representations of basic human emotions, either fear or hunger or a craving for attention. After the hour or so in the mornings, she would walk back up with the tablet to the desk where the nurse was chatting with one of the ward guards, usually about vacation plans. The rehab center employees received generous vacation packages as part of their employment plans, and they liked to take them in condos in the Mediterranean. Gibraltar and Ibiza were popular destinations Corrag heard mentioned. She stilled her thoughts and handed back the tablet with a blank look, a slightly dazed expression on her face. She was cultivating the persona of that lost girl from Democravia, a victim of circumstances beyond anyone's understanding. She didn't believe in destiny, only in the set of circumstances that had led to this. Poor choices, as Alana used to say, and Ricky would hush her. Democravia was built on the presumption of eliminating the possibility of human error, and here she was, the emissary, imprisoned in the lunatic asylum. Surely there had been a mistake. But Corrag had already learned she was not alone in the night here either.

In the afternoons they let small groups up on the roof to play with a basketball or just stand in the thin December sunlight. The roof space was surrounded by black mesh to prevent people jumping. On the third or fourth day, the city beyond the river was finally calmed, no sound of firefights or explosives. Flocks of wheeling pigeons were in the sky above Brooklyn water tanks, along with plumes of smoke from still burning buildings. Corrag liked to get right up to the wall and look through the mesh into the distance. The Rand Center stood as a reminder of the night she'd been picked up and the last she'd seen of Beithune. She thought hard, listening for a word from him, but she heard nothing. The redheaded girl was in a wheelchair by the wall, staring at the gravel on the ground and the glinting pieces of molybdenum left over from some building project.

"Hi," said Corrag. "You like the sun?"

"No." The girl looked up at her, squinting. It was the first word Corrag had ever heard her say.

"What's your name?"

"Emma."

"Emma. That's a pretty name. Where are you from?"

"I don't know."

Corrag had the sudden sense that she knew more than she let on, that Emma was someone, not just a victim.

"Do you hate it here? Do you want to go home?"

Emma looked at her, squinting again. There was a searching in her look, something beyond the words.

"I don't want to go home. I'm crazy. Look at this."

Emma shoved her arms out of her lap where they lay surrounded in a blanket against the cold. Scars and still raw lines of razor cuts ran from her elbows to her wrists, marking her pale bare skin.

"Why do you do that?"

"I don't know."

"Oh, Emma."

She had never encountered melancholy so muted, so fully incorporated into a personality. People like Emma did not exist in Democravia, or they were hidden away so successfully that they might as well have never existed. Corrag felt like she was drowning in sadness. For several days, when she awoke first thing in the morning with the sudden hissing of steam pipes, she checked herself, running an inventory of the heart, before she felt ready to get out of bed. The days went by in a blur, with medication rounds followed by group talks led by the nurses. Corrag had avoided any medication stronger than Milof, a mild tranquilizer, and by the end of that week she felt she might be able to survive this strange place. In the evenings, when the prisoners/patients were allowed to gather in the main room and play ping-pong and smoke cigarettes, Mendez sat in a circle with an ever-changing constellation of acolytes and dispensed wisdom and hope.

There were new people in every day, and towards the end of that first week they brought in a woman, about thirty, very pretty, who had been a broadcast personality with the Air Nueva Apple news organization. She was pretty in the classic Repho mold, and defiant. She and Mendez hit it off well. She had been gathered in a moment of weakness, walking in the park around the Onassis reservoir after dark. She admitted to the police that she had been drinking. But she was also suspected of disaligner sympathies.

"What business do they have trying to stop what I put in my body or what my personal opinions are? This is a goddamn police state," she said, wild-eyed. Coming from her, a well-known personality, it meant something, and Mendez smiled with a clarity that Corrag loved.

Corrag felt a part of something important. She even tried a cigarette, a filter-less Lucky Hit, filling her lungs with the black smoke and gagging, to the amusement of the others. Even Emma laughed.

Mendez and the new woman, Vicky Jones, told stories of people's ability to overcome impossibly ridiculous circumstances. There was a feeling that the Gheko administration and its policies would not survive very long if people could come together and organize a counter to the ruthlessness of the crackdown they were seeing.

That night Corrag dreamed of the destruction of her body and the immutable nature of her soul. In the dream the doctors were the ghosts of former patients that still clung to the building, the site of their tortures in bygone days, and chose to inflict their pain on the living rather than move on. They tied Corrag to a bed on her stomach and carried out unspeakable acts. She cried out in her dream, but the monstrous shouts of the doctors drowned out her protests. When she awoke, she was still whole. It had all been a dream, very vivid and horrifying, but unreal. The light coming in her window soothed and reassured her. She was alive, and the ghosts of the dream had vanished, leaving behind a trembling but unscathed living person. It hit her with the weight of reality that the simple evidence of her senses would always be something that could save her, that ghosts of her own or of others' invention would not shake her grip on sanity.

She rose and dressed in the Wards Island jumpsuit that she'd been given. The ever-present green was a way they had of bringing the prisoners down. Corrag yearned to wear anything else besides the color green, and it was only her first week. She went out to the stairs and began to descend one floor to the cafeteria.

Nobody was eating. Mendez's eyes were red. Corrag sat next to him. The others at the table were silent and stared at their plates or into the distance.

"What's wrong?" asked Corrag.

"Vicky's dead," said Mendez.

"'What? How?" asked Corrag.

"In her room, a belt. The staff cut her down and brought her into the lounge."

"She was done, Mendez. That was a hit made up to look like suicide." The man who spoke was a former police officer, a fifty year old with thinning hair, Cooper Lytle. Like Mendez, he was a long time resident on the ward. Corrag had suspected him of being a Gheko plant because of his usual silence. But now he was angry.

"Yeah. That's the way I see it too," said Mendez.

"It's time we had a shut down," said Lytle.

"That's a tough call."

"Are you with me?"

"It's going to be hard on a lot of folks."

"We've gotten too comfortable with the system. We need to save some of these kids," said Lytle.

Mendez looked around at the tables and then to Corrag.

"What is it? What's a shut down?" asked Corrag.

"We shut the place down, and some people get out. The punishment for the rest, the folks who stay behind, is pretty harsh, almost like a death sentence," said Mendez.

"How do you do it?" asked Corrag.

"Never mind that," said Lytle.

"We have the knowledge. The *how* part is taken care

of. It's the *what if* part that bothers me. What do you think Corrag? Do we take the chance? Would you chance a breakout if you knew the consequence of failure were basically you end up either dead or a vegetable?"

"I don't know."

"Look," said Lytle. "If we don't fight back there will be others like Vicky. Every day now. It's going to get worse. They can't use this place as a slaughterhouse. They've gone too far."

"I agree," said Corrag. From what she had seen: the mass tazing, her arrest and detention, the treatment on Ward's Island, it was clear the Repho was not in the business of promoting individual liberty and freedom as it advertised. It seemed to be increasingly about greater control and manipulation of the masses for the interests of a distant elite. She wanted to get out and somehow find Beithune. Anything was better than staying in Ward's Island. She loved Lytle now for his defiance. He would rather fight. His spirit was infectious.

Mendez called a group together at the mid-morning break. They were on the roof and it was a brisk day with a wind. They could see whitecaps out on the river. The distant spires of midtown looked like the icy towers of some fantastic future planet. Corrag was excited but shivering with nerves and lack of food. She wished she'd eaten some breakfast. Mendez was speaking, explaining to a group of them what the drill would look like. Lytle had a skeleton key he'd been saving for just such an event. In the afternoon, during the down hours, which they usually whiled away in their rooms, a group of them would go floor by floor and alert as many as they could. The floor wardens usually played cards or gamed together at that time. It wouldn't be difficult to get as far as the third floor. Shortly before dinner, Lytle, who was already there waiting, would set off an explosion in the boiler room and that would be the diversion they needed to rush the third floor barricades and get down to the ground and out. Then they would need to overpower the security system at the gate and get to the water's edge, where there would be boats waiting to get them away.

After Mendez was done talking, he hugged several of them.

"How do you know the boats will be there waiting?" asked Corrag, when she had a moment alone with him. They were standing at the roof's edge, looking out the mesh at the water and beyond at the northern boroughs.

"Corrag, in case this fails. I ... there's a communication link inside. Lytle and I have kept it a secret for many years now. I'm going to show you in case you get left you'll know."

Mendez and Corrag walked together nonchalantly down the stairs to the recreation room on the fifth floor. There was a gaming console against the wall nobody used because the games it contained were about two decades out of style. But Mendez sat down and took up a game of Mario, pinging the balls back and forth across the screen.

"See, this is kind of fun," he said. Corrag agreed. The guard left the room pacing slowly in his heavy black shoes. Mendez looked behind and out of his pocket took an old USB cable and plugged it into the computer and then the other end into a jack half hidden by plastic curtains.

"Okay," said Mendez, scooting in his chair, rebooting the computer and playing with the code to bring up an old Internet link with a blank portal. Mendez's face appeared on the screen, lit up by the glow of the screen in front of him, then he disappeared and another face took his place, this one darker, harder to make out.

"This is Mendez. Wards Island. Is Korazan there?"

"He's getting the boat ready."

"One boat?"

"Three boats."

"Okay. This is Corrag. I wanted to introduce her. She's good."

"She's made. I'll let Korazan know. Corrag. Where you from, dude?"

"Democravia."

"Nice. Korazan likes them chick dudes from Democravia. Just kidding."

"Okay, we're done," said Mendez.

"Never done. Just kidding. Over and out, bud."

Mendez pulled the cable and stuffed it in his pocket. He smiled wisely up at Corrag.

"Simple as that," he said. "The most secure communication link in the city. Probably the only two Macs left with the old Leopard OS on the install."

"Who's Korazan?"

"Korazan? Sudanese cartel boss. Not the type of guy you'd want to bring home and introduce to Mom, but the man's got street cred, and we have a common enemy."

Corrag stared hard at Mendez's wizened face and sunken eyes. There was still a spark glowing in them despite the years he carried. She felt like hugging him, but she didn't. Later she regretted not hugging him then.

That evening, as she was daydreaming about Durkiev Drive and the Rosaleses and her parents in their old house, wishing she could speak to them for even a minute on an emosponder, missing them and the smell of synthetic floor oil on the tiles and the sound of the bot whirring down the otherwise silent stairs, the explosion went off somewhere in the bowels of the building. It sounded with a deep bass thud and then the floor shook and people screamed. For a second Corrag did not know what had happened, and then instantly she picked up her feet and ran for the stairs. Then she stopped. She was supposed to gather as many people as possible, shepherd them down to the third floor. She spotted Emma in her wheelchair and ran over to kneel in front of her.

"We're getting out now, making a break. You want to come?"

"It's against the rules."

"There are no rules now, Emma. We make the rules."

"I just don't ... leave? Where would I go?"

"Just come with me, Emma. Trust me."

Emma scowled, looked confused and began to shout. Corrag did not hear the words at first, concentrating instead on the muscles of Emma's face tightening, turning the skin a bloodless white, tinged with yellows and greens, and the anger rising in her eyes. She understood the term boiling blood because it seemed like the blood was causing a liquid froth in her eyes, and they might pop from their sockets. Then she began to hear the words intermittently, as if from a distance.

"Whore! ... Bitch! ... Ruin everything! ... How dare you!"

Corrag stood and backed away.

"Sorry, Emma," she mouthed, and she turned and ran for the stairs.

The nurses and wardens made feeble attempts to hold certain prisoners back, but the desire to flee was an overpowering tidal wave of emotion. Corrag could see even the weakest break away and bolt from their would-be captors. The crowd on the stairwells surged through the doors on the third floor. A couple of floor mates held the doors open, giving instructions:

"Don't stop! Get through the gate. Get outside and head for the water!"

The guards darted around, trying to stem the human tide, but for everyone they grabbed and pushed back five ran by. Someone jumped one of the guards from behind and brought him down, and that was the last Corrag saw of him. From a side door appeared Mendez, and beside him was Lytle, leaning against him, his large belly unhindered, face bloodied. He was shirtless, and his pants were hanging in shreds. Corrag weaved through the throng until she was beside Mendez.

"What happened?"

"Don't mind. Run, Corrag. Get yourself out."

"But we can't leave without you. Come on. I'll get him."

On either side of Lytle, they managed to get the wounded man past the third floor barricade and down the two flights of stairs to the exit. Corrag struggled to support Lytle's weight. People shouted and surged back through the door. She could see out past the huddled mass; two driverless armored vehicles were pulling up to the entrance. A spray of bullet fire sounded. Full panic seized the mob. Corrag huddled dizzily with the two men, who seemed strangely calm, as if they'd lived through all of it before.

"In a minute now they'll run for it again," said Lytle.

"When boiler number two blows?"

"That's right."

Seconds later another explosion went off, this one sharper, more concussive than the first. Shards of flames appeared on the walls, as if materializing by magic, as the combustible electrical wiring and plastic ducting in the wall space caught fire from below and blew out the vents. Once again panic took hold of the mob, and there was a sudden surge out the door. Bullet fire and screams filled the dusk. Lytle removed his backpack and handed something to Mendez.

"Now's a good time as ever, brother," said Lytle.

Mendez looked at him and at Corrag.

"Go, Corrag. Run far and spread the word. You only get what you fight for."

He and Lytle went out the door, Lytle hobbling and Mendez staying serenely by his side. They walked behind the crowd of escaping patients, emptying onto the entrance plaza and falling in waves to the fire from the two armored bot vehicles. Corrag saw the two men walk up to the first vehicle and begin to scale the armored plating, both of them struggling and then lifted by inspired escapees who could see what they were trying to do. The vehicle tried to shrug them off, reversing and spinning on its swivel track like a trick pony. Then Mendez raised the hatch on the roof and tossed something inside. The muffled explosion halted the bot in its tracks. It sat simmering like an angry, wounded insect. The other vehicle swiveled around and fired off a tank round at its companion. It sent the bodies of Mendez and Lytle flying amid shards of metal and reverberating balls of flames.

In the resulting confusion, the escapees surged to the water's edge. Some clambered on the rocks and fell into the river. In the dark, they could see boats approaching, black silhouetted hulls bouncing silently and breaking the water ahead, then slowing and coming alongside the rocks where the people stood, balancing precariously, holding each other, some of them sobbing and screaming for help. The boats took on as many as they could, rocking awkwardly and gunning the engines, reversing the propellers to stay steady in the swirling tidal currents. Corrag was among the people clambering on board. As she was falling into the black mass of the East River, a strong pair of hands picked her up under the armpits and hauled her over the gunwales. They pulled away from the island, and she looked back at the flames enveloping the first floors of the main building and the drones circling in the sky above the inferno, their neon colored lights blinking, seeing everything.

A short ten-minute ride over the choppy river saw them at the piers of the Mount Vernon projects, a camp of homeless, illegal refugees huddled by barrel fires in Van Cortland Park in the distance. The boats came alongside without tieing off, and the people swarmed onto the dock. Men and women with high caliber guns and ammunition belts hanging around their shoulders led them to an emergency medical tent at the edge of the park where rebel doctors would treat their wounds. Then the guerrillas resumed their positions staked out around the park, firing at the drones they were sighting through night vision goggles. Corrag sensed the excitement of these men and women fighters. She imagined they had planned for an insurrection of this type for years and hauled out guns and ammunition from secret spots in the tenements where they had long laid buried for this moment. She was headed aimlessly for the medical tent, following the crowd. It was obvious many were simply melting into the streets, disappearing from the scene. At that moment the screech of Repho fighter jets sounded above them, and the ground seemed to open up around her. With slitted eyes and a scream in her throat she felt her legs pumping, while at the edge of her vision the buildings blurred. A string of explosions rocked the night, and then there was silence broken only by moans. Where the medical tent had been just instants ago there now was an open crater. The buildings around the park had been pounded into rubble. Corrag wanted to run but felt as if her legs were mired in cement. She wanted to fly. A hand grabbed her shoulder. She turned, and a scarred face with intelligent darting eyes met her gaze.

"Come," said the black man, and Corrag followed, glad to have some direction.

The man gave her a bucket and told her to start digging. There was a line of people that had assembled, and they dug away at the rubble of what had once been apartment buildings, putting what they could in the buckets and passing the buckets down the line until they came across an arm, legs, severed pieces of encrusted flesh still wet and warm. These they placed carefully aside in the park.

Corrag leaned into the blackness under the rubble, hoping to hear voices, signs of intact life, miracles buried under the shards of glass, twisted beams and concrete chunks. They dug for hours and took turns running the emptied buckets back up the hill of rubble, careful not to fall into the gaps of blackness where life oozed itself away in silence and shame.

Corrag's arms were burning with fatigue. She could hardly open her hands to get them around the bucket handle when it was full. Her hands were bleeding. She was thinking of ways to exit the scene, and how she would never forgive herself if she did. Mired in self-recriminations, she suddenly heard a cry, a voice below. She yelled back. "Who's there?" And popped her head and shoulders deeper into the crevice. "Help!" she heard.

Corrag stood and called out for help. A boy with a searchlight passed up the line. Corrag took the light and told the boy to hold her by the legs. She leaned into the chasm, coughing in the dust. The light showed up a length of a corrugated I beam. Underneath it she thought she saw something move.

"Are you there?"

"Yes," said a squeaky, scared voice.

"We'll get you out. Don't worry," said Corrag.

Ten hours later the light was showing in the sky and the rescue teams were wiped out with exhaustion. Several tons of debris had been moved by hand. An excavator bot had been located in a sand and gravel depot in Bridgeport and was on its way, but the volunteers had to keep working without stopping for food or water. Corrag felt only one thing, a constriction in her throat that almost blocked her breathing, but not quite. Everything else was numb. She couldn't lift the buckets, but somehow dragged the empty ones back from the dumpster on the boat on the dock. The guerrilla soldiers were smoking khat and listening to jihad rap. They had come up from Philadelphia, they said. About fifteen or so had disappeared in the bombing. Then someone yelled that the girl was out. They'd rescued the little girl. Everyone wanted to see her; she was wrapped in a nanofoil blanket and whisked away on a zip bike before Corrag could get to her. Corrag was crying as the sun came up, sitting down where she was at the edge of the rubble pile. At least she could feel the tears. One life was saved; a small victory had been enacted in the midst of all the useless, evil destruction. There was some celebration, but there was also word coming down that the survivors of the Korazan Brigade had been ordered back. The soldier, the black man with tribal scars, tapped her on the shoulder and pointed to a porter truck, one of a line of vehicles that had appeared suddenly on the edge of the park. They were evacuating, and she was going with them. She was giddy, elated. She wanted to fight whatever or whoever had been bombing the neighborhood hours before. Her identity as a Democravian did not immunize her from feeling a part of this. On the contrary, it impelled her to seek to destroy the evil before it got away with worse.

She was barely able to walk. She was so tired, but full of a sudden joy and excitement at the cold December sun glinting off the aluminum roofs of the trucks. The men and women piled in after clicking on the safety latches on their rifles. Corrag sat on a utility bench with no backrest. One of the soldiers offered to switch with her. She stayed where she was. Everyone was exhausted.

They drove in a convoy across the GW Bridge and out to the Delaware Forest. The truck had no windows and was decaled with the markings of the Lambertville Chinese Vegetable Growers cooperative, a celebratory, drunk looking New Year's dragon festooned above the lettering. The parking lot was on the edge of the highway. Across the highway was an A frame at the edge of the woods. Dead oak trees alternated with low, dying pines strangled by invasive tropical vines. They crossed the road at a trot after checking for clear with one of the soldiers on an emosponder. Corrag could see beside the A frame, as she got closer, there were pup tents set back in the bushes. A couple of others who, like her, had been volunteered into the trucks now were brought inside the

A frame by the soldiers, holding their rifles up and urging them up the rotted plank steps.

Inside the door, a black girl smiled. She got them inside and then closed and locked the door. She was about twenty, with sharp features and broad shoulders in her camouflage jersey. A man with a face that held almost no recognizably human features sat on a beat up sofa in the dark room.

"These are the new inducts, General."

"Well, introduce us, then," said the man on the sofa.

"Guys, this is General Korazan. Welcome to the Korazan Brigade."

"Come closer to where I can see you," said the man.

Corrag and the three others beside her, all young men, complied. General Korazan had the tribal scars that a lot of his soldiers had and flat, lifeless eyes. There was a stink about him of rotted flesh that reminded Corrag of a vulture she'd once seen in the San Gabriel Mountains up close above the cloud line. It had been sitting on a rock as they'd almost reached the summit of some climb, she couldn't remember which, maybe Sentinel Ridge, and the smell of it had been overpowering. Ricky had chased it away by hollering, and it had flapped its huge wings and dropped several dozen feet into the chasm before achieving some lift and clearing some outcroppings and veering away out of sight. The memory was a powerful one, and Corrag thought it providential that it should resurface at this time, so far from her childhood and those family hikes. She wished she'd never seen General Korazan. He seemed devoid of emotion and therefore either extremely untrustworthy or their promised redemptor.

"Okay. Now I can see you. Tell me who you are and why you want to fight with me."

They were quiet, shuffling in a line in front of the sofa. Corrag turned around. The black girl was standing at the door clutching her rifle.

"You first," he said, pointing at her.

"Me?"

"Yes."

"Well, I'm from Democravia, Edmundstown. And I don't know why I want to fight with you. Honestly, I lost my cousin. I would like to find him and maybe by joining up with you I can. I'm not really a fighter. Beithune is. I'm sure you could use him. Why are you fighting?"

"Why? We're fighting to rid the world of the oppressors, child. No other reason. The scum who want to kill our future. Make slaves of us and our children. They running this circus they call the Republican Homeland. It's only a homeland if you call this shit a home with 25 percent homeless and over half with no access to the Augment."

"Okay," said Corrag.

Korazan stood and walked over to the door.

"What's your name, child?" he asked.

"Me? Corrag Lyons."

He whispered something to the girl and she got on her emosponder. They both looked back at the sofa at the inductees who shifted their weight, waiting for another cue from the general. The girl got a response on the emosponder and relayed it to the general in a rapid patois that was impossible for Corrag to understand.

"How about you?" Korazan walked back to the sofa and questioned the next volunteer, a boy with sandy brown hair and thick, tattooed arms. He sat back on the sofa and resumed his grasp of the khat pipe he'd left teetering on the sofa's arm.

"Billy Gansky."

"Why are you here, Billy?"

"I don't know how you want me to say it."

"I don't want it in any way. Just tell the truth."

"They ... k ... killed my parents," he stammered. It took him awhile to get his words together.

"My Mom and Dad were st ... strawberry growers. From Graftonburg. That's in P ... Pennsylvania. They wanted to grow in our own way, using our own people. We always made our own harvest until they said we had to use the S ... Sandelsky scalers. The government and S ... Sandelsky are trying to run the table all across this country."

"Okay. And you?

Korazan turned to the last boy.

"I don't know. I hate the Repho," he said, in a quavering voice.

"Come here."

"Why?"

"Just do as I tell you. What's your name?"

"Ivan."

"Ivan, how old is you?"

"Twenty five."

As he questioned, Korazan flipped open his emosponder and held it up to the inductee's face. It shone a light into his eyes.

Korazan checked the emosponder down close, squinting his eyes at the screen held in his hand. He looked at the door and the black girl guarding it, and his glance caused her to move to the door and open it. Three soldiers shuffled in, lightweight sniper rifles with night vision sights slung across their backs.

"Ivan, did you know you have an augment? We don't like that at all."

"I hate what they've done to me. I want to kill all of them!"

"Take him away," Korazan said to the soldiers and placed the pipe in his mouth.

"No, you don't get it. I'm on your side!" Ivan made a dash for the door. The black girl jumped in his way and ducked as he swung a fist at her. Then the soldiers jumped him from behind as he was going through the door and pinned his arms behind his back and cuffed him after he went sprawling forward down the steps. They manhandled Ivan through the trees. Corrag could see it from her spot inside the room. Then the door closed, and it was dark as the general spoke. Korazan sucked at his pipe. He was talking, telling them about the Korazan Brigade and the fight against the Repho that had broken out across several hotspots. They were part of a broad alliance of rebel groups who fought under different banners and different causes. Some of them were against the Augment because they were opposed to the immortality project that it fit into, others were fighting the corruption of the Sandelsky/Gheko alliance because the power that had once belonged to the traditional political institutions was now concentrated in the hands of cronies, the friends and relatives of the two autocrats. But the Korazan Brigade took on the fight on behalf of the downtrodden, the powerless. Many were the sons and daughters of migrants that had been refused access to any commercial or government augment because of a lack of documentation or finance.

A shot was fired. Nobody said anything about it. Corrag felt herself go numb, as if the blood had drained out of her body. She didn't see herself getting along with a bunch of people who executed volunteers in cold blood. But there was nowhere else to go. She was in the midst of a war. Sides had been chosen. She squeezed her arms, trying to keep her spirits up.

She trained in the use of the Bograd, a flamethrower that used compressed hydrogen. She had been chosen, not for any particular predisposition she didn't think, but rather because it was a weapon that depended on the strength of a unit, two loaders and one director, and she seemed to be able to communicate well with the different sorts of volunteers that were coming in -- from rural refugees to urban working class, disaffected youth.

There was a distinct religious cast to the unit's basic culture. Male and female priests set up in a makeshift shed almost every day to lead evening prayers. Corrag attended these services, drawn to the solemnity and the richly colored robes the priests wore, different from the

Unitarian church services she'd attended with the Hunnewells in New Albion and the blue-jeaned pastor there. Although there was no mention of it, she was pretty sure it was the Church of Peter the Rock. The priests in the camp had companions that traveled with them, and some of them had relationships with some of the soldiers.

The black girl, Gillema, aide to Korazan, who had assigned Corrag to the Bograd, came by at meals to make sure she was all right. The other two boys that were the rest of Corrag's unit usually ate with her, and they also shared a tent that they pitched beside hers. Their names were Cesar and Kevin. Cesar was Guatemalan. And Kevin, the black soldier that had tapped her for duty back in Van Cortland, had originally been a child soldier in the wars of the African Horn. He was Somalian. Kevin knew the names of the stars in his language. *Benadir, Xidigta*, he said, and tried to teach Corrag. Corrag listened in the dark without looking him in the face, and tried to repeat. There was the Big Dipper. He pointed and said *Aquila*. The eagle. Corrag shivered. She couldn't look him in the face because it scared her to see his eyes, even in the dark when she could hardly see them. She could tell instantly what he was thinking by the light in his eyes, like an eagle's, voracious and unstoppable. She wished Beithune were there to learn the names of the stars. He would be better than she was about remembering.

At the end of the second week she went over to find Gillema in her tent. She was sitting outside the flap nursing a small fire and drinking tea from her vintage aluminum cup that she'd picked up at the swap shop in

Lambertville. Jokingly, she called it her Korazan Brigade chalice.

"Hi Gillema. Can I see you?"

"Yes, of course. Sit, girl. Talk to me. How is your Bograd unit?"

"We're fine. We're getting along well. But, I don't know. I feel funny. My heart is twisted inside me. Do you know what I mean?"

"Well, that is a strange condition. Tell me more."

"You know Kevin and Cesar?"

"Yes?"

"They're both very special to me. I feel funny."

"You like them. Which one better? Are they fighting over you?"

"No, please. I don't want them to fight. But Kevin is very nice. He teaches me things. Like new words for everyday stuff. Did you know that Kevin always prays at noon? Because he believes that the words travel up to the sun. Words are related to light. Light decays and becomes night, but just before the night, once it hits the upper atmosphere, the light is able to materialize our prayers, the prayers inside the light, and be heard by God. But I don't know if I believe in God, Gillema. I wasn't brought up to believe. I certainly don't think my soul should belong to him."

"Only if you want. It's your *free* choice," said Gillema, shifting and making a spot beside herself on the log. Corrag sat and pulled her legs up into her chest as far as they would go.

"There's so much new information. I'm having a hard

time processing it all. This is the way I always wanted to live. I feel strong. I have a purpose. But I'm scared. I don't want to die. Kevin says some of our allies use suicide squads, but we don't. Is that true?"

"That's right. Albert ruled out suicide as an effective strategy. Imagine dying inside yourself in order to accept your own death. Anything is possible for such people. That's why we don't trust all the allies."

"Is that why you don't accept augments?"

"Exactly. They're not to be trusted either. They've already died as humans in order to accept themselves as immortals. It's the same idea. They have no real allegiance to the living. The best fighter is a man or woman in love with life."

"But why did you have to shoot Ivan? Couldn't you have sent him back?"

"Albert doesn't believe in taking chances with our safety. He's more than a military man, Corrag. He really cares about us."

The next battles would take place inside the city itself. They were planning an attack on the Sandelsky offices. By infiltrating small units one at a time, units able to live and take cover for days on the street, they would assemble a force at the very doorsteps of the powers that ran the Repho, the brain and neural coordination, the underlying network of greed and death that was responsible for the hard-line police state the Republic had become. Corrag and her Bograd unit could assemble and disassemble the flamethrower in a matter of minutes. They listened to lectures from cartel veterans on techniques for living without being seen, disguised as panhandlers or harmless disruptives. The night before they were to ship back to Manhattan, Corrag attended mass with Kevin. Cesar stayed in the main building. He was going into Lambertville on the bus to call his mother in Quetzaltenango from a Chinese restaurant that had an interface some of the soldiers had figured out how to use. In the sermon, the priest, a thin man with a grey ponytail, spoke about the different types of love represented, and the ideal of friendship.

"For we have chosen. And now the task is to accept our responsibility to each other as the highest calling. There is no greater love," said the priest and gave the sign.

Outside it was cold, and the sky was cloudless. A crescent moon gave just enough light to shine through the leafless branches that they walked under. At the top of the hill was a treeless circle where an old fire tower still stood, rusted cables anchoring it to the outcroppings of bedrock.

"I want to go up it," said Corrag.

"Go up," said Kevin.

"Will you come?"

"If you want me to go up, I will."

Corrag pulled herself over the barbed wire barrier and reached the stairs that wound on the inside of the tower's frame. Kevin caught his pants and tore a gash in his leg getting over the wire. He sat on the stairs and stanched the bleeding with his hand.

"Are you okay?"

"I think so." He stood, looking at her with a funny

smile like a little boy. Sometimes she thought she was like a mother to him.

Corrag continued to the top, where the stairs let out on a platform above the tree line. She could see the Delaware River glinting in the thin light of the crescent moon, and beyond the hills of the Poconos was the hinterland where the Korazan Brigade hoped to one day establish a free state for unaligned, unaugmented humans, a country where the guiding principles of social cohesion and sustainable technology would balance human striving with planetary well being. She believed Albert Korazan when he talked. He seemed so convinced that they could do it, and one day live free, not slaves in a system that took care of you if you sold yourself to the lowest bidder. They would fight the Repho in its home and prove that they were not the weaklings that the Gheko controlled media outlets made them out to be. By confronting Sandelsky and Gheko with the urban campaign, they hoped the weakened Repho state would not want to commit resources when they declared their home ground. But that was years off. In the meantime they had other safe havens and would be moving camp after this next phase of battle. Only Korazan knew where. He was in consultation with the leaders of paramilitary groups up and down the land as far as Panama, he claimed. It was amazing how committed Corrag was to the struggle after so short a time. It was like she'd been planning all along for this without knowing it, all the years of her childhood feeling like something was wrong. The fight wasn't just about the corruption of the

Republican Homeland. It was about a state of affairs that was shared with the Democravian Federation as well, a system of governance that depended on passivity, on individuals allowing themselves to be manipulated in the name of security and comfort. What were the good citizens scared of? Was it of knowing the truth, that the ease promised by the two respective systems was a sham? After all was said and done, there was no escape from death in augmentation; there would be no colonies in the distant stars, only the gentrified suburbs of Juarez and Lima, or in the case of the Repho, the exclusive vacation condos of Madagsacar or Croatia with their repetitive, anaesthetizing luxury. If only more people could allow themselves to feel the sweetness of brotherhood. Now Corrag had tasted it for herself, she knew the shared struggle was the only way to live.

It was cold, bitter cold. When the slightest breeze ripped through the hills it felt like her breath would freeze inside her lungs. But Kevin was warm with his arms around her. She couldn't look at him still, but when he kissed her she felt her heart beating in her throat and his heart beating in his, and her senses sharpened like an animal's. They climbed down, and this time Corrag caught herself in the barbed wire, and Kevin helped her get over, pushing her from below so she wouldn't cut herself as she extricated herself from the barbs. They laughed together as she fell and he caught her. His face was a sieve through which blew the hot African desert winds that had erased his childhood. His laugh was forced, a man in exile from himself. She loved him. They found a hollow under the pine trees. The water of the swamp was frozen into a sheet of silver at their feet. It was snowing, and they covered themselves with their coats and made love on the ground, blood pumping their mingling heat, blood and salt and then their bare skin becoming a painful reminder of where they were. Kevin laughed and sat up, pulling up his pants.

"Tomorrow we fight, so tonight we make love. We fight better."

"Yes," she said. "That's the theory anyhow. We'll see."

"No, don't doubt. It's bad luck to doubt."

"I don't doubt."

"If you doubt, Cesar will also and then we will run like scared dogs. You are the *quful* for us. You must not bend to anything."

Corrag's tears froze on her cheeks as they walked back down the hill through the trees. The wind whispered a song. Corrag listened hard, thinking of Ben, the first time they'd made love, in the park at night at the end of Unity Drive, but all she heard was a beating heart and then the music of the Korazan camp before sleep, the melodies of distant lands uniting in a common dream of a brighter, more human future.

Five -- The Battle for Alpha

The streets were thick with sad people carrying the repressed expressions of hidden allegiances and identities. Others looked straight at you as if they knew you even better then you knew yourself. Corrag, Kevin and Cesar dressed as street people with nondescript Huff boots and scuffed canvas flat soles and their black PeopleMart packs on their backs. A close observer would have noticed the way the packs sagged despite the tightness of the straps and the way they leaned forward when they walked. They took care to follow the rush hour crowds on this midday getting on and off the canal porters. The nanowalls on the newsstands were full of stories about the mad Chloe sisters and their escapades in Athens before performing there for the assembled members of the Committee for Growth, the exclusive trillionaires club. Corrag stopped and browsed at a corner shop while Kevin and Cesar reconnoitered the area around the Sandelsky Center. The canal porters belched out their crowds of commuters at the 96th and Broadway jetty. After getting her fill of meaningless but oddly comforting news, Corrag sat on the marble steps and placed her pack beside her and began to panhandle with the aluminum cup that had belonged to Gillema. A policewoman came by and asked her to move. But there were so many people around the plaza it was easy for her to move a few feet before sitting again.

The policewoman had disappeared. Then Kevin and

Cesar glanced at her and she stood to follow. They walked along the canal in single file on the backside of the building going west. The sun was shining on the upper glass. Corrag imagined the ignorant conclaves of assembled power, not knowing that forces were gathering at their feet to sweep them into the dustbin of history.

The water was choppy, and Christmas party boats plied their way up the Hudson for dinner cruises. Corrag, Kevin and Cesar sat at the promontory of Morningside Park and watched the boats full of seasonal revelers passing far below.

"It's Christmas tomorrow," said Cesar.

"We never celebrated it in Democravia. We had Academy Night when the students gave concerts and performed in plays."

"No, it's big in Texas," said Cesar. "Lot of believers in the communities there. Whites and Latinos, but the Spanish baby Jesus had a soft spot for parties."

"Oh come on, Cesar," said Corrag.

"No, I'm serious."

Kevin laughed.

"This is a good place. We stay tonight," said Kevin.

"Seems quiet enough. I'd feel better if there were more people," said Corrag.

"Look there," said Cesar, pointing up the hill to a group of what looked like laughing teenagers, pushing and sliding on the snowy ground. Corrag recognized some Korazan fighters among them.

"We're everywhere," she said.

She had an idea of buying Christmas presents before

nightfall. It was Christmas and Cesar had inspired her to celebrate. She thought of Beithune and whispered his name to herself, still hoping to hear something inside her head, some response from her cousin. She feared he might be dead; it had been so long since she'd heard from him. The hardest part would be waiting for the word from Korazan about the start of battle. Kevin read her mind.

"You want to go, go. We'll stay here and wait for you."

"No, Kevin. You need to go with her. I'll stay here with the stuff," said Cesar.

"No. Two with the Bograd. One can go and look for food."

"You two stay. I'll do that," said Corrag. She left them and walked down the path and over the footbridge to the intersection of Amsterdam and the West Side Canal. From there she continued up Amsterdam, the water of the canal sloshing and mixing with the falling snow to form a slushy mix on the walkway. Municipal bots were putting down scrap boardwalks along the worst of the flooded pedestrian ways. Corrag stopped at a little shop selling toys for children. There were metallic post-diluvian insects that jumped and chirped familiar melodies. There was the popular Birdman jigsaw puzzle and the Buzzhead vibrating jokesters for the little boys and the little ballerinas that danced on the head of a pin. It made Corrag miss her home and her friends. If she got through this stretch alive she vowed she would get a new, fully charged emosponder and find her parents. Instead of presents, though, she thought it would be better to get food for the night, knowing they only had a few more hours before being summoned to the fight.

A few blocks further along Amsterdam there was a food market. Corrag bought some fresh Brooklyn bread, some hydroponic mangos and a block of modified kefir cheese that was on sale for half price. They didn't have a lot of money to spend. Then she splurged on a bottle of New Albion maple wine, in honor of Beithune. Walking out with the bag hanging from her hand, a young man, hatless, just a thin, flannel shirt on despite the cold stopped her. His eyes were slits of pain and close set like a fox.

"Remember the whale. I'm guessing you know the answer by now."

She took another, closer look at the face -- a thin, raw face that once, not so long ago, had belonged to a young man. It was Lars from the Butterfly Club.

"Lars. What are you doing up here?"

"Getting by. How about you?"

"It's a long story."

"You're alive and well and out on the street. That's good."

"What happened to you?"

He had a red gash on his cheek that looked like it had recently been a bleeding wound.

"Tracer round. You know how it is. Been on the run now. All of the Bonanza crew."

"Was that your name? Beithune said you wanted us to join. Your posse."

"I did. Good thing you didn't. Beithune said he'd lost you. Went off the deep end."

"Where is he?"

"Picked up. Sent off to the Nenkaja."

"For disruptives?"

"Sure."

She'd known the Nenkaja as a top security prison for disruptive activists. "How do I get there?'

"What, the Nenkaja?"

"Yeah."

"Nobody goes up there. It's up past all shit. Probably I'd forget about Beithune. You'll never see him again."

"How do you know?"

"Don't get angry. Who's the wine for?"

"Not for you."

The way he tried to reach into her bag to take the bottle made Corrag angry. She grabbed it back out of his hand.

"Don't ever take things that don't belong to you."

"Guess you've grown a backbone." He smiled sheepishly.

Corrag gave him a disgusted look and then felt an instant wave of pity. Something about him reminded her of their days of struggle in Williamsburg. Beithune and she had still been under the spell of Beithune's dream of gaining inside access to the world of power and creative mastery. At one point Beithune had genuinely believed that Lars was someone with the key. Now Lars looked like someone who had given up on any means of building a life. Instead he depended on his wits and criminal gains.

His sense of entitlement had disappeared, leaving just a risky bravado.

"Don't go, Corrag. I know how I can help you."

"How? Make it quick. I'm short on time."

"I can get you inside Sandelsky. Isn't that what you and Beithune wanted?"

"Not me. Beithune. How?"

"They have a party tonight for the bigwigs."

"And you're a part of it."

"I just got lucky. One day I was on the street, you know really hungry and tired and I asked this lady for a bit of food. She was eating this big loaf stuffed with meat and olives and sun-dried shit and she told me to come with her and that's how I got the gig. Been going every night for the last week. That's where I'm off to now. Come with me and I can get you in."

"Sorry. I've got to get back to my friends. They're waiting."

"Forget about them. Three or four in the morning after cleaning up'll do you, and they'll have you back every night for the whole month if they like you. Come on."

All the rules of life were upside down. Cesar and Kevin were not going anywhere without her. She went along with Lars, a sense of foreboding mixing with excitement as they approached the back of Sandelsky Plaza. A detachment of Repho military police lingered around the bays that let out on the canal. Corrag dropped her bag of food in an alcove that had once been a storefront. The retractable bimini tops on the boats lined up at the bays were coming down, and men and women in scanty, unseasonal party outfits lounged on leather cushioned berths, conversing and laughing. A few pedestrians approached the entrance along with Lars and Corrag, dressed sensibly against the cold. Inside the arches of the bays, continuing around on the walkway above the water, Corrag spied a security checkpoint. A policewoman with a tablet was checking names and performing scans. Behind her stood two private security guards. Corrag thought she recognized one of them from her first day in the Repho, when Beithune had challenged Shulder inside the Sandelsky showroom. It was the blond giant, the man who had given Beithune the *Absolution* in-tabs. Corrag averted her gaze as Lars approached the policewoman, hoping not to draw attention to herself. If she backed away now it would be suspicious. She had to go through the checkpoint.

"Name?" said the policewoman.

"Lars Guvner," said Lars, looking into the scanner. "Food service. She's with me."

"Name?"

"Yula Kosh."

Corrag looked into the scanner. She heard a beep on the console at the desk. The policewoman stepped away and looked at the console. A boat going through the bay revved its outboard props and popped its bow into the air and the people on board cheered raucously. The policewoman looked over at the two private goons. They smiled at her and shouted at the people in the boat. Corrag looked at Lars who looked back at her nervously.

He looked like he might run in a second, and Corrag tensed, thinking she might have to do the same. The policewoman smiled. Some comforting, warm thought related to the boats and the two guards and the people onboard went through her mind. She looked at the console again, and her eyes glazed for a second, bringing her appointed task back into her consciousness despite the Christmas season. Lars looked at Corrag and almost imperceptibly jerked his head. Corrag scooted past the desk to catch up to him. The policewoman mumbled, and looked up to wave onward the next person in line.

Inside the elevator, Corrag looked at her reflection in the mirrored wall and let out a relieved breath. She did not recognize herself. She smiled at Lars. They had gotten in. If only Beithune could see her now, she thought. She seemed older, her face harder, looking more like Ricky than ever before. She had the Lyons chin that she'd seen in pictures of Ricky's father, Al, on the jacket covers of the books he'd written, one about aviation and one about the natural history of birds. Ricky had always wished she would turn out to be the writer in the family to follow Al. Maybe at last she would do something meaningful that would make him proud.

The party was in full swing on the upper floors of the Sandelsky complex. A man in a white suit grabbed Lars as the elevator doors opened and pushed him towards the back.

"Hurry. Get changed. We need you now."

"She's with me."

"Fine. Get her a fucking frock and get her out there,

too. These people want it all and they want it yesterday!"

In the back rooms where the food was being prepared an Asian woman handed Corrag a frock and smiled when she put it on.

"You're good to go, girl. Just pin your hair back," she said, taking Corrag's hair and sweeping it behind her ear. "Now keep your mouth shut and stay out of people's way. Don't listen to the conversations and you'll be all right. Lots of pretty girls do okay. But lots never come back. Don't be one of those. Come back in here if you need a break. Remember, you're here for a reason. Don't forget what that reason is. Christmas money, baby."

Corrag couldn't help smiling to herself. This was like some book they would read in Miss Schilling's class. Under the flashing lights, in room after room she held her tray aloft and wandered, serving the food and drinks. People called her over in a frenzy of feeding, dancing and talking all at once. The music piped in on the sound system was a blend of patriotic Repho standards and funkier world beats cauterized of their defiance. Corrag's eyes were drawn to the gold and jewels, furs and scrubbed suede animal skins draped from bronzed shoulders and thin arching necks. She noted the lines of mouths, the half smiling, twisted lips of feigned deep contentment betrayed by the eyes. The eyes glanced everywhere at once in a collective hunger that could not be contained for long by any words or points of contact.

"Here, girl," called a young man with a blunt, fuzzy goatee.

"These are very good."

"You must try the rock chevrets."

The guests crowded around, jostling her. Corrag smiled and tried not to make eye contact. She felt her head swirling, about to explode with the music and the lights. Her hunger for real nourishment heightened her sense of the surreal atmosphere of the Sandelsky office party. The walls draped with neon bunting and the transparent columns filled with red and green lights seemed to sway and throb. On the way back to the kitchen she saw Lars with a tray of canapes, his mouth moving, emitting absurd, self-serving bits of randomness. She watched his back and well-oiled mannerisms. Their lack of augmentation gave them both a hunger, she realized, of looking out for themselves in a potentially dangerous environment. Despite herself, she found his attempts to win over the clientele sympathetic. The crowd of Repho elites, all on the Augment, all inside the whale, buzzing on a common chord of impulse and prompt, held people like Lars and her in contempt, a secret not-so hidden behind their wall of shared innuendoes and numbed emotional responses.

Drawn by some kind of inbuilt magnetism down the halls of rooms and alcoves, Corrag continued onward with a fresh tray of drinks. An old man in a grey spandex suit tried to pull her inside a room by the shoulder, but she broke away, barely able to keep the tray from spilling. Before the door closed she caught a glimpse of a dark pile of bodies on furniture. That was enough to make her gag. Even worse were the fighters inside a glass cube, greasy bodies streaming sweat and blood, and the men and women placing bets on the matches. Then somebody vomited and a door swung open. There was a large pool table and an overhead light. Someone called for a drink. Corrag went in and the door closed.

Her tray was empty. She slunk against the curtained wall, unbelieving and wanting to stay. Maxwell Gheko and Samael Chagnon smoked a shared hookah in two fat recliners while their closest aides played pool around a table lit by neon overhead lamps. It had to be them; Corrag was sure, despite never having seen likenesses of either. A sort of halo of power, a nearly visible glow surrounded them. Gheko, the younger of the two, was the more ordinary looking. He seemed like a military man, with thick jowls and long red hair tied in a back bun. Chagnon had the look of a seal, *lobos del mar* as they called them in Rosaria, a sleek fat forehead and a sweeping widow's peak of silver hair, brilliant dark eyes that seemed to take in everything about the room with a single glance. Even though no words were directed at them, every move of the pool players was somehow connected to the two men in the chairs, as if they were black holes bending the visible and invisible around themselves, absorbing the energy into their negative spheres of influence.

"Hey, girl," said a pool player. "Fetch us a bottle of vintage. Enough of the cheap stuff."

"Moet if you please," said another.

Corrag stepped away from the shadows where she'd been leaning against the wall. She thought she would silently leave without bringing further notice to herself. If they only knew who she was they would surely hurt her. And if she only had a weapon she could do away with the crooked leadership of New York in a single blow. As if reading her thoughts, the seated old man she thought was probably Chagnon looked at her with a dour expression. She couldn't help staring back, looking into his eyes for a clue to his humanity or lack thereof. The secretive power behind the Gheko administration's ostensibly democratic governance of the largest, most important city in the Repho, Chagnon had an expression that suggested a sense of inviolable power, but also a curious probing and sorting, as if he were at once dismissive and trying to fit her into a mental scheme.

"Come here, child. You look familiar to me."

Corrag approached, thinking hard about what he could possibly see in her.

"What's your name?"

"Corrag."

His eyes searched hers. They were so cold and bottomless they made Corrag think of a different sort of being, an alien intelligence.

"And you are?"

"With the caterers."

"Unaugmented."

"Yes."

"By choice?"

"By circumstance."

"Where is your home?"

"Edmundstown."

"Ah. You are aware your country is under martial law

and has approached the Repho for military assistance."

Someone around the pool table laughed. Just then the nanowall display lit up, and a man's face appeared on it. Corrag recognized President McKinsky; the receded jaw line and protruding black eyebrows were unmistakable. Walter McKinsky was on his third term in Washington, almost as long as Gheko had been in power, sustaining himself in office by the same opportunistic and shoddy manipulations of public opinion and media control. McKinsky was about to declare an internal war, putting the Korazan and other allied national groups on the terrorist enemy list. As the Repho president's tremulous voice resounded through the soundproofed room, she felt Chagnon grab her wrist.

"Take her down to the desk. Have her searched. We can't take chances at this point, Samael," said the other man she thought was probably Mayor Gheko. He pulled on his hair, fixing the ponytail and leaned back in his seat with the hookah pipe.

"Don't leave. I'll have a word with you when this is over," said Chagnon. Corrag complied, standing limply by his side as the men sucked at the hookah and listened to their ostensible commander-in-chief on the nanowall. The pool players stopped their game and leaned against the table.

"Maxwell, what's happening?" McKinsky asked.

"Not much, Walter. We have to stop meeting like this," croaked Gheko.

"Yeah. Ha. Listen, uh. Maxwell, we have word from intelligence, scraping of media that there's something coming from the KB and associates."

"What, the riffraff are getting uptight. What's new?"

"Listen, man. You know we're going ahead with the cleanse, right? We're moving the schedule up to meet the increased threat level. You need to consult with Hinkle and see that your police units are aligned on this. This is going to be a massive mobilization to make it work cleanly and effectively. The scope of the operation cannot, must not be leaked. Another reason to move the timing up."

"We're in the middle of a big fiesta, Walter. Thought you'd at least send your Vice President to be in on this. Nobody parties like us here in the Big Apple."

"Sorry I missed it. But if we want to maintain our status with the whale we must be ruthless and now is that time, Maxwell. Are you and the Chagster capable of cleaning this situation up? Otherwise we are more than willing to send battle carriers from the Mediterranean with additional air support and personnel."

"That won't be necessary at all, Walter. We've got this tied up. I can't believe you even doubt it."

"I don't. Just doing my due diligence."

"Understood," said Gheko. Then the face faded from the screen and the piped in music resumed.

"Party hardy," said Gheko, grabbing the hookah pipe from Chagnon's outstretched hand as the men and women around the pool table cheered.

"Let the ball drop," said Chagnon, slumping back in the chair.

Two of the men at the table looked at each other.

They approached Gheko. One of them spoke.

"Plans for Operation Alpha?"

"Let Hinkle know we're set to go. Countdown," said Gheko. The two men turned at the same time and walked out of the room. As they went out the door Corrag moved stealthily after them, and Chagnon croaked.

"Wait. Stop her."

Corrag stopped. Chagnon stood shakily. Everyone looked at the two of them, especially at the lizard-like old man as he lurched over to her and held her shoulder with his long-boned, stiff fingers.

"Where are you going?" asked Chagnon.

"To get you more drinks, sir. There was a request for more champagne, I believe."

"I told you I needed to see you. Come with me."

"But, sir."

Chagnon pulled her by the elbow.

"Do you know who I am?" he asked her.

"Yes, sir."

"Then don't say another word. Do you understand?"

"Yes, sir."

He had her elbow in his grip and walked unsteadily out the room and down the hall, past the fighting cube, past the red and green columns, through the crowds and to the bank of elevators. People turned and parted for them. Soldiers at the elevator stood down.

"She's with me," said Chagnon, waving away a policewoman with a scanner at the door. Corrag shivered despite the jets of warm air blowing through the elevator's ventilation system. Chagnon's fingers were unrelenting in their grip. She felt helpless, like a rabbit caught in the jaws of a predator, relaxed and oddly unafraid prior to the mortal bite. The elevator climbed. When it stopped, they were on the top floor of the Sandelsky complex. The elevator door opened, and Corrag recognized at once the black obelisk from MandolinMonkey, with its darkened reflective walls and negative spaces. Chagnon's smile lit up his teeth in a neon glow. She was really on the inside, but unlike Beithune had no desire to be there and, even worse, no plan as to how to get back out.

"Relax your mind. Don't think of anything. Don't try to block it. You could black out if you do. The neutrino wave will overpower any resistance."

They were sitting on opposite sides of a box of inbuilt scanners, staring at each other over the top. Chagnon continued:

"This is my latest design. The Memory Sponge. Demand is soaring. It can establish connectivity between any two people, sieving memory banks and correlating patterned nodes.

"So? What does that mean?"

"You and I, Corrag, will establish the links between us."

"Links?"

"That is right. The times and manners we have been together in multidimensional space that may have transpired either with or without our conscious knowledge, or without leaving a strong enough memory marker. If I told you I needed to see you, it was because my extraordinarily attuned senses detected something familiar about you."

"Will you have access to all my memories?"

"I could, but that's not my intent. So don't worry. I don't really care or want to have a read-out of your entire life taking up space in my mind, even in the cloud. Although there are uses for that. But I just want to know if and how we are linked. I want to prove a hunch. See if my mental apparatus is as sharp as I think it is. Is that understood?"

"How long will this take?"

"Just a few minutes. Relax. Otherwise I'll have to strap you in and force a reading. You don't want me to do that."

She had no choice. She leaned forward into the box and opened her eyes. A strange light flashed. She lost consciousness. When she came to her senses again she was sitting in a metal chair at a plain white table, and Chagnon was sitting beside her wiping her forehead with a damp cloth.

"Some people have a stronger reaction than others."

"Are we linked?" mumbled Corrag, dreading the response. The thought of being in any kind of a relationship with Chagnon was repellent to her.

"No," he said. He sounded disappointed. "Although there was a hint of an echo correlation. Sometimes the patterns are quite complex. One of the possible answers is the multidimensionality of time, along with space. My next advance will be to take the memory sponge into parallel frames, using a quantum dark matter tracer. Dark matter remains embedded at the quantum level, even in offspring, and leaves a time stamp of decay which it may be possible to read."

He stopped talking to wipe his own sweating forehead. Corrag had the sense that he was not even very aware of her physical presence. He was talking to himself. He stared into the console.

"You really need to be augmented, kid."

"I'm not interested, really."

"Why not? You want to be part of the future, don't you? History has no time for losers. The unaugments will be rounded up and forcibly made to choose between ignorance and reason. Some of them, the recalcitrant or delusional will be terminated. There is just too much at stake. It's a shame. I am not in favor of violence. Do you know that all of our actions leave quantum tracers in our genes that get handed down to our children? That's why I have decided not to procreate. Please, do yourself a favor. Don't have children. And become an augmented citizen of the Homeland before it's too late."

"Funny. For all your technological wizardry and intellectual brilliance," said Corrag, smiling to herself. She remembered Kevin and Cesar, her friends, waiting for her in the park, and the bag of food she'd hidden outside the building. "I need to go, sir," she said.

"You can't. It's too dangerous. I must make sure you're safe. Stay with me, Corrag."

"Without a choice, without freedom, without a history? What would it be? There are bots for that."

He was silent, and Corrag waited.

"Promise me you'll come back. Here. This is my

access card. I have many more. Get yourself into Sandelsky if you're in any trouble, any at all, and I'll make sure you have the best augment in the world."

"And which one is that?"

"The Sandelsky Gold Plan. Everybody knows that."

"Okay. I promise." She took the shining card from his outstretched hand, invisible in the negative light. He stared hard at her, with the gleaming whites of his eyes surrounding the black holes of his pupils. But she felt safe inside her head. He couldn't reach her now.

She rode the elevator to the ground floor with three Sandelsky security officers, their emosponders crackling with bits of heightened information. Outside the main entrance, a unit of Repho National Guard troops had assembled in the square, carrying snub nosed, laser assault rifles and nanofiber shields. Quadcopter bots bristling with missiles shot down the canyons of midtown in the night sky. Corrag hurried, pressing up the avenue to get back to the park.

An air of imminent panic had taken over the city. There were people rushing in all directions, and the boats in the canal were all headed north out to the river. Corrag didn't notice the silence that had fallen until she heard her name in the shadows and realized she was alone on the sidewalk. There in a doorway were Kevin and Cesar, the Bograd and supply bags at their feet.

"Corrag. Here."

She ducked in beside them and went to her knees. She didn't say anything, just holding her breath, holding their hands, eyes closed in prayer, not believing in the luck she'd had to run right across the Korazan Brigade's front line. As her eyes adjusted she could see figures crouched in the doorways across the canal up and down in both directions. Occasional pedestrians continued to run by on the sidewalk, oblivious, not wanting to know what was going down.

"The Alpha battle will begin with you, Corrag. When we fire, that is the signal," said Kevin, his hand on her shoulder, bringing her to her senses.

Corrag knew that.

It would be her call to set the match to a fight that would certainly destroy lives and hopefully the corruption of the Repho. The enemy, she now knew, were small men, old and feeble in their desires, straddling the world with large shadows cast by their technology and their delusions. If only Korazan could see Chagnon up close in his frailty and uncertainty, would he still seek this war? She wanted to say something, but Kevin would not understand. His face was set in hard lines, his eyes casting into the distance for the sight of a predetermined vision. They had trained and prepared for this. Again she had no choice.

"Come on, then," she said. "Follow me."

The streetlights went off after a tremulous last flicker. She took them as far as they could go back down the darkened avenue, until the National Guard troops on Sandelsky Plaza were within earshot, the sounds of the officers' communications on their emosponders coming out of the night along with the faint glow of lithium lightsticks that must have hung around their necks. Then, without speaking, they put into practice what they'd learned in the weeks of drill, assembling the Bograd by feel, in the dark. They worked seamlessly, and Kevin had the hard drive and the hydrogen tank connected and tapped the ground with his foot as a signal. Corrag turned and lifted the mid-barrel to Cesar's shoulders and placed herself in front to handle the sighting lens, cranking up the extension with one squeeze of the grip.

They were out on the sidewalk in full view of the plaza. It was dangerous, but with effort she forced the thought of fear from her mind, replacing it with the words of the Edmundstown Upper School mission: "*Smile all the while*". The image of Ricky appeared in her mind then superimposed on the words of the motto as they appeared on Ms. Schilling's nanoboard. The quadcopters of the Repho National Guard's 44th Air Wing stationed across Long Island Sound slowed in their reconnoitering over the plaza, then dipped before they picked up speed, telegraphing their direction. When the box went green she pulled the trigger. A bolt of ions established the path for the fireball. The quadcopter fragmented at a distance of about 900 meters above street level. The explosion's remnants, balls of flaming destruction, screwballed into the side of the Sandelsky building, and sent the soldiers in the plaza diving for cover.

"Corrag!" It was Kevin calling her. She turned, and he was pointing behind them into the sky where a quadcopter had settled, hovering. Cesar and Corrag maneuvered the barrel around and Corrag quickly sighted. She pulled the trigger. The quadcopter fired at the same time. The water in the canal emptied over their heads. Through the water she could see another ball of fire come floating down to earth. She turned, and Kevin and Cesar were urging her along. The dim figures of Korazan fighters moved up the sidewalk, hunched over with their Sig Saurs in their hands, pumping their free fists in the air in encouragement. She heard a long burst of automatic fire from the plaza. They fell, taking cover in the doorways. When her Bograd team reached the bridge, Corrag could clearly see the National Guard troops not more than 100 yards away, setting up rocket stations and piling sandbags as quickly as they could around the perimeter of the plaza. She turned to Kevin.

"Set it to Scorch." There were two settings on the surger, Tangent and Scorch. Scorch would burn everything in the path of the ions out to a preset distance. It would also use up the hydrogen propellant at a much quicker rate. Kevin gave the thumbs up. Cesar lifted the barrel, and he and Corrag stepped around the stone column of the bridge. Corrag set the crosshairs on the main door of the Sandelsky building and pulled the trigger. She knew she would never forget the cries of pain and anger of the National Guard soldiers as they were engulfed in the Bograd's blue flame. The fire swept the plaza from right to left, burning everything combustible on it down to ash in a matter of seconds. The heat was overwhelming. The smell of burning plastic mingled with the smell of charred flesh. The flame ball turned blue, and the fire receded back along the ion path as the hydrogen in the tank ran out. Corrag dropped the end of the barrel and doubled over. She fell wretching and stumbling down to the water's edge. Kevin grabbed her from behind, stopping her before she tumbled over the low wall.

"Get it out. It's in my eyes."

"Relax, Corrag. It's just smoke."

"My eyes are burning, Kevin."

"Relax."

Corrag could see in her mind's eye the canyon wall of the San Pedro dam behind Ben Calder. She could see Joan Hunnewell in the doorway of the Northern Lights farm. Her legs were heavy and she felt a strange weakness overcome her. Immediately she sensed the root of the sensation -- a new life stirring inside her, the flowing water that Abel Marin had urged her to follow. When she opened her eyes again, she could see Cesar against the stone column working the hard drive on the surger. Kevin turned her to face him. He looked determinedly into her eyes, his expression as enigmatic as ever to her. Behind him there were cargo boats coming up the canal from under the GW Bridge, barely visible in the distance. They were Repho troop transports. She was seized with a new thought; the threat that these boats posed was more dangerous than anything they could have foreseen. She heard Cesar's voice insistently breaking in on her musings.

"General wants us falling back right away. I relayed initial attack and that's all he wants. 'The day is done,' he said. Fall back at once is the orders."

"We can't. Let the others know to follow the orders. We go on. Inside."

"What?" Cesar was incredulous.

"I know where the network center is. We can liberate all the augments today. Destroy the Repho's surveillance and control capabilities."

"Corrag. You don't disobey the General when he says fall back."

"I know what I'm doing. You're free to go. Both of you." Corrag's look took in both men. The boats were now approaching the stone tidal barrier lining the avenue. They could see the orderly movement of troops on the decks. Cesar turned to Kevin.

"Brother, you can stay with her if you're crazy."

"I am."

Cesar took no longer than was necessary. He unlocked the hard drive from the surger and spoke into it as he moved with it slowly back to the corner of the avenue.

"Korazan troops disengage from the fight. Orderly retreat to base positions and assume street cover."

Kevin and Corrag stood together on the bridge over the canal, holding their bootleg Chinese made Sig Sauer .40 calibers. Ahead of them were the plaza and the burning remnants of the National Guard deployment. Behind them came the sound of armored zipbikes cranking up on the Hudson River landings. The men on the decks loading the zipbikes with ammunition and modifying their programs with mental synchronizers had the look, Corrag guessed, of augment shock troops, a development in the Repho state's arsenal of force -- augmented men, drawn from the prisons and rehab centers, who voluntarily or involuntarily gave themselves over as human-bot hybrids and were said to constantly receive superhuman doses of serotonin and dopamine supplements as a reward for their services.

It was too late now for them to join the retreat. There was only one way to go and that was dead ahead across the bridge, which would take them to the back of the plaza nearest the main entrance to the Sandelsky building. The bridge was nearly empty except for the strewn bodies of burnt soldiers concentrated at the opposite end. Corrag looked at Kevin. He was unhurried and calm, waiting for the right moment to act. Corrag took heart from his demeanor. The hardest part would be getting across the plaza without taking fire from survivors of the Bograd attack.

"Kevin, follow me."

"Yes, Corrag."

Corrag tucked the gun back into the shoulder holster. She broke into a run and Kevin kept up at her side. Together they reached the other side of the bridge without breaking stride. They dodged the casualties of the Bograd assault, still writhing and smoking where they had fallen. Corrag felt herself flying as they reached the main entrance and pushed through the revolving glass doors. It felt like a moment ago that she had done the same with Beithune upon arriving for the first time in the Repho after her tubid trip from Democravia. Ahead of her were the same blond giant that had greeted them and the Mongolian looking boy, Shulder, that Beithune had successfully fought in a barrier challenge. They were standing amidst a group of armed men and women that comprised the Sandelsky private security arsenal, half of them on emosponders and the other half standing around looking dazed, as if in a state of shock. Corrag swallowed hard and strode forward barehanded. Kevin stepped up beside her silent and stone-faced.

"Howdy, folks. Uhm, who's in charge here?" she asked. The group turned as one and stared at the two of them. "It's us. The reconnaissance unit," she continued confidently. "Ranger Brigades. Operation Street Clean. We need to secure the network center here. Orders from Hinkle."

"How'd you get here?" asked the giant.

"The Navy, man. I didn't call a water cab. Fares too high this time of year." There was suppressed laughter, and Corrag could sense some of the danger dissipate. One of the Sandelsky guards got on his emosponder.

"Look, I don't have time. Tell the people upstairs we need to secure the building against further attacks, and we need to move fast."

"You'll need to do the security scan first. Just procedure," said the giant.

"I have this from General Hinkle," said Corrag, flashing the Sandelsky access card. The giant took it from her and inspected it closely, turning it over several times in his enormous hands.

"We'll accompany you." He motioned with a nod of his head to Shulder, and the boy stepped forward eagerly, feeling for the emosponder strapped to his throat. They followed Shulder over to the elevators. Inside, the low hum of the generators told her the area power grid had been affected by the fighting. She looked at Kevin and he looked back with a slight question on his face. Shulder was making him nervous. But she gave a minimal shake of her head to put Kevin off the idea of any action to take Shulder out. They needed to get to the top of the building, across several layers of security, to the hall where she believed the network's main servers were housed. The elevator was sure to have cameras and motion sensors installed.

After a long journey of vertical, horizontal and then vertical ascents, the elevator stopped at the top floor. Shulder stepped aside and let the door open beside him. Then he stopped and waved them ahead. As Corrag stepped beside him at the door she had her hand on her gun. Without pulling it from its holster, she leaned against Shulder and coldly pulled the trigger. The shock of the gun blast pushed him back against the far wall of the elevator where he slumped to the ground as the doors closed.

Wordlessly, she led Kevin down the darkened hall. At the junction of corridors a team of high-level advisers walked quickly past them. Corrag recognized several young men from the poolroom the previous night. Their well-fed good looks had been replaced by fearful, browbeaten expressions. Corrag saw at close range the effect of the Korazan attack in the faces of the swiftly walking young Gheko administration aides. The orderly structure on which their lives of comfort had been based had been pulled out from under them, leaving a chasm in their hearts that they had never before imagined. Pale-faced, terrorized, they did not even give the two intruders a passing glance. Corrag looked in both directions down the corridors and thought she saw the door she was looking for. It was, she hoped, the entrance to the dream laboratory, where she had been tested in the Memory Sponge. In the door was an eye scan. Corrag put her face to it. Kevin held her arm. In his other hand was his gun, ready to blast his way in.

"No. It's okay, Kevin. This is what we have to do. We're almost in."

"But you can't have the clearance."

"I'm on the data banks."

"You are?"

"Yes."

As if on cue the door latch made a clicking sound. Corrag pulled it open and they both slipped inside. There was the Memory Sponge, Chagnon's latest toy, and against the far wall the long series of output boards for the cloud server's hard drives, the central nervous system of the Sandelsky dream machine. It now fed the augmentation program of the entire North American grid, Repho and Democravian. Bar graphs alternated with colored flowcharts monitoring minute-by-minute energy and informational throughputs. If she could locate the actual servers there would be nothing standing in the way of her improvised plan to decimate the augment system that Sandelsky was now relying on to install itself in power, via cloud server mind manipulations from coast to coast in a bloodless, anti-democratic coup. Her mind was clear with the resolution to act and a secret joy that she would not be deterred by fear of failure. This was Ben's gaming advantage, what he'd tried to teach her. Any false move she made was sure to bring on a massive response from the company's security apparatus. Once they began, it was most likely they would not end. There would be no way to get out safely; just the slimmest chance that with a successful attack they could leverage any subsequent chaos in the chain of command to mount an escape. Still, she could not look back; only trust herself.

"Okay Kevin. We need to locate the servers."

"Where are they?"

"I don't know. Somewhere in here."

She sat in a swivel chair and the Memory Sponge lit up like a Christmas tree. Kevin sat down opposite.

"Is this it, Corrag?"

"No, Kevin. This isn't it. I'm just thinking." She sounded harsh and impatient. Kevin looked hurt.

"What is this, then?"

"This is the Memory Sponge. To determine unknown links between people. They use it in interrogations."

There was no sense testing their links. It was too far-fetched to think of any way they could have crossed paths back in time before the Korazan training camp. She couldn't believe she was even thinking of something so preposterous. She tried hard to refocus, puting her hands on both sides of her face and staring at the ground between her feet. How to determine where to start? If she thought hard enough, the idea would come. That was the best method. The funny thing, she realized, was that the link between them far outweighed anything the Memory Sponge could pick up.

"Kevin. There's something you need to know. I'm sorry I've been somewhat distant lately."

"What do you mean, Corrag?"

"I mean we have a baby. I'm pregnant."

"What? Corrag. This is ... this means..."

"Don't say anything, Kevin."

"Corrag. It's my child. Our child, I mean. We have to get out to safety."

"There's only one way out. Let's find the servers."

"Where?"

"I don't know."

"Look for them. Come on."

Kevin began to move around the room, waving his gun nervously, jerking and changing direction. It hurt Corrag and put her in a foul mood.

"Kevin. Stop."

She stood from the Memory Sponge and walked over to the output wall. The graphs never varied their displays of colored bars and lines. It all meant the Sandelsky machine was functioning as normal, regulating the hopes and dreams of half a billion people, the combined subject populations of the Repho and Democravian states; issuing the behavioral cues that aligned the population with resource flows and market demands. The display synthesized the internal, secret lives of her countrymen in a neat and reasonable fashion, but Corrag could almost smell the rot represented behind the graphic display: the mind control systems on both sides of the continent that had melded and warped to the interests of the elites sitting on Council Boards, Legislative Advisory Units, Citizen's Desks and other such apparatuses of rule to keep themselves and their cohorts in comfortable, superior, augmented safety.

"I'll shoot it, Corrag. Fuck it." Kevin was crazed, waving his gun at the output wall as if at some demonic force. Corrag had no idea where to go. She walked over to the wall and began to feel her way along with her hands, knocking with her fist, hoping for a soft spot in the synthetic tiles. It was crazy, she had to admit. It had to be here. The servers had to be in this top floor hidden away somewhere.

Then she saw it, a straight vertical line in the pattern of tiles on the next wall. She walked closer and examined the line and saw that it turned perpendicular overhead, a gap just a few microns wide. She pushed all around but felt no give. She pulled her gun and took careful aim at the edge of the frame where a door latch should have been and fired. The gun kicked back in her hands. She looked at the panelled, secret door. It had swung open.

The open door revealed an immensely long warehouse space filled with interminable stacks of six-foot tall, glass-encased brown wafers set on edge and lit by green LEDs. These were the circuit boards. The glass cases were connected by thick strands of multi-colored cables that ran everywhere along the floors. Above the stacks were wide pipes of coolant that came down in J bends and looped around in U bends to form an intricate maze of rigid nanofiber ductwork in the ceiling space.

The entire room gave off an almost undetectable background hum that filled Corrag and Kevin with an awesome dread, as if some strange insect life would assume the shape of a swarm and attack. Corrag walked deep into the stacks and shot at the glass casing. Her action had no effect. The casing was bullet proof. She tried tugging at the cables, but the lengths seemed to disappear into the ground. There didn't seem to be an obvious grouping that would power the whole warehouse down; instead there was just an amorphous network of lookalike, thick colored strands as far as she could see. Kevin jumped up to see what was beyond the row they were in. Corrag ran, panicked, down the rows of glass encased circuitry, the innards of a demonic maze. She was running out of time. There was sure to be an alarm sounding somewhere and Repho bot troops rushing in to gun them down.

"The pipes, Kevin. Can we shut them down?"

"How?"

"Lift me up there."

Corrag held herself against the glass and stepped up on Kevin's shoulders and from there into the ceiling space, swinging herself onto the aluminum girders that shelved the pipes. Then she crawled in the darkened roof space along their tops. Some were warm, carrying away the excess heat from the servers. Others were ice cold, filled with seawater pumped from the harbor. She heard stamping boots and saw the helmeted heads of hybrid troops from off the Navy troop carriers. There was a blast of gunfire, and she heard Kevin's gargled scream. A chill of numbing panic ran through her body, threatening her balance. For a few minutes she wavered on the edge of consciousness, lying flat, hugging on the warm pipe with her cheek against it. She was on her own now, but determined to do what it took to sabotage the Sandelsky machine before they brought her down. She went at the rubberized U bend expansion pipes with her combat knife and renewed vigor, hacking into their skins. Then water began to flow, falling in a pressurized hiss onto the floor. She crawled slowly and then faster as she gained confidence to the next section, jumping the space between the rows of pipes along the girders without attracting attention from the bot-men below, as they wordlessly stalked up and down the rows. They had cameras mounted on their helmets, swiveling in all directions under the centralized direction of the human handlers on board the transport ship.

Meanwhile, Corrag's work with the knife was having an effect. The human-bot troops began to slide and fall on the slick floor, and she could see the haze of LED lights from the stacks blinking and changing color. Flashes of red and orange from around the warehouse warned of grid rerouting amid load failure from overheated network branches. She had gotten the hang of slashing through the pipe bends with just a few draws of the serrated knife blade, and the satisfying gush of water was a signal to keep moving. Then a shot rang out near her, and she froze again in fear. She heard a voice call her name. She pushed off with her foot to get away. She slipped.

Floodlights came flashing on, blinding her, as she lay

stunned on the ground, expecting at any moment to feel a flood of metal ripping her apart and sundering consciousness from the body that had gotten her so far. She heard her name.

"Corrag. Are you all right? Your father and I have been sick with worry."

She looked up slowly. Silhouetted in the light was the figure of her mother in a long evening dress as if she were about to entertain in the old house on Durkiev Drive.

"Mom? Is that you?"

"Yes. I've come. How could you involve yourself, Corrag? An emissary after all, does not bite the hand that feeds her."

"But Democravia no longer exists, Mother. Or does it?"

"It's the principle of the thing, dear. Who are these people you've been helping? It's going to be all right. You must tell me."

Alana was kneeling. Her copper hair was a little greyer, but her eyes and face looked just the same, the proud cheekbones and thin lips with the slight Hunnewell twist. Corrag stayed where she was, sitting with arms around her knees. The warehouse was silent, just her and Alana talking. She had so many questions for her mother. But the coiled spring inside her, wound tight, ready to fight for her survival, was keeping the words from flowing freely.

"Tell me dear. Where are they?"

"I can't tell you, Mother."

"If you don't there will be repercussions. Your father

and I, Corrag...”

"Where is Father?"

"Your father and I have been worried sick, dear. Now tell me where I can find them."

"Who?"

"The Korazan."

"Why, Mother?"

"Your father and I have been worried sick."

"I can't tell you. Get me out of here, Mother."

"Where is the Korazan Brigade?" Her voice went a shade darker suddenly and she stood, backing away.

"Mother!" Corrag screamed as the illusion faded. A pair of arms grabbed her from behind and put her in a chokehold as she fought to escape. They had her down on her stomach, and then were cuffing her wrists together, putting a bag over her head. She couldn't breathe. They let up and stood away and were talking. Lifting her up by the wrists, they lead her away in the total darkness. That hurt, the way they lifted and dragged her. But nothing compared to the pain in her head. She had fallen for it. It had been Alana, but only a hologram. Of all the cheap tricks, that was the worst. A projection to get her to talk. It had fooled her. She felt let down by her own mind, usually her most reliable ally. It had been turned. And now she was a prisoner again. And alone. Corrag weighed her options. If she had a chance she would attack her captors and force their hand. Death was the best escape, her most reliable ally now.

She was strapped into a seat and left alone. Hours later she could hear the pilot speaking the staccato commands associated with flight permissions and routes. The lift off was straight up, then the rotors tilted and the plane accelerated horizontally. After some minutes, Corrag drifted off, sleeping fitfully, resting her head as best she could in her shackled position. But she kept jerking awake, feeling as if she was falling from the overhead pipes in the server warehouse and about to get shot. So she couldn't tell what direction or for how long they'd been flying when someone shook her roughly awake.

Wordlessly, they were pushing her out through the hatch with her hands still shackled and head covered. She went down some rickety stairs into a bitterly cold air. Her skin, where exposed, felt like it would freeze and fall off. There was some sunlight, though. It must have been morning. She heard English spoken on the ground by the airport workers greeting the plane's crew. She had some hope for an acceptable outcome, some civilized answer to the question of where she was and what was to be expected of her. She wasn't sure she would fight when the hood came off, or whether or not an attempt to escape was still the best answer. The hours of darkness and fitful dreaming had acquainted her with a new reality. She was not alone. She had a baby. There was a life inside her. Everything was changed. Before the flight it had been an unreal dream, an idea of a different country that she was bound for with no strict travel schedule. But the enforced sensory deprivation, the surrender to fate of the long flight and the arrival in a new morning, despite her captivity, her status as a conquered prisoner, had opened her to this strange flowering. The timing of her awakening had all the markings of destiny, a destiny she still did not believe in, but now could not argue with. She was in a mess.

Six -- The Nenkaja

The country was long and flat and in the ice floes of the sea there seemed to reside a monumental despair that breathed out mists and inhaled sick laughter. There was very little light to work by, and yet they made the prisoners work long eighteen-hour shifts, lit by halogen lamps powered with the snowmobiles. It was cold, and every night some died before they could get back inside at the end of a shift. They left the bodies to be recovered in the spring when the ground would melt to bury them or burn them in the garbage pits. The food rations, raw whitefish soaked in vinegar served on dinged-up metal plates and occasional breakfast rolls flown in from the Repho in the C-22 Navy transports out of St. John, were doled out according to work rate, so that if you were strong you could get stronger. The weak ones died. There were many that died. In a short time Corrag became hardened and stopped keeping track. She was in the women's camp, and Beithune was surely in the men's camp which was somewhere beyond the long, flat ice and darkness that surrounded them in the Nenkaja.

Their job was woodcutting. There were piles of logs they chopped out of the ice and then chainsawed to length. The chainsaws were recharged in the generator house. It was a place to get out of the cold and thaw out fingers and toes. But Corrag didn't like to hang out too long. It took away time from the cutting. There were women who said it was better to stay warm then to eat, but Corrag was eating for two. As soon as the feelings returned to her fingers she grabbed her chainsaw and headed out the door into the darkness and silence of the night broken by the headlamps and the mechanical sounds of the saws burring against the grain of the spruce logs. Her quota was twenty logs for the night. She was about halfway through. The enforcers were staying in their tent. That was unusual. They usually liked to roam through the cut yard and goad the women, even when it got below zero. Most of them had risen through the ranks of the Nenkaja, had had the augment and the opportunity to rejoin the Repho, but had chosen the life of enforcers. They said it got under your skin. Corrag didn't think that would be her case. She would get out somehow. Her term was the standard five years at the end of which her case would be set before the commander and the board of trustees in New York, and if she was deemed a good prisoner she would be given the chance for an augment and rehabilitated back into society on good terms. Or at least that was the promise made by Dr. Juarez-Knoblock, the camp commander.

"You're doing good, Corrag," said Betty, one of the older prisoners. She had survived three stretches, back to the beginning of the Nenkaja with the first Repho administration under President Ryan, when it had housed just a few high-ranking jihadists from Guantanamo and Federation sympathizers. Betty was slowing down, and had lost three toes to gangrene, but there were other prisoners who would help her out, make sure she had socks. The key to survival, said Betty in the bunks at night at the end of a shift, nursing her blackened feet, was keeping one good pair of dry socks at all times. That and eating. Corrag already noticed that some of the women had lost their appetites, and the others would swoop in like vultures and steal their food as soon as they turned their heads. They didn't seem to mind, had accepted the fact that they were on their last legs. They called these girls the ten-milers because they all had a ten-mile stare into the blankness. Corrag swallowed hard and smiled at Betty.

"Cold though."

"You go, girl. You beat the cold."

"Thanks, Betty."

Corrag switched on the saw and it started up without a hitch, running strong after the recharge. The chain was still sharp, and it bit into the frozen spruce with a satisfying pull. Despite the menial nature of the work, Corrag took pride in her ability to judge the length of the cuts and stack the cords neatly. There was satisfaction in a job well done, no matter the recompense. She thought Ricky and Alana would be proud of her. The chainsaw pulled straight through the two-foot diameter log, and Corrag was grateful for a good tool. They sharpened their own chains, and Corrag had become an expert, filing the burrs by the glint of petroleum candlelight and sighting with squinted eyes in her bunk. She slept with her boots by her side under her hands, not wanting to have them stolen away by jealous fellow prisoners, and the file went under her pillow. During the day she hid it between cracks in the floorboard under her bunk, covering it with her pile of clothes. The older prisoners, and even the younger ones, offered to trade her bread for a sharpening job. Sometimes she accepted and sometimes she did not. She stopped, set the chainsaw down and crunched the snow in her rubber boots, pulling the chopped lengths of log out of the snow, piling them four or five at a time in a wheelbarrow and wheeling the barrow to the center of the yard where the cords were stacked. The enforcers were charged with keeping track of everybody's cut rate and used this responsibility to set the women up against each other, cheating one out of wood to favor another. It was just the way it was in the Nenkaja. To expect human decency was a fatal mistake. At some point in the night it was just you and the cold fighting it out, no other thoughts allowed. A voice, an appeal to common language and its emotional content, stole the life energy that could spell the difference between survival or death. It was that way, night after night. And it would be until the spring. That was Corrag's goal, to survive long enough for the spring to give her baby a chance.

"You. Take your wheelbarrow over to Chicago."

The enforcer was talking to her. Chicago was in a lumpy sector of fir and black spruce saplings that had never been properly cleared and was covered with drifts of snow some eight to ten feet thick. She would never get her quota there.

"That's not my sector, sister. I've already been assigned."

"You heard me. Any more lip and it'll be the Bunkhouse where you finish off the night."

The Bunkhouse was an ironically named naked rock, a glacial erratic that sat unusually high off the water's edge surrounded by ice floes. Women assigned for punishment were chained there sometimes in shirtsleeves to face the winds coming off the water. It was a death sentence. Sometimes in their bunks, in the cinderblock hangar that was their shelter, the women could hear the cries of a prisoner, the last lungful of reproach before succumbing to silence, the wail of a living ghost, coming from the Bunkhouse. Corrag had never seen it and didn't ever want to. There were many ghosts in the camp, but especially the enforcers. Corrag did not know what this one looked like under the fur hat and the long thick felt, fur-lined overcoat. She hated her, but even hatred was superfluous. She dumped the load and went back for her chainsaw and trudged across the cutting yard with it, crossing paths with other prisoners who avoided shining their lights up at her face.

There was a pickaxe leaning at an angle in the snow. Corrag put her chainsaw down. Nobody had been at work here all night, she could see, by the absence of boot prints in the freshly layered pallor. In the light of the headlamp she could see the barest evidence of wood under the ice, the curve of a log here and there. She walked up and down. A warm glow spread from her chest. It was anger. It spread down her arms into her wrist. The pickaxe felt like an extension of her arm. She swung it hard at the ice along the edge of the curve of dark log. It bit and split off splinters of sharp wet that hit her in the face. There was a chance she could get at the log. There was a chance she could find others logs buried in the ice. There was absolutely no chance she would make her quota in the remaining time before the end of her battery charge. But any bread was better than no bread. Corrag would not be denied. For the sake of the life in her she swung again and again, feeling the fire in her chest and the sweat breaking out.

She stopped. Too much sweat was a danger. That meant chilled skin and hypothermia and incapacity and starvation -- the end. The quick way of the end was preferable to the slow. The quick way was a fever and unconscious and then being left out in the yard in your underwear for what they called the night cure. The slow way was sickness, shitting your guts out with dysentery and your body too weak to recover and slowly in your bunk taking leave of your possessions and your food ration, willing them to the survivors and drifting off in a moaning bad dream. There was never a pleasant or decorous death the slow way, whereas the quick way, they said, left a smile on the face in the mornings when the clean up detail was charged with taking the body and dragging it to the burn pile. The hardened prisoners liked this detail because sometimes the dead held their most prized possessions still clutched in their hands, hidden away until the end, a ring or gold earring, a remnant of femininity as a token for the passage.

Her clothes would only dry out back in the hangar. She would have to be strategic. In this way Corrag balanced herself. The decisions she made were crucial. And failure was by no means inevitable. She had to know this in order to think clearly.

It took her more than an hour to get enough of the log free of the ice to make a cut. But instead of sawing she climbed on the end, straddling it like a horse and began to buck up and down on it with bent knees so as to keep her weight off the ground. She made a strange figure if anybody had been watching, a jockey on some imaginary mount. The log was immobile, trapped solidly and permanently at the starting gate. But imperceptibly and slowly she felt it giving way, and then at last it broke free by a couple of inches, enough space to get the end of the pickaxe in and heave with all her might. It rolled over the lip of the ice and came to rest a few inches from its previous alignment. Corrag rested, breathing hard, leaning on the pickaxe. Only then did she start the chainsaw up and set it to work on the closest end.

It took almost the entire rest of the shift. When Corrag wheeled her first barrow load of cut logs to the center of the yard, a thin band of light was visible coming over the flat tundra to the south like a window facing out on sweetness and music. All the enforcers emerged from the charging shed to watch her as she dumped the load and began to add the logs to the stack. The fiercest among them, an old battleaxe named Marilyn Muslkick, a former policewoman in Tampa Bay, Florida who had originally been sent up for drug dealing and murder, came walking out to where Corrag was stacking. They said she had killed with her bare hands several of the toughest prisoners during her time as an enforcer. Even Juarez-Knoblock, the camp commander, feared her. Often he walked through the kitchen and dining room chatting to the prisoners, but when he saw Muslkick on duty he made his walk through quickly and quietly, hands behind his back like a professor, albeit a professor with old school heavy metal tattoos covering half his face. Muslkick was known to disapprove of Juarez-Knoblock's predilection for intermittently picking one or two of the younger prisoners as favorites and using them as staff in his office. It was a coveted duty despite the hatred it could engender and the danger of reprisals. Muslkick was said by some to be a jilted lover of Juarez-Knoblock's, but others denied this vehemently, and there were fights that started among the prisoners still over this element of the camp's mythology.

On this dawn in particular Corrag sensed her ambivalence. Muslkick carried her tablet in one hand and pretended to make notes with the other, using her gloved finger to tap at it. The sun on the horizon behind Corrag lit up the condensation emerging from Muslkick's nose in wisps, like a dragon. She looked up and stared at Corrag with eyes lit red.

"You are short of quota. You know that, right?"

"Would have made it," said Corrag, saving her breath.

"Would have and could have do not earn the bread in the Nenkaja. Maybe you should just abort the bastard and lighten your load."

"Never."

"Don't expect any sympathy from me."

"Then give me the check and let me go."

"You're not done."

"I'm done. I can't do any more. Just short me the bread."

Muslkick stared hard at her with eyes that gave off an unbroken hostility.

"I will break you, you little whore, if you so much as raise your head above the ground. You understand me? Now I'm going to give you a little hint. Save your white ass a whooping and listen to me. There's only one way to survive the Nenkaja. Toughness is not that way. Kindness is not that way. You need to be wicked. North Country wicked."

Corrag stared back, feeling the air fill her lungs. That was better than words.

"Is that it?" she asked at last.

"That is it." Muslkick turned and walked back to the shed. The women left standing at the door included prisoners and enforcers. Sometimes there was little to distinguish between the two groups at a distance.

Three more barrow loads. The sun was higher in the sky. The wind picked up and froze Corrag's face a little harder. She wiped it with the sleeve of her coat and noticed the chainsaw oil mixed with hardened snot on the back of it. It had to be all over her face that she'd been wiping all night long. She dropped the chainsaw at the charging terminal after unclipping the chain. She was the last one back to the hangar. Inside the door, the blast of heat from the woodstove greeted her with life saving intensity. She dragged herself over to the bunk and sat on the edge and held herself from crying. Someone had messed up the pile of clothes under the bed. She fell to her knees. When she reached under she noticed the file still in the crack. Thanking the eternal power of Providence, Corrag felt the creature twist inside her. It was hungry. She was famished, on the edge. With all her strength, she undid the buttons on her coat with cramped hands and fell back on the bed.

Hours of a dreamless sleep later, there was someone tugging at her feet. She opened her eyes. Betty was loosening her boots. She sat up like a bolt of lightning.

"You gotta keep dry socks, Corrag. How many times have I told you?"

"Oh, yeah." She tugged off her boots and socks with her hands.

"The girls are talking about you."

"What are they saying?"

"Apparently you pulled a hard one last night."

"I don't know if I can go back out there. I didn't make quota."

"Don't worry. Get some sleep. I'll wake you up for dinner time."

"Thanks, Betty."

The older woman pulled the thin sheet over her and she pulled herself into a ball and instantly fell back asleep. When she awoke she felt sick, disoriented and thirsty. Her legs felt bloated and unable to move. She fought the urge to lie there in the dim light when she knew there was a lineup in the dining room. She could hear the voices, the clanking of dishes on the crude hewn tables. The smell of warm bread rolls and cabbage filled the hangar. That bread and the soup, cabbage and potato in a thin gruel, was the eternal Nenkaja winter ration. Corrag had never imagined being as hungry as she was now. Betty talked often in the dark in the next bunk about the food in the summer. They were allowed to gather berries in their free time and they boiled them down in makeshift pits, using cups as pans to make jam. The idea of jam was like a promise of eternal life to Corrag now.

She struggled to get her boots on and joined the line with her plate in her hands. The tables were filling with the women prisoners, smirking and pulling faces despite the exhausted and deep set eyes, the hair tied back with little care or let loose to hang raggedly in disarray. There were little touches of friendship, scooting over to make room on the benches, the camaraderie of the damned. But there was also a wariness, a fear or unwillingness to show weakness. Nobody knew who would turn and inform to the enforcers about some cheating, sharing, display of friendship or love, for a little bit of favor, a better chainsaw, a slightly warmer blanket, all that could mean the difference between life and death.

She got to the front of the line and the woman on duty looked at her with a quick appraising glance as if she knew her entire life history. It was a damning glance. Corrag knew that what was coming was going to be even worse than she'd expected. Her heart sank as the guard woman opened her mouth and cleared her throat. A hush seemed to come over the hall, but Corrag thought that might be her imagination.

"You didn't make quota."

Corrag nodded, looking at the tray behind the steamed glass counter. She counted the rolls quickly. There were about thirty left and about a dozen people behind her.

"There's also a warning on behavior with associated penalties. You go down to six ounce ration."

"For the day, right? Just for the day."

"Take it up with the staff. I'm just the food server."

Instead of exploding with anger, Corrag saved her energy. She took the half roll on her plate and a pat of butter in its nanofoil case and moved down the line. She filled up her glass with water from the bucket, ladling it slowly and not spilling. She wondered how long she could last on half a roll of bread and a pinch of butter a day. Her hands didn't waver, though. She was proud of herself for that small grace, the left over inheritance of her smile-all-the-while upbringing. There was not the slightest hint of weakness in her. She vowed to not break easily.

A second later, for the first time, a deep fear hit her in an instant like an arrow in her chest. She might not make it. She might not be tough enough. Her life and that of her unborn child might be the casualties of this system of injustice. The world of the Repho and Sandelsky and the Nenkaja would win. There would be no markers or memorial plaques, nobody to even remember she had once passed that way. That, she realized, was the worst fear, of being erased, forgotten, of never actually having existed. There was only one way to materialize in the world, and that was to be remembered by somebody, to have left a discernible mark on the world in the living memory of a friend or a child.

All of this went through her mind as she sat on the bench at the first table she came to. The other women stared at her and were silent. She looked around at their faces, modest, diffident, embarrassed for her pain and suffering but unable to change anything, too full of their own woes and fear to reach out and alleviate hers. Corrag buttered her token of bread and methodically chewed, swallowed and drank from the glass. The silence in the hall was remarkable, she thought. What were they waiting for? Somebody would begin to shout soon enough that something had been stolen. Every night there were fights, accusations, vows of vengeance. Then the enforcers on duty would stop their chat at their table and sweep in, lock the room down, send them out into the cold while they searched for homemade weapons. Sometimes they would only let them in with a couple of hours left before the night shift went on, so that they would have to work without having gotten any sleep. But this morning there was none of that. Not yet.

The silence was truly deafening. Betty walked by with her plate. Corrag looked up just as she dropped a piece of bread. Then Marina, an older Inuit woman, also a long timer, did the same. Then Candia. Corrag's hands dropped involuntarily to her side. A line of women prisoners walked silently by her at the table, dropping scraps of their bread on her plate until it was full. Corrag felt like laughing suddenly, it was such a solemn moment, but the spirit of defiance was also one of humor. She did laugh, a surprised giggle escaping her at the riches that had suddenly appeared as if by magic, a very special magic. She could feel the enforcers at their table, glaring and humorless, Muslkick among them, calculating the angle, the amount of solidarity they could afford to let coalesce around her at this moment. The best thing, the most powerful act was to eat and enjoy the food. Soon enough she would repay their generosity.

There was a little bit of light coming through the gap between the wall and the ceiling plate uner the southern eaves. Corrag's bunk was aligned so she stared out at the light on sleepless days. Betty couldn't sleep either.

"She said that to you it's because she admires what you did, Corrag," she whispered.

"I don't think so. Basically she threatened to kill me. It was a very clear message."

"No. You don't understand. She doesn't need to threaten you. The fact that your life is in her hands, that's understood. She singled you out for those words because she fears you and that's because she admires you. You threaten her armor. If you can get under her skin it would do us all a favor. This is a war that can be won only by emotional subterfuge, Corrag. You are our hammer. Right now you have tremendous power. More than we have for a long time."

"I don't see how we can win."

"I've been here a long time, Corrag. Trust me. Sometimes there's no difference between us prisoners and the enforcers. They're just as hard up as we are. Even worse because their prisons are maintained with their own collaboration. It's a form of self-mutilation. That's why they are so full of hate. The Repho knows what they're doing. They're doing a job on all of us."

She loved Betty for her words. They soothed her in a way that went beyond comfort. There was strength in them that could form sinew and add bulk. Corrag felt herself stretching in the bunk with two things, reflections of each other -- the new life, the baby growing in her and the idea of herself as a force, willing a way of being into the world. She did not know which she cared for the most.

But the enforcers had the final say.

Two days later was the end of the work month. The camp reported its production totals and adjusted its goals every month. That night, before their shift went on Muslkick entered the bunk room and announced a walk through inspection. Five minutes later, they barely had had time to finish dressing and tighten the laces on their boots when Juarez-Knoblock walked to the middle of the hangar, between the two sections of the bunkhouse and cleared his throat. He clicked the microphone attached to his collar and began to speak, but not before the feedback sent an earsplitting shriek through the hangar. Languidly turning it down with a tap at his throat, Juarez-Knoblock proceeded to announce a rise of the quota to twenty-five logs per night as a minimum for the basic ration. He said it was an emergency measure in order to meet the entire Nenkaja's needs, as the wood supplies had run low and the electricity generating pool had increased due to expanding prison populations in all the area camps. The women prisoners groaned and looked at each other. If it seemed unlikely that they would be able to meet the new quota, he wanted to remind them that it was their patriotic duty to meet their responsibilities unquestioningly as part of their rehabilitation in the Repho. Every individual would strive to be a self-sufficient worker and the weak links would find appropriate retraining opportunities in due time. Betty stifled a laugh. As Juarez-Knoblock spoke, Muslkick stood at his side, glaring at anyone who dared to meet her eyes. She had daggers for eyes. Corrag felt her heart sink. Not so much for herself but for Betty and the other older prisoners who did not stand a chance of coming close to the new workload.

That first night with the new quota, Corrag had it relatively easy. She worked in the New Jersey quadrant with clean piles of logs, and her partner in the quadrant was Marina. They worked together, one hauling and the other sawing and between the two of them came very close to quota in just ten hours. Corrag was exhausted. Before dawn, Muslkick was at the center pile where Corrag and Marina were stacking. She announced the tally, which was Corrag's fourteenth log. Corrag knew that was at least half ration; she could survive on that.

"North Country wicked? You're not even close," said Muslkick.

Corrag found herself afraid to respond. She dutifully went back to the New Jersey sector, but then asked Marina to cover for her.

"If they come by say I went back to the hangar."

"Be careful, Corrag. Don't be caught. We need you."

"I won't."

Corrag put her chainsaw down behind the log pile. She trusted Marina to watch over it and make sure nobody would steal it. She walked away through the trees, slipping silently, crouched beneath the branches, being careful to stop when a floodlight came swinging by the yard. The first woman she saw was Candia, working alone on a fairly depleted pile. She looked tired but not defeated. Candia was about thirty, a former programmer for Anabot, a Sandelsky rival in the Midland states.

"Hey, Candia."

"Corrag. What are you doing?"

"We're helping each other out tonight. If you get close to quotas, check someone else out who might need help. What goes around comes around."

"I like that. But be careful. Not everyone is down with helping out."

Corrag kept going through the trees, looking for Betty or someone else who needed help.   Grace was in her fifties, a financial writer who had made the mistake of levelling charges of insider trading against some futures company. She could barely keep the chainsaw up at the log. It was getting stuck. Corrag stepped forward. Grace sat down in the snow.

"Let me see that."

"Sure. I can't move any more."

"I know."

Corrag started up the chainsaw, let it run, checked the charge level. She cut a couple of sections of the log and pulled the rest away from the snow. Grace addressed her.

"Why are you doing this?"

"Payback. We help each other, we can get through this."

"Someone's going to snitch on you. You're a very foolish young woman."

"This is how we turn it around. Stick together."

"Okay. You might be wrong. But go ahead. I won't tell."

"Where's Betty?"

"She's over in Arizona."

"Where's that?"

"Directly opposite us."

Corrag cut a couple more logs for her. She was at six. Two more would get her enough bread to sustain her. Not much, but enough to keep her alive. When she saw the enforcers had retreated back to the charging shed she set off across the yard on the run.

Betty looked like she was in trouble. She had about five sections of a single log cut, but she was sitting against the back of a tree. Her pile was half submerged in ice. Corrag knew she had to do something to keep her alive.

"Betty, where's your chainsaw."

"Back there." She raised her gloved hand in the dark to point. Corrag flashed her headlamp on, and saw the chainsaw. She retrieved it and started it. She got it to work and cut a few logs. Betty would have to wheel the barrow over to claim them.

"Are you okay?"

"Am now. You are an angel, Corrag."

"You saved my life a couple of nights ago."

Betty stood on wobbly legs and hauled the barrow over to the center of the yard. Floodlights showed Corrag the transaction in the distance. When she got back, Corrag instantly started up the chainsaw and continued to work. There was about an hour left in the shift. Corrag cut five more logs in that time.

"Corrag, you're as strong as a man."

"Not really."

"Who is the father of your child?"

"A man named Kevin."

"He must need you. They always need us more than we need them.

"True. But he's dead."

"I'm sorry. You'll find another. The best of them are capable of teaching us something about the higher virtues. Like my friend Frank. Did I ever tell you about Frank?"

"No."

"Frank Ash. A three-time Nenkaja survivor. Last I heard he was in the jungle. We can learn from them. Corrag. They can inspire us. The way you inspire me."

"Come on, Betty. It's the least that I can do. You've taught me that it's possible to grow in a desert."

When they got back to the bunk room, Corrag felt a twinge in her belly. It felt like she had strained several abdominal wall muscles. She knew she needed to sleep it off. But first she would eat. There was a feeling of elation in the air. But also, in retrospect, she thought later, something like dread in the air also. Nobody had made the quota, but everyone had at least made some level of the ration. She pulled off her boots and looked in the bag beneath the bed. Some of her bread there had gone missing. It must have been the enforcers, because the day shift was out and nobody else had been around.

That was the first sign that not all was right. Then she heard the news. It spread instantly. Candia had been caught out of her section and been dragged off to the Bunkhouse. Muslkick walked between the bunks. This was her time to shine. The hatred in Corrag sapped her of any feeling, as if her heart had been vacuumed out of her chest.

"You all know what a violation of the Code means here in the Nenkaja. She was caught helping others. Out of her section. There is no higher law in the Nenkaja. Survival of the fittest. That's the bottom line here and always will be."

Corrag slumped to her bunk. She was too tired. Sleep was the only solution, even in the face of this horrible news. But she couldn't sleep, knowing that Candia's undoing, the crime that had taken her out of her section to seek out others in need of help, had been her idea. About noon, while everyone slept, Corrag sat up and pulled back on her boots and put back on her coat. Half delirious with desperation and exhaustion, she made her way to the door of the bunk hall, unguarded, and fumbled with the latch. From behind, she heard footsteps. It was Betty, in her long Nenkajah coat, dishevelled, barefoot, coming at her with head down like a charging bull. Corrag put her hands out reflexively as Betty tackled her.

They both landed on the ground with a thump.

"Help me, girls," cried Betty.

"What are you doing?" cried Corrag.

Betty reached over where she lay half crazed and clamped her hand on Corrag's mouth to silence her.

"You're putting the entire shift at risk, Corrag."

Women prisoners surrounded them, blocking the thin light from the eaves.

Corrag struggled free. "I just want to go see Candia. I can't leave her out there," she said. "It's my fault. We can't just leave her."

"No, Corrag. There's nothing we can do. You don't understand. If they think it's gone beyond a certain point they'll kill us all. They'll put us all to death. Is that what you want?" asked Betty.

"They won't do that. They'd have to close down the camp. It's free labor for them," said one girl standing at the edge of the crowd.

"They've done it before," said another woman.

"We can't let her go," said Betty determinedly.

Corrag struggled to her feet. "Look, this is just wrong. We can't just let Candia die. What will that do to us? Let me go out there and try to get her loose from the chains. I'll set her free, and she'll have a fighting chance to get out of here."

"To where, Corrag? There are no settlements for 500 miles," said someone in the darkness.

"She'll have a chance," insisted Corrag. "That's better than dying in chains while we sleep. I can live with that. I won't settle for less." She drew her file out of her coat pocket and held it up to the small bit of light from the eaves. Already the day was dying.

"Okay, Corrag. Say you do get out there and help Candia get free. You won't get back inside."

"That's fine. I'll miss you guys," she said.

The prisoners that had been standing in a blockade came closer, surrounding Corrag. Many were crying quietly. Someone gathered two blankets and an extra coat and someone else rolled a pair of boots up in them and tied it all with with twine that had held a mattress together. Someone else found a box of matches and a tin cup. Elise, the toughest of them all, handed over her prized possession, a knife she'd fabricated from a spoon. There was a collective intake of breath at this unexpected bit of generosity. Life in the Nenkaja could never be the same.

Corrag's hands trembled as she untied the roll, put it all together, tied it again and then put the blanket roll on her back, hanging the loop of twine against the collar of her coat. With her hood up she focused only on what lay ahead. It was time to say goodbye to prison life and the attachments to people she had made. She counted these as the closest bonds in her life. She would get free or die trying.

"Bye, Betty. Keep these girls going for me."

Some of the girls looked envious. She was breaking out with the slimmest chance to actually make it to freedom.

"Hope we never see you again. Good luck, Corrag."

Marina stepped forward through the crowd.

"Look, Corrag. Take this."

Corrag looked at the carving of a fish with a man's head in its mouth.

"What is it?"

"It's a Jonah talisman. If you stay along the shore it will be milder at night. And you won't freeze if you light fires with fallen branches and lichen. Boil water with berries you'll find under the ice on the rocks near the shore. When you get to Red Bay, show them this. They'll know who made it and they will take care of you."

"Thanks, Marina."

Corrag didn't have any more words to express her gratitude. There was no better love than what she felt at that moment for her fellow prisoners. Like the wind in her sails, it would keep her going through the passage ahead. Reason alone would not lead her. Faith was not blind; it was spurred by the providential power of this love.

"Go on then. Be free for us," said Betty, reading her thoughts.

She stepped out the door. The floodlights were on in the yard and the enforcers were in the charging shed. Maybe they would see her, but most likely they were sitting in the folding chairs sipping a hot drink with vodka in it. That was their main pastime, drinking Nenkaja vodka laced tea and trying to stay warm. Corrag felt their presence like a blast of diseased air. She avoided the yard and walked behind the bunkhouse to get to the rocky slopes. She made her way along the ridge of the slope. She could see that beyond the hangar was the ice-clogged strand, and beyond that lay the flat vast ocean lit up by the stars and moon shining a silverish green, eerie spell over everything. There was a stillness that masked the ceaseless motion of the universe. Underneath the dull buzzing of chainsaws she thought she heard something else, an anguished moaning, keening sound. She headed in a circuitous route for the shore and the locus of that pained expression.

The rock was black, like an obelisk. Candia was silent, just a lump swallowed up in the even greater blackness of the rock. Corrag hoped she was still alive and ran the last quarter mile through the trees with a sudden bout of anxiety, dodging the branches that whipped her in the face.

She climbed the rock on all fours and fell down, roughly shaking the body there beneath her hands.

"Candia. Can you hear me?"

She repeated the question and rubbed up and down her spine and head, trying to revive her.

"Candia. Please listen."

Candia stirred, as if awakening, and rolled her head over.

"Where am I?"

Corrag unrolled the blanket.

"Sit up and I'll wrap you."

"Can't move my arms."

"Okay."

Corrag did the best she could getting the blanket around Candia's body with the chains on her wrists and ankles pinning her to the ground. She talked all the while, telling Candia about the resolution she'd made to get her free and how the entire prisoner population was counting on them making it.

"It's Christmas," said Candia.

"Not exactly. But we got to get this for them, Candia."

Corrag examined the chains and the plates against the rock, covering up the bolts that screwed down into it. She used the file on a chain link, but found it difficult to hold the chain steady enough to get a cut started in the metal. Then she worked around one of the plates, seeing if she could shift the stone. Some of it came away. She wasn't sure if it was dirt, but kept poking to get some more.

"This might work," said Corrag.

She couldn't feel her fingers. It would take too long to get the bolt out of the rock this way, and there were three others to go. There had to be a better solution. The link of the chain nearest the bolt stayed in place against the rock. She tried filing on it and found she could get the file in a groove. It might take an hour or so to cut, but that was the best chance. Corrag stopped.

"You hungry?"

"I'm so hungry, Corrag."

Corrag gave Candia some bread, placing it in her mouth and waiting patiently for her to chew. She moved her jaw with difficulty.

"I think I can do this, but you need to stay with me, Candia. Do you think you can?"

"I think I can, Corrag. I'll try."

"Okay, then. I'll try, too. Absolutely."

Corrag got on her knees and placed all her weight against the file. The pain in her side had returned, but she ignored it. The burring of the file was everything. Every ounce of her being was concentrated in her fingers and hands, feeling the way to deepen the groove in the metal. The cold was her ally, making the iron brittle against the sharpened edges of the file. Her fingers and ears together found the perfect angle, feeling and listening for the greatest advantage against the metal of the chain. Eventually she got close and stopped. She sucked the file to clean it and stuck the opposite end of the file into the link and stretched with her wrist and budged it apart enough to slip away from the plate in the rock.

"That's your left arm free."

"Almost."

Candia sat up and used her free arm to wrap the blanket tighter around herself. The distant buzz of the chainsaws in the cutting yard had ceased momentarily while stacks were made and accounts settled.

"Do you think they'll come looking for you?"

"Pretty soon they will. They'll notice I'm gone. We have a few hours."

Corrag took a deep breath. Her arms trembled with fatigue as she set them to work again under the weight of her upper body, leaning against the next link in the chains that bound Candia. She knew it was fear more than physical depletion that pained her and fought as hard with her own mind as she did with the file. When the second link snapped, she sighed with pleasure.

"We're going to do this, Candia."

"Good. I'm in."

"It's not done yet."

"No. I want to meet somebody. Have a baby like you. When is it due?"

"I don't know. Summer sometime."

"I'll be there for that."

"I hope so."

"There's lots of women around to help with it, Corrag. Maybe Juarez-Knoblock will let us have a christening party."

"I don't think so. Anyway, we're not going back. But keep talking."

"A party. What a concept."

Candia babbled on for an indeterminate time. It took much longer to get the two last links cut. Corrag had lost track of the time. The sound of the chainsaws had stopped. Candia stood and kicked her legs around, getting the blood flowing, while Corrag remained on the ground, wondering what came next. The wind blew swirls of snow that registered in the dark only by hitting them in the face.

"Which way, Corrag? Are you okay?"

Slowly Corrag stood, coming back from a dream, and put the file in her pocket. She removed her gloves for a brief instant and massaged her fingers and put them inside her pants between her legs to get the feeling back in them. The shooting pain in them was almost unbearable. She rolled the provisions back in the extra blanket after Candia switched it for the spare coat and tucked in the ends to keep it secure and slung it like a pack over her back again. The cutting yard lights were off. They needed to move quickly. Then the alarm sounded, letting all the camps know that Corrag was missing. She had heard of escape attempts, none successful, and none in the depths of the winter. But here they were, half frozen and about 500 miles to trek to get to the nearest civilization if they got lucky. What would they eat? She had no idea. How long would it take? There was only silence. Corrag consoled herself with the familiar thought that every impossible journey began the same way, with a footstep into the unknown. The task was made more difficult for Candia by the chains hanging from her wrists and ankles. She wrapped them around her arms and Corrag tucked them in on each other like a slipknot. It made it possible, but difficult. But there was nothing except the snow in their face to hold them back. For both of them this was a charge of courage, a wisp of hope that pushed them towards either freedom or death. Either choice was better than the slavery of prisoner life.

"It's better this way," said Candia.

"Yes. It is," agreed Corrag.

The two women slipped down the Bunkhouse and away from the camp. When they reached the edge of the sea ice where the wind whipped overhead and out into the infinite emptiness they veered towards the south and the suggestion of light. After a few hundred yards the frozen ice reared up in blocks surrounded by the chop of waves. They cut along the shore, avoiding the sea ice. By now it was light and they were headed west, by Corrag's estimation. But there was no way. They seemed to be going in circles. It was impossible following the convoluted, boulder-strewn, frozen shore. They would have to move inland. Then they came to the fence that marked the boundary of the Nenkaja.

"Wait," said Corrag. "There's something I need to do. Wait here for me."

Candia did as Corrag instructed. She waited. Corrag disappeared over a slight incline. In the distance she thought she saw a structure. Something -- an instinct, a hope, told her the men's prison house lay in that direction. As she approached, she could see her hunch had been right. There was a building, and the shapes of men huddling under the eaves, readying to go out, maybe a hunting party to look for her and Candia. Corrag decided to come closer and see them. Making a zigzag pattern, varying the speed of her approach like a wild animal, Corrag approached the men until, lying on her belly, she could make out the faces underneath the hoods of their Nenkaja coats. One of them spotted her, and a group of three walked over to where she lay. Corrag stood, preparing to fight, grasping her knife inside the coat.

"Woman, are you okay?" asked one of the men. They were all prisoners, like her.

"Yes. Do you know Beithune?"

"Beithune. He's with us. Inside there. Asleep." The man spoke for all of them. The rest were saving their breath, staring at her incredulously.

"Tell him I'm okay. I'm leaving. I tried to see him. Tell him to be strong."

"We'll do that. Get out of here. They'll be sending out guards looking for you."

"Good." Corrag turned and went off in the direction she'd come. The dawn's light reflected a swirling grey light that soon covered up her tracks in the wind.

Winter storms had weakened the boundary fence. Candia and she stood at one side of it. It was possible to cut around the end by climbing down a cliff and back up on the other side. It took the two a couple of hours to complete this traverse climbing with hands and feet. Only when they were back on the other side, following a snowmobile trail through the low woods, did Corrag think that she was leaving everything behind. It was really her alone now with just the thought, the memory of her past, a communication with ghosts. But Candia was good company and strong. And there was the life inside her that was still just a seed creature, metamorphosizing into a human with every second that passed, entirely trusting that there was a purpose to this run. This presumption of the unborn, larger than everything in the world, certainly larger than the Nenkaja, which had receded into insignificance, was already shaping every choice Corrag made, every step she took. There could be no mistakes now. She panicked when she thought they had no idea where they were, just following the trail hoping that it led somewhere where they could find safety.

Candia did not like the woods. The trail petered out, and often they had to bushwhack through the spruce, the branches whirring back and smacking them in the face. For Candia this meant dropping the chains and dragging them. She was tired, not complaining, wanting the trees to finish, but the expanse of them seemed considerable. The other problem with the trail was the ease it gave trackers in following them, since the marks of their passage in the tree-sheltered snow were so visible. So Corrag was glad when they came out on a treeless, windy expanse as the sun began its descent below the horizon, vanishing in a blur of diffuse yellow light. The way ahead lay across the corrugated fabric of the northland, mountains running vaguely parallel and twisting in the voluptuous folds of the braided rock, reflecting and absorbing the solstice sun in stripes.

The cloud cover overhead meant there was no need of a panic, despite the freezing wind at their backs. A good fire would keep them warm enough through the night. They stopped before long, and Corrag dropped her pack and began to search in the moonlight for branches. There were bushes in the folds of rock with deposits of broken kindling hidden in their interiors and larger wind-whipped trees hugging the crevasses that had dropped branches in the storms. Corrag amassed several pieces of drooping, brittle wood while Candia dug out a pit in the snow as best she could, kicking and scraping with her boots and chains to get down to the frozen rock. After assembling the wood in the pit, Corrag lit a match to the driest piece of fibrous, rotted pulp she could find. Several matches were wasted, but eventually a piece of wood no biger than a quarter caught flame and she set it next to some other larger pieces, cupping her hands over it and watching the flame flicker, widen and lick, spreading around itself and then rising to get at the larger structure of branches until the whole thing was ablaze and the two of them sat together, backs to the wind, rejoicing in the moment and luxuriating in the warmth that thawed out their faces and massaged the limbs they held over it.

Corrag reached for the bread in her pack. There were two intact rolls and some crumbled bits. She shared it out evenly between them. That was the last of the easy food. They debated where to go.

"If we follow the shore, it will be warmer. Up here on the ridges it might drop so low some nights there's no way we can stay alive."

"Even with a fire?"

"Well, what if we don't keep the fire going?"

"We can keep it going. The shore is too crazy. There's the ice and then rocks. It'll take forever to get anywhere."

"It might be easier to hide out up here."

"Let's stick to the ridges. We can see which way we're going," said Candia. She put her head in Corrag's lap. Despite being almost twice her age, Candia was like her child. Corrag felt a sense of responsibility for her. The other advantage of the high country she did not mention to Candia for fear of alarming her was that the greater visibility would be crucial if they wanted to have some warning of pursuers. Better to be prepared to make a stand then to be caught by surprise, she thought.

So it seemed an eternity, an expanse without beginning or end that they trekked the interior, following the ridgeline away from the coast. The third day had dawned, she thought. It had been no more than three, but might have been less. Two days and three nights, she was sure. In the distance, to the south, was a landscape that included mountains and icy canyons. The red clouds that lined the sky portended worse weather. In the fire, still burning, were the feet of a bird, some kind of petrel or tern blown off its migratory route in a storm. Corrag had found its frozen body at her feet, hidden half buried in ice, and carried it with her on the traverse the previous day, plucked it, split it and roasted it. The bits of charred flesh had gone a long way to restoring their strength. Candia had complained. It was a disgusting thing, but eating was key to surviving. Still, it was hard to get Candia up. The wind was ruthless, and Candia blamed her for the decision to follow the ridgeline. She complained of the pain in her wrists from carrying the chains, her frozen hands, and the impossibility of regaining strength in her legs. Corrag spent some time with the file trying to cut the clamps of the chains loose, but she wasn't making any progress. The file seemed to have lost its bite. Candia wanted to know where they were going. The truth was Corrag didn't know. She had to make Candia understand that what they were attempting was a miracle. Any place of arrival was a victory. For Corrag, every day of freedom on the run was a day she'd won against the death camp and for the women they'd left behind. Candia just wanted to rest. She wanted to stop, and for her a return to the routine of the camp was preferable to the misery of trying to cheat death on their own. The vastness of the unknown had defeated her. She had forgotten already about her night on the Bunkhouse. Corrag marvelled at her ability to put out of her mind the certain death she had faced. For this reason she promptly discounted Candia's whining.

"Come on, Candia. We have to keep moving."

"The wind is so strong, Corrag. It's coming right at us. Can't we just wait a bit for it to die down."

"It's not going to. It's going to pick up. The south wind means storms coming. Look at the clouds. Let's hike for as long as we can today until we find some shelter before the storms hit."

Reluctantly, Candia stood and readied herself for the march, wrapping her head and shoulders in the extra blanket and tieing the arm chains one by one around the sleeves of her coat. Corrag packed up the knife and the file and the bird carcass together in the pockets of her coat along with Marina's whale bone carving already stored there for safe keeping. Then she heard it at the same time as Candia. The high-pitched whine of a motor, just the hint in the whistle of the wind. It was sooner than expected. But that was how destiny worked, Corrag knew. When you weren't expecting it, that's when it made its appearance. Before you had time to think.

"What is that?" asked Candia, whispering soberly.

"Snowmobile."

"Who?"

"Don't know. But they're probably looking for us by now. They've probably spotted us already."

"How?"

"I didn't want to tell you but there was a drone

yesterday, just before the night. It came up from behind us when we were arguing about who was going to eat the bird and flew over us."

"Why didn't you say something?"

"I didn't see it until it was too late. I didn't want to scare you. I just wanted to let you sleep last night. You looked so peaceful and seemed so happy, Candia."

"Well, I would have liked to know. So what's the plan?"

"The plan is we fight. We have time. Somebody's giving us a fighting chance; we take it. I'm not going back."

"Corrag, you are frigging crazy."

"No I'm not. I'm just calculating. What would you rather do?"

"Get these chains off me."

"Exactly. Listen to me, Candia. We can do this."

Corrag closed her eyes and thought of Ben. Here's what he would do. First climb the rock they'd come along just before nightfall and see who was coming on the snowmobile.

"Then what?" asked Candia.

"Then we'll jump them."

"Where do you come up with this shit?"

They picked the way up the ice-covered back of the wall along a route that Corrag discovered, feeling for finger holds with her bare hands. The top of the wind-blasted rock revealed the entire Labrador coast, and to the northeast, coming up on the trail they had made, popping above the ridgeline and bucking into the air, were three snowmobiles in a line. The engine noise was louder now, the high-pitch of hydrogen powered engines working at full revolutions per minute.

"There's three," said Candia.

"Master of the obvious."

"So much for your plan."

"No. We let the first go by and take out the back two."

"And what happens when the first turns around?"

"We'll have weapons."

"I don't know how to shoot."

"I do. I'll show you sometime when we have a minute. Come on."

Corrag handed Candia the homemade knife.

"You know how to use this," she said.

"I'll try," said Candia gamely.

They climbed out on the ledge and positioned themselves ten feet above the trail they'd made along the mountainside. The trail climbed at a steep angle above the valley that stretched eastwards towards a series of headlands that jutted into the ocean, lit in blue by the sun. Corrag marvelled at how beautiful it all was. She felt breathless, gripping the file in her hand. She wondered whether she was dreaming. She turned and looked at Candia.

"I can't do this," said Candia.

"You have to. Just smile all the while," said Corrag, grimacing.

"Do you think it'll work?"

"I believe it will. "

The snowmobiles appeared on the trail. The first one

was green and carried a heavyset man wearing a fur hat. The two following had on helmets and were slowing as the first snowmobile slowed, closing the gap between the three of them. Corrag tensed.

"For freedom," she said, before straightening and hurling herself out into space. She sensed Candia falling behind her. Her feet and legs took most of the shock on the front of the machine. The rest of her collapsed with full force against the front of the driver. The file tore through flesh and bone somewhere in his chest. He went off the machine. She rolled off before it went over the cliff. Then she crawled back and found the man in the snow clutching at his chest, doubled over on his knees. She put her hands together and hit him on the back of the neck. He stayed down. Then she rolled him over and found his gun strapped against his hip in a holster. She pulled it out and looked up to see the first snowmobile bearing down on her, coming back on the freshly laid trail. Aiming and firing at once, Corrag made one shot on her knee. She was about fifty feet away when the explosion rocked the ridge country.

The last snowmobile had come to a stop against the canyon wall, riding up an ice protrusion and twisting sideways. It looked like it had been glued into place. Candia and the driver had rolled themselves into a ball a little further back. Corrag approached the two with gun drawn. Candia had wrapped herself around the man's body, gore all over both of them. She could hear her crying. Corrag picked up a leg chain dragging in the snow.

"You're a mess," she said. She sat in the snow next to the amalgam of the dead body of the snowmobile man and the live Candia and waited for Candia to compose herself. The snowmobile's engine was still running. Eventually Candia stopped crying, unsticking herself from the bloody corpse, and Corrag gingerly reversed the snowmobile away from the canyon wall. The gears worked the same as a zipbike. Then Candia climbed on behind her and gathered up her chains.

The snowmobile continued down the trail with two new riders as it got dark. The headlights went on. They plunged down the mountainside into the valley. The snow was swirling thickly around them, and the visibility was non-existent. The blizzard dropped about twelve inches of snow in less than an hour and then petered into a fine mist of ice for the rest of the night. The temperature remained constant at just above minus twenty degrees Celsius. The snowmobile had a dashboard of gauges. They were headed south by southeast. Corrag's gloved hands on the bars had no feeling in them. Neither did her face. She had just enough strength to focus on the beam of light ahead and steer. She dared not accelerate for fear of throwing them both off. They seemed to be riding along a road of sorts; there was a sign. Highway 510, it said. They were on a twelve-foot wide clearing that ran along a river and then crossed a suspension bridge. There were lights ahead, dwellings, the outskirts of a town, according to the global positioning gauge that had just recently come on. Corrag stopped on the far side of the bridge. They could hear water rushing under the ice.

Everything else was frozen solid, even, it seemed, the twin beams of light up ahead. They both stood unsteadily beside the bridge. Corrag felt herself losing consciousness and leaned against the stone column until the blood returned to its normal course and she could see again. Then she pointed the snowmobile at the river in first gear, walking beside it, and gunned it, releasing her grip on the handle bar. It sauntered over the lip of flood mark ice and disappeared into silence. It was like Cortes burning his boats, Corrag thought, remembering that story. It had ended badly for Montezuma, but she couldn't remember how it ended for Cortes. Presumably it had ended well, although the idea of burning your boats had never sat well with her. In this case it was a necessary precaution against detection by agents of the Repho who were surely everywhere and far less accommodating than the Aztecs. Candia walked alongside her, clutching at her chains like a bad disease.

"We're going to have to do something about those things."

"Please, God. What do we say?"

"I'll do the talking."

"I need to know what our line is, Corrag. What if they separate us and interrogate us? Our stories need to line up."

"Look, Candia. Story line is not our strong suit. We need to appeal on an emotional level. I don't know what we're going to say yet."

The town, when they reached it around a bend in the road, sat above a sheltered bay lit by the stars. It was comprised of an odd array of boxy wooden houses with very little in the way of architectural interest. But there was a store and a dim, faraway sort of light on behind the etched glass. Nobody else seemed to be present or even accounted for. Corrag was giddy with delight, however, at the sight of a light, for it signified warmth. Her toes had long ago stopped feeling pain, which was generally known to be a danger sign. The door to the store, which sold iconic hardware and processed food items, was painted red in thick globs of ancient coats over the original wood, and it had a latch for a handle, which she pushed down with her useless, frozen thumb. When she pushed it creaked. They stepped forward inside onto the ancient faded linoleum of Frenchie's Home Goods. Corrag pulled off her gloves in a civilized gesture. The two men inside, one behind the counter, did not react to their presence, but rather continued to talk as if nothing had just happened. Corrag stopped her forward progress to listen. Candia pretended to be interested in an item on a display stand located in the middle of the floor. It seemed to be some sort of engine part she lifted from a crate of similar parts. Corrag wriggled her toes. There was no feeling in them. The men continued talking.

"They're holding their toes to the fire on that one."

"Oh, yah. The council boys don't give in that easy."

"And the McHenry boy scored twice on the power play."

"But the Kings need a clue. That coach is..."

"I don't know what you call it."

"Then the other day he had a shit with the Goose Bay

crowd."

"It's Mercier driving the whole Salmon deal."

"Yah."

"Can I help you?"

The man behind the counter was the older of the two, although his grey hair was still thick and curly. The other man wore a felt hat and his face gave little away in terms of emotion. Corrag grabbed a box of frosted donuts and stepped to the counter.

"How much are these?"

"Those? About whatever it says on the box. Can you read it for me? My eyes are fading. Yours are probably better, although you look like you've been out in the cold a spell."

"Yes. I have. I'm freezing. It says three dollars ninety-seven. Is that in Canadian?"

"Oh, are you part of the college crowd up for the cross-country tri-motor sports event?"

"No, not quite, but sort of. I can pay with this."

The other man whistled the start of *Hark the Herald Angels Sing* and faced Candia and then looked away and stepped off balance to the side in embarrassment at the state of her appearance. The arm and leg chains were wrapped absurdly up in her sleeves and her face was black with dried blood and engine grease. Corrag slowly pulled out Marina's whalebone carving and placed it in her palm upon the counter. The man studied it and his muscles almost imperceptibly froze. He closed her palm for her.

"Your hands are freezing."

"Yes, we've been outside. It's cold out."

"Bring the donuts. Both of you come into the back. Julian watch the door for me."

"Yes, sir," said Julian, recovering a bit of his composure.

The back room had no heat, but the man wasted no time turning on the spare baseboard gas-fired unit along with an ancient flat screen on the wall that came up with some spreadsheet of inventory figures. He switched it to the provincial news channel and scanned rapidly with finger touches.

"Nothing here. Where are you two running from? Be honest with me. You have a Jonah token so I am trusted with your safety."

"The Nenkaja," said Corrag.

"Have the donuts," he said, and disappeared back in the store. Corrag ripped open the box and handed it to Candia. She fiddled with the screen until she got a home page and found some news from the main Repho channel, the Mann Report. There were disturbances in Democravia and the Council had been seized by something called the Union of Concerned Beings. Corrag sat on the faded sofa and took the box of donuts from Candia and popped a sugarcoated donut in her mouth. The newscast droned on about the rise and fall of stock prices on the Repho exchange. Sandelsky was doing well.

"They're still there. Democravia's gone. It's all been for nothing," said Corrag.

"But we're safe," said Candia. "That's good, right?"

"For now. Totally dependent on the kindness of strangers."

"What's a Jonah token?"

"I have no idea. Something about the carving Marina gave me. Said they'd know about it in Red Bay. She was right."

"God bless her," said Candia dreamily.

Corrag was drowsy, and as the heat in the room grew she found it almost impossible to keep her eyes open. At one point she bolted to her feet and opened the door back to the store. Nobody was there and the lights were off. She went back in and closed the door. The hum of the water pump kept the memories of their recent ordeal away. The flat screen had gone blank. Candia was asleep. She thought she might as well be also. She sat and stretched out as best she could next to Candia's grimy chains on the sofa and closed her eyes, and instantly she was dreaming. She was running on open ground, free, in the warmth of a Democravian summer. Beside her was a child, brown skinned, face like an angel.

Seven -- The Haven

Red Bay was an unaugmented town almost in its entirety; the people fished for sustenance and exported the dried herring and blues off to the Repho via airlift from St. John's. Many were part of the Jonah cult, which as Corrag learned, had spread along the Atlantic periphery out of the Hebrides and down into the Repho in pockets. The members of the cult were bound to old-style communication channels and wrote long missives to members in other seaboard towns and identified themselves with homemade letterhead stationery with the graph of a whale and the letter J flat in the belly of the whale. The letters were transported in fishing boats that ran along the coasts and crossed the blue waters in season. The cult leaders in Red Bay were Charles Fugel, childhood friend of Wilders Gersome, the owner of Frenchie's Home Goods and Fernanda Fredricksen. The two women, Candia and Corrag, by escaping from the Nenkaja, were accorded celebrity status among the members. They moved into a room in Fernanda's attic, and when the spring finally came at the end of April, Corrag had put on twenty extra pounds with the baby and continued to fatten on the fish stocks and squash dishes that Fernanda prepared in her kitchen. Fernanda's children had moved away to the Repho in search of other lives. They were augmented and never came home. Fernanda was lonely, but resigned to her loss. She took solace in the Jonah cult, which preached the Day of Atonement and release from the Belly of the

Whale in the third generation.

The town youth stared at Corrag in awe and some in fear. The sun was climbing higher every day. There was a park next to the bay that Corrag liked. She was getting heavier and shorter of breath on the steps carved into the hillside, the earth held in with hemlock beams soaked in copper green. Candia had a boyfriend who worked on the fishing boats. She waited for the evenings, sleeping late, then went out to the quiet water, standing on the rocks encrusted with mussels, and watched the boats perform their docking maneuvers. The boats went out early in the mornings before dawn and returned at dusk and sometimes later depending on how far they had roamed in search of catch. There was an ebb and a flow to the life in Red Bay that made for a settled sort of momentary contentment. Corrag felt oddly restless despite herself, despite the need for calm to make a good place for the baby. It kicked and danced in its little world, responding to her thoughts and pronouncements. She sat on the bench at the top of the cliff and pulled up her shirt to let the sun play its tune. It was July.

By August the mosquitoes descended in clouds when Corrag poked a fork into the ground to retrieve some early potatoes from Fernanda's garden. She filled a bucket with the little pearls as she swatted at the air. Straightening, she heard her name being called from the house. It was Candia. She was hardly ever around. Corrag headed back to the house, and halfway there was hit by a sudden urge, a cramping that made her pick up the pace. By the time she was at the house her water had broken.

She sat down on the back steps, spilling the potatoes, as the waves of shooting pain overtook her.

"Candia," she called. Fernanda poked her head out the back door and the little grey house cat slipped inside, startled by the sudden air of surprise.

The two women and Euclive, a member from Goose Bay, got Corrag inside onto the sofa, and Candia went for the midwife. Fernanda did not have an emosponder. Most of the town did without, although there was a nanofiber line onto the North American circuits installed by the provincial government about ten years previous.

The midwife arrived with Candia. Corrag was feeling a little better. She sat up and smiled. The midwife took her temperature and ordered more blankets. Then Corrag felt the sharp overwhelming labor of childbirth. By the late afternoon, about six hours in, the baby's head emerged, a whorl of black hair in tight little curls. Candia gasped. Corrag bit her lips so hard they bled. The pain blanked out all thought. She felt like she'd been buried under a rockslide. When the baby burst out into the midwife's capable hands, with eyes in slits of black rage, Corrag took one look at the bundle of fibers and muscles wrapped in mucous membrane as it opened its mouth and gasped a bleating complaint. Her heart went out to the raging boy that it was.

"There now," said the midwife, putting him on Corrag's chest.

He took to feeding with ferocity, a good sign, and Corrag felt an even deeper contentment at the dropping of the milk in her breasts. His name would be Arthur. She thought Kevin would like that too.

Arthur's eyes changed from black to a hazel backlit by the same flame of enthusiasm as they had displayed on the day of his birth at the fountain of Corrag's full breasts. Weeks in, the members were concerned at his lack of a father. Fernanda lectured Corrag on her need to find a suitable marriage partner from the bachelors of the coastal towns. Corrag was quite happy alone in Fernanda's attic. She felt anchored against the possible storms that might come their way.

"I think I can do this."

"Yes, but the boy..."

"He is different."

"He will need a male."

"He will have males. There's Childers. There's Charles. There's Euclive."

"I won't argue. It's something we believe. A male and a female can do the job."

"What about two males. Or two females?"

"Not as good. Not as healthy. Period."

"Why not? Can't we accommodate to it?"

"We can, of course. But it's the ideal we want if we're talking about resisting the Whale. Our children don't have all the supports of the augmented world. They have to have it all, the resources our ancestors have always relied on. Inside here." Fernanda tapped her chest.

"But everyone is different."

"Okay, Corrag. I'll let you have the last word. But why not attend the Fishermen's Association ringo this Friday at the hall?"

"Okay. I will."

Fernanda left her alone in the attic with Arthur after that. Corrag thought about what she'd said. It didn't make any sense. She had known women in the Nenkaja, like Betty, who were fiercer and braver than any man. And she had known men, like Beithune, more deeply in tune with the natural and psychic worlds than any woman. The sources of a child's personality, the influences on their development, were impossible to predict or contain in any formula, no matter how time-honored. Arthur would have the benefit of the best of everything. She would never settle for just a man for the sake of conforming to anyone's outward picture of perfection. That was the same as accepting augmentation as the only ticket to adult advancement. She stroked the baby's cheek softly as it looked up into her eyes with growing understanding. The infinitude of possibilities would be his to discover, just as Corrag had seized it for herself from a world that had tried to shrink her to its predetermined dimensions.

That Friday in the afternoon, after Corrag's walk along the seaward trail, observing the slow progress of the icebergs in the bay and the profusion of boats in for the ringo, Fernanda accepted the baby from her outstretched hands at the door of the house. Candia and her boyfriend, Eddie Fox, were waiting a little further down the road, talking in a little, intimate huddle. Arthur began to cry, but Fernanda expertly calmed him, bouncing and rocking and cooing breathless endearments.

"You do love him, don't you, Fernanda?"

"He is adorable. Of course I do. You'll be fine. Go on."

Corrag felt that Fernanda understood how special Arthur was. She was lucky to have her. She felt like she was almost a mother to her and a grandmother to the baby she now held in her arms at the door. And Arthur, conceived amidst hate, would have the peaceful contentment of a settled childhood in a community of hard-minded, visionary resisters. But he would always be different, an extension of her own journey of discovery, and she doubted that any man could understand that continuum. It was no longer just Corrag alone. It was her and Arthur. A man would have to love the two of them undivided.

"Ready, Corrag? This will be fun," said Eddie.

"Ready as I ever will be," said Corrag in a dubious tone.

They approached the Fishermen's Hall, a large red building that housed the town offices along with a large barn used for meetings and storage of town equipment such as lifeboats. The line outside the hall ran along the side of the building and consisted of fishermen in for the weekend and the festivities of the ringo. The lifeboats had been moved outside and along the strand side of the hall. There were boats from up and down the seaboard and as far afield as Greenland and Machiasport, Maine. The three waited their turn, and when they got up to the front of the line there was some joking comment from one of the men at the door about the local girls. Corrag cringed. Once inside, they headed for the tables along the back where there was food. As they reached the table, the announcer on the rickety stage asked for silence and began to introduce the visitors assembled there with him. Corrag grabbed a lobster roll and turned and stared at the lineup, undifferentiated dignitaries on a military mission, a combined delegation from the Union of Concerned Beings and the Republican Homeland. The announcer, a friend of Euclive's whose name Corrag could not remember, droned on. Apparently it was important and they were all to be grateful for the visit. They were touring the region with the promise of future money for a deep water port to be constructed as part of the joint Arctic development program that the UCB and the Repho were now engaged in and which promised jobs and opportunity as fishing stocks continued to rebound from recent warm years. He finished his comments to polite applause and some jeering from the fishermen, who were generally not fond of government projects and in the case of the Jonah, covertly opposed to the expanding influence of what they termed the North American cyber-mind, or just simply the Whale. The announcer smiled.

"Now they'll start the music, right Eddie?" said Candia, shaking herself at the prospect.

Eddie laughed and hugged her around the shoulder.

"Any minute now. Corrag?"

But Corrag wasn't listening. She was stepping towards the stage to inspect the faces. She couldn't believe what she saw. There was Ben Calder, with a thinning crew cut, his face lined and drawn and in the uniform of a high-ranking officer of the new rulers of Democravia, the

UCB, shifting his weight distractedly on stage with the slight forward slouch he had never outgrown from his teenage years. She looked at his face carefully as he looked out over the crowd. Then the lights dimmed and the contingent of visitors disappeared off the stage. Had she imagined it or had his face revealed a bored look of cynical disbelief? She wanted to believe in the old Ben, the wise-cracking high school kid who'd convinced her to trust her own lights and not the adult, received version of who she might be. But this was a different Ben, a Ben of power and prestige, passing through the world at a remove, entrusted with the gears of governing, the mechanisms of control, an augmented man. If life were playing this kind of trick on her, she would have to play back. She had to know if it was Ben.

"Where are you going now, Corrag?" asked Candia disapprovingly.

"I'll be back," she answered, and breezed through the crowd as the music commenced. It was *Hall of Waves* by Okinawan, but nobody was dancing. She remembered at school dances in Edmundstown the flurry of activity that this song would set off with its power harmonics and lyrics about the surfer boys and the escape from the hall of waves that seemed to be a fate that they were all destined for. How ironic that it would come on now, to remind her of how far away and long off those days now were.

Outside the door she spied a knot of people headed down the hill to the water's edge. A twenty-foot whaler waited on the jetty to take them out to the torpedo boat docked out on the edge of open water, its bow just visible beyond the cliffs. She ran after until she was up on the shoulder of the man on the edge of the crowd; his crisp uniform and the jagged walk gave her a moment's jolt of uncertainty. But he couldn't have forgotten who she was. She touched his arm.

"Ben."

Ben turned around. He looked her in the face, and his blank, rigid features melted. He stopped walking as the group of men moved on down the hill. He said nothing, just searched her face quizzically. She got up as close to him as she could without revealing an inappropriate intimacy that might embarass him.

"Do you remember me? Corrag?"

He still said nothing, but his expression became distraught, as if she had reminded him of something deeply troubling. The he knelt and put his face in his hands, rubbing his eyes.

"Ben," said Corrag, kneeling beside him. "Are you alright? I just couldn't believe I saw you in there. After all these years. Do you remember, Ben? The last time I saw you, the dam, Abel Marin? I was given a probation sentence and you got sent back to the Basin. I tried to contact you. I prayed and prayed you'd be all right."

"Who'd you pray to, Corrag?"

"I don't know. God?"

"God?"

His look was angry. It was Ben. For an instant all the time dropped away. They looked each other in the eyes, and the search for solace and understanding was the same for both. A man ran up and called out.

"Colonel Calder, sir. You'll miss the boat." Ben stood and gave her a chilling look, a deathly look just before his focus faded and he turned.

"You're right. A common acquaintance. A boy we once both knew. Thanks for coming back for me, Kurts."

In that final look and turning away Corrag had seen all she needed to see. She was left with the portrait of a tortured soul, trapped in a world not of its making. The augmented mind had claimed a crooked victory, stealing away the boy of her youth, the dream she'd once had of completeness in another human being. For the second time Ben had been lost. This time Corrag saw a way out. She knew what she had to do to put the sting behind her and carry on. Her child was the completion of her purpose, and in her dedication to his well being she would find the way forward. It was a simple formula, but effective and true for her. She walked back to the Fisherman's Hall and smiled at the men and women mingling at the door with drinks in their hands, the look of connoisseurs, savants, victors against the common enemy -- the winter, the icebergs and the endless Atlantic. Corrag joined their party, but not without the feeling of a heavy heart, of a weight not shared.

What had Ben traded up for, what was his life like? She wondered occasionally, but less and less as time went on. The summer gave way to the return of the lengthening night. She took Arthur out and showed him the stars, remembering the names his father had used for the constellations. He seemed to respond to the sounds in her mouth of those strange words, the desert words that had spawned the idea of his creation in her mind. She loved the way he would look at her but not look at her, looking beyond her as if waiting for more, as if the words for the stars were their own source and they would appear in the air self-generated, and sometimes she believed they would.

In the mornings, Corrag walked Arthur in a stroller down the road to the water's edge, going slowly to savor the sun's light on their faces. Arthur asked the names of things he saw, and Corrag pronounced them. There was a flock of geese in a wavy V flying overhead. There was a seal ducking under the water. Arthur loved the town road worker who filled potholes on the road with the excavator's claw full of steaming, smelly asphalt. A group of schoolgirls gathered at the entrance to the town's high school, giggling at them. There was a new, mean-spirited edge to their laughing, brought on by the coming winter. Corrag was not hurt by their sly taunts, she realized that there was a fault line in the town between the Jonah cult and the others, and none of the girls in the school entrance belonged to the Jonah. That fault line, the division that ran through every group of people she'd lived among, lay inside human beings, not in the settings in which they lived. It was part envy, part pain, and it ran as deep as any love. The pleasure of its expression was as great as the joy of human solidarity. She rushed Arthur along, not wishing to expose him to the corrosive elements in the air.

On Sundays, The Jonah congregation, calling itself

the New Church of the Remonstrance, met in Fernanda's large living room, which spilled out onto an enclosed porch. Corrag was beginning to recognize the many hymns. She sang along with a voice that was gaining in strength. Afterwards, the congregants surrounded her, and Arthur was passed around from person to person as he smiled silently and craned his little head to see where he was. They treated her and Arthur like royalty. Eventually the meeting dispersed and Candia, Corrag, Fernanda and Euclive were in the living room putting up the folding chairs and sweeping the floor. The baby was in a pen playing with some toys. Charles Fugel, who led the service most weeks, and Mrs. Green, the music teacher at the high school, were watching him. When they were done tidying, Fernanda brought out a tray of chocolates that they passed around the table.

"He is a joy," said Mrs. Green, referring to Arthur, who just laughed at Fernanda's Cairn terrier Joey.

"He loves that dog," said Candia. She was waiting for the opportunity to excuse herself and see if Eddie was outside, lingering, as was his recent habit, by the remains of the picket fence destroyed by several consecutive years of winter storms. She and Eddie had decided to announce their engagement publicly at the last fishermen's ringo scheduled at the end of the month. Eddie was not a Jonah, but Candia had told Fernanda she thought he could be pressed into a commitment, that he wasn't actively hostile.

"Yes, he does," said Corrag, helping the conversation along without pressing. There was always an expectant air to these Sunday gatherings, as if Arthur and she were about to perform a sign of the coming age.

"He loves it here in Red Bay if I do say," said Fernanda. "He is really a happy little fellow."

"Shame he doesn't seem to have any father figure in his little life," said Mrs. Green.

"That's not important!" said Charles, shocked. "Corrag, are you happy here?" he asked.

"Yes, of course," she said, a slight, defensive tremor in her voice.

"You would leave, though, if you could," he said.

"I don't know."

"The body of the Jonah has many needs. The evangelists are the wings of the Jonah message, spreading it to the four corners, preparing the way for the Third Day."

"What are you suggesting, Charles? The girl is hardly in a position." Fernanda acted shocked, picking the lint out of the folds of her skirt.

"She is in a position. She hasn't been home to Democravia. It's a very unsettled country where the Whale has been resisted. It's back in full control, yes, but there are great opportunities for us to win many converts, people who need to hear the truth about the Jonah and the hope of salvation we bring. For Corrag it would be a risk, yes, but also an opportunity to continue her spiritual growth in the service of the Gospel. Would you like to go home, Corrag?"

Corrag didn't answer, picking Arthur up out of the crib, as he was about to cry. She took him in her arms and rushed to the window. The sight of the little finches flitting in the trees where Fernanda had placed a feeder always distracted him. As the conversation continued behind her, she felt her heart beating in her throat. She couldn't tell if she was more frightened or excited by the possibility of going home to Democravia. The prospect had dropped out of the blue so suddenly. It was as if her childhood home no longer existed except in her memories, and she feared going back to find only the ruins, an unrecognizable land, and her parents dead, or worse, in such a desperate condition that her presence and Arthur's would not bring them relief. She had failed in so many ways to come to an adult, stable place, that going home was a shameful proposition. And yet, behind the fear was a rush of undifferentiated emotion, of longing and pain. She was scared to admit it, but she wanted to go very badly.

"Papers and what not. Emund Montaquila can fix it with his work. It would have to be soon. The passage will be shut in a month."

"But we can't just send her in blind."

"Of course not. We have people. Known friends."

It happened quickly after that. Every day there were sessions with Fernanda and Charles Fugel reading with her from the tablet of the Book of Remonstrances, channeled originally by Ian Winterstone, a truck driver living in Surrey, from the angel Yuriel. Winterstone had been a sickly child, picked on by his peers, and one day, after being thrown in a lake on a school picnic to Wales in 2015, he had heard Yuriel urging him to write down what he said. Winterstone went on to record the Book of Remonstrances on several versions of early tablets of Indian and Chinese manufacture. On this point Charles expressed some minor distaste. He was a purist who wrote his letters by hand in an elegant cursive he'd learned from his father, the first principal of the Red Bay elementary school. Mrs. Green had been his music teacher.

The B of R, as the Jonah members called it, basically told of the rebirth of civilization following the dark ages of the Whale. Life inside the Whale's belly was full of bile, an acidic reflux born of waste and wantonness, especially the luxuriousness of the virtual life. For the Jonah, bile was a metaphor for the toxic lifestyle of the Repho, the competitive individualism rooted in original sin that had been reborn. They held the old Democravian system in equal contempt for its liberal fluffiness, the lack of moral fiber. Now of course it was moot as the old order in that part of the country had withered on the vine.

Like her time of indoctrination and training with the Korazan, Corrag took to the daily sessions with Fugel and Fernanda with a natural passion for Winterstone's prophetic vision, the large ideas, the way she could easily see the world changing with her entrance into the secret life of the elect.

"The islands have seen it and fear. The end of the Whale is coming and the earth trembles and the seas rise up to wash away evil in the last hour. That's how it goes, Corrag."

"Yes, I know."

"Can you see it?"

"I think so."

"'And they aproach and come forward and help one another and say be strong. And that's where you come in."

"I do?"

"Exactly. You're a midwife and will help in the birth of the Jonah people and Arthur will be a shepherd with a flock of his own."

"Yes. I like that."

"You like that."

"I do."

The readings were all on tablets that were handed around from congregation to congregation in the Maritimes and beyond. The Jonah people wrote letters to each other on the snail mail and afterwards the letters were transcribed into the tablets of one of the leaders of the respective congregations before they were carefully burned. Fernanda couldn't see very well and so she had handed the duty of transcription to Candia. Corrag was breastfeeding Arthur in the back of the house while the dog played with a bone, the ham bone left over from the Sunday dinner with the elders of the Red Bay congregation. Fugel looked out the window.

"The dog is playing with that bone left by the Ebionites," he said. He always smiled sadly when he called the Jonah members that. Corrag asked Fernanda about it as Fugel was using the bathroom.

"Fernanda. What are the Ebionites?"

"They were a people who were wiped out by the

Romans. Charlie has confessed to me that he believes we've all been Ebionites before. We get our souls from them. That's what he believes," she whispered.

"Do you think so?"

"I don't know. Why not?"

Candia called her over through the open back door. She was typing from the letter on the portable keyboard with the tablet propped on the top step.

"Look at this, Corrag."

"What is it?"

"This is where you're going. Big-time, girl. You and Arthur are going to be stars."

"Don't keep it to yourself. Let me see."

It was the letter from Edmund Montaquila they'd been waiting for. Everything must have been arranged in Quebec for Corrag and Arthur to come. Corrag put Arthur down. She read aloud:

Dear Red Bay Crowd,

Keep your remonstrances coming. Have no fear about us here. As they say in the best families: Laissez Le Bon Temps Roulez. There is no life without death. It is a cause of terror to the sinner.

I know you are wondering if we have room at the inn for the travelers. That and more as we also have the necessary documents and passage for Corrag and her boy. We await word from you. Note that the feelings are running very strong here against the recent consolidation of the augment/mind/whale vis a vis Kupertini-Chagnon merge. We have had some major falling back in strength with the deaths of our lay deacon Osorio Benjamin due to an aneurysm that struck in the night. His final days were spent planning retreats in the Iron Range of Michigan for our missionary teams. Hundreds attended the wake and we gained some new conversion candidates who are currently in the evangelizing house out near the Norm Lavecque.

You were asking about getting some money from the treasury for small-bore training. I believe that would be possible but I must ask in return for accountability since you well know we have had instances of the old three card monte in some of the Jonah. I am not naming names, but when I say Goss Falls, New York you will know what I mean.

Corrag stopped reading. Candia had stood up and put her arm around Corrag's shoulders. There were tears in her eyes. Arthur was trying to climb the wooden steps. The dog was pulling at his diapers. It was a scene of domestic bliss, but something was not right. The letter dropped from Corrag's fingers.

"What's wrong?"

"I'm scared."

"You scared?"

"Yes. I don't know who I am. What am I supposed to do?"

"Take it one day at a time, Corrag. Let it happen. Just concentrate on the little things. Don't worry about the big things."

"They wanted me to be an emissary, Candia. I never

accomplished much of anything."

"You don't need to. Just be you. Look at me. I'm happy. Eddie and I want to be happy. You just need to want something bad enough. You taught me that, Corrag. Do you want to be happy?"

"I want everyone else to be happy. I don't care about myself."

"Care about yourself more, Corrag."

The two were crying and Arthur started bawling also. Even the dog started in howling. Fernanda came to the door to see what was the matter.

Two weeks later the boat was ready at the pier early on a cold morning. Seagulls screeched over the houses and along the cliffs. Charles Fugel, Mrs. Green, Wilders, Euclive and Eddie Fox stood on the road by the remains of the picket fence. Fernanda and Candia were going to walk them down to the water. Corrag was trying not to cry and urging Arthur to wave. The little boy was dressed in a jumpsuit that Fernanda had found in an old plastic bag in the spare closet where all her old childrens' clothes were kept.

"Everything good comes to an end," Charles was saying. "Corrag let this end be a beginning. Breathe in the salt air on your journey. Fill your lungs with goodness, and you will carry us all with you on your way."

Corrag walked around to them all and had Arthur grab their fingers. Corrag tried to personalize her farewells.

"Charles. I love your words. Keep them coming. Mrs. Green, I will always remember your voice, especially on

Morning has Broken. Wilders, if it weren't for you, I probably wouldn't be here. Eddie, you better take good care of Candia."

"I'll try, Corrag," he said and stuck his hands further in his pockets. Corrag loved all of them. She turned to where Candia had her bag and Fernanda stood out on the road and stepped away from the fence. She had always been a good Democravian girl, a star in the firmament of her parent's world, but nothing had prepared her for the dissolution of that world and the long road she had embarked upon when she'd stepped away from the Spring Fest with Ben Calder almost three years before. She felt like the aspects of her personality that had kept her alive through the recent past had been hidden, laying dormant, unsuspected, and she was still not sure they were hers.

The boat was a fifty-foot Scottish schooner retrofitted with Yanmar solar electrics and nanofiber icebreaking shields in the bow. It was called the *Belle Enfant*, homeport of Trois Rivieres. It sat low at the pier rocking slowly while the tide came in and icebergs congregated out in open water. The captain, Bob Anselm, was a bearded veteran of the Canadian brigades that had fought in the Basin with Democravian troops in the first decade of the Nativist wars. His wife Beth was his first mate and there was a deckhand, a boy with slitted green eyes named Oddgeir. Beth was a nurse from Vancouver. Corrag and Arthur were the only passengers, but there was a load of Greenland rock in the hold that they were bringing to several parties south of Quebec City, as Bob put it when asked. They welcomed Corrag and Arthur aboard. They would have the forward cubby in the bow while Bob and Beth slept aft next to the engine room and Oddgeir took the berth in the galley. Arthur cried all the time down below, so Corrag took him on deck, sitting in the cockpit behind the wheel while Oddgeir steered by the compass setting and watched for icebergs. The icebergs came alongside and then slipped away, their ice faces revealing rainbows in the sluicing fractures. The clouds on the horizon were an exotic bestiary that Corrag and Arthur tamed by giving them the names of people they'd known. Since Arthur's knowledge of people was limited to their Red Bay circle, Corrag took the opportunity to introduce him to the people of significance in her past. There was Ms. Schilling in the front of the class lecturing on the significance of the word solidarity in the song by the same name by the Grupo Chumaya, one of her favorites. There was Ricky about to sit down to his dinner and Alana dressing for a dinner party, applying synthetic pearl dust to her face in the bathroom. There above them was Beithune, flying through the air in a swirling high kick. She couldn't see Kevin anywhere.

"It doesn't matter," she told Arthur. "You have his face so you'll get to know him by looking in the mirror."

She couldn't see Ben anywhere either.

"The fact is, Arthur. We don't know where we're going or what will happen when we get there. The past is just a comforter. It's better than sucking your thumb, though."

"Why don't you come below and have some tea," said Beth, poking her head through the companionway.

""But what about the icebergs? Oddgeir can't do it alone, can he?"

"I'll take the watch."

Corrag accepted a steaming mug from Bob and sat at the chart desk while he watched the instrument panel and listened to the crackle of the maritime satellite channels he had hacked into on the Loran receiver. She set Arthur down on the pillow beside her and he flopped over into her lap and proceeded to fall asleep.

"How's the wee one?" asked Bob.

"Finally asleep," said Corrag.

"He's a great little guy. Congratulations. Who's the father?"

"Long story. Lost him in the Nenkaja. Actually never saw him again after Alpha battle. We were knocking out the augment system in Sandelsky when they took us both prisoners."

"The Korazan insurgents?"

"Yes."

"Put a scare into the Repho, didn't you? Too bad they're back stronger than ever with that Kupertini douchebag out of the Democravian state. What does he call it, the Union of Constipated Bastards?"

"I don't know. I just want to live a normal life."

"No such thing anymore, Corrag. You could lay low with us on the boat for awhile, but we're scheduled to deliver you over to Montaquila's crowd."

"Why?"

"Why what?"

"Why do you do this?"

"Money. A life. Everyone has to fight their corner. I don't trust the Repho. I don't trust the rebels. Anybody who pays me, I trust them until the job is over. When we sail out of port, out of sight out of mind, as far as I'm concerned. And the blue water is still a haven for the lawless."

"What about the Augment?"

"What about it? Not for me or Beth. I don't have anything against it on moral grounds, just hasn't got good enough. Some day, when it's right, I might get it done. I might care about living forever some day. Right now I like living every day as if it was my last. More fun that way."

Oddgeir cracked the hatch open and shouted some words that she couldn't hear. Bob followed up the ladder, and when he came back down he ordered Corrag up.

"Get into the bunk and pretend you're asleep with the baby.

"What is it?"

"Repho coast guard cutter. You're my daughter and we lost your emosponder."

Corrag did as she was told, skirting into the bunks forward of the hold, with Arthur in one arm, his head slumped in exhaustion. She got into the berth and pulled the blankets over herself and Arthur. It was cold. Arthur nuzzled into her side, seeking warmth. And the boat popped and swayed, breaking the waves with its bow. She could sense them slowing, falling back. The pounding of the water against the hull grew louder. She closed her eyes. If this was the belly of the whale, she would one day wake up and there would be sunlight and warmth. She just needed to hold on a little longer. It wasn't, strangely, in God that she trusted. It was in Arthur. His presence by her side was all she needed to feel calm. Not that she could keep him safe if there was a danger of being captured and returned to the Nenkaja. Only she couldn't even think of that as a reality. She listened hard, and when she didn't hear anything except the constant reverberations of the muffled water she fell asleep.

Marina handed her the whale carved out of bone. It was morning. The sensors were ringing in the chapel offices, and when she turned her head she could see Alana disappearing around the corner and up the entrance ramp for the disabled. The prisoners were running from the shed and scattering and the guards were doing nothing about it. Corrag walked up to Marion Muslkick and asked her why she was doing nothing to prevent the prisoners from escaping. The Nenkaja would disappear if all the prisoners escaped, just evaporate into the mists that were rising all around from the swampy ground. Muslkick pulled off her shirt and freed her large breasts and began to dance. She was crazy, and the Nenkaja could disappear and take them all up into thin air with it. Corrag went inside the chapel offices and saw Alana with Kevin. Kevin was asking Alana if he could marry her, but then Dr. Juarez-Knoblock intervened and announced new quotas for the log cutting.

"But it's summer," said Marion Muslkick.

"Put your shirt on and get back to work," said Juarez-Knoblock. It was too late to do anything about all the

escaped prisoners. Corrag wondered if it was really Alana who had disappeared back outside. Muslkick refused orders and all the remaining people in the chapel offices, Corrag included, began to sing Morning Has Broken. *She wondered if it was Alana and what she wanted. Was she escaping? Would she make it? Kevin stood there looking brave and maintaining a guarded silence. Corrag felt guilty about him and wanted to hug him and somehow urge him up into a higher level of participation, but his best days were behind him as was true for everyone she knew.*

Then she was on a carousel and Ricky was standing at the fence watching her as the carousel spun. She was holding tight to the reins of the pony as it bucked slowly up and down. She was wearing a dress, a light blue dress that Alana had bought at a yard sale in Petaluma. There were still yard sales in those days and people's funerals. As the carousel spun and the pony bucked, the music playing was Fire to the Rain, *an old song Alana used to sing to her when she was just a baby. She remembered. The carousel stopped. Corrag dismounted from the pony and she straightened her blue dress and looked around for Ricky. He was gone. Everyone was gone. There was just an empty beach and a man at the end of the sand holding up a dead fish that had washed up in the storms. She could smell the salt air, and it was wet, raining, and she had nowhere to go. She began to run. Her feet were stuck in the wet muck, and it took all of her strength to get them to move. Then the waves began to strike the beach with greater strength, and she could hear the rumble of thunder. The man was still there. At the end of the beach. With a pile of dead fish he had collected. She was coming closer and she could almost see his face. But the sand was sucking at her feet. It was getting harder and harder to run. She willed her legs to move faster, push harder, and her heart was beating so fast it hurt her chest. But the man wanted to show her something. About the fish. They were all dead, lying on the wet sand and rotting. Something had poisoned them. But she would never know what it was because he would fade away. Always fade away before she got back to him.*

She woke up. It was Ricky's dream. She shook her head. This was not a dream. The boat was pitching violently, and she could hear the wind whistling somewhere. Someone had left the hatch open. She decided to get up and leave Arthur asleep. She piled the pillows and blankets between him and the rail on the bunk so he wouldn't roll out. She staggered along the passage, and there was nobody in the galley and the hatch to the pilothouse was open. She climbed the ladder. The wind was deafening. The stars were whirling in the sky, and the boat was bucking up to them like a wild horse. The light from the pilothouse revealed the hulking waves all around, their skins crabbed and frothing from the wind.

""Forty knot winds astern," yelled Beth. "Nor'easter. We'll ride it out and take turns on watch. You have time before it's your turn."

"But all of you are up here."

"We're reefing the sail. Once that's done we'll be okay."

Bob yelled at Oddgeir, who was working on getting the mainsail down and reefed. He held onto the boom for dear life as the waves crashed over the hull, threatening to sweep them all away. Beth shone a flashlight on him, and he wore a headlamp. A massive wave rose beside them and pushed the boat up in the air and set it back down almost on its side. Bob spun the wheel inside the house, adjusting the track manually to fight the water's takedown. Corrag couldn't help it. She ducked inside and fell back down the ladder, not without taking a spray of icy cold water all over herself. Oddgeir looked down after her and laughed when he saw her sprawled in the galley as pots gimbaled cockily on the stove.

"Give her a hand, Oddgeir," said Bob.

With a swift jump and holding onto the map table, he reached her as she tried to stand and extended his hand for support. She was glad to take it, suddenly feeling sick.

"You look like you could use some coffee."

"No thanks."

"This is really good. Try it."

Oddgeir took one of the pots off the stove and poured some of its contents into a mug with the name of a Parisian kebab house, *Le Sanctuaire de Baal*, and handed it to Corrag, who had stayed seated on the sole. Corrag took it gingerly, unsure of releasing her hold, and sipped it, slobbering a bit onto her shirt. It tasted of spices, cinnamon, and a hint of garlic.

"I don't want to be sick."

"Don't think about it if you do. It's good. Even the

best sailors get sick on this passage."

"How old are you?"

"Sixteen."

"You seem really young."

"How old are you?"

"Seventeen."

"You're not much older."

"No, not much."

"You know how old Bob is?"

"I'd guess forty five."

"Fifty-seven. Beth is thirty-five. They've sailed around the freaking world seven times."

"Really?"

"Yeah. We did the Suez Canal and around the Horn this summer and back up to Europe. We specialize in the trade of ideas. That's what Bob says."

"Oh."

Oddgeir's eyes were making Corrag feel even worse. They were impossible to focus into, small slits of hazel. She wondered if he was a part of her dream, the man with the fish. She decided to share it with him and see. If he was a dream, he would recognize the man and be able to tell her who it was.

"Do you believe in dreams?"

"Lucid or what?"

"No, I mean, am I dreaming right now."

"No this is real. I know what you're feeling though. My first trip with Bob I was so sleep-deprived. It was sick."

"Where are you from?"

"Me? I'm from Grindavik, Iceland."

"I'm from Edmundstown. Democravia. Do you miss your family?"

"Yes. But this is life. You have to apprentice to something."

"I don't know. When I get old I want to live someplace quiet and nice with a picket fence, but not washed away. Someplace warm and far from the ocean."

"The desert. You should check out Namibia. It's really nice and there are some cool people living there."

"You have been all over."

At that moment the sickness snuck up and hit her. As she began to retch, Oddgeir slipped a slop bucket from underneath the galley stove in front of her and she held it with one hand. When she was done, she lay down on the fold out berth and slept and woke in a fright, thinking of Arthur. She somehow got forward in the total darkness. The wind was still howling and the boat was being tossed around like a bit of flotsam in the apocalyptic rage of an elemental meltdown. Arthur was still sleeping, as soundly as any child in a crib on the rock solidest foundation of middle Repho. She lay next to him and prayed. Not knowing to what or how, her prayers took the form of a pure supplication to transcendent mystery in charge of the storm. If they could just somehow ride it out and if she could avoid getting hit by a wave while on watch, that would be the most merciful outcome and appreciated with every fiber and nerve cell in her body.

But for four days and nights she stayed in the berth. Beth changed Arthur's diapers, wiped Corrag's head with one of the damp cloths, assured her it would be all right. She wasn't able to take any watches, or join them in the galley, barely able to lift her head to sip at the broths made from frozen calves' livers. Beth brought them for her. They were making their way down the seaboard with the wind on a broad reach and that meant a faster passage into the shelter of the gulf of the St. Lawrence, she said assuringly. Then one day the wind stopped and they were motoring past cliffs on the starboard, the mountains behind them. Corrag made her way out on the deck with Arthur. His eyes blinked at the unfamiliar sun. The water was a gently rolling field of blue, and the little fishing boats plying their way out to the traps reminded Corrag of the print hanging on the wall of the bathroom in the Hunnewell farm, a vintage marine scene by John Cleveley, *View of a Seaport*.

Nobody was saying much. They were exhausted. The radio was crackling with messages not intended for the *Belle Enfant*. Bob sat at the map table with the screen on and stared at nothing in particular. Oddgeir was in the pilothouse steering and Beth sitting beside him on the stool, her legs crossed and a mug of something steaming in her gloved hands.

"Ah, there it is," said Bob, stroking his beard and then rubbing his hands together. He shut off the screen and leaned out the hatch.

"It's on for tonight," he yelled. "Bring it around north by northeast and we'll aim for the channel buoys."

"Where are we?" asked Corrag, once he was back inside. She had Arthur in her arms. Her legs felt wobbly.

"Sit down girl. You're not well. Thank God we're here. You couldn't have gone on much longer in that way."

"I was pretty sick, wasn't I?"

"Not too bad. This is Ille Royale. We're putting in here. We're to meet our people here soon. I've let them know. Have your bags packed."

Bob was excited, with the air of a quiet man on the verge of a major coup. Corrag was not surprised when, after they'd pulled alongside the jetty on the island once intended for container ships picking up agricultural produce, with large eroded cement columns rising from the murky, silty waters of the tidal river, two boxlike trucks pulled up and spilled out a half dozen men in regular clothes but a common fitness level that spoke to her of military training. Oddgeir tied off the hawser on the rusted cleat and the men approached him. Bob, sitting in the pilothouse, focused on cutting off the motor. Arthur peered out the porthole in the galley in Corrag's arms. Then he wanted to be put down. Corrag had her bag in the galley berth there with her, and Beth did something at the stove. It was about mid-morning, and Corrag wondered aloud if they were coming for her or the cargo or both.

"What do they look like?" asked Beth.

"Chinese,"said Corrag. They're all of them Chinese or something."

"That's the Triangle Shimwa. They're here for the rock not for you."

Three of the men came aboard talking jovially with

Bob. They went below and lifted the planks off the cargo hold. They began hauling the heavy metal boxes off the boat with Oddgeir's help. It took two men to a box. They loaded them in their trucks and Bob was handed an envelope with his payment in Republican dollars, still the strongest American currency. As they worked, Bob and Beth conferred in the galley, planning their route southward. They wanted to be in Bermuda in two weeks and then Recife by the middle of September. The problem was the Gulf Stream, to determine which way was it running. Sometimes it ran in reverse and sometimes it stalled and sometimes it ran full force up to the Scandinavian lands. It was the sign of a planet trying to shrug off a sickness. Then a man appeared on the jetty pushing a bicycle. Corrag leaned out of the hatch to see who it was whistling. She thought he had also a vaguely Asiatic air, with a thick head of white hair and a still black goatee.

"Are you the young mother?"

"I might be."

"Yes. Let me introduce myself although there is little time for pleasantry. The local constabulary is just now coming off the Ille Royale bridge. My name is Montaquila, Edmund. The Cicero of the Laurentian Plain."

"Let me get my baby."

"Yes, forget the rest of your shit and post haste, chicky."

Montaquila owned a zipbike, but it appeared to be non-functional. As he pushed it up the hill away from the water's edge, he grunted and cursed. Corrag followed at a safe distance, with Arthur tied to her front in a sling. When she looked back, the *Belle Enfant* was motoring away from the jetty and the three trucks' doors were sliding closed. Montaquila was making hard for a dirt trail leading away through a narrow gate into a children's park of slides and swings. He got the zipbike off the road and stopped. Just then a convoy of siren sounding, bot-driven armored vehicles with the insignia of the Quebec Provincial Guard came roaring down the main road past Corrag. She stepped onto the hard shoulder and covered Arthur's ears with both her hands. The Shimwa trucks below made squealing turns off the pier and headed in the opposite direction. Gunfire sounded and the QBP responded with automatic lasers from their roof-mounted cannons that exploded one truck and disintegrated the tires off another, sending it careening off the pier and into the river below. The lead truck turned a corner onto a street of summer residences, the house owners soon returning to open windows and mulch the hydrangeas.

The streets quieted down. Corrag picked herself up and dusted Arthur's knees and legs with her hands. He needed a diaper change. One Shimwa truck had escaped. Military choppers circled above the pier with searchlights on, looking for survivors. The sun was sinking in the western sky behind the lineaments of the ancient city of Quebec. Corrag helped Arthur down the slide. He was an intrepid climber and had gotten stuck halfway up the incline and lay on his belly and laughed while Corrag pulled at his feet. Montaquila was on his emosponder, pacing with a bedraggled look, speaking loudly, repeating to make himself better understood to the person on the other end of the connection.

Hours passed and the sky was dark except for a thin sliver of a waxing moon. Montaquila had gotten her to talk about herself. He asked her to trace the roots of her faith. She hedged a little, but mentioned her Democravian upbringing with its respect for religiosity if not any particular religion as responsible for her sense that some kind of *faber* was ultimately responsible for all. Montaquila, surprisingly, was agnostic although he sympathized deeply, he said, with people's right to believe in any kind of self-perpetuating system.

"So why are you ... why do you support the Jonah?" asked Corrag

"They're an effective bunch of people," he answered curtly.

"Wouldn't you like to believe?

Montaquila paced. She had the sense that the conversation was taking a tack that he didn't quite find favorable.

"Not necessarily. Look, the idea of a messianic victory is very nice, and might in fact be in the cards. But that's not where I place my bets. However, the Jonah rocks when it comes to rocking the boat, and that's my game. I'm a disruptive from way back, baby. Rock and roll just never died with me. I will shake the Whale with a shimmy in the belly. What about you? Do you honestly believe that stuff about the three generations before the system dissolves with the approach of the man god on the pale horse and the hordes of angels driving out demons into the stinking river that divides the good souls from the bad souls? Isn't that slightly medieval?"

"It's in the Book of Hebrews. Much older than the Middle Ages. Have you read it?"

"No. Have you?"

"I've listened to some of it."

"We have some people who have genuine visions. You'll meet them. They think you are the root of Jesse or somebody. The red heifer. Except this will be a new temple in a barren land."

"Listen, I really just want to get back to Edmundstown and find my parents at this point."

"You can't shake the weight of history once it comes bearing down on your head, Corrag. Just roll with it. That's my advice."

Corrag walked Arthur around in her arms under the starry night. He was miserable and wouldn't stop crying. Montaquila's friend showed up finally. The two men worked on the zipbike with flashlights and a rolled out bag of tools. Then Montaquila stood, and it started up.

"Battery chamber sprung a leak. It'll get us home," he told Corrag. "Listen, he added. "All that stuff I told you about my very shakeable belief system? Keep it to yourself. There would be a whole lot of sorry pilgrims if that got out."

"No worries there, Edmund. Your secret's safe with me," said Corrag.

His friend James Romney, a Jonah with a laundry

business on the island, rode away up the hill from the park. Corrag tied the baby in the sling again and slung him so he straddled her back. His head lolled. She assured Montaquila they would be all right. They mounted the idling zipbike with the repaired battery and rode away across the island, the bridge and down the congested highway towards the thin sliver of moon.

Montaquila lived below the old city, in a neighborhood of new apartment buildings and squares of cobblestone. They parked the zipbike in the basement of the building and walked across one of the squares to get some food items and diapers for the baby in a MarcheAmi. The people in the square looked like young, hip couples wearing black leather.

"Don't let them fool you." said Montaquila, reading her thoughts. Most of these are plants, hybrids, or worse. What we call *robotes informateurs.*"

"What are they?

"Non-humans. Subjects of the great experiment to subvert the delicacy of creation. The immortal monsters of the age."

"Sandelsky implants?"

"No. The next step, Corrag. If you are a loyal augmented servant you can be uploaded into the shape of your choosing and live out the rest of time as a machine, your thoughts and reaction constantly refreshed in the cloud."

"Hybrid bots."

"Something like that. For the few and humble. The chosen who will populate the stars with their manufactured offspring. The idiot bastards of Satan."

Once up in the apartment, Montaquila ran a bath and went back out, leaving her and Arthur. Corrag dipped Arthur in the lukewarm water and bathed him. With a fresh pair of diapers she put him to bed in the spare room across the hall. Then she went back and took a steaming hot shower and dried herself, patting her arms and legs with a cotton towel and putting on a t-shirt and sweatpants Edmund had set by the door. Revived, she finally felt like relaxing, like she was on solid ground again.

The view out the window was of the river and the lights of a riverside esplanade. Again the young untrustworthy people were strolling along it. They seemed sinister and yet eerily appealing. Edmund gestured towards an empty goblet on the coffee table with the bottle of wine. She nodded. Montaquila poured and handed her the glass of dark red wine, and she took a sip.

"Delicious."

"It's a Democravian vintage. To your return home."

"Thank you. Are there no real people out there anymore?

"Very few. The government will have an easy time rounding up the remnants of the unaugmented. They're all cowering in their homes like rabbits in their burrows. Not like the Repho cities with their huge underclass. There are disadvantages to a settled, good French Canadian working class people, I'm afraid."

"But hasn't Gheko been rounding up unaugments?"

"The Korazan resistance in the outer boroughs has

set them back. They tried, but it's proven unfeasible. Don't forget that augments have family connections, relatives, especially older relatives who haven't gone over and when they end up in the cargo hold of container ships for weeks on end it becomes a very uncomfortable thing for all concerned. The answer obviously is Sandelsky gaming and entertainment systems that anesthetize the population. But eventually they will get around to it again. And when that happens, we will be ready."

Corrag looked at his eyes as he talked They were a dark color with hints of deeper lights, and his words were comforting to her with the flavor of their vintage. She was very tired, however, and when he announced that there were people coming over she balked. But there was nothing he could do. Word had slipped out, probably Romney the laundry owner had told someone that she was here, the Nenkaja prisoner who had appeared in Red Bay bearing the whale, with her miraculous child.

"You give us hope in the darkness, Corrag. I can't tell you how important that is in these days of peril. Just bear up for our sake. All they want is to say they saw you and wish you well."

A crowd of people spread through the apartment, probably around fifty of the Jonah people, a good percentage of which were under forty, men and women in casual yet chic clothes belying their heightened state of alertness. They had grown up in the shadow of the Repho and now wanted nothing more than a chance at a normal life as the Whale spread the power of the augmented elite through the world. Corrag met the bearded former college professor of linguistics who had lost his job to a bot that could present the material and test more efficiently than he. There was someone else who testified that legislators in Indonesia were being urged to vote themselves out of office as the population clamored to be ruled by bot overlords with no corrupt party affiliations. The major networks were withholding the news because it would be too upsetting for the population in Canada, with only 45 percent augment penetration, as opposed to the 65 percent in the Repho/UCB union. The writing was on the wall, said the professor. Montaquila nodded his head.

"We are in a good position. We have been dispelled of our illusions for some time. Unlike many others who thought to buy time by currying favor, we have spent our energy wisely, organizing for this day. Corrag, your journey home will be as a missionary for us, the Jonah, as we seek to keep the light of a humane culture alive in these coarsened lands," said Montaquila.

"I understand the Jonah. I'm not sure I can be successful," said Corrag.

"Success is sacrifice in the name of God, the One and Almighty," said the professor.

It was Corrag's turn to nod.

People filed through on their way out. They wished her well. They really seemed as if they were happy just to have seen her and touched her arm and said something, anything to acknowledge this special occasion. Corrag wondered if it was real or if maybe they were all under the spell of some hugely ill-conceived illusion. It was not of her making, if they were. There was no way of knowing. There was no certainty. They seemed to concur on that point, and it seemed to be the basis of their resistance and their hope.

Eight -- Circuitry

Montaquila sat her down on a stool in front of the nanoscreen in his study and took high-resolution photographs of her eye. It was eight o'clock and the bells of the basilica were chiming. Out on the river a barge floated past and a circus set up shop in the park across the esplanade. Her irises radiated out blue and yellow in swirls from the center like undulating cords. There they were blown up on the nanoscreen.

"Classic rattlesnakes. This should be straightforward."

Montaquila went into the database. It was a highly sensitive operation as it had involved hacking the biometric records of the Library and Archives Office. There he found the eyes of Sonia Pivak, who had died in 2019. They were similar in pattern, although a brownish hazel in color. He blew up the irises side-by-side and played with matching the two patterns by shifting the value sticks. Corrag watched him work on the photoshop template on the screen. He had to take into account the dilation and contraction due to lighting to get the ends of the ranges right, he said. Working with silver salts in a hydrogel solution and incorporating light sensitive ground quartz with chromium oxide and iron oxide for color, he was able to make up a reasonable facsimile, he said, wearing a jeweler's magnifying glass and talking while he worked. Then he printed out several copies of lenses and had Corrag try them on and inspected her eyes in a scanner he had there.

"So much easier when you have the actual subject in front of you to work with," he said, satisfied with himself.

"Do you think it will work? she asked.

"Man versus machine. Still not a contest, sweety, in the game of life. I could be wrong, but I'm probably right. We'll give it a try. That's our basic strength, isn't it?"

She didn't answer what she hoped was a rhetorical question.

"Give me the afternoon to work up a Canadian birth certificate and get it e-stamped."

"Okay."

Corrag took Arthur out on the esplanade. They walked through a marina, looking at the sailboats, and then an empty market with the stalls set up and ornate fruit rinds still littering the concrete floor. A police van zipped around the corner and the ceaseless rounds of bot vehicles and delivery trucks glided by like syrup enveloping the afternoon. A young couple sat on a nearby bench as Corrag played with Arthur around an empty fountain. The little girl ran up and admonished Arthur for playing with a scrap of leaf blowing in the dusty fountain.

"That's dirty," she said.

Her mother chased her.

"Come now, Lillian. Don't be a bother."

"She's not a bother," said Corrag. The young woman and her male companion wore matching light blue windbreakers. Her male friend pulled out a can of some refreshment and popped the seal. The young woman smiled with reticence at Corrag. Her smile masked a shared knowledge, but what was it? Corrag wondered if she knew her from somewhere. The little girl tried to get into the fountain, and her mother stopped her.

"You never know what kind of germs. What kind of people ... "

She didn't finish her sentence. Then she walked off with her girl and returned to her bench. Corrag picked up Arthur from the fountain. The little birds in there came back once he was out of their way. Corrag felt suddenly lonely and lost. The young couple and the little girl had spooked her with some reminder of an essential exclusion. She wanted to go up and start a conversation. Learn more about them. But what was the chance they were not even human? The thought sent a chill up her back, a pallor of distrust that settled over the day like a filter, robbing the light of its essence so it seemed dark and cold. She thought of Alana and Ricky and felt sorry for herself but not for long. Arthur snuggled in her lap and fell asleep.

She got back to Montaquila's apartment in the rush hour, after walking with the crowds of people getting off the trams. They had seemed hurried, afraid, unable or unwilling to focus on their surroundings instead of their emosponders. She got the sense of their basic unreality, like a tide of some kind receding before her very eyes. She wanted to describe this feeling to Montaquila, but he interrupted her as he opened the door.

"We've had a visit from the QPB. Someone's tipped them. We need to hurry. Annette will take you out to the

Norm Lavecque tonight for the 8:05."

Annette was a young woman with hair pulled back in a bun sitting on the living room sofa. Corrag recognized her from the get-together the night before.

"What? Tonight?"

"Yes. We have no time to play around. You are Sonia Pivak, age 19, from Thunder Bay, visiting your parent's old college friends Ernestine and George Smith in Fresno. Here are the important facts. Memorize them and then get rid of the paper. Here is an emosponder with your necessary documents. Here are the lenses. Here is your birth certificate in case you need to produce paper evidence."

"Is he still Arthur?

"Yes. Arthur Pivak. Your son. There is no record of him anywhere so he is a clean slate. Just tell them you are planning on getting him officialized in Edmundstown. No problem. The odds are you won't be questioned once you go through the initial scan. Travel requirements have been eliminated for the former Democravian cities. You'll tube into Ryanport and connect there for Lax. Ernestine and George will be there. They are a very sweet and very loyal older Canadian couple who moved out to the coast years ago and they are absolutely thrilled about hosting you."

"Okay."

"We have your bag already packed with clothes and essential toiletries, some books and things on the emosponder for you."

Underneath the calm optimism, there was a tremor

in his voice. He had been bothered by how fast the police had appeared. He hadn't expected things to move so fast. For Corrag, it was not as surprising. Once again the war was here.

"You know what's expected of you."

"Right now?"

"Right now, just stay alive. In the future, we'd like to see you help bring in new members. A growing base on the West Coast is a priority. We have the resources to support you. Stay in touch through the snail mail. If you need immediate help, Ernestine and George have contacts. Commit my address to memory. It's on the paper."

She helped Annette and Edmund make dinner, just a salad and some shiitakes in a bacon and onion sauce and some more red wine, this time an Australian Pinot Grigio that Edmund poured into a decanter while they set the table in the kitchen. They laughed and told stories about the foibles of young adulthood. Edmund was, besides a superb cook and counterfeiter, a great host who could put anybody at ease. Corrag couldn't help feeling a twinge of jealousy of Annette.

Then Corrag took a shower. Afterwards she checked the bag that had been packed. The clothes looked like they could belong to Sonia Pivak, a Canadian girl on her first trip to the former Democravia, halter-tops and tee shirts in the primary colors and form fitting neoprene pants.

"This could be fun, Arthur," she said. Arthur looked up and smiled at her. She loved the way he responded to her words. It was funny the way that things could be so normal and on the verge of catastrophe at the same time, she thought. She couldn't remember any longer how her childhood had been. Were there never any signs of a coming disaster? Perhaps her disillusionment in school those last few years had been a warning that the path ahead would not be fully marked. But everyone had always been so sure of themselves. That was probably the sign, looking back, that decay had gotten the better of the collective consciousness. She picked out what was a sensible traveling outfit, loose pants, a long-sleeved cotton blouse and put on a suede coat draped on the cot. There was still time, about a half hour before they were set to leave, so she picked out the utility tablet from the bag and searched for news icons. There were reviews of the latest Sandelsky gaming platforms and stories about the Hoselier twins that had starred in the absurd science fiction series, *Imperfect Settings*, about aliens and human expeditions coexisting on Gliese 581g.

On the ride out in the taxi, she and Annette sat together silently in the back. Corrag took out the plastic case and put on Edmund's lenses. She turned and Annette smiled at her.

"Looks good," she said.

"Thanks. I feel good, I guess," said Corrag.

She wanted to ask Annette what her life was like, how she had met Edmund, but felt the questions would be too compromising in the taxi, even with the nanoscreen shield up between them and the driverbot. When they got to Norm Lavecque, Annette led her to the entry desk and waited while Corrag checked herself in under the name Sonia Pivak. There was an eye scan. It seemed to go all right.

"So. This is it?" asked Annette.

"Yes. I guess it is."

"Good luck."

"You too."

Annette smiled and turned. Corrag proceeded to the embarkation gate. There were two bots and a bored looking woman in a brown security uniform checking ticket stubs on the platform. Corrag went ahead and showed her the tickets for herself and Arthur.

"Is the child going to need any special meal such as the nutritional for under-5 year olds?"

"Yes, please. The child's nutritional."

The bot pushed some keys.

Corrag took her seat on the tubid, placed Arthur in her lap and her bag in the seat next to her and settled into reading on the tablet. She got some stares from some of the other passengers, but otherwise nothing untoward. The rest of the passengers finished boarding. A man in a white business suit with a tan stopped and looked at the seat number.

"I'm afraid I'm going to have to ask you to excuse me. I have the seat there."

"That's fine," said Corrag. He put his carry-on bag in the overhead and made himself comfortable, leaving Arthur's empty seat with Corrag's bag between them.

"How old is the baby?" asked the businessman. He smiled in a friendly, alert manner. Corrag found to her surprise that she was in the mood for talking. She smiled back.

"Oh, he's not even one year old. He's just a baby, really."

"Very handsome. Reminds me of my daughter. Her name is Janacar. She's half Zimbabwean. She's 25 now."

"Oh, wow. How old are you, if you don't mind my asking?"

"I'm 67. But technically I have no age because I've been uploaded, you see."

"Really?"

"Yes. So technically I'm immortal."

"Oh, cool. What's that like?"

"It's better than the alternative. Mostly just like before. I have almost all my functions. I mean I can't have sex. But that's sort of liberating."

He laughed, and so she did also.

Corrag looked at him. He smiled a sad sort of smile. He seemed almost comical in his honesty.

"Well. That must be sad," she said, embarrassed.

"Well, not if you don't think about it, and of course I don't," he smiled.

"I see. What do you think about?"

"Anything I want. I have my memories, and I'm learning all the time, taking courses and attending seminars. I'm headed to a writer's conference in Malibu. Do you know it?"

"My dad used to take me out there before. When I was very little. He liked to surf.

"What was his name?"

Corrag swallowed, realizing she had been about to reveal more about herself than was safe.

"Not important," she said. "But what about your privacy. Doesn't it bother you that your thoughts are not your own?"

"What do you mean, not my own? Why, of course they are, I am a writer. Charles Decour. My books are world famous. I have a contract with Berger and Sons." His eyes, the pupils never dilated, she realized, looking closely. Also, his skin perfectly stretched across the chin and neck, like a mannequin's.

"What about the Cloud?"

"Well, of course there could be a backdoor. That doesn't bother me. Small price to pay."

"I guess."

"Are you augmented yet?"

"Not yet."

"And they let you travel? With things being the way they are? The filthy unaugments. What those people did to Rand Park is beyond description. You must get yourself done, honey. As soon as possible."

"Oh, I will."

He looked at her quizzically, and for a brief instant, Corrag felt a chill. His glance had made a secret appraisal that had not been favorable. Without excusing himself, the man took out nightshade glasses and plugged a wireless auralscape bud in his ear and leaned his seat all the way back. Arthur was hungry and began to fidget and cry. Corrag put him up to her breast and he suckled while the tubid took off and slung itself into top speed. Then the meals were served. The man beside her did not eat. Arthur was not a good traveler. He wanted to get down and crawl around, exploring. On their way into Ryanport, her aisle mate finally took off his eyeshades and gave a scowl at the sight of Arthur standing on his toes on his seat beside him and looking at the rows of passengers finishing their food towards the back of the container. For all his vaunted augment advantage, he didn't seem all that tolerant of others, thought Corrag. Then, when they stopped at Ryanport, he stood and switched seats and she never saw him again until they were in Lax and walking to the baggage desk and she passed him in the hall where he was standing very still and looking at nothing in particular against the wall. She realized in that instant, with bristling armed UCB troops thick at every crosswalk and every boarding gate, that she would never find her hosting couple Ernestine and George.

"Arthur," she said. "Get ready to run."

She picked up her pace. In the elevator going down, she stood in the middle, away from the glass walls, surrounded by people of every persuasion and physical type. In the main hall she walked by the rows of market customer agencies that had sprung up since the Federation had been deposed by the UCB. She picked one with no other clients at the desk and arranged for the rental of a zipbike, thinking she would enjoy greater security and anonymity on it. They were harder to spot in traffic from drones. She paid with the wad of Repho dollars Edmund had given her and the man at the desk had her sign a dingy old insurance screen with a stylus.

Then he gave her the magnetic tab with the lot location printed on nanofilm. She put it in the pocket of her coat, picked Arthur up in one arm and slung the bag over her shoulder and marched out of the terminal.

The Democravian air greeted her with its once-sweet scents of youth and possibility now gone underneath the haze of the contaminated afternoon sky and the ever-present gaze of security cameras and circling drones. With Arthur in the sling tight against her back, she started out on the zipbike through the lot. At a checkpoint, a bottleneck at the terminal exit before everyone headed in the cardinal directions down the still solid Democravian infrastructure, the officer gave her a quick glance, took the nanofilm receipt, and waved her on. She kept behind a line of bot delivery vehicles in the slow lane headed up to the Mono Valley on 498. A couple of times she spotted surveillance drones crossing the sky ahead and pressed even closer to the convoy, but she presumed she had been marked and was being followed. She got off at an exit for Davisville and then tracked diagonally on little used county roads through Ysidro. She stopped at Ysidro state park where she and Ben had met Abel and Sandy. She pulled onto the shoulder. Nobody followed behind on the road for at least a half hour. She thought it better to press onwards to her destination. She continued on the back roads as the day began to wane behind her into Edmundstown, with its placid, suburban streets and its quaint commercial district and into the hills on the eastern end -- the ritzier neighborhoods of St. Michael's and Endura.

The zipbike slowed silently and stopped a block or so away. She would walk the rest of the way just to be safe. There was the house, its carport with the brown asphalt tiles still slightly moldering with age and the cracks in the curb just the way they'd been all her life. But the front door was new, in a blue pastel color that Alana would never have chosen. And instead of Ricky there was a stooped Asian man of an advanced age walking in slippers on the front lawn in the setting sun. Corrag walked with Arthur along the sidewalk and rang the doorbell of the next house. She heard the opening beats of *Holly Jolly Christmas* and realized with growing hope that it was the signature doorbell tune the Rosaleses had always used. And there was Mrs. Rosales in curlers and some yellowish cream smeared across her face. She was a lot older and frailer than Corrag remembered.

"Mrs. Rosales. Hi, it's me. Do you remember me?"

"Corrag?"

She did remember. Corrag was surprised that she remembered her name, She didn't recall having much first name basis contact with the Rosaleses.

"Hi. The house looks wonderful and the yard too."

"How nice of you to stop by and visit."

"Mrs. Rosales. Do you know where my parents are?"

"Well, they're not here."

"No, I know that. There's a new man in our house."

"Oh, he's wonderful. Shokuro is a wonderful neighbor. He's a lovely man. Shokuro!" She began to call the man. She wanted him to meet Corrag.

"No. Mrs. Rosales. I don't have a lot of time. I'd

rather not."

"Shokuro! Hi there!"

"Mrs. Rosales, stop! My parents. Did they leave an address with you when they moved?"

"Well. The Mister would know about that. If they did, the Mister would have that information."

"Could you ask him for me?"

"Yes. You stay and talk with Shokuro. He's a lovely man and has a very good job with some information business downtown."

A few minutes later, Mr. Rosales appeared at the door. He was wearing a brown corduroy jacket and smoking a cigarette. He was unshaved. He looked worried.

"Corrag. Why are you here?"

"I don't know."

"Do you and the child want something to eat before you move on?"

"That would be nice."

Mrs. Rosales set out a plate on the little kitchen table that folded in between the appliance bank and the wall when not in use. They had a new cat whom she called Luigi that jumped up on the folding table while Corrag sat there spooning gelatin and whipped cream into her mouth and Arthur's.

"Is he okay with that, dear? It's the special hyperfroth from that company, I forget its name, the doughboy."

"Pillsbury."

"Yes, from the Repho. We're getting all sorts of Repho goods nowadays. The cheap stuff is even cheaper than before. Somehow the good stuff is even more expensive. Of course for the majority life has always been hard, no matter who is running the show. But I like this hypercream. He seems to like it. His mouth reminds me of a neuralscape I saw once, when I was a lot younger. Do you like ice cream?"

"No, that's fine. We really need to get going, Mrs. Rosales. I appreciate this so much."

"Are you sure?"

"Yes."

"Your mother and father were so nice. Such nice people. Good people. I was so sorry to see them go. Where are they? Ricky and Alana. They were always a joy. And they had a daughter. I forget her name."

"That's me, Mrs. Rosales."

"Are you sure there wasn't another one. You can never truly be sure, dear."

"I'm pretty sure."

Mr. Rosales stood by the door with an absent look on his face.

"No. Don't go yet. Have another thing to eat."

"Why? You've been very kind to me."

"I must hold you here." He suddenly looked like he was winding down.

"Mr. Rosales. Have a seat. You look ill," said Corrag.

"They will be here soon."

"Who?"

Mr. Rosales did not say anything else. He took his wife by the arm and led her back into the kitchen. Corrag could hear them talking to each other. Mrs. Rosales kept repeating the question why.

"Why? Because that's what they require," bellowed Mr. Rosales. Corrag understood that he was speaking about the Augment. She and Arthur needed to get away. Just then she heard the sound of vehicles pulling up to the curb. She went through the kitchen and yanked at the knob of the back door. Mr. Rosales walked over to stop her.

"Get away, Mr. Rosales. I don't appreciate what you've done." Her threat stopped him in his tracks and he sat at the kitchen table with his head in his hands. Mrs. Rosales was crying soundlessly.

Corrag got out the back door and felt her way along the back garden wall. She remembered there was a door there. She unlatched it and slipped away with her baby.

Corrag got back on the zipbike. Arthur was a good sport. He fell asleep before she even started the motor. She rode past her old house. There were soldiers swarming all over it and the Rosales residence. It struck her that the scene before her eyes would only ever be just a memory. It was the one possession that was truly hers. Not even Arthur, because he belonged to God. And there was nothing to do for it but take a final glance. The details would fade away in time, but the idea of that house contained all of herself in it, the receptacle of her earliest metamorphosis where she'd shed childhood like a skin.

Four hours later she and Arthur were idling in line at the Tijuana crossing. If they asked her to pull over she would try to get away into Tijuana and ditch the zipbike. It was dark. The customs agent pulled the mobile scanner over and she looked into it. She was still Sonia Pivak in the eyes anyway, and that still seemed to be okay. They were either being very canny or they had slipped up. There was no way of knowing which it was. Five hours of solid biking on Ruta Uno and after that she was in Rosaria, where the Coop had its greenhouse operation and where she knew she would find Alana and Ricky. She had been coming here for as long as she'd been alive for Ricky's surfing vacations.

There was a campground with popup campers and tents set up for the migrant workers who came from as far as Peru and Colombia to find work on the vast vegetable fields of the Cooperativa Popular. There were always surfers from all over. There was still a sign at the gate that had been made by Edmundstown VocAg classes featuring the Edmundstown Wildcat, a panther like creature adopted as a branding by the Coop.

She walked in a circuit among the cinder block structures and the more settled looking of the metal-sided campers. She looked for clues like laundry or a telltale flowerpot. But in the end, it was a voice, Alana's voice, admonishing her father for something. It was unmistakable. She couldn't hear the words until she got closer to the window.

"What could we do, Ricky? What could we do? Life goes on. Yes, on and on and you can choose. Choose. That's what I said. It's a choice. Of course it is."

Corrag felt like hugging herself, hugging the wind, the ocean beyond the beach, all of the expanse ahead and behind her. The world had filled again, and astonishingly it was Alana's voice that had filled it. She knocked on the metal frame of the front door. When it opened a crack she spoke.

"Hi, Mom. I love you."

"Corrag?"

Epilogue

The doctors at Xen Kai Matamoros Hospital had botched the operation to remove Ricky's augment. Without proper maintenance, Alana's had faded out on its own. But they'd had to cut into the cerebellum to remove his. In the evenings Corrag took him out through the surf and spoke to him while the waves rocked their boards, trying to get him to remember. Alana had a Nicaraguan friend, Mariela with a bad leg, who wasn't working in the fields, who took care of Arthur on the beach.

She stopped looking out past the beach, expecting a disaster.

The work was not its own reward. But she got used to the hours in the greenhouses training tomatoes to their trellises and setting out blocks of kale and arugula into their humps of corrugated soil. It was enough for the Cooperativa to grant her a pass to the social and cultural events. She thought she might try at some point to get on the *comite* that determined the calendar of opportunities for advancement, as they were called.

The UCB under Hans Kupertini actually seemed to be doing a good job consolidating popular support in the old Democravia. Ricky and Alana still got the PNS news on their emosponders, and there were several stories that featured the name of the up-and-coming minister of state, Benjamin Calder, who had been involved in the negotiations over Arctic rare earth mining between the UCB and the Homeland. He seemed to be having a stellar career.

There never was a push to round up the unaugmented people. Instead, there seemed to be a tacit acceptance of an evolutionary divergence, of a lingering commonality of interests that would prevent violence or turmoil or upset of the status quo. So they proceeded into uncertain times.

Arthur liked to see the rising humps of the great whales in the distance, migrating with their calves to their summer feeding grounds. It was one of his earliest memories. And he jumped and ran down the beach towards a man standing there. Ricky smiled as if in recognition.

"Don't you worry about your baby?" asked Alana.

"No. Not really. I'm thinking he's going somewhere good."

Corrag was at that place that she had sought in her desperate moments, of being called for something hopeful that made life worthwhile and dying seem a lesser evil.

www.ingramcontent.com/pod-product-compliance
Lightning Source LLC
Chambersburg PA
CBHW030402180626
46812CB00005B/1891